Standard Deviation

Standard Deviation

KATHERINE HEINY

4th ESTATE • London

4th Estate
An imprint of HarperCollins*Publishers*
1 London Bridge Street
London SE1 9GF
www.4thEstate.co.uk

First published in Great Britain in 2017 by 4th Estate

First published in the United States by Alfred A. Knopf,
a division of Penguin Random House LLC, in 2017

1

Portions of this work originally appeared, in different form, in the following publications:
Chapter one has appeared as "Fluent in Her Language" in the *Antioch Review*,
Winter 2012; chapter two appeared as "The Seamy Side" in the *Southern Review*,
Summer 2013; chapter three appeared as "We're Here" in the *Southern Review*,
Winter 2013; chapter four appeared as "Lame Duck" in the *Gettysburg Review*,
Summer 2014; chapter five appeared as "Leviathan" in *Glimmer Train*,
Issue 90, Spring/Summer 2014.

A catalogue record for this book is
available from the British Library.

ISBN 978-0-00-810552-5 (hardback)
ISBN 978-0-00-818988-4 (trade paperback)

Printed and bound in Great Britain by
Clays Ltd, St Ives plc

MIX
Paper from
responsible sources
FSC® C007454

FSC™ is a non-profit international organization established to promote
the responsible management of the world's forests. Products carrying the
FSC label are independently certified to assure customers that they come
from forests that are managed to meet the social, economic and
ecological needs of present and future generations,
and other controlled sources.

Find out more about HarperCollins and the environment at
www.harpercollins.co.uk/green

FOR *Ian*

Before you became my mistress I led a blameless life.

LAURIE COLWIN

Standard Deviation

One

It had begun to seem to Graham, in this, the twelfth year of his second marriage, that he and his wife lived in parallel universes. And worse, it seemed his universe was lonely and arid, and hers was densely populated with armies of friends and acquaintances and other people he did not know.

Here they were grocery shopping in Fairway on a Saturday morning, a normal married thing to do together—although, Graham could not help noticing, they were not *doing* it together. His wife, Audra, spent almost the whole time talking to people she knew—it was like accompanying a visiting dignitary of some sort, or maybe a presidential hopeful—while he did the normal shopping.

First, in the produce section, they saw some woman with a baby in a stroller and Audra said, "Oh, hi! How are you? Are you going to that thing on Tuesday?" and the woman said, "I don't know, because there's that other meeting," and Audra said, "I thought that got canceled," and the woman said, "No, it's still on," and Audra said, "I wish they wouldn't double-book this stuff," and the woman said, "I know," and Audra said, "Well, if we don't go, will everyone say bad things about us?" and the woman said, "Probably," and it wasn't that Graham wasn't paying attention, it wasn't that he missed the specifics—it was that there *were* no specifics, that was the way they actually talked.

He took his time thumping melons and picking over grape-fruit and was actually rewarded for being forced to linger by remembering to buy green grapes, which weren't on the list.

"Who was that?" he asked when Audra rejoined him.

"Who?" She was peering into the shopping cart.

"That woman you just said hello to."

"Oh, she has a girl in Matthew's class," Audra said, selecting an apple. "And a five-year-old *and* a toddler *and* that baby, if you can believe it. But no more, because when the baby was only a week old, she had her husband get a vasectomy. Just made the arrange-ments and woke him that morning and said, 'Guess what? You've got a doctor's appointment.' And he went!"

She took a bite of the apple. Audra was forty-one—a slen-der woman with a not-quite-perfectly oval face. In fact, Graham sometimes thought, *all* of Audra was not-quite. Her eyes were not quite brown but had stalled at hazel, her lips were not quite full enough to be lush, her eyebrows were not quite high enough to be called arched, her chin-length hair was not quite auburn, and its messy waves were not quite ringlets. She'd worn her hair this length for as long as Graham had known her. Apparently, if she cut it shorter, it curled up around her face and made her head look overly round, and if she grew it longer, the ends got too heavy and she had to have lots of layers put in. (This was marriage: you started out thinking you'd married the most inter-esting person in all the world and twelve years later, your head was full of useless hair facts. Of course, there was other stuff in there—some milestones, having a baby, buying a house—but that was basically the essence of it.) Audra was not quite beautiful but her liveliness kept her far away from plain.

One aisle over, in the breakfast cereals department, Audra

suddenly stopped the cart. A young man behind them glared but Audra paid no attention.

"Oh! Hey!" Audra said. "Look! Hello! Hi! Whoa! How are you?" You would have thought she was greeting a whole soccer team instead of one lady in a T-shirt and jeans with her hair pulled back into a bun.

"Hello, Audra," the lady said.

"So sorry I missed yoga this morning, Beverly!" Audra said. She cleared her throat. "Or, um, I mean, Maninder Prem. Sorry, again, I forgot that you go by your spiritual name now, right? Even in the supermarket?"

"You can call me Beverly," the lady said neutrally. "But please remember that I have a no-refund policy for late cancellations and no-shows."

"Of course," Audra said. "It's just that this morning we had a slight—well, I don't know if you would call it a family emergency, more of a family *situation*—regarding my mother-in-law and an ancient jar of capers in her fridge and a trip to the hospital—"

Audra's tendency to lie could still shock Graham. His mother lived in Ohio, and as far as he knew, she was perfectly healthy, although she did have a habit of leaving things in the refrigerator for a terrifyingly long time.

"I'm sorry to hear that—" Beverly said. There seemed to be more to say but she wasn't saying it.

"Yes—" Audra said. There seemed to be more for *her* to say, too, but she wasn't saying it, either. Finally, she made a fluttery little gesture and said, "Beverly, this is my husband, Graham. Graham, this is my yoga teacher, Beverly."

Graham smiled politely and shook hands with Beverly, who looked him up and down, her eyelids flickering. He was fifteen

years older than Audra and he could tell that Beverly was thinking, *Oh, it's one of those marriages.* Graham wanted to tell her that
it wasn't one of those marriages, that his relationship with Audra
was so special and unique even *he* didn't know what it was, but
he'd given up on trying to communicate that long ago. He was
tall and in good shape, with the hair at his temples just starting to
go gray, but he suddenly felt tempted to stand up straighter. (Was
it just Graham or was Beverly awfully judgmental, especially for
a yoga teacher?)

"So anyway," Audra said, "see you next week, Beverly."

They moved on, and as soon as they went around the corner
and out of sight, Audra said, "I completely forgot about yoga this
morning!" as though that hadn't been as obvious as a bumper
sticker.

"I think Beverly could tell that," Graham said.

Audra sighed. "Maybe so. I don't know why I ever thought
yoga class early on a Saturday morning was such a good idea. I
guess I must have been feeling particularly empowered when I
signed up."

They saw their appliance repairman, Brady Shannon, in the
ice cream aisle, and Graham knew that Audra would have an
extra-long talk with Brady because she believed that if you were
very, very nice to repairmen, they responded very, very quickly
the next time you needed something repaired. The fact that this
theory had proved very, very untrue had not shaken her belief
in the practice.

"Brady Shannon!" Audra exclaimed.

"Well, hello, Ms. Daltry, Mr. Cavanaugh," Brady said. He was
a slight, balding man wearing a gray sweat suit and those black
padded kneepads that skateboarders wear. Every time Graham
had seen him, Brady was wearing those kneepads, presumably

because he was always having to get down and crawl around people's refrigerators and washing machines.

"I was thinking of you just this morning," Audra said. "In fact, I think of you every morning when I get in the shower!" Brady had recently fixed their shower head. "I think, *This feels heavenly and I owe it all to Brady Shannon!*"

Brady smirked at Audra and rocked a little on the balls of his feet.

Not for the first time, Graham wondered if there was some sort of processing unit—some sort of *filter*—missing from Audra's brain. She said things like this all the time without realizing how they sounded, and now here was poor Brady Shannon, getting turned on in Frozen Foods.

"Anyway," Audra said, oblivious, "how have you been?"

"Oh." Brady sounded disappointed. He probably hoped that Audra would go on describing what she did in the shower. "I'm all right."

Audra touched Brady's arm. "And please tell me how dear Ellen is."

Okay, now first of all, Graham happened to know that Audra didn't say things like "dear Ellen." Except that she just did. Second, Graham would have bet that Brady didn't like it when people said things like "dear Ellen." But he had just liked it when Audra said it. Third, Ellen was a cat.

"She's coming along, I guess."

"Bladder infections can be very serious," Audra said.

"Don't I know it," Brady said, shaking his head and tsking.

Audra and Brady talked some more about dear Ellen's urinary tract, and health problems among the elderly cat population in general, and the astronomical cost of veterinary care, and Brady's aunt Linda, who had had a bad run of UTIs herself recently, and the time Audra drank cranberry juice nonstop for a week and turned out *not* to have a UTI at all and—

Finally, finally, they got to the checkout lines.

Audra said, "Now, let me see if Jordan's working. Oh, yes, he is! Let's get in his line. Come this way."

"Who's Jordan?" Graham asked, maneuvering their cart with some difficulty.

"The checkout guy."

"Well, yes, but why do we need to be in his line?"

"Just a minute," Audra said. "Here." She pulled the front of the cart to a checkout line near the door. The customer in front of them was just putting the last of her groceries on the conveyor belt.

"Audra," Graham said again. "Why—"

Audra squeezed around the front of their grocery cart so that she was standing right next to Graham and spoke in a low voice. "I thought I told you this but maybe not." Her breath on his face was as warm and soft as clover. "I was here a couple of weeks ago and Jordan was ringing up this man's produce and the man had bought some pears but Jordan accidentally hit the wrong button and rang them up as these superexpensive *Asian* pears and the man got very huffy—he really was the most awful man, Graham, very coarse and uncaring—and told Jordan to take the Asian pears off his order and Jordan tried but he'd never done it before and the cash register froze and they had to call the supervisor and the man hollered at Jordan and stormed off without even buying his groceries! I thought Jordan was going to cry. I honestly did. He can't be more than twenty, and he's so sweet and defenseless-looking. So, anyway, now I always make sure to go through his checkout line and tell him what a good job he's doing."

Perhaps this was the fundamental difference between them.

Audra was worried about Jordan's self-esteem and Graham was wondering if Fairway still had the special Asian pears. If so, should he go get some so they could have Korean short ribs with pear marinade for dinner?

Audra edged back to the front of the cart and began unloading their groceries onto the conveyor. Graham peered around her to look at Jordan. He was a tall skinny African-American guy with neatly cornrowed hair and the large scared eyes of a deer. He was painstakingly checking out the purchases of the customer in front of them.

When they got up to the cash register, Audra said, "Good morning, Jordan!" so suddenly that Jordan fumbled the can of peas he was holding and had to lean down behind the counter to pick it up off the floor.

He looked at Audra cautiously. "Good morning." He began scanning items.

"How are you, Jordan?"

Jordan paused, a bottle of ketchup in his hand. "Pretty good." He scanned the ketchup and reached for a box of cereal.

"I was hoping you'd be working today," Audra said. "You always do such a good job."

Jordan stopped again. It was clear he couldn't work the register and talk at the same time. Graham estimated that they had at least fifty items in their cart. So if each conversational exchange took thirty seconds—

"Thanks," Jordan said finally.

He scanned a carton of orange juice and a box of pasta—Graham's hopes rose microscopically—before Audra said, "You're so efficient!"

Jordan stopped. Graham sighed. The man in line behind Graham sighed, too.

Jordan swallowed nervously. His neck poked out of the too-large collar of his tan uniform, narrow and vulnerable. "Thank you, ma'am," he whispered.

"Audra," Graham said quickly.

"Hmmm?"

"We forgot to get Parmesan cheese."

She frowned slightly. "Did we? You want to run back and get some?"

That was the last thing Graham wanted to do, but at least Jordan had managed to scan another three items while Audra was distracted.

"I think we also forgot toothpaste," he began again, but she had already turned back to Jordan.

"Excellent, Jordan!" Audra told him. "Look at you go!"

(Try to imagine having sex with someone so universally encouraging. It was, like almost everything about Audra, both good and bad.)

Graham sighed again and rested his elbows on the handle of the cart.

They had left Matthew, their ten-year-old son, at home with Bitsy, and when they got back from the supermarket, they found that Bitsy and Matthew had built a domino line through every room in the apartment, including the bathrooms.

Bitsy had been living in their den for about three weeks. It wasn't accurate to say a *friend* of theirs named Bitsy or even *Audra's* friend Bitsy because Graham had never seen Bitsy before she moved in and Audra had only met her a handful of times at book club. Graham had thought the only people named Bitsy were bubbly teenagers, but this Bitsy was in her early fifties—

with a long, narrow face and close-cropped salt-and-pepper hair, and the sinewy body of a devoted runner. She looked more like a greyhound than like someone named Bitsy.

The reason (if you could call it that) Bitsy was living in their den was because about six months ago, Audra, who was a freelance graphic designer, went to deliver a mock-up of a menu to a restaurant client in midtown and when she came out of the restaurant's office, she happened to see Bitsy's husband—she recognized him from the time Bitsy hosted book club—having lunch with a twenty-something girl in a miniskirt. (Audra had described the girl to Graham at length and was apparently upset because the girl was wearing a pair of knee-high Frye leather boots that Audra had tried on once and had been unable to get zipped over her calves.) Graham had told her that there might be an innocent reason for Bitsy's husband to be having lunch with a girl in a miniskirt, but Audra'd just given him a withering look, and then about a month ago, Bitsy's husband had moved to Ithaca on a creative sabbatical. ("Creative sabbatical?" Audra'd said to Graham. "He's a bank manager! I never heard of anything so suspicious in my whole entire life.") Audra had felt so bad—so responsible in some weird way, she said—that she'd offered to let Bitsy move in even though Bitsy and her husband owned a nice brownstone in Brooklyn. Bitsy didn't like to live alone.

"Hey, honey," Audra said to Matthew now, carefully stepping over the line, "some kids are playing in the lobby. Why don't you join them?"

She said this type of thing at least once a day, apparently not having realized in ten years that Matthew was not a social person, that he would never go and join some kids who were already playing. He probably wouldn't go even if the kids came to the door and asked for him. He was like Graham, not like Audra, and Graham thought that sometimes they both frustrated her endlessly.

"I don't want to," Matthew said. "Me and Bitsy are going out to buy batteries for her camera and then she's going to film it when I knock over the domino line."

"Okay," Audra said, and sighed.

"Thanks, Bitsy," Graham said.

She smiled at him. "No problem."

Bitsy and Matthew left. Graham followed Audra into the kitchen and began unpacking the groceries. "How's it going with Bitsy and her husband these days?" he asked.

"Oh, he's still feeding her all this nonsense about the creative sabbatical," Audra said. "And she believes it! I honestly don't think she understands that she and Ted are acting out this sort of cliché. I don't think she *knows* that men have been making fools of themselves chasing around after girls in miniskirts for hundreds of years."

"You seem to be forgetting that you were a miniskirt girl yourself," Graham said. "My miniskirt girl, in fact."

"Oh, I never forget that," Audra said. "That's how I understand about these things, insider knowledge."

It was true that Audra had a lot of insider knowledge. And it seemed like everyone wanted to trade on it. Sometimes Graham felt like he was married to Warren Buffett. Well, a female Warren Buffett who knew about everything except finance. (Maybe Audra and Warren Buffett should be married to each other and have every possible base covered. They would be the most sought-after couple in the world.)

People came to Audra for advice—well, no, not *advice,* that was the wrong word. They came to her for secrets, for gossip, for connections—for *intel,* that was the term—about everything. Friends sought her expertise on their job interviews, on their children's chances of getting into private schools, on marriage counselors, on hairdressers, on au pairs, on restaurants, on shops, on neighborhood watches, on gyms, on doctors, on internet providers. People asked her about local politics and she didn't even know who the mayor of New York City was! (Well, she probably did know who the mayor was, but it wasn't a certainty by any means.)

Right now, Audra's friend Lorelei had called and said she was on her way up to ask Audra's advice about a client meeting.

Lorelei was Audra's best friend, had been her best friend since they were both twenty. She lived on the third floor of their building and Graham sometimes saw her in the lobby and about once a month Lorelei and her husband and Audra and Graham had dinner together, and they often spent Thanksgiving together, so Graham *saw* Lorelei fairly often, but it *felt* like he was married to her because for fourteen years now, Audra had been giving him Lorelei's opinion on everything along with her own. "Lorelei thinks you're too old for me, but I don't," she'd said when he first met her. Or "Lorelei and I both think you shouldn't have given in to your first wife about those maintenance fees."

Audra did this constantly, and not just to Graham. She even did it to people in shops and restaurants, saying, "Lorelei would never pay so much for a jacket, but I love it," or "Lorelei and I both like scallops so I'll try the special." (Did people think she was schizophrenic and referring to some person only she could see? Graham wondered suddenly. Or did they think she had multiple personalities and Audra was the dominant self who spoke for both?)

The buzzer sounded and Graham went to let Lorelei in.

"Hey, Graham," Lorelei said, and smiled. She was a petite, dark-haired woman with freckles and the greenest eyes Graham had ever seen.

Graham knew Lorelei's opinions on everything from their bathroom tiles (too dark) to his mother (passive-aggressive) to his recipe for beef stew (beyond delicious), and all of that was very tedious, but he also knew some interesting things about her. He knew that she was saddened by the invention of colored contact lenses because now everyone assumed she wore them, and that her husband had made her cry once by making fun of the way she walked in high heels, and that when she was fifteen, she had made out with her boyfriend in a lake and when the boyfriend ejaculated, his semen had floated to the surface and followed them around like a jellyfish.

Of course, Graham realized that it must work the other way around and that Lorelei must know everything about him, too, but he had always sort of enjoyed that. How many people could have such intimate knowledge of another person and yet never really say anything beyond *The salmon here really is excellent*? It sometimes stirred in Graham a profound affection for Lorelei.

And yet, even Lorelei, who was a client service director with a big social advertising agency, was here, humbly seeking knowledge from Audra, a part-time graphic designer!

It was not the graphic designer bit that made it odd to Graham that someone would want Audra's advice because he actually thought Audra was very talented. And it wasn't the part-time thing, either, because that was sort of necessary at least until Matthew went to high school (or possibly until Matthew got married, at age forty-five). It was more just *Audra*, who had recently wondered aloud to Graham where the fuse box was (they'd lived in their apartment for ten years) and had often said she considered herself privileged to live in the age of the hair towel.

But there was no doubt that Audra knew people, and she knew things *about* people, and often she knew things about people who knew *other* people who knew people who had brothers who worked in the State Department and it was very helpful when your passport got stolen.

Lorelei went into the living room to talk to Audra, and Graham went into the kitchen to make tea for all of them. He knew just how Lorelei took hers—a single Ceylon tea bag, steeped for four minutes, with one sugar and a dash of lemon. He even knew which mug she preferred—an old-fashioned turquoise one with white enamel lining—and that she liked gingersnaps with her tea, although they didn't have any gingersnaps right now.

Graham liked making tea. He liked cooking, he liked baking, he liked food, he liked kitchens. In another life, he would have made an excellent owner of a safe house in the Underground Railroad. He would have always been happy to get up in the middle of the night and poke up the fire, listen to the fugitives' tales while he fried ham steaks and made hot biscuits. And although Graham had been a teenager in the seventies and never attended a consciousness-raising group, the idea had always deeply appealed to him. Political activism while you stirred the spaghetti sauce? What could be better?

He had started out as a medical researcher—Graham liked routine and order—and now he was in charge of medical ventures for a venture capitalist firm. There was just no market for underground safe houses anymore.

"So this very junior person in our office," Lorelei was saying to Audra, "basically the girl who makes the coffee, tweeted something without approval—"

"What did she tweet?" Audra asked.

"Oh, just something about how the clients' shoes are guaranteed not to give you blisters," Lorelei said. "She didn't realize the word *guarantee* was legally binding language and now the clients are furious, and I have to meet with them tomorrow."

"Who are the clients?" Audra asked.

"Superguardian Footwear," Lorelei said.

"Just a sec, let me look them up," Audra said, and there was the muted clatter of her laptop keyboard.

Graham tried to remember how conversations like this went in the pre-Google world and found he couldn't, although the pre-Google world was only what, ten or twelve years ago? (Some people, like his mother, still lived there.) Before Google, it seemed to Graham, there was probably a great deal more topic changing. Or maybe conversations were just shorter. Maybe you said, *Have you ever heard of a company called Superguardian Footwear?* and the other person said, *No,* and you said, *Oh. Well, anyway, I'll see you tomorrow.*

"All right," Audra said in that half-present, half-absent sort of voice people use when they're looking at a computer screen and talking at the same time. "Let's see. Here's their website—wow, I really do *not* like that color blue."

"Go to their company page," Lorelei said. "Maybe you know the vice president or someone." She sighed. "I wish you could go to this meeting *for* me, the way you broke up with Jeff Mayberry for me in college."

Audra sounded puzzled. "I broke up with Jeff Mayberry for you?"

"Oh my God, yes, don't you remember?"

"No, not at all."

"I wanted to break up with him," Lorelei said, "but I didn't want to hurt his feelings. So you and I were doing a lot of role play and pretend phone calls, with you being me and me being Jeff, but whenever he called, I couldn't quite do it, and finally you got impatient, and the next time he called, you pretended to be me and said, 'Listen, Jeff, I'm just in kind of a crazy situation and I can't see you anymore.'"

"Did it work?" Audra sounded amused.

"Yes!" Lorelei said. "That's the most amazing thing about it."

"Jeff couldn't have been that attached if he didn't even recognize your voice—"

"I can't *believe* this," Lorelei interrupted. "I have, for years—literally, for decades—been going around telling people I couldn't do things because I'm in kind of a crazy situation. It's been my all-purpose answer to almost every awkward question and now I find out you don't even remember saying it."

"Who all have you said it to?" Audra asked.

"Everyone!" Lorelei said. "I'm sure I've said it to people who were collecting money for UNICEF, and my mother-in-law when she asks why I haven't had children."

This was the pleasure of twenty-year-old friendships, Graham thought. Tracing a memory back to its source. Like following a stream through the woods and up a mountain until you find the spring trickling from a rock and you clear away the dead brown leaves of the intervening years and the water flows as sweetly as ever.

Audra's voice came clearly from the living room. "Really, the only connection I have at Superguardian—and it's not much help—is that their chief operations officer is a man named Columbus Knox and I believe I gave a man by that name a blow job once outside the Raccoon Lodge in, like, 1990."

"*What?*" Graham said, startled.

"It was a long time ago," Audra called soothingly. "And I didn't know him terribly well."

You know, actually, it was nothing like being married to Warren Buffett at all.

The very next day, a woman ahead of Graham in line at the deli ordered a Reuben sandwich with French dressing instead of Russian, and Graham recalled that his ex-wife had often ordered that very sandwich, and then he realized the woman *was* his ex-wife. How could he not have recognized the back of her head? The long slender neck and smoothly gathered French twist? Her hair was the color of corn silk and Graham knew that it felt like corn silk, too—so soft it seemed to disintegrate when you rubbed the strands between your fingers.

"Elspeth?" he said. ("Stupid name," Audra had once commented, she of the friends named Bitsy and Lorelei.)

The woman turned and yes, it was definitely Elspeth, same blue eyes, same pale face and delicate eyebrows. She looked older, but of course, she *was* older. Her skin seemed very slightly grainy, like the finest grade of sandpaper, like tiny calcium deposits on an eggshell. He realized abruptly that his eyes were crawling over her face and how unpleasant that must be. He forced himself to stop.

"Graham," she said. She didn't say anything else. He was glad she had her hands full—napkins, a can of soda, and a glass—because that prevented him from having to hug her or shake hands with her. He wasn't sure which he'd do anyway. Did you shake hands with someone you'd been married to for eight years?

A silence spread between them like a puddle of oil, shiny and dangerous. Graham was certain that if he looked down, he would see his shoes beginning to blacken.

But then the deli guy slapped Elspeth's sandwich on the counter. She turned to Graham. "Why don't you join me?"

"That would be great," Graham said. "You go find a table and I'll order a sandwich and be right with you."

He ordered his sandwich in such a slow, distracted manner that the deli guy kept sighing and rolling his eyes. Graham was busy trying to remember how many times he'd seen Elspeth since their divorce. Not many. Once he'd passed her going through the turnstiles at the Columbus Circle subway station—she was coming in and he was going out. She hadn't seen him but he had glimpsed her expression and she'd looked so unhappy that he'd stopped and turned to watch until she was out of sight down the stairs. He'd told himself that she wasn't unhappy about *him*. They'd been divorced for four years at that point. She could have been unhappy about anything. And then once when he'd gone to the funeral of a mutual friend. Elspeth had been sitting near the front of the funeral chapel, tall and slim and regal in a black suit. Somebody must have whispered to her that Graham was there, because she had swiveled her head—like a pale blond swan breaking formation—to stare at him. Then she'd looked forward again, and Graham, furtive as a poisoner, had slipped out before the service was over.

The deli guy handed him his sandwich—Graham was so flustered, he almost forgot to pay for it—and he joined Elspeth at a table in the corner.

She smiled when he sat down and Graham recognized the smile. It was a gracious, for-company smile that she put on sometimes, the way another woman might get out her Spode china or whip the dustcovers off the best sofa.

Graham smiled back and then took a big bite of his sandwich to buy himself some time.

"So," Elspeth said. "How are Audra and Andrew?"

Now Graham regretted the big bite because he had to chew for a while before he could answer.

"They're good," he said at last. He didn't bother to correct her about Matthew's name because he wasn't sure if she'd said the wrong name as some sort of passive-aggressive thing. "And you? How are work and—things?"

"Work is good," Elspeth said, lifting her sandwich with long fingers. She was a lawyer at a midtown firm.

"Still at Stover, Sheppard?" Graham asked.

"Oh, yes."

"And do you still live in the same apartment?" It occurred to him suddenly that he didn't know her address or phone number or email. He had a moment of disconnect—was she even real? What tethered her to the world?

"Actually, I'm moving," Elspeth said. "Or trying to. I want to buy a place in that building over on Seventy-sixth and York? It's called the Rosemund. Do you remember that?"

Graham nodded, although he didn't.

"Well, anyway, I want to buy there but it's very tough—the board has to approve you."

"I can't imagine a better tenant than you," Graham said sincerely, and then faltered for a second. He had been *married* to this woman, and the best thing he could say about her was that she'd make a fabulous tenant?

"I've heard they don't like lawyers," Elspeth said. "Too litigious."

Graham had a sudden flash of how Elspeth would come across in an interview: cold, hard, perfectionistic. Her favorite drink was a gimlet, and she was not unlike a gimlet herself, in either sense of the word.

"Anyway," she said. "What about you? Where do you live?"

Graham told her about his apartment and they compared mortgage rates.

There didn't really seem to be anything to say but they both still had half a sandwich to go, so they talked about the privatization of workers' comp in West Virginia and Nevada, and pretty much the only personal thought Graham had was that she was still the tidiest eater he knew.

When he told Audra that night that he'd seen Elspeth, she got so excited that she accidentally poured half a bottle of syrup onto the waffle she'd made for Matthew.

"I can't eat that," Matthew said.

"Sure you can." Audra put it in front of him. To Graham, she said, "What did she look like? What did she *say*?"

"Is it going to be squishy?" Matthew asked. He wouldn't eat anything squishy, or lumpy, or crispy, or spicy, or really any food that could be described by an interesting adjective.

"If it is, I'll make you another one," Audra said absently. "Tell me, Graham!"

"Well, she looked the same, only sort of older," he said slowly. "She still wears her hair the same way."

"And?" Audra prompted.

"And what?"

Audra made an impatient gesture. "What's her life like? Is she happy? Why has she never remarried? What does she do for sex?"

Graham glanced at Matthew, who was, amazingly, eating the soggy waffle.

"Well, I don't think I want to know the answers to any of that," he said finally.

"Then what was the point of even having lunch with her?" Audra asked. "You could have had a more meaningful conversation with someone at a bus stop!"

That was Audra's view. But Graham was not so sure. He thought that sometimes just having a polite conversation with someone, just surviving thirty minutes in that person's company, just realizing that that person did not dislike you enough to sit at a separate table—sometimes that was a major triumph all on its own.

In a way, it was very nice having Bitsy live in their den, because she was so good with Matthew. She was unfazed by Matthew's picky eating, and patient with his slowness at homework, and gentle with his refusal to pick up his room. And she had endless energy for origami and paper airplanes and dominoes, which were Matthew's main passions, and which Graham and Audra had tired of long ago.

And in a way it was *not* very nice having Bitsy live in their den, because Audra knew about the miniskirt girl and Bitsy didn't. The trick was not to reveal it, but Audra felt they had this responsibility to bring Bitsy around to the idea, slowly and gently.

"I think that's Bitsy's husband's responsibility," Graham said.

"But he's not *doing* it!" Audra protested. "He gives her all this nonsense about the sabbatical and she *believes* him. She's in denial."

And so they had long awkward dinner conversations with Bitsy during which Audra tried to bring Bitsy around to acceptance—a process akin to steering a river with a spatula.

"Tell me more about Ted's sabbatical," Audra would say.

"I don't really know," Bitsy would answer placidly. "He says it's very private. He does a lot of yoga."

"What else?"

"I think it also involves massage therapy."

"I'm sure it does," Audra would say and Graham would bite back a groan.

Or Audra would say, casually twirling spaghetti with her fork, "Is it, um, *common* for bank managers to take creative sabbaticals?"

"Ted's the only bank manager I know," Bitsy said. "His company has been very generous."

Twirl, twirl. "Where does he live in Ithaca?"

"A very small studio," Bitsy said. "He sleeps on a futon and uses a board on sawhorses for a desk."

"That sounds like a young person's apartment," Audra said.

"Yes, it does," Bitsy agreed calmly.

"It sounds like, well—like an apartment a girl in her twenties might have."

"He's subletting from a college student."

Audra made interested eyes over a mouthful of spaghetti. "A *female* college student?"

Bitsy nodded. "Yes, her name is Jasmine."

"Jasmine what?"

"I don't know," Bitsy said, cutting her spaghetti. (You sort of knew ahead of time that she was a pasta cutter the way you knew Audra was a pasta twirler.)

Audra looked disappointed. Graham was sure she'd hoped to do some pleasurable Jasmine cyberstalking. He cleared his throat to indicate a change of topic, but Audra was not so easily diverted.

"You should go visit Ted," she said to Bitsy.

"Oh, no," Bitsy said. "I don't want to intrude on his creative process."

"A surprise visit!" Audra said. "Think how romantic—"

"More garlic bread, Bitsy?" Graham asked. "More wine? More water? More butter? No? Matthew, what about you? Well, I know you don't drink wine—that goes without saying—but water? And tell us about school! What happened today?"

And on and on, until his voice rasped.

Later that night in the bathroom, he said to Audra, "I wish you wouldn't do that."

"Do what?" she asked, clipping her hair back.

"Have those conversations with Bitsy." Graham began brushing his teeth and then stopped. "What if she actually agreed to go to Ithaca and surprise Ted? Think of the mess you'd make."

"I can't help it," Audra said. "She's so delusional!"

"You know that business about leading a horse to water," Graham said, rinsing his toothbrush. "You just can't make it drink."

"But you can pop an ice cube into the horse's mouth!" Audra protested. "You can moisten the horse's lips with a wet washcloth! That's all I'm trying to do here—just prepare Bitsy ever so slightly for the inevitable."

She turned on the taps in her sink and began soaping her face.

There were other questions about Bitsy, lots of them. Was she really so blind when it came to Ted? Would it, in fact, be better for her to know the truth? What if she didn't *want* to know the truth? What if they told her and by some miracle, Ted actually *was* on a sabbatical? How long was Bitsy going to live in their den? Why was Bitsy here if Audra didn't even like her? Why did someone from Brooklyn belong to a Manhattan book club? Was it true that she could run an eight-minute mile?

Don't ask Graham about any of it. He didn't have a fucking clue.

To be totally honest, Audra wasn't the only one who enjoyed a good cyberstalking session. Right now, right this second, *Graham* was the one settling down at the dining room table with his laptop and that first magical whisky of the evening, preparing to devote half an hour—thirty minutes of his life that he could never ever reclaim!—to cyberstalking his ex-wife. And yes, he was looking forward to it.

Again, he wondered, what exactly did people *do* before the internet? Oh, all sorts of studies existed about how people used to read more books or watch more TV or make more telephone calls or snowshoe or keep bees or make marmalade, but Graham was not sure he believed those studies. It seemed to him that people *still* read a lot of books and watched a lot of TV and talked on their cellphones all the damn time, especially in restaurants when you were trying to read the newspaper.

Maybe, before the internet, people just lazed around pointlessly more, or threw tennis balls at the wall to hear the pleasant *thwock! thwock!* sound, or wondered idly what kind of mileage their friends' cars got. It didn't seem to Graham any sort of great loss. Not when he could sit here and snoop on his former spouse without even leaving his own living room, and no awkward questions about what you were doing watching the neighbors with binoculars, either (which was what they did instead of searching the internet when Graham was a teenager, now that he thought about it).

Graham took his first sip of whisky and typed Elspeth's name into the search engine.

"What are you doing?" asked Audra. She was sitting on the couch with her own drink beside her, sewing a badge onto Matthew's Cub Scout uniform.

"Just looking something up," Graham said absently.

Elspeth didn't have a Facebook page, but that wasn't really surprising. If someone asked her if she was on Facebook, she would probably say, "Why do I need to be on Facebook?" (She had always been a conversation-stopper kind of person.)

She wasn't on Twitter or Instagram, either. Graham had to content himself with going to Stover, Sheppard's website. There she was: Elspeth Osbourne, partner, mergers and acquisitions. Elspeth's photograph had been Photoshopped so aggressively that it didn't even look like her. Maybe it *wasn't* her, Graham thought suddenly. Maybe it was just a stock photo of a blond lawyer. He read the little blurb beside her picture: *Ms. Osbourne practices in the Mergers and Acquisitions Group. She advises U.S. and international corporate and private equity clients on a full range of transactions . . .*

This was so boring that Graham was beginning to wish he'd spent the last ten minutes throwing a tennis ball at the wall. He took another, bigger drink of whisky and tried to remember the apartment building Elspeth had said she wanted to move into. The Roseland? No, that was a ballroom. The Rosemund, that was it.

And here it was, the Rosemund website, at his fingertips. Graham clicked on some floor plans and photos—chrome, glass, marble, stainless steel. Everything as bright and hard and shiny as the sidewalk after an ice storm. No wonder Elspeth wanted to live there. She had an intense dislike of carpeting—or anything soft, really. Graham clicked on the "Amenities" page. Billiards Room, Concierge, Fitness Center, Heated Outdoor Pool, Parking Garage, Starbucks. Did that mean there was an actual Starbucks in the lobby? Audra would never leave the building if they lived there. He clicked on the somewhat ominously titled "Our Application Process" page and scanned the building's board of directors.

Then he glanced over at Audra, still sewing in a little pool of lamplight, the auburn in her hair glinting like tinsel.

If you were married to Marie Curie, you might ask her what

the atomic weight of lithium was from time to time. Not to keep her on her toes, but just because you could. And now, in that same sort of spirit, Graham said to Audra, "Do you know any of these people?" and he read her the list of board members:

Francis Ray
Gordon Richards
John Palmer
Marco Luxe
Connie Sharp

"Oh, for God's sake," Audra said. "Marco Luxe is the doctor who delivered Matthew."

Graham frowned. "I thought that was Dr. Medowski."

"It was *supposed* to be Dr. Medowski," Audra said, holding the shirt closer to the light and then putting it back in her lap, "but he was grouse hunting! Don't you remember? I called his office to say that my contractions had started and to ask him to meet us at the hospital and his receptionist said, 'Oh, Dr. Medowski isn't here, he's grouse hunting in the Adirondacks,' and I said, 'Why on earth does he want a house in the Adirondacks?' and she said, 'No, *grouse* hunting,' and started telling me about grouse or partridges or what have you, and I'm like, 'Fine, whatever, but I'm having a baby here and I need Dr. Medowski,' and she says, 'Well, you can have Dr. Luxe,' and I said, 'I don't want Dr. Luxe, I want Dr. Medowski,' and she says, 'It *is* the first day of grouse season, you know,' in this very *blaming* sort of voice, like I should have planned better—"

"Do you think Dr. Luxe would remember you?" Graham asked.

"Oh, I'm sure he would," Audra said serenely.

Actually, Graham was sure he would, too. Audra had talked nonstop during labor and even through the delivery. He remembered the doctor (apparently it was Dr. Luxe) saying to the nurse, "The epidural has really thrown her for a loop," and the nurse saying, "No, that's just her personality."

"Do you think you could call him?" Graham asked. "And ask him a favor?"

"What sort of favor?"

"For Elspeth."

"I don't see why not," Audra said. She sighed suddenly. "I think I've sewn this shirt to my jeans. God, I hate Cub Scouts. Get me another drink, will you?"

Matthew wanted to join an origami club that met on Sundays at nine in the morning on the Lower East Side that Bitsy had helped him find on the internet. Was it fair to *blame* Bitsy for this? Would it be fair to ask Bitsy to take Matthew to the club meeting every Sunday for the duration of her stay in their apartment, and possibly years beyond that? No, probably not. Graham sighed and called the number on the website.

Later Graham would tell himself that he knew just from the way Clayton answered the phone that there was something not really—not exactly—not quite—*normal* about him. But the truth was that he wasn't really paying that much attention and he didn't pick up on anything until they were at least four or five exchanges into the conversation.

"Hello," Graham said. "Can I speak to Clayton Pierce, please?"

"This is Clayton speaking."

"Well," Graham said. "I'm calling about the Origami Club—"

"All right, all right, just hold up a second here," Clayton said. "First, how old are you?"

"I'm calling for my son," Graham said. "He's the one who wants to join."

"And you?" Clayton said. "Do you fold?"

"No," Graham said, and there was a small frosty silence on the line, the same kind of silence that might follow someone at a swingers' party asking if you swing.

"I see," Clayton said. "How old is your son?"

"He's ten."

"Mmmm-hmmm," Clayton said, obviously writing something down. "And his name?"

"Matthew Cavanaugh."

"Is Matthew aware that we are an invitation-only club?" Clayton asked.

"Well, no," Graham said, startled. "We didn't know that."

"Now, look here," Clayton said. "This isn't the YMCA, where any sort of riffraff can walk in and join. We have *standards*. We're *exclusive*. Like White's in London."

"Or the Marines," Graham said. The few. The proud.

"Oh, hey now, I don't hold with any sort of military action," Clayton said hotly. "I'm a pacifist and the club is strictly non-political."

"Yes, of course," Graham murmured, wondering if it was even possible for an origami club to *be* political. What were they going to do—fold a fleet of paper airplanes and invade Libya?

"All right, before we can even *consider* Matthew as a member, I have a few questions," Clayton said.

Graham, like all parents of special-needs children, had a range of stock phrases that he used when talking about Matthew to other people. The phrases ranged from polite euphemisms ("We prefer to think of him as reserved") to gentle sidestepping ("He can be very independent in the right circumstances") to outright lying ("Matthew *loves* new experiences!"). But the odd thing was that, in this conversation, Graham didn't need to use any of those phrases, not a single one.

"I assume Matthew can do a general swivel fold," Clayton said.

"Oh, yes."

"An open sink?"

"Yes."

"What about an open *double* sink?"

"That too."

Clayton made a reluctant impressed sound. "And a closed sink?"

"I think so," Graham said, frowning. "He spent weeks learning something called an unsink, or maybe a closed unsink. I can't remember."

"Well, there's a tremendous difference," Clayton said tartly. "We're not talking about making omelets here, where you can by guess and by golly. A closed unsink is a very difficult fold."

"I believe he was making something called a—a tarantula?" Graham said. "Lang's Tarantula?"

Silence on the other end of the line, except for a slight noise that could have been a pencil tapping. "Is Matthew free this Sunday?" Clayton said at last. "We'd like to meet him."

"Yes, he is," Graham said.

Clayton gave him his address and told him to have Matthew there by nine.

Graham hung up feeling absolutely confident that Matthew would dazzle them. He would never admit it, not even to himself, but it was a wholly new sensation.

War is hell, yes; but so is Cub Scouts. Or at least being the parent of a Cub Scout is. A subtler kind of hell where the people have no sense of irony, and they make you go camping in cold weather, and you have to carve small race cars out of blocks of wood, and sing songs that have a lot of verses, and attend den meetings, and help your child obtain all sorts of useless (and nearly unobtainable) badges. And then, after years of encouraging your kid to like Cub Scouts, you have to quick *dis*courage him from liking it around age twelve so it doesn't adversely affect his social life. Plus, they ban alcohol.

And now Audra wanted to attend the Cub Scouts party!

"It's not an *official* Cub Scouts party," she said to Graham. "It's just for adults."

"Why would we want to go if Matthew isn't even invited?" Graham asked. Matthew wasn't invited much of anyplace. It was something that worried him.

"Think of it as networking," Audra coaxed. "Almost everyone there will be the parent of a boy in Matthew's class. This is a great way to get to know people and make him feel more a part of things. Besides, I already promised Matthew's Akela we would go."

This was another thing about Cub Scouts: you started out using all these scouting terms ironically—*Akela, Webelo, woggle, camporee, Okpik*—and you ended up using them sincerely. Before you knew it, these words had crept into your vernacular and you said them to prospective clients or sex partners.

So they went to "network," leaving Matthew with Bitsy, and walking over to the Akela's very nice eight-room apartment on 108th Street. (The Akela was married to an investment banker.)

The Akela herself answered the door. She was a tall, large-boned woman with sharp blue eyes and blunt-cut blond hair. Graham was used to seeing her in the ill-fitting and unbecoming khaki Scout uniform, but the long red velvet dress she wore now was no more flattering. And what's more, she had the slightly sweaty, shaky look of someone hosting a party. Graham's heart went out to her at once.

"Graham! Audra! Welcome!" she cried, and Graham realized he had no clue what the Akela's name actually was.

"Maxine," Audra said. "Thank you for having us."

The Akela was carrying a wineglass—the sight of it lifted Graham's spirits like a scrap of paper tied to a weather balloon; alcohol wasn't banned at *this* party!—which she used to gesture vaguely down the hall. "Just help yourselves to a drink . . . we have, you know, whatever . . . and I'll introduce you . . ." She trailed off as the buzzer sounded again and took a big swallow from her glass before she answered.

Graham and Audra walked into the living room in search of drinks. Indeed, alcohol was in abundance; in fact, there wasn't even food. The long white-clothed table in the living room held a huge punch bowl of ruby-red rum punch swimming with raspberries, a tray of frosted tumblers filled with mojitos as cool and green as a shady lawn, another tray of sugar-rimmed cocktail glasses of margaritas garnished with mint, a dozen pineapples cut in half and filled with creamy piña coladas, three fruit-clogged pitchers of sangria, long lines of bubbling champagne glasses, and a towering pyramid of small plastic cups of red Jell-O with a small sign that read *Vodka Shots!* in a cheerful handwriting propped in front.

Audra helped herself to a margarita and squeezed Graham's arm. "Network," she whispered, and slipped away into the crowd.

Graham took a glass of champagne and backed up until he was standing against the sideboard. A large man with wide flat hips was standing there, too, talking to another man about how his GPS was getting frustrated with him.

"So it'll say, 'When possible, make a legal U-turn,'" the man said. "And if, for some reason, I don't make a U-turn, it says it *again,* but with, you know, this little pause, like, 'I *said,* when possible, make a legal U-turn.' It *sighs* at me."

The man stepped forward to get another champagne glass and Graham gasped, because the man's midsection had completely hidden *another* bar set up behind him, which featured the largest bottle of Johnnie Walker Red Label whisky Graham had ever seen in a private residence.

Graham set his untouched champagne aside with a brief apology to the poor starving children in China (or whoever suffered when you wasted alcohol) and filled a cut-glass tumbler with ice. It took both hands to lift the Johnnie Walker bottle, but Graham held it steady as he poured the whisky into the glass. It glowed a soft amber, as fine and warm as your best childhood memory. His respect and admiration for the Akela was growing by leaps and bounds.

Graham took his whisky glass and began to circulate. He approached people standing alone or in groups, introducing himself, asking about the names and ages of their children, comparing teachers and classroom experiences. He talked to fathers about tuition costs and to mothers about cafeteria food. He talked about math homework and reading logs. It was intensive labor, similar to panning for gold—patiently sifting through sediment and muck while your back ached and cold river water numbed your ankles. The whisky helped, but only so much. Graham didn't find a gold nugget, but much patient conversation shifting revealed a tiny gold flake: one woman told him that if Matthew wanted to play an instrument in the band, he should choose the trumpet or the French horn because the music teacher sprayed saliva when he talked and it was hard on the woodwinds up there in the front rows.

Graham poured himself another whisky, thinking briefly of the fairy tale where the man's servant drinks an entire lake, and went in search of Audra. He found her sitting at the kitchen table drinking with the assistant cubmaster, a short burly man with thick gray hair. Graham circled close enough to hear their conversation, and found that she wasn't networking at all. They weren't even talking about children or scouting!

"Now, the man who owns the liquor store on Ninety-seventh Street is *very* kind," Audra was saying earnestly. "Very caring, very friendly. He always waves at me when I walk by, although once he waved at me when I happened to be walking past with my neighbor Mrs. Gorsky and Mrs. Gorsky said, 'I don't think it reflects well on the building's reputation for you to be so chummy with the liquor store owner,' and I said, 'If you're so worried about appearances, maybe *you* shouldn't put a million empties out every Tuesday.'"

A bell clanged suddenly in Graham's head. He hadn't known this conversation had taken place, but he discovered he was able to pinpoint exactly when it must have occurred: last September, when Mrs. Gorsky had suddenly turned silent and squinty-eyed when he met her at the elevator bank.

"Mrs. Gorsky sounds extremely unpleasant," the assistant cubmaster said, stretching his arm across the table to add more Don Julio to Audra's margarita, which was now so strong it was nearly transparent.

"The liquor store on Seventy-fourth is owned by a Serbian couple," Audra continued. "They aren't quite as *compassionate* but they often have better prices."

The crowd shifted, pushing Graham back out of the kitchen. He talked to someone about furnace maintenance and blocked air vents. He had another whisky and talked to someone about traffic and how at first audiobooks seem like the solution to your commuting nightmare but they're actually not. He talked to someone else about the Whole Foods and the difficulty of finding kosher M&M's.

Then he had a long boring (that is to say, even more boring than the previous conversations) discussion about diabetes research with a woman who had what Matthew would call "angry eyebrows," and at the end, when he said innocently, "Now, whose mother are you?" she got even angrier-looking and said, "You don't have to be anyone's wife or mother to have an identity," and it turned out she was single and from out of town.

He decided it was time to go and went to find Audra, who was still sitting at the kitchen table.

"Wait, wait," she was saying to the assistant cubmaster. She had a little froth of margarita foam on her upper lip. "Exactly what is the difference between Tinder and Grindr?"

Graham sighed. "I think we should be going," he said loudly.

Audra and the assistant cubmaster gave him twin looks of annoyance, but he stood firm. Audra shrugged slightly, and the assistant cubmaster pushed back his chair reluctantly.

"It has been my *sincere* pleasure talking to you," he said to Audra, clasping one of her hands in both of his.

"Mine—too," she said warmly, with just a little bit too much space between the words. "A sincere—pleasure."

It took the combined efforts of Graham and the assistant cubmaster to haul Audra to her feet, and then Graham led her out of the kitchen. He propped her against a bookshelf the way you'd lean a broom against a wall while he checked his pockets to make sure he had his wallet and phone. He waved a hasty goodbye to the Akela across the room and propelled Audra out the door.

In the elevator, Audra pressed the button for the lobby with great concentration.

Graham regarded her silently for a moment. "Did you talk to anyone besides the assistant cubmaster?"

"Hmmm?" Audra peered at him, her eyes beady with tequila.

"I said, did you talk to anyone? Did you *network*?"

She looked thoughtful. "Well, yes, there was a woman at the beginning of the party. I can't recall her name, but she had wild frizzy black hair. Did you talk to someone like that?"

Graham shook his head.

"I must say, I found her quite—*intrusive*," said Audra, who had once interrupted a complete stranger on a crosstown bus to say that the symptoms she was describing sounded like bacterial vaginitis. "She kept asking what Matthew's *issues* were, what *medications* he takes."

When the elevator came to a stop, Audra swayed in an alarmingly loose-jointed way, like one of those spring-loaded string animals that collapse when you push the button in the base. Graham took her arm and led her into the street.

He had planned to take a taxi home, but it was no fun having a driver holler at you because your drunken spouse had vomited in the back of his cab. (Graham knew this from experience as bitter as raw aspirin.) They would have to walk. But the weather was fine, and the whisky had stoked a red-hot sort of pleasure-furnace deep within him. Now that he was out of the party, Graham felt like he could walk for miles. He linked his arm through Audra's.

All hail the Akela, he thought.

The next morning, Bitsy took Matthew to an origami demonstration at a mall in Garden City and Graham and Audra got to sleep in, which was good, considering Audra's hangover. Graham got up eventually and walked down to the corner and bought some brioche and two coffees and a hair magazine for Audra.

Audra was pleased by the hair magazine, which she took to be a sign of his love and affection for her, although actually Graham had bought it for the amusement of watching her devour it. She was like a stock analyst studying the big board. He thought Audra had great hair already.

"Any developments with Bitsy and her husband?" he asked. He had to ask once more before she heard him and then she still didn't take her eyes off the magazine.

"Oh, no, same old, same old," she said, folding over the corner of a page.

Graham had been wondering lately if it was a good idea to let Bitsy have so much access to Matthew. What if she found out about her husband's relationship with the miniskirt girl? For all he and Audra knew, Bitsy could decide to run down her husband with their SUV while Matthew serenely folded an F-16 in the backseat. But before he could say anything, the phone rang.

"Oh, hi, Maxine!" said Audra.

So Graham read the newspaper while Audra had a fifteen-minute postmortem of last night's party. Clearly there were a few blanks in Audra's memory—"I'm so sorry I didn't get a chance to meet your husband . . . Oh . . . Did he happen to mention what we talked *about*?"—but, in general, Audra was very supportive and told the Akela that it was a fabulous party; and no, the Jell-O shots were *retro*, not vulgar; and Audra was pretty sure everyone there was too old to be posting drunk selfies on social media this morning, so don't worry about your judgmental colleagues. Then she said, "Tuesday would be super!"

When she hung up, she poked Graham and said, "That was Maxine, wanting to know if Matthew could come over for a play-date with Joey this week. I told you it would pay to network."

Graham did not know what to say. He wanted to tell her that eventually Matthew was going to have to do this on his own, that she could not get him through life on the force of her own personality. But she was too happy. And she wouldn't have believed him anyway.

Sadly, Graham was not home when Audra called Dr. Luxe, and so he had to imagine how the conversation went. All Audra told him was that Dr. Luxe was "delighted" to hear from her, that he remembered her "vividly," that they had a "marvelous" time catching up, and that Dr. Luxe was "tickled pink" to be able to do them the small favor of recommending Elspeth to the Rosemund board. Graham didn't believe that anyone under the age of seventy—and possibly no male of any age—used the phrase *tickled pink,* but he supposed that was about the gist of it.

In fact, Audra and Dr. Luxe were now such good friends that Dr. Luxe had invited Audra (and Graham and Matthew, even) to his son's wedding the next weekend to bulk out the number of guests—something to do with a lot of guests canceling at the last minute.

"I don't want to go to a wedding where I don't know the people getting married," Graham said. "I don't even want to go to weddings where I *do* know them."

It seemed to Graham that one of the benefits of getting older was that your friends stopped getting married and having expensive boring weddings that wrecked your budget and ruined your weekend. (There aren't a *lot* of benefits of getting older, but that was one of them. Also: you don't have to pick up cans and bottles for beer money; and if you stay out late, you don't have to sneak back into your house through the basement window to avoid waking your parents. That's pretty much it.)

"You're the one who wants a favor from him," Audra said mildly. "Besides, we can give them those horse-head bookends that my cousin Susie gave us as a wedding present."

"We still have those?"

"Oh, yes," Audra said. "Somewhere. I didn't feel right giving them to the thrift store, but I didn't want to give them to someone we actually *liked,* so they've been hanging around forever."

And so, a week later, they drove out to Long Island on a perfectly good Saturday, all three of them (or five of them if you counted the horse-head bookends). Audra wore a short pale blue dress with a matching bolero jacket and a big white bow at the collar. This dress had always struck Graham as vaguely pornographic—it looked like a man's fantasy of what a librarian would wear—but it was very pretty. Matthew was wearing khaki pants and a white shirt with one of Graham's ties knotted at his throat. He had the same almost-auburn hair as Audra but much thicker and not as curly. Matthew's hair was Audra's delight—she said it was so perfect she didn't even have to brush it.

Graham allowed himself a grudging approval of the wedding venue as he parked the car in the gravel parking lot of the church. The reception would follow immediately in the stately home next door—no drive, no re-parking the car, no waiting around. Ten minutes from wedding vows to a drink in every guest's hand. Just as it should be.

"Tell me the bride's and groom's names again," Graham whispered to Audra as soon as an usher had seated them.

"Bryant and Michelle," Audra said in her normal speaking voice. "Bryant went to law school at Georgetown and now he works in multisomething finance in Boston."

"And Michelle?"

"I know virtually nothing about her," Audra said, "except that she gets very wet during sex. Don't fidget, Matthew."

An elderly couple in the pew in front of them suddenly sat up very straight, and the woman snapped the clasp on her purse shut with a startled *click*. Graham sighed. Perhaps Audra had once had a filter, but gossip overload had destroyed it.

It turned out to be an old-fashioned wedding with a receiving line, and Graham had to shake hands with the bride and wish her every happiness, all while trying very hard not to think about the only thing that it was really possible to think about now, or probably ever, in her presence. Audra seemed blissfully untroubled by this and hugged Bryant enthusiastically, saying, "Welcome to the world of marriage!" and then hugged the bride and said—actually said—"I've heard so much about you!"

The elderly couple were right behind him in the receiving line, and the man gave Graham a sort of sickly smile when he heard that.

Graham shook hands with the bride's parents, and then Mrs. Luxe, a large woman in a battleship-gray dress, from which her satin-covered bosom protruded like the prow of, well, a battleship.

Next in the receiving line was Dr. Luxe. Now Graham remembered him—a big olive-skinned man with a large nose and abundant silver curls brushed back in what Graham's mother called "finger waves." His wife, clearly the second Mrs. Luxe, was much younger, blond, and timid-seeming.

"I'm sure you remember my husband, Graham," Audra said

to Dr. Luxe as Graham shook hands with him. "His ex-wife is the one who wants to move into your building."

"Ex-wife?" Dr. Luxe looked startled. "I thought it was a friend."

"Friend *and* ex-wife," Audra said smoothly. "We're extremely close."

(This was possibly the biggest lie anyone had ever told in that particular church. Elspeth had refused to ever even meet Audra.)

"I admire that," Dr. Luxe said.

"I didn't want us to be one of those *acrimonious* couples," Audra said. "That's so hard on everyone. Actually, we enjoy Elspeth's company immensely. We all go to lunch together and sometimes the movies. She even helped us with our kitchen renovation."

"How refreshing!" Dr. Luxe said.

"Often Elspeth goes on vacation with us," Audra said, completely carried away now. "Not if we're going somewhere romantic, of course, like the Bahamas, but more like long weekends and things. You know, like if we're going to the Berkshires, then we think, *Why not take Elspeth? She's so much fun! And so knowledgeable about nature and hiking and bird-watching.*"

"That is the most civilized arrangement I've ever heard of," Dr. Luxe said. "I think it's marvelous."

The second Mrs. Luxe's eyes were huge. She was obviously terrified that she would now have to go mushroom hunting with the first Mrs. Luxe.

"But perhaps just maybe don't mention my name to Elspeth," Audra added in a soft rush, touching Dr. Luxe's arm. "She's terribly independent. She would want to think she got the apartment on her own."

"My lips are sealed," Dr. Luxe said.

"Anyway," Audra said, "this is our son, Matthew! Matthew, Dr. Luxe is literally the first person who ever held you."

Graham closed his eyes. Sex, divorce, lies, obstetrics—would this conversation never end?

But Dr. Luxe seemed delighted. He shook hands with Matthew and exclaimed over how tall he was while Graham shook hands with the second Mrs. Luxe. By then, there was such a traffic jam of wedding guests behind them that a kind of crowd surge pushed them out of the receiving line and into the bar, where Graham grabbed a glass of champagne from a waiter's tray and drank it in one swallow.

But the rest of the wedding was okay, even more than okay. The manor house had French doors opening onto the grounds. It was a beautiful summer day, and teenage girls had been hired to organize all the children. Most of the children happily ran out onto the lawn, but Matthew stayed sitting at the table. One of the teenage girls—a pretty brunette in a soft lavender dress—sat next to him and Matthew made an origami tree frog that had 101 folds out of a cocktail napkin. The brunette ruffled Matthew's hair and asked him to fold something else, and Graham thought perhaps there might be an upside to this origami business after all.

Graham and Audra even danced a little, and it was as they were dancing that it suddenly occurred to Graham to wonder *how* Audra had known anything about the bride's sex life.

"Hmmm?" she said sleepily, her head resting on his shoulder. "Oh. Because it turns out through some weird coincidence that Bryant knows Doug's old roommate and he told Doug and Doug told Lorelei, and she told me. In fact, Lorelei thought she and Doug might get invited, too, but they didn't."

Graham held her closer, and saw that Matthew was alone now. The brunette had wandered off. Still, it had been a better day than expected. Graham was relieved that Lorelei hadn't come to the wedding, because if she had, she and Audra would have devoted the whole day to the most intensive type of conversation imaginable (they once talked so much they blew out the candle in a restaurant) and then he wouldn't have had Audra to himself.

Graham's and Audra's were not the only universes. There were also other universes—hidden ones, secret ones. Little pocket universes scattered around and you slipped into them unexpectedly, like when you stopped into a bodega for milk and discovered a cardboard display stand of Sucrets or Love's Baby Soft perfume or some other long-defunct product. Origami Club was in one of those pocket universes, and Graham and Audra had to take Matthew there on the day after the wedding. (At nine o'clock in the morning on the day after the wedding, to be precise.)

Origami Club was held in Clayton's apartment, and the first unusual thing was that Clayton's apartment building was on a street Graham had never heard of and he thought he knew every street in Manhattan. Walter Street? Where the hell was that? On the Lower East Side, as it turned out. And although the building looked like all the other low red-brick buildings around it, it had a bright green door, which made Graham think of enchanted forests. There was no doorman and the hallway had black-and-white hexagonal tile and smelled deeply of cabbage and rent control. Matthew gazed around curiously, as though they were on the set of a play.

They rode a creaking elevator up to the fourth floor and pushed the buzzer for apartment 4A. A thin, excitable-looking man in his late fifties answered immediately, giving the impression he had been crouching right behind the door.

"Come in, come in!" he said. "I'm Clayton Pierce."

They shook hands with him and then he led them down a hall through a cluttered apartment. The doors to the rooms that opened off the hallway were all open, and glancing in, Graham saw that every single object—every bedspread, lamp shade, picture, curtain, hand towel, tissue box, wastebasket, vase, throw pillow, candleholder, hamper, and doorknob—either was made out of origami or had a picture of something made out of origami on it. It seemed that possibly the only thing *not* made out of origami was the white-haired woman who popped out of the kitchen to greet them, although she was wearing earrings made out of itty-bitty origami cranes.

"Hello," she said cheerfully. "I'm Clayton's wife, Pearl. You must be the Cavanaughs. We've been looking forward to meeting you."

"We've been looking forward to this, too," Audra said. "Matthew especially."

In the dining room, two other men, also in their fifties, were seated at the table. Clayton made a sweeping gesture and said, "Everyone, welcome Matthew!" He glanced at Graham and Audra. "And . . . non-folders."

"Matthew," Clayton said. "This is Manny and Alan."

"Hello," Matthew said in his soft clear voice.

"Is it true you folded Lang's Tarantula?" the man named Manny asked.

"Yes," Matthew said. "But I couldn't do it the first time and got all frustrated and cried a long time."

Graham closed his eyes. He remembered that evening well. He would have preferred Matthew had been up all night with the croup or whooping cough.

"That happens," Manny said. "Did you try it again?"

"Uh-huh." Matthew pulled out a chair and sat down. "But the creases weren't sharp. I like the creases to be *sharp*."

"Well, naturally," Clayton said.

"That's neat paper," Matthew said.

"It's imported from Thailand," Alan said.

Matthew hauled his backpack onto his lap and unzipped it. "I have some regular paper. Should I get it out?"

"He does have very small fingers," Alan said to Clayton. "That might be useful when we do Kamiya's Wasp."

"We can use tweezers like we've always done," Clayton said testily. "We accept new members on the basis of skill, not finger size. Otherwise we'd have a roomful of—of—I don't know what."

"People with very small fingers," Matthew said softly.

"Exactly," Clayton said. "Now, Matthew, today we're going to be making Ermakov's Mantis Shrimp and that has box-pleating collapses. Do you know how to do those?"

"Yes," Matthew said. "Will you help me if I get stuck?"

"Of course," Clayton said. "Well, within reason."

Something was wrong here. So obviously wrong that Graham almost could not figure it out. But he glanced at Audra and saw she felt it, too.

Normally, Graham and Audra (especially Audra) had to act as a sort of lubricant for any social interaction Matthew had. And not just a mild lubricant, like Vaseline or butter—we're not talking about anything as minor as a stuck zipper here—but a heavy, industrial lubricant, like motor oil or axle grease. Oh, the playdates and lunches Graham had sat through with Matthew and another child, while Audra said things like, "Matthew loves the Wiggles! Don't you, Matthew?"

"Yeah."

"He especially likes the red one. Murray, I think. Who's your favorite, Jimmy?" Or Tommy. Or Zachary. Or Ross.

"I like the yellow one."

"Matthew likes him, too! Right, Matthew?"

"Not really."

"Well, he sort of likes him. I mean, he doesn't *dislike* him. But I guess he probably likes the blue one best. And he really loves that song about fruit salad. What song do you like, Timmy?"

"The one about the car."

"Matthew, too! Right? Toot! Toot! Remember, Matthew? Listen, maybe after we finish lunch, you guys could watch *The Wiggles* together? What do you think, Matthew?"

And on and on. Until you understood—truly *understood,* on an emotional level—why simultaneous interpreters have the highest suicide rate of any profession. And now here was Matthew, chatting away, holding his own, while Graham and Audra stood there, as superfluous as the leftover screws that roll around on the floor after you assemble a bookcase.

As if realizing this, Pearl turned to them and said, "Now, you two run along and enjoy your day. Matthew will be just fine here. You can come back and pick him up around four."

"Four?" Audra said, glancing at Graham. "But what about lunch?"

"We'll give him lunch here," Pearl said calmly.

Oh, well, now that was a problem. Matthew did not eat lunch at other people's houses. It had been tried; it could not be done. It led to tears, often on the sides of both Matthew and the hostess. Other people's mothers didn't understand that Matthew would not eat their brand of ketchup, their flavor of potato chip, their variety of cereal, their make of apple juice. It had to be utterly and completely familiar or he wouldn't touch it. No sandwiches cut in triangles, no generic Oreos, no off-brand grape jelly. And then there were the people who actually expected Matthew to sit down with their families and eat meat loaf or chicken pot pie. (The world is full of reckless fools—Graham had not realized that before Matthew began trying to eat meals at other people's houses.)

"It would be better if we stopped back and picked him up before lunch," Graham said.

"But I don't want to leave early!" Matthew said. Honestly, this day was full of surprises.

"Well, maybe we could come back and bring you something to eat—" Audra began.

"I'm sure we can manage lunch," Pearl said, obviously unaware that Matthew's past was littered with the corpses of women who said "I'm sure we can manage lunch." "I always make the boys something to eat."

"It's just—" Audra said, biting her lip. "It's just—he's really terribly fussy."

"All the boys are fussy," Pearl said calmly. She began to list their meals off on her fingers. "I usually make Alan a grilled cheese sandwich on white bread with the crusts cut off. Manny has already told me he wants plain rice and a banana cut in slices and a glass of whole milk. Clayton, of course, will have pancakes because it's Sunday. I also have both creamy and crunchy peanut butter, and saltines."

Oh, at last, at last! These were Matthew's people! They spoke Matthew's language! Why then did Graham feel so sad?

"Well, if you're sure you don't mind," Audra said. "And if I could just take a quick peek at your pancake mix and syrup and make sure it's a brand Matthew likes?"

"Of course," Pearl said graciously. "Just come on into the kitchen. And be sure to tell me if there's some particular way he wants the pancakes made."

Audra stepped into the kitchen to give Pearl a crash course in the way Matthew liked his pancakes—milk instead of water in the mix, syrup served in a separate cup, no butter ever—while Graham watched Matthew and the other members of the Origami Club begin folding sheets of green paper so thin they were almost transparent. Graham had thought the shrimp would be folded out of coral-colored paper, but evidently not. Alan was complaining about his mother, which was reassuringly normal.

"So my mother's having her garden club over to lunch," Alan said, "and she wants me to fold all their napkins into hydrangeas, and I say, 'Fujimoto's Hydrangeas? You want me to make *six* Fujimoto's Hydrangeas? Out of napkins?' and she says yes and I say, 'Napkins that these ladies are all just going to shake open and wipe their mouths with?' and she says yes and I say, 'Do you have any idea, any *real* idea, how difficult it is to fold a tessellation?' and she says, 'Do you have any *real* idea how difficult labor and delivery are?'"

"I think we're all set," Audra said, coming out of the kitchen. "Matthew, sweetie, call us if you need anything at all, okay?"

"Okay," Matthew said, not looking up. His tongue poked out to touch the middle of his upper lip—the sign of his greatest concentration.

"Goodbye, everyone," Audra said. "It was so nice to meet you!"

The folders sort of nodded and grunted, and Pearl walked them to the door. "Don't worry about a thing!" she whispered, squeezing Graham's arm. "Matthew's going to fit right in!"

Well. Yes. So much had to go unsaid there.

In the elevator, Audra wrapped her arms around Graham and leaned against him. In these dingy surroundings, she smelled as fresh as a bar of soap just broken in half.

"Promise me we won't let Matthew turn out like those men," she whispered, "and if he does, that we'll still love him anyway."

. . .

Elspeth sent them a change-of-address card. It was just a small white note in a plain envelope with her name and new address at the Rosemund.

Graham stood in the lobby of their building, drops of summer rain glinting like diamonds on his overcoat, and tapped the card against his palm for a long time. He wondered if she would ever know he'd helped her get that apartment. Probably not. Bad deeds—even anonymous bad deeds—came home to roost eventually in the form of a speeding ticket or a court summons, but anonymous good deeds generally went unacknowledged forever. Unless the person you had done the good deed for was extremely resourceful and tracked you down via Craigslist Missed Connections.

He brought the card up with the rest of the mail and handed it to Audra in the kitchen.

"Oooh," she said eagerly when she saw the return address. She pulled out the card, scanned it, and looked at Graham expectantly.

"What?" he asked.

"After all this time, she finally writes to you and it's this?" she said, exasperated. "Not even a written message. It's so—so unforthcoming."

"That's sort of her personality," Graham said. "She's not a forthcoming person."

"But it's still sort of a window into her life," Audra said, her cheeks pink with indignation. "She may as well send everyone blank pieces of paper, because this says nothing about her."

"Well, actually it says a lot about her," he said. "It says everything about her, in fact."

And didn't it say a lot about Graham, too, that he used to be married to such a person? That such a person (oh, involuntary but still-so-disloyal thought!) had suited him much better than Audra?

Friday afternoon, and Graham was in his study in the apartment, waiting for a phone call from the Origami Club.

When Graham and Audra had picked Matthew up last Sunday, Clayton had given them a somewhat pompous speech about how the club would have a special meeting during the week to discuss potential new members. He said this in a way that simultaneously implied there were *many* potential new members to discuss and indicated that Matthew was the first new potential member, ever.

Anyway, Clayton had said he would call Graham and let him know their decision on Friday, and Graham had been so certain of Matthew's success that he'd gone out and bought a bottle of sparkling cider, which was now chilling in the back of the refrigerator. (Graham would have liked to celebrate with real champagne, and even let Matthew have a sip. But last May, Graham had removed a tick from Matthew's scalp using Bombay gin and a pair of tweezers and Matthew had told his science teacher he got drunk over Memorial Day weekend, so now Graham tended to err on the side of caution.)

Graham's cellphone chirruped and the screen read CLAYTON PIERCE, ORIGAMI. Graham had programmed the number into his phone—that's how sure he was.

"Hello?"

"Graham Cavanaugh?"

"Yes."

"This is Clayton Pierce," Clayton said. Then he cleared his throat and continued grandly, "The members of the Origami

Club would like to extend a cordial invitation to Matthew to join our organization and help us maintain the high quality of life that origami allows us to enjoy. We are a dedicated group who meet each Sunday for origami and fellowship."

The word *fellowship* gave Graham a post-traumatic Cub Scouts–related flashback, but he just said, "Matthew will be very pleased."

Then Clayton said in his regular voice, "Oh, and we're updating the website, so tell Matthew to wear a red T-shirt on Sunday for the group photo. Goodbye."

"Goodbye," Graham said.

He left his study, intent on finding Matthew, but the first person he bumped into was Bitsy. She was wearing running clothes, and her cheeks showed hectic spots of color like a teething baby's. Her breath was ragged and loud, as though she were just returning from running instead of just starting out.

"Bitsy?" he said uncertainly.

He reached out to touch her shoulder, but she brushed past him as though he weren't there and thumped out of the apartment.

Graham started toward the kitchen and met Matthew coming out of the bathroom. "Hey, Matthew!" he said. "I just got great news. You made the Origami Club!"

"Okay," Matthew said. So much for him being very pleased.

Graham sighed. He went to find Audra. She was in the kitchen, opening a bottle of wine.

"Oh, God," she said as soon as she saw him. "Can you make fettuccine Alfredo tonight with full-fat cream and all the butter? Maybe even double the cheese?"

"I guess," Graham said. "Why?"

"Bitsy!" Audra said as though this was an obvious answer. "Didn't you see her?"

He nodded. "What's wrong? She seemed upset."

"Upset?" Audra said. "Jesus, Graham! She found out about Ted and Jasmine like one minute ago!" She saw his alarmed look and added, "No, *I* didn't tell her."

"How did she find out?"

Audra pushed her hair back from her forehead. "She was just here in the kitchen with me, doing her prerunning stretches and talking about hip flexors and round-the-world lunges, and I said that round-the-world is also something men ask prostitutes for, and she said, 'How do you know that,' and then her phone rings. So she digs it out of that little running belt she wears, and it's Ted, and right away Bitsy says, 'If it's about that insurance claim, I still haven't been able to find it,' and then he says something and she says, 'Can we talk about this later because I like to have my mind calm before my run,' which was kind of a surprise to me because I thought calm was Bitsy's baseline—"

Yes, oral history is a wonderful practice—a powerful way to preserve traditional customs and confront contemporary problems. Graham firmly believed that. But he also believed he knew what it was like to be married to a tribal elder whose storytelling is a bit on the long-winded side.

"—and then Ted says something and then Bitsy says, 'Yes?' in this very sharp voice and then he says something else, and suddenly she pulls out a kitchen chair and sits down and then she says, 'I *am* sitting down,' and she listens again and then she says, 'Yes, someone is here with me,' and she looked over at me, and I thought something was wrong with her eyes for a minute. But then I realized that her pupils were so dilated that her irises looked black. She looked like—like a shark. And she listened for a longer time and then she said, 'I will never forgive you for this, Ted.' And then she hung up and tucked her phone back into her belt."

Audra leaned back against the refrigerator. Its blank white-ness made her look like a riot of color—burnished hair and red blouse and flushed cheeks. Like a winter sunset.

"I said, 'Oh, Bitsy, that sounded awful,' and sort of held out my arms, but she just stood up and she still had the shark-eyes and she was moving like a shark, too, sort of—of cruising. It was like she was swimming through the air too fast and might crash into the wall. And she said, 'I want to go for my run,' and I said, 'Bitsy! Your mind's not calm at all! You'll be hit by a car or at the very least pull a hamstring!' and she said, 'Just two miles,' in this faraway voice, and then she left— Oh, Graham, I thought I would be relieved, but I feel so bad for her."

Graham sighed. "Me, too."

He did feel bad for Bitsy, more than he had thought he would. He realized that he, like Audra, felt responsible for Bitsy. She was a member of their household, and she was in pain. And the fact that Graham and Audra had inflicted this same pain on Elspeth all those years ago did not make them hypocrites.

And yet—and yet—he could not help wishing it hadn't hap-pened on the same day they were celebrating Matthew's accep-tance into the Origami Club. Because Graham had come to believe that people were only happy when they could feel one emotion at a time. That was the reason that things that had pro-voked such pure joy in childhood—fresh chocolate-chip cookies, a sweatshirt warm from the dryer, a perfect sand castle—did not offer the same joy in adulthood. You were too busy having all these other tiresome emotions about income tax and drunken texts and varicose veins and how much money was in the parking meter. People in love were happy because being in love blocked all the other emotions out. And righteous anger felt so good, for a few minutes anyway, because it burned so hot that all other feelings were cleared away. And now Bitsy's heartbreak would over-shadow Matthew's triumph and in the ten years of Matthew's life so far, triumph had not come easily—oh, my, no.

"Hey," he said, trying to make his voice enthusiastic. "At least I have some good news. Matthew made it into the Origami Club."

"Really?" Audra smiled shakily. "Then we should be opening the sparkling cider, not the red wine. Matthew! Come here!"

Matthew came into the kitchen and stood there shuffling his feet while Graham popped the cork on the sparkling cider and filled the three champagne flutes Audra lined up on the counter.

"To Matthew," Graham said, lifting his glass.

"Cheers," Audra said.

They clinked glasses and all took a sip. Graham allowed the sparkling cider to roll around on his tongue for a moment. Nope. Absolutely no mystic rejuvenating power whatsoever. It just wasn't like champagne.

"Sweetheart," Audra said to Matthew. "I am so *proud* of you."

Matthew glanced down, and when he looked back up, his expression was radiant. Only Audra could bring that out. It was as though Matthew's face had been dipped in sunshine, Graham thought—and Graham was not normally a person who gave him-self over to mawkish metaphors.

The apartment door banged open. That would be Bitsy, back from her run. (Evidently, she really could run an eight-minute mile.) They would give her lots of red wine and Graham would make fettuccine Alfredo using full-fat cream. It was the most they could do for her. It was, unfortunately, the most anyone could do for her right now.

"Bitsy!" he called. "Come on into the kitchen and join us!"

Graham looked at Audra. She was looking back at him, her

eyelids so heavy with gratitude that her blinks were long, sensual movements, like a cat's stretches.

It occurred to Graham suddenly that whatever happened with Bitsy tonight—if she decided to leave Ted, or murder Jasmine, or just stay up very late listening to Luther Vandross—Graham would actually be right there while the drama was unfolding. He wouldn't have to hear about it later.

He did not feel, at that moment, standing there in the kitchen, that he and Audra were living in parallel universes. Or, if they were, she was at the very nearest edge of her universe and he was at the very nearest edge of his, and they had found a thin spot in the fabric of their worlds, a meeting place, and a way to stay there, touching, floating, together.

Two

"You won't believe what happened!" Graham's secretary said.

Her name was Olivia and she had long dark hair with heavy bangs. She always looked out from under the bangs like an excited cat peering from under a chair when you're about to throw a ball of yarn. She was twenty-three, freshly emerged from college, although Graham sometimes thought she could be freshly emerged from the womb, given how naïve she was. Graham had had to show her how to read her bank statement! He had had to explain the difference between local and state taxes, and that food could still go bad in a refrigerator, and even daylight saving time. How could you not know about daylight saving time and live on your own? What were her parents thinking? But for all that, she was a pretty good secretary—an extremely fast typist and she never ran out of cheerful, friendly energy. (Graham's previous secretary had been a woman in her fifties who sighed heavily, like a dog or a teenager, whenever he asked her to do anything.)

"What?" he asked now.

"I've locked myself out of my apartment!" Olivia said. "Just as the door clicked shut behind me this morning, I thought, *Wait!— wait!* And sure enough, I'd left the keys sitting on the kitchen counter."

Graham recognized that feeling. "Call your roommate," he

said. He knew Olivia had a roommate. It was the only reason he could, in good conscience, stand to let her go home at night.

"She's in Kentucky visiting her parents," Olivia said.

"What about your neighbors?"

"What about them?"

"Do any of them have a key?"

She looked puzzled. "Why would I give a key to my neighbors?"

"In case you lock yourself out."

"Oh! I see what you mean. But keys are expensive to make—like twenty-five dollars just for the one for the dead bolt."

This was another thing about Olivia—how she and her roommate seemed to live on no money at all. Although she brought a giant Starbucks Frappuccino to work every single day, so Graham suspected it was not lack of funds but how those funds were spent.

"What about the super of your building?"

"Luis, you mean?"

"If that's your super's name, then yes."

"But I don't have his phone number," Olivia said, "and he hardly ever answers when we knock on the door."

"Well, then I guess you're going to have to call a locksmith," Graham said gently.

Olivia's eyes got very wide, and she nodded gravely.

She went back to her desk and Graham could hear her pressing buttons on her phone and an instant later she said, "You won't believe this! I locked myself out of my apartment!" and then she had basically the same conversation she'd just had with Graham. "No . . . She's in Kentucky! . . . No . . . No . . ."

She hung up and dialed another number. "You won't believe this! I locked myself out of my apartment!"

Graham sighed and got up to close the door to his office. He supposed that when Olivia had called all her friends, she would get around to calling a locksmith. He could still hear the beginning of every call, even through the door, with Olivia squawking the word *believe* like a pterodactyl.

Almost as soon as he returned to his desk, Olivia buzzed him on the intercom. "Phone call for you on line one," she said. "Esp—Els—Elsp—"

"Elspeth?" Graham said. "Elspeth Osbourne?" (Like he knew more than one.)

"Yes," Olivia said. "Can I put her through?"

"Go ahead," Graham said.

Elspeth had never called him at work before. Well, not in ten years, at least. Imagine: it had been over a decade since he had spoken by phone to a woman he had once married. People were not meant to live like this, he sometimes thought. It was too confusing. He lifted the receiver and punched the button.

"Graham Cavanaugh," he said, figuring that it was best to start out formally.

"Hello, Graham," Elspeth said crisply, causing Graham to have an unexpectedly vivid image of her. Audra and every other woman he knew tilted their heads slightly when they answered the phone, so they could slide their handsets under their hair. But Elspeth always wore her hair pulled back in a French twist. She answered the phone without any nonsense. He could visualize the rest of her, too: her perfect posture, the silk blouses she favored, the narrowness of her shoulders, the way she always sat with her feet tucked slightly under her chair because she believed that crossing one's legs caused varicose veins. ("It *does*?" Audra had said in a horrified voice when Graham had told her this years ago. She'd lost nearly a whole night of sleep worrying about it before deciding it was an old wives' tale, like that thing about leaning on your elbows making them ugly.)

"Hello, Elspeth."

They sounded like characters from *Mister Rogers' Neighborhood*, Graham thought. *Won't you be my neighbor? Won't you please?*

"I'm sorry to bother you," Elspeth said, "but—"

"It's no bother," Graham said, interrupting without meaning to.

Elspeth paused for a moment. She didn't like to be interrupted. "I'm calling because my great-aunt Mary died—"

"I remember Aunt Mary," Graham said, interrupting *again*. He seemed to have forgotten how to talk to Elspeth. "I'm so sorry."

"Yes, well, this is slightly awkward," Elspeth said, "but Aunt Mary left us a joint bequest. She hadn't updated her will. She had quite advanced dementia for many years."

The implication was clear: only someone with advanced dementia would leave anything to Graham, after what he'd done to Elspeth. But Graham decided to ignore that.

"I see," he said.

"So," Elspeth said. "I was wondering if you might be able to meet me at the estate lawyer's office so we can both sign for the bequest."

"Certainly," Graham said. "When?"

"How about tomorrow?"

She gave him the address and he wrote it down and they agreed on three o'clock and it was just like a normal phone call really. Almost.

Elspeth was waiting in the lobby of the estate lawyer's building when Graham arrived. Her ash-blond hair was pulled back neatly, and she wore a tightly belted pale pink trench coat over a matching pink turtleneck and white wool pants. She was still Elspeth, still absolutely immaculate.

"Hello, Graham," she said. "I'm sorry to put you to so much trouble."

"It's no problem."

They took the elevator up to the lawyer's office and signed together for the bequest, which turned out to be a small marble statue of a cat. Graham recognized it instantly—it had arched its marble back on a shelf directly over Aunt Mary's head at the dining table during a dozen Sunday lunches.

"Oh, right, that cat," Elspeth said flatly.

The lawyer explained that they could have the statue evaluated and then one of them could buy the other one's half, or they could sell the statue and split the proceeds.

"I know," Elspeth said. "I'm an attorney."

The lawyer's secretary boxed up the marble cat, and Graham and Elspeth took it with them, along with a sheaf of papers for each of them, the top one of which had a photograph of the statue paper-clipped to it.

"You can have the cat," Graham said as soon as they were on the street. "I only came because the lawyer needed my signature."

"I don't want it," Elspeth said. "I think we should sell it."

"Okay," Graham said. "But you sell it and keep the money."

"Oh, I wouldn't feel right about that," Elspeth said, and Graham knew enough to realize that it wasn't that she felt she owed him anything, it was that her lawyer's mind had leapt ahead to the potential problems that might arise from such a casual arrangement.

They went into Starbucks to talk about it, and finally agreed that Elspeth would take the statue to Sotheby's to have it valued and put up for auction.

"I feel like we're on *Antiques Roadshow*," Graham said.

"I can't stand that program," Elspeth said. "It's so depressing how they always choose people whose whole quality of life hangs in the balance of the value of some knickknack."

They had finished their coffee and began moving toward the door.

"I guess you should know," Elspeth said, pulling the belt on her coat tight. "I'm living with someone."

Actually, there was no reason he should know that. He and Elspeth had no children. In lots of really important ways, it was like they'd never been married at all.

"That's great," he said. "Who is it?"

"Oh, you don't know him," Elspeth said. "His name is Bentrup Foster."

What is the very best thing about him? Audra would have asked. *Where did you meet him? What did you think when you first saw him? Is he the type of person who thinks a bowl of cereal counts as dinner? How many times does he hit the snooze button in the morning? Would he ever do a shot of tequila to get drunk quicker? Does he watch game shows? Does he give good back rubs?*

But Graham did not want to start channeling his second wife in the presence of his first wife, so he only said, "What does he do?"

"He works in the shoe department at Barneys," Elspeth said.

"I'm glad for you," Graham said. "That you have someone."

"Yes." Elspeth looked thoughtful. "With is better than without."

He wondered if she would ever—*ever*—say anything that didn't make him feel automatically guilty. He doubted it.

When Graham got back to their apartment that night, Audra was helping Matthew with his homework at the dining room table.

"What the heck is bus station division?" she asked Matthew,

wrinkling her forehead as she read the worksheet. "Can we Google it?"

"Hi, Daddy," Matthew said.

"Oh, hey," Audra said. "How was it? What did Aunt Mary leave you?"

Graham dropped the sheaf of papers on the table, and Audra glanced at the photograph of the statue. "A marble kitty cat," she said, clearly not impressed. (Honestly, Graham was starting to feel offended on the cat's behalf.) "Did you see Elspeth?"

"Uh-huh."

"Who's Elspeth?" Matthew asked.

"Daddy's first wife," Audra said.

"I didn't know you had another wife," Matthew said. He looked at Audra. "Did you have other husbands?"

"Only other people's," she said cheerfully. (She claimed she couldn't censor herself around Matthew or she'd go crazy.) "Now finish up your homework. It's only seven problems. Just do them the regular way, I guess."

She followed Graham into the kitchen. "How was it, seeing her?"

"It was okay, actually."

"Did you have the sense she wanted to murder you?" She said this in a normal sort of voice; they might have been discussing whether they had any lemons.

"No, of course not," Graham said.

"You used to say that," Audra said. "You used to hang up the phone with her sometimes and say that you could tell she was hoping you'd drop dead."

Had he said that? It was hard to remember. "Well, that's different from wanting to murder me," Graham said. "She was actually perfectly friendly. She's living with someone."

"Perfect!" Audra exclaimed. "We can go on a double date!"

"I don't know about *that*," Graham said. "That might be pushing it."

"Oh, please," Audra said. "It would be the most natural thing in the world."

Well. Graham was not so sure it would be, not sure at all. "You seem to be forgetting," he said, "that you were the cause of my divorce in the first place."

"Oh, but that's ancient history," Audra said. "That was all twenty years ago."

"Thirteen," he corrected. She had a tendency to round up. It was almost a way of life.

"Well, whatever," she said. "Surely she's over it by now. She's living with this other man. Aren't you the least bit curious to meet him?"

"No," Graham said, knowing full well that she would find this attitude incomprehensible.

Audra sighed loudly. "But I'm dying to meet *her.* Just think, you were married to her for a decade"—it had been eight years—"and she and I have never even laid eyes on each other!"

That was only half-true. Elspeth had seen Audra once but Audra didn't know that. He and Audra had been on their way to Macy's to register for wedding gifts and they'd come up out of the subway on Thirty-fourth Street, and dashed across Seventh Avenue into the store, and in those brief moments, Elspeth had seen them. Graham knew because she told him the next day on the phone. (This was when they were first separated and still talked bitterly on the phone every few days.) "I saw you and your girlfriend going into Macy's yesterday," she'd said. Graham still remembered what Audra had been wearing that day: jeans and a silk blouse and a little rabbit-fur vest she'd bought in a secondhand store. She had looked unbearably pretty and young, so young. He'd seen her through Elspeth's eyes and felt guilty all over again.

"Maybe that's for the best," he said now.

"Why?" Audra said. "Are you ashamed of me? Ashamed of her?"

"No, neither," he said, realizing as he said it that it was true.

"Then, please, just ask her," Audra said. "The next time you speak to her, just mention the idea and see what she says."

"Okay," Graham said. Sometimes it was easier just to give in.

So when Elspeth called to tell him that the marble kitty cat had been valued at four thousand dollars, he said, "I've been thinking we should all have dinner together."

"Dinner?" Elspeth repeated. She sounded startled.

"Yes," Graham said. "The four of us. You, me, Audra, and Bentrup. Like a double date."

"A double date?"

(This was a problem when you lived with people who had strong personalities; you started to sound like them.)

"That's only an expression," he said hastily. "I just thought, you know, the four of us could have dinner. But we don't have to if you think it's too, ah, unconventional." He'd been about to say *kooky* when he realized that was an Audra word, too.

"Of course it's unconventional," Elspeth said. "We're divorced."

"There are a million ways to be divorced," Graham answered. Which was *another* thing Audra said: *There are a million ways to be married, there are a million ways to raise a child, there are a million ways to run a household.* It so happened he agreed with her.

"I guess," Elspeth said slowly, like someone struggling to comprehend a difficult concept.

"It doesn't have to be a big deal," Graham said. "We could—" He was about to say *go out somewhere casual,* when he remembered that Elspeth didn't like to go to restaurants. "You could just come over for dinner," he finished.

She was quiet for so long that he finally said, "Elspeth?"

"I'm thinking," she said.

Graham remained silent, and after a moment, Elspeth said, "Okay. Let's do it."

"Good," Graham said. This had to be the most lukewarm meeting arrangement ever made.

He wondered what factors she had been weighing during her silence. He was, he realized suddenly, very happy not to know.

How do I look?" Audra asked, as she and Graham stood in the front hall, waiting for the babysitter. It had somehow worked out that they were going over to Elspeth's new apartment for dinner, something to do with Bentrup's work schedule.

"You look great," he said, and she did. She wore black jeans and a thin fuzzy white angora boatneck sweater. The wide neckline showed her collarbones. Graham did not have the heart to tell her that she couldn't win tonight—if she looked pretty, it would be assumed he was with her for her looks; if she didn't, it would seem like she had let herself go.

"Now, remember," he said. "Don't say anything about helping her get the apartment. In fact, don't even mention the apartment."

"How can I not mention it if we're standing inside it?" Audra said. "Won't that seem sort of ungracious? What if, after we leave, Elspeth turns to Bentrup and says, 'That woman was so odd! She didn't say one word about our home.'"

That seemed to Graham to be possibly the *best* thing Elspeth might say about them after they left.

Audra had arranged for their downstairs neighbors' daughter Melissa to babysit Matthew while they were at Elspeth's. "It's strange that Melissa's always available," Graham said. "It must say something about her social life."

"Or else her boyfriend's some married guy she can only see at, like, lunchtime," Audra said, knotting a scarf around her neck.

It surprised Graham, still, how quickly Audra could access the seamy side of life.

There was a soft knock at the door and it was Melissa. Graham studied her while she slipped off her shoes, but he couldn't picture her with a married lover, or any lover, in fact. To him, she just seemed like a cheerful, freckled teenager, almost without a gender. He could barely imagine having a conversation with her, let alone an affair.

(Audra had about two hundred stories of all the lecherous fathers of children *she'd* babysat in high school, including one father she'd actually had an affair with, a man named Edward. Edward used to pretend to walk his dog in the evenings but he would actually sneak over to Audra's house on nights her parents weren't there, and one night Edward's wife drove by and saw their dog tied up in front of Audra's house, looking cold and forlorn. So the next night, Edward's wife called Audra up and said, "Just tell me the truth, has Edward ever—ever touched you?" and Edward picked up the basement extension and whispered, "Say no, Audra!" which was just about the stupidest thing anyone could've possibly done, in Audra's opinion, and it blew up into a big scandal and she was blacklisted as a babysitter by the whole entire neighborhood and— You know, actually, maybe it wasn't so surprising that Audra's mind always leapt to some sort of sordid answer so quickly after all.)

"Hey, Melissa, how are you?" Audra said. "I love those boots. Are they new? Are they Uggs? I've never seen that color before. Matthew's in his room, he wants to show you something on Google Earth. He wants a peanut butter sandwich for dinner— you know how he likes that, right? And he can have chocolate milk with dinner, and he can watch half an hour of TV, and read a little before bed but lights out by nine, and keep going back in to check, because otherwise, he'll turn the light on again."

Melissa said nothing, just nodded gently. Graham had noticed that shy people loved Audra because she talked so much, and she frequently did both parts of the conversation.

"Okay, great," Audra said now, though Melissa had not actually said a word. "I guess we're off."

Melissa smiled. "I know the drill by now."

"Well, good," Audra said. "Because I feel like I was machine-gunning you with information there."

Melissa laughed. They said good night, and as they walked out, Graham thought that if he had made a joke like that to Melissa, it would have been awkward, not funny. It was as though Melissa could not see or hear him. That was the real reason he couldn't imagine having an affair with her. He was dead to her, but Audra, at barely forty—Audra was still young enough to move in the real world.

Bentrup answered the door of Elspeth's apartment, and Audra said, "Goodness!" in a startled voice. (It was even ruder than it sounds, if that's possible.)

But Graham knew what she meant because he was shocked by Bentrup's appearance, too. It wasn't so much that Bentrup was in his early sixties, or that his hair was bright silver, or that it was slicked back from his forehead in a pompadour, or that he had a deep artificial-looking tan the color of toast, or that his eyes were caught in nets of wrinkles, like a reptile's, or that he was wearing a green velvet smoking jacket and an *ascot*—it was all of these things. All those details added up to make him someone entirely other than Graham had expected.

"It's so nice to meet you," Audra said.

So that, technically, she'd said *Goodness, it's so nice to meet you*, except with a long pause in the middle and the intonation all wrong.

"And you, too, my dear," Bentrup said, taking one of her hands in both of his. His voice was another surprise: British and fulsome and taking too long to get to the ends of words.

Then he shook hands with Graham and took the bottle of wine they'd brought and there was a little flurry of conversation (Bentrup asking how their trip over was and Audra saying, "Well, you won't believe this but the cabdriver told me how to program our TV remote") and then they followed Bentrup down the hall.

The Rosemund was just as Graham thought it would be—glossy and hard-edged, with so many chrome and stainless steel fixtures that it seemed as though the apartment were wearing braces. It was the kind of place that had to be kept aggressively clean, otherwise all those reflective surfaces would double any messes you left behind.

Elspeth was in the kitchen. "Graham, hello," she said, and kissed his cheek. He wasn't expecting that. "And you must be Audra," she said. Was he imagining it or was there just the slightest bit of mockery in her tone? Like *You must be Audra, unless Graham's moved on to someone else by now.*

"Hello," Audra said, and her voice was warm and pleased. "I've heard so much about you."

"Likewise," Elspeth said, and turned to stir something on the stove.

This was something he'd forgotten about Elspeth, how she tended to be very minimal in conversation sometimes, and a certain kind of person found that minimalism uncomfortable and rushed in to fill the void with revealing chatter.

"You know, I think I was in this building years and years ago for an alcoholic intervention," Audra said. "I was working as this woman's personal assistant and she asked me to participate. She was arranging the intervention for her husband, and I think she wanted to up the numbers. I was afraid she might fire me if I said no, so I went and then we all had to get up and talk about how the husband's drinking was impacting our lives and I didn't know what to say. I mean, I *wanted* to say, 'Well, it's impacting my life because I have to be here on a Friday night when I could be out drinking with my friends,' but I didn't feel that would be overly helpful."

Bentrup was twisting a corkscrew into a wine bottle. "Did it work?" he asked.

"Hmmm?" Audra said absently, as though she had already moved on to thinking about something else. "Oh, no. It turned out that the husband was in an alcoholic blackout that night and didn't even remember there'd *been* an intervention." She turned toward Elspeth. "So if you don't mind my asking, why don't you like restaurants?"

Elspeth pursed her lips slightly. "Why don't you like Chinese food?"

"I do like Chinese food," Audra said.

"Well, name something you don't like," Elspeth said.

"People's breath after they've eaten Doritos," Audra answered so promptly that Elspeth blinked.

"Okay," she said, still stirring the pan on the stove. "Why don't you like people's breath after they've eaten Doritos? It's the same sort of question."

"Not really," Audra said. "Because, I mean, have you ever *smelled* someone's breath after they've eaten Doritos? It's really unpleasant, but restaurants are, on the whole, pleasant experiences."

"Unless the waiters have been eating Doritos," Bentrup said, and Audra laughed.

"Now I have to ask *you* something," she said to him.

"Certainly," he said.

"If you work in the shoe department, why are you wearing slippers?"

Bentrup was indeed wearing slippers—or maybe they were moccasins. They looked new and stiff, nothing like the ones Graham wore at home, which bulged out at the sides like a hamster's cheeks. Bentrup smiled. "I don't like to be too predictable."

During all of this, Graham was very distracted by the blouse Elspeth was wearing. It was black silk and had a *picture* of a white bow on it, but not an actual bow. Graham liked analogies and he couldn't help thinking that there was some way in which the blouse suited Elspeth perfectly. It was not that she was a two-dimensional person, he knew her far too well to ever think that. It was more the self-contained, insoluble, impenetrable nature of it.

Bentrup raised his wineglass. "To your very good health," he said.

"Cheers," Audra said, clinking her glass with his.

Graham and Elspeth raised their glasses. Graham glanced at Elspeth and saw that he could read her expression as easily as he read a clock face: she was amused at her own expense. *Who would have ever thought I'd be socializing with these two particular people?* She was thinking that, or something close to it, he could tell.

It was amazing, really, that after so many years apart, he and Elspeth still spoke in marital code.

He called the day after dinner to thank her and she said, "It was a pleasure. Audra is certainly vivacious." But what she meant was *She talks too much, however do you stand it?*

"I enjoy that about her," he said. "Bentrup is extremely dapper."

"I like the way he looks," she said spikily, having understood him correctly to mean *He looks like a dandy.* (Actually, Audra had said on the way home that Bentrup reminded her of a sexy snake-oil salesman, but Graham wasn't going to go there.)

"I'm sorry I didn't get to meet Matthew," Elspeth said, which didn't make much sense because Matthew hadn't been invited.

"Well, it was a school night," Graham said.

"Audra told me he goes to the Laurence School," Elspeth said. "I didn't realize he was autistic." *I guess everything didn't turn out so hunky-dory for you and Audra after all.*

"He's not autistic," Graham said, his voice rapping out more sharply than he'd intended. "He might not even have Asperger's. No one knows. But he's a visual learner and he does well at Laurence. Lots of kids there have exceptional IQs." And, as anyone with a special-needs child could tell you, that sort of defensive speech is code for *Watch it.*

"Yes, of course," Elspeth said. "And Audra showed me a picture. He looks like her, very handsome." *I can give compliments, even about your second wife. I am not a small, vindictive person.*

So Graham said, "Matthew reminds me of your father, actually."

"My father?"

"Yes," Graham said. "Very bright and mathematical but not

terribly good at picking up on social signals." *Take that.* Actually, it sort of described Elspeth, too.

"My father did not have Asperger's," Elspeth said, emphasizing every other word slightly. *You never liked him.*

"Not diagnosed, no," Graham said. "But remember the first time you took me skiing with your family and he asked me to calculate what temperature water boils at at ten thousand feet? That was his idea of small talk." *I know how strange your family is, don't forget.*

"And you did it," Elspeth said. *Who are* you *to accuse my father of having Asperger's?*

"Yes," Graham admitted reluctantly. And even more reluctantly, but also involuntarily, he supplied the answer again. "One hundred and ninety-four degrees Fahrenheit. For each thousand feet above sea level, the boiling point of water drops two degrees."

"And I married you," Elspeth said. "So there you go."

This last part was a little cryptic, even for code. Did she mean, *I married you and look how horribly it turned out,* or *I married you because you reminded me of my father, so it serves me right,* or even something more general, like *For want of a nail, the kingdom was lost?*

Graham didn't know how to respond, so he said, "Thanks again for last night. The red snapper was delicious."

"Thank you," she said. "I took an Asian cooking class last year."

There was a moment of silence when they both seemed to realize that they had actually meant what they were saying. They weren't speaking in code anymore. Graham felt a needle of fear: God only knew what she might say now.

So he said he had a meeting and that they should all have dinner again soon and he would be in touch, and she said the same sorts of things back, and—safely cloaked in code again—they hung up.

Can I just ask," Audra said that night. "Is Elspeth in or is she out?"

They were sitting on the sofa after dinner and she was drawing dolphins freehand for a brochure she was designing for a scuba diving school. Dolphins in left profile, dolphins in right profile, dolphins looking straight ahead, smiling, staring, laughing. She tore each sketch out of the book after she drew it and threw it on the floor. It was how she got inspired.

"What are you talking about?" Graham asked.

"It's just something I've noticed about you as you get older," she said, sketching. "People are either in or out with you. Either you accept them as a friend and someone you're interested in, or you want no interaction with them."

"You couldn't be more wrong," Graham told her. "It's not something that's happened since I've gotten older. I've always been that way. I don't need to be friends with the doormen and the man at the bodega and the dentist."

"I'm not friends with the *dentist*," Audra said. (They had their own marital code.)

"You had lunch with him."

"Never!" She looked scandalized. "I think you mean Dr. Medowski." She'd had lunch with her gynecologist? This seemed even worse on a number of levels, but before he could say anything, she continued, "And you should be friends with the doormen, Graham. They'll do anything for me—call me a cab in the worst weather or carry the teeniest package."

"I can call my own cabs," he said. "And carry my own packages, too."

"You miss out on a lot, though," Audra said, tearing another sketch out of her book. A drawing of a dolphin talking on the phone floated to the floor. "They know so much gossip about everyone in the building. You know that couple on Two with the little redheaded boy who keeps pulling leaves off the plants in the lobby? Well, they hired a nanny last week and she quit after half an hour. *Half an hour.* Can you imagine? Anyway, you never answered—is Elspeth in or is she out?"

Graham considered for a moment before he answered. He and Elspeth had not made a very successful married couple, but maybe they could be successful friends. Didn't they have all the ingredients for that: a shared history and common interests and similar intellectual outlooks? Certainly if Audra could be friends with the checkout girl at the health-food store, he could be friends with Elspeth.

"In," he said finally. "She's in."

And so they began, cautiously, occasionally, to do the things that couples do.

Graham and Audra had Elspeth and Bentrup over for brunch and introduced them to Matthew.

"Do you know who Satoshi Kamiya is?" Matthew asked them.

"The head of Toyota?" Bentrup guessed.

"No," Matthew said. "He's the best origami guy in the world." He turned to Elspeth. "Did you know who he is?"

"No," she said. "Do you know who Alexander Fleming is?"

Matthew shook his head. "Does he do origami?"

"No," Elspeth said, never one to volunteer information.

"Do you do origami?"

"No."

"Who *is* Alexander Fleming?" Audra asked.

"He discovered penicillin," Elspeth said.

Audra frowned slightly. "I thought that was Jonas Salk."

(The rest of brunch went a lot better.)

But mainly they walked. They walked through Central Park and had hot dogs; they walked through Little Italy for the cannoli; they walked across the Brooklyn Bridge.

Since four people can't easily walk together, they tended to divide into pairs, and the formation of these pairings and subsequent conversations were fascinating to Graham.

Sometimes he walked with Elspeth and they updated each other on mutual friends' lives. (He and Elspeth never spoke directly of their marriage, only of the times before and after. Graham imagined it would be this way if you had a relative who went to prison.) Some of their friends had done so little in thirteen years that it was boring to hear the updates—"He still works in finance, his mother lives with them now"—but others were intriguing: Elspeth's cousin had left his wife for the teenage pool boy; one of their former neighbors had started a healing ministry after his eczema mysteriously improved; another friend had invented a self-propelled vacuum and was now a multimillionaire. It amazed Graham that he had forgotten some of these people completely, and yet they were still around, still in touch with Elspeth. He in turn told her about his mother and her sciatica; about some people he worked with whom she'd always been fond of; about a friend from high school who still called drunk at three a.m. sometimes. Every time they exchanged information about someone who had chosen sides in that long-ago split, Graham felt a little less responsible, a little like he'd repaired some tiny bit of damage.

He wondered sometimes why Elspeth agreed to these outings, and even suggested them. Surely *she* didn't feel guilty about their divorce. He thought maybe it was because she was, and always had been, a difficult person socially. He didn't mind her quirks, and neither did Audra, but how many other friends did Elspeth have? Not many, was Graham's guess.

Graham and Elspeth talked about the marble kitty cat sometimes, too, and speculated on its fate. Three months had gone by and Sotheby's had yet to sell it.

"I feel bad for it," Graham said.

"And for Aunt Mary, too," Elspeth said. "She thought it was this treasure and no one wants it."

"She should have had it buried with her," Graham said, and wondered suddenly if he'd gone too far and offended Elspeth, but she only laughed.

While he talked to Elspeth, Audra and Bentrup strolled ahead, deep in conversation. Graham thought privately that Bentrup was in awe of Audra—her flirtatiousness, her prettiness, her forceful personality. But Elspeth never seemed the slightest bit jealous, even though Audra always tucked her hand into Bentrup's arm as they walked, so maybe Graham was wrong about that. Later Audra would tell him that Bentrup was sixty-two, and that he grew up in Portsmouth, England, and that he used to go to tanning booths but didn't anymore, his skin just sort of stayed that color. Also, he'd been married twice, the first time to a woman named Tillie, who had an unshakable belief that dishcloths should be folded a certain way to avoid bad luck, and the second time to a woman named Margaret, who disliked it when Bentrup spat in the rhododendrons.

Sometimes Graham and Bentrup walked together, but they never spoke of anything personal. In fact, Graham found Bentrup almost maddeningly *im*personal, like some tour guide they'd hired and now regretted bringing along. He said things like, "Chinatown is the largest Chinese community outside Asia," and "While much of the foliage in Central Park appears natural, it is in fact almost entirely landscaped." Even worse, it took him easily—*easily*—five minutes to get to the end of any sentence with the way he drawled in his British accent. Was this the kind of conversation he had with Elspeth at home? Was this what she liked? But Graham never paid much attention to Bentrup because he was too busy trying to eavesdrop on Elspeth and Audra.

How opposite they were! How could one man have fallen in love with both of them?

"My grandmother always said that you should be totally packed and ready twenty-four hours before a trip," Audra said. "But I don't think she had so much *stuff.*"

"I agree with her," Elspeth replied. "You should be organized." Her use of *you* did not sound general.

And once Audra said, "Lorelei used to work at Baskin-Robbins and she believes your choice of flavor reveals all sorts of things about you."

"Who's Lorelei?" Elspeth said. Then a moment later, as though she were unable to resist, "What does my choice reveal about me?"

They had just come from Baskin-Robbins, and Graham had a moment of profound gratitude that Elspeth had not ordered vanilla, because God knew what Audra would have made of that.

"Oh, Lorelei says women who order Pralines 'n Cream are almost always PMSing," Audra said. "They are craving the salt and the sweet at the same time."

Salvation came from an unexpected source when Bentrup said, "Did you know there is a physiological basis for food cravings during premenstrual disorder?"

"Premenstrual *syndrome!*" Audra laughed. "It's not a personality disorder, though I guess maybe it seems like one."

She moved up to talk to Bentrup, and Graham dropped back to talk to Elspeth, as smoothly as partners in the Virginia reel.

One day they were having coffee at the High Line and Graham sat on a bench between Audra and Elspeth. He was eating a croissant with his coffee, and a flake of croissant stuck to the side of his mouth. Elspeth and Audra reached to brush it away at the same moment.

"Oh, sorry," Elspeth said, and it was the closest to embarrassed Graham had ever heard her sound.

"Hey, be my guest," Audra said. "I get to wipe crumbs off his face all the time." This seemed to Graham like a dangerous thing to say, but Elspeth only smiled and brushed the bit of croissant away.

"There," she said with satisfaction.

"I was looking forward to eating that," Graham said, and both women looked at each other and laughed, a sound that was lost quickly in the wind and the screech of seagulls, but one that seemed to Graham to linger on and on.

For some reason concerning Lorelei's apartment being renovated and unfit for company, Graham and Audra were having to have Lorelei and her husband, Doug, *and* their priest over for dinner so that Doug and Lorelei could get their godson baptized in their local church and not have to waste a Sunday driving to Staten Island. Or something like that. (Apparently the priest was outside Audra's direct sphere of influence and a mere phone call wouldn't suffice, hence the need for dinner.)

Graham didn't mind—he was just happy that Doug and Lorelei weren't moving in with them while their apartment was being renovated. (The den was available as guest quarters once more, now that Bitsy had finally gone back to her brownstone in Brooklyn—a move prompted solely by Bitsy's desire to prevent Ted from moving back to the brownstone first. It was strange now to think that Bitsy had left the magnifying glass of their apartment and gone back to being a teeny beige tile in the huge glittering eight-million-tile mosaic of New York City. It always surprised Graham when houseguests left and resumed their lives elsewhere.)

"We should invite Elspeth and Bentrup, too," Audra said.

"Why?"

"Because we, you know, *owe* them." Audra made a vague circular motion with her hand, presumably to indicate—what? The vast confusing ocean of who owed what to whom?

But Graham understood. Now that they were friends, Graham and Audra had to shuffle Elspeth and Bentrup into the friendship deck of cards, to be dealt back out again evenly in the form of social commitments. A dinner party for seven was just as much work as a dinner party for five, so okay.

Audra left it up to Graham to call Elspeth and ask if she and Bentrup would be interested in spending an evening helping them emotionally seduce a priest. He thought he was calling Elspeth's mobile, but it must have been her landline because Bentrup answered.

"Good evening," he drawled. It was less of a spoken word and more like a sticky drop of amber resin that flowed slowly down the line.

"Hello, Bentrup. It's Graham Cavanaugh."

"Ah, Graham, what a pleasure." Bentrup took nearly a full minute to round off the word *pleasure*. It made Graham want to snap his fingers in irritation.

"Yes, well," he said. "Audra and I are having a kind of impromptu dinner party tomorrow and we were hoping you and Elspeth could join us."

"How very kind of you," Bentrup said. "I will have to check with my lady."

Lady? Did he mean Elspeth? (Of course he did, because who else would Bentrup have to check with—the cleaning lady?) But did Elspeth know he referred to her this way? Did she *like* it?

"However, if I may be so informal," Bentrup continued, his voice lingering over every consonant, "I'm sure she and I will be delighted to come to your soiree. Please consider us a soon-to-be-confirmed yes."

"Okay, great," Graham said hastily.

They said their goodbyes and hung up. Graham felt that if there'd been a snare drum handy, he would have beat out a staccato rhythm just to get the sound of Bentrup's voice out of his head.

The buzzer sounded the next night and Graham went to answer it, expecting it to be Doug and Lorelei, but it was the priest, Father Hicks, a friendly, white-haired, round-faced man wearing a suit with a clerical shirt and collar under it. The only unusual thing about him was that he was very short, possibly under five feet, and Graham kept unintentionally talking to the area about six inches above Father Hicks's head.

Audra came tap-tapping in high heels down the hall from Matthew's bedroom. She looked very pretty, in a dark red dress, her hair pulled back in a gold clip. "Oh, my goodness," she said as soon as she saw Father Hicks. "I know you! You're the man I cut in front of in the supermarket checkout line. I'm sorry, I didn't know then that you were a priest or whatever."

Graham blinked, not sure where to start objecting. Father Hicks was a priest, not a *priest or whatever.* Did she think he was a vicar? Also, she seemed to be implying that she would have no remorse about cutting in front of a layman.

But Father Hicks only smiled and said, "That's perfectly all right."

And then, fortunately, Doug and Lorelei arrived. Doug was a big fleshy man with pale crew-cut hair you could see his scalp through. No matter what shirt Doug wore, his neck always squeezed over the collar in the back. He looked to Graham like a not-very-bright midwestern high school football player who now sold used cars. Actually, he was a native New Yorker and the chief commercial officer of an international company. Graham liked him a lot.

Bentrup and Elspeth arrived a minute later and there was a little burst of introductions, with everyone sort of talking over each other, and Bentrup saying, "The pleasure is entirely mine" *twice.*

Graham had to go into the kitchen and get dinner ready, so he missed whatever it was they found to talk about, though he could hear Audra offering wine to everyone. He prepared seven plates of tomato-and-mozzarella salad and then called them all into the dining room.

"You're so lucky Graham cooks," Lorelei said to Audra as soon as they were seated. "Doug can't cook a thing."

"Neither can I," Audra said. "Really, next to nothing. But you're a great cook, Lorelei. Now, Elspeth, tell me, when you and Graham were married, who did the cooking?"

Elspeth gave Audra one of her long looks and then she said, "We took turns."

"And do you cook, Bentrup?"

God, it was like being on some endless, awkward talk show.

"Oh, not at all," Bentrup said. "Not one bit, I'm afraid."

Audra looked thoughtful for a second. "So if Lorelei came to live with Graham, and I went to live with Doug, who would gain more weight? You guys, from cooking delicious meals for each other, or Doug and me, from ordering pizza all the time?"

Graham wasn't sure they should be talking about wife swapping, even of the culinary sort, in front of a priest, but to his surprise, Father Hicks joined right in. "Oh, you'd get tired of pizza pretty quick," he said. He pointed his fork at Graham and Lorelei. "But they'd just keep trying to outdo each other with lavish meals and get fatter and fatter."

"I think so, too," Audra said, giving him her most approving smile. "Now tell me, who cooks for you, Father?"

This topic carried them all the way through the chicken masala, though it did reveal a large amount of ignorance on Audra's part. Apparently, she thought Father Hicks lived in a kind of rooming house for priests (that was how she described it) and that the church paid some woman to cook for all of them. She was surprised to learn that he lived in an apartment and cooked his own meals.

"And what about laundry?" Audra asked.

"I have a washer and dryer," Father Hicks said. "I do my own laundry."

"Just like a regular person," Audra marveled.

Graham thought Doug and Lorelei's godson's chances of getting baptized in Father Hicks's church were probably low and falling.

Then Bentrup and Lorelei had a brief discussion about the price of mozzarella and a deli Bentrup knew of somewhere in Queens. "You must remind me later," he said to Lorelei. "I will give you the address forthwith."

Not for the first time, Graham wondered how successful Bentrup was as a shoe salesman. Did people get up and leave rather than listen to him? Or did they buy a pair of shoes just to shut him up?

He glanced across the table at Elspeth and their eyes caught for a second, like two coat hangers before you shake them free of each other.

After dinner, they moved into the living room. Audra sat next to Father Hicks on the sofa, and said, "Do you mind if I ask you a question?"

Without really meaning to, Graham held his breath, and he was pretty sure everyone else did, too.

"Go ahead," said Father Hicks.

"Well, I went to your church charity shop this week to buy a dresser," Audra said, "and I was wondering if you'd noticed that the man who works there looks just like a young Charlie Manson?"

"Oh, absolutely," Father Hicks said.

"I'm so glad it's not just me," Audra said. "But really, it was so unnerving being alone in the shop with him! I kept thinking, *Is he going to kill me, or brainwash me, or just sell me a dresser?* But he was as nice as could be. And going to school in social work, too."

Father Hicks nodded approvingly. "He's a good kid."

Audra took a sip from her wineglass. "And do you know our dentist, Dr. Alpen? I believe he's a member of your congregation."

"Oh, yes," Father Hicks said. "He's an usher."

"Well, I can't understand why Dr. Alpen is not off treating lepers somewhere," Audra said, "because he has absolutely saint-like patience when it comes to cleaning Matthew's teeth. Do you go to Dr. Alpen, Father? Or someone who, like, specializes in priests?"

"No, no," Father Hicks said. "My dentist is a Lutheran."

He seemed charmed by Audra's interest in his life, and not offended like a sensible person would be.

"Now, let's see," Audra said thoughtfully. "Who else do I know from your church? What about the Mosebys?"

"Oh, yes," Father Hicks said. "David and Carol and their five kids."

Audra leaned forward slightly. "Maybe you don't know this, but when their oldest son, Bobby, threatened to burn down the house unless his parents bought him a motorbike, *they bought him a motorbike.*"

"I'll have the community pray for him," Father Hicks said.

Audra laughed. "I think it might be a little late for that."

They both sounded very merry.

Graham said nothing and drank his wine. He understood that Audra was using this gossip to include Father Hicks, to draw him to her in a warm silk net that felt, for this evening anyway, like friendship. The gossip was all gentle and harmless, though Graham had no doubt whatsoever that Audra knew things about all these people that were far more shocking than anything Father Hicks had ever—*ever*—heard in confession.

"Perhaps you can tell me something," Father Hicks said to Audra. "Do you happen to know a former parishioner of mine named Brice Breedlove? Because he and his wife stopped coming very abruptly about a year ago, and they used to be such regular churchgoers."

"Oh, yes, I know what happened to Brice," Audra said unexpectedly. (Well, sort of really expectedly, actually.) She leaned forward to refill her wineglass and Father Hicks's. "Apparently God spoke to Brice one morning last year and told him that he was making a big mistake with his adjustable rate mortgage. And Brice was like 'What are you saying? You think I should get a fixed rate mortgage?' And God said, 'No, no, I want you to move right out of that beautiful expensive condo to a studio apartment in Queens and have no mortgage at all.'"

(She kept saying *God* as if He were some friend of hers, the way another person might say *Sheila.*)

"Heavens," Father Hicks said, looking a little startled.

"And furthermore, God wanted it done by his forty-sixth birthday!" Audra said. Then she touched Father Hicks's arm. "I mean, *Brice's* forty-sixth birthday, obviously. God is, like, seven hundred million years old."

"Did Brice do it?" Lorelei asked.

"Oh, yes," Audra said. "I don't think Brice's wife wanted to, but how can you argue with your husband and say you know more than God? Literally, more than God? So she went along with it and God made them have an estate sale to get rid of most of their earthly possessions and I bought their brand-new waffle iron for fifty cents, which is when Brice's wife told me all this. And now they live in Queens with almost no stuff and I guess they go to some church out there. Although maybe they don't really *need* to go to church at all, what with God talking to Brice directly."

(Now Audra was saying *God* somewhat ironically, as though it had quotes around it, but the way someone might say *Sheila* if Sheila were a poodle, or perhaps a rosebush.)

"Can we just back up for a second?" Doug asked. His eyes were sharp with interest. "You say God was against adjustable rate mortgages but did He say anything about jumbo loans?"

"You'd have to ask Brice that," Audra said primly.

"But why didn't God tell Brice to buy Apple stock ten years ago?" Elspeth said suddenly. (Trust Elspeth to find the loophole even in divine intervention.) "Then Brice could have afforded any house he wanted."

"I thought of that, too," Lorelei said.

"Well, Apple or Microsoft," Doug said to Elspeth somewhat critically. "Apple ten years ago or Microsoft twenty years ago."

"Indeed," Bentrup said. "It does seem there could have been some more forward thinking."

"You know, maybe God wasn't involved in people's finances before now," Audra said slowly. "He may only have started to think about finances extremely recently, since, in God's lifetime, the stock market is a very new thing. Maybe He wasn't sure it would last. Maybe God thought the stock market was like, I don't know, break dancing or cocaine."

Father Hicks's eyes were huge. "I think that is absolutely profound," he said.

He was gazing at Audra adoringly, and it seemed to Graham that he looked torn between wanting to convert her and wanting to pounce on her.

Finally, at ten-thirty, Doug and Lorelei made reluctant noises about going home, and Elspeth and Bentrup agreed. They all went to the front hall together. Elspeth had the deeply reflective air of someone who has just seen a particularly savage wildlife documentary, and Bentrup had taken on the seedy, shellacked look of a late-night convenience store shopper.

"Thank you for a delightful evening," Father Hicks said, hugging Audra. His head fit under her chin and he seemed to rest his head on her breasts for a moment.

Lorelei hugged Audra, too, and Graham heard her whisper, "You are the most *wonderful* friend."

Graham shook hands with everyone, and he and Audra watched them walk out into the hall toward the elevator, Father Hicks looking none too steady on his feet.

Audra shut the door and leaned against it. "Do you think we should give Matthew some sort of late baptism?" she asked.

"No," Graham said. "I definitely do not."

"Thank God," Audra said. "Because I don't think I have another such evening in me."

And she went straight to bed without even clearing the table.

You won't believe who I ran into today," Audra said one night a few days later.

"Who?" Graham asked.

"Bentrup!"

They were in the kitchen. Audra had promised to make something like two million cookies for the bake sale at Matthew's school tomorrow, and she was melting chocolate in the double boiler while Graham unwrapped caramels.

"Where did you see Bentrup?" he asked.

"At Barneys."

"Ah," said Graham.

"I went there to buy some mascara," Audra said, "and then I thought I would just mosey up to the shoe department and see if he was there and he was!" (Toward the end of the sentence, her voice had picked up speed, making it sound as though this were some amazing coincidence.)

"That makes sense, given that he works there," Graham said. "Did he see you?"

"Oh, yes," Audra said. "I went in and said hello and he was so nice. He took me through the whole store and introduced me to tons of people and let me use his employee discount to buy some scented candles and I told him he should buy one for Elspeth but he said she didn't believe in them. How can you not believe in scented candles? They're not like UFOs."

Audra loved scented candles, which was something he'd always found slightly incongruous in her personality. "Why?" she'd asked once. "It's not as though I like *Yankee* candles." Graham had often tried to find the perfect comparison for the way she'd said that, something to do with champagne or caviar or maybe even real estate ("It's not as though I live in *Queens*"), but he could never come up with anything that had exactly the right inflection. He had eventually concluded that it depended on some insider knowledge of scented candles he didn't possess.

Audra was still talking. "And then we had coffee in the employee restaurant—did you know there's a whole other café that the normal customers don't even know about?—and then he had to go back to work."

"What was more exciting, the employee discount or the employee restaurant?" Graham asked.

She did not even have to think about it. "The discount, of course. Though we had a very interesting conversation over coffee. He told me that when he and Elspeth go to dinners and stuff for her law firm, she wants him to tell people he's retired, instead of saying he works at Barneys. Sadly, I was unable to find out what kind of sex they have."

"What do you mean, what kind of sex?" he asked.

"Well, you know, how often and what position and does she make him wash his hands first and does he fetch her slippers in his teeth," Audra said. "Really, I'm so interested, any little detail would have thrilled me. Aren't you curious?"

"No," Graham said. "I don't like to think about it." This was half truth and half lie because he honestly didn't like to think about it, but he was very curious. To him, Elspeth and Bentrup seemed an entirely platonic couple, like Bert and Ernie. "And have you ever, *ever* made a man wash his hands first?"

Audra shook her head. "But she's so fastidious and I'm so notoriously unfastidious."

Notorious to whom? The general population or men she'd had sex with or what?

Audra stopped stirring and looked at him. Her hair was pulled back in a ponytail and her skin was flushed from the heat of the double boiler. Graham would not have improved one single feature of her face.

She gestured at him impatiently. "I can't believe that in this entire time you've unwrapped three caramels. It goes much faster if you use your fingers. The way you sit there with your bifocals and a penknife!"

"What's wrong with a penknife?" Graham asked. "And why shouldn't I wear my bifocals? Otherwise, I'll cut my hand and bleed all over the caramels and you wouldn't like that, either."

Audra moved the double boiler off the burner and came over to help. "It's more the picture you create," she said. Her fingers were monkey-quick on the caramels, unwrapping three more in the time it took her to say that. Her voice was amused. "It's like, I don't know, you're a patient in an old folks' home and this is some project I've given you and you don't know how to do it." She laughed. She had a habit of laughing at her own jokes.

Graham laughed, too. He was glad, suddenly, that she was teasing him about seeming old, because, he realized, when she stopped teasing him about it, it would be because he really was.

They met Elspeth and Bentrup for dinner in a small French restaurant on the Upper East Side that Audra knew.

"Is this okay?" Audra said to Elspeth while they were waiting to be seated. "It's not freaking you out?"

"No," Elspeth said. "I don't have a *phobia* about restaurants. I just don't particularly like them."

Audra looked intrigued. "Is it because you're paying someone? For something you could do in your own home?"

"Yes, sort of."

"I'll bet you don't like getting massages, either," Audra said.

"Correct," Elspeth said.

"I *love* massages," Audra said. "I don't mind that I'm paying someone to touch me. That doesn't extend to hookers, though." She glanced at Bentrup with an apologetic expression, as though to imply that everyone present knew Bentrup had a heavy prostitute habit but that they all liked him anyway.

Bentrup smiled reassuringly. "I don't go to hookers, either," he said.

"I think being a hooker would be the worst job in the world," Audra said, and her voice took on a slight relish. "Well, except maybe cat food salesperson. But honestly, imagine all the unattractive men you'd have to have sex with if you were a hooker. Just think about it."

"I am, I am," Bentrup said. He seemed to have gotten the knack of conversing with Audra, the knack being that you had to pretend you were talking to someone in the time before society had formed and social boundaries had been invented.

"If you *were* to go to a hooker, though," Audra said to Bentrup in a slow, considering voice, "what-all would you ask for?"

Bentrup looked alarmed and another man waiting to be seated looked delighted, but fortunately the hostess came to lead them to their table just then. Audra went first, followed by Bentrup, but

Elspeth lingered for a moment to give Graham a hard look. Her eyes reminded him of a certain kind of gravel, the type that bit your feet when you walked on it barefoot. She probably thought this was the kind of conversation he and Audra had at home all the time. (It sort of was.)

The hostess seated them at a table. They ordered wine and listened to the specials and then they were left to study the menus.

"What are you having?" Audra asked Bentrup.

"Well, now," he said, rolling the words around in his mouth like a merlot. "I believe I'll have the baked clams and the pork tenderloin."

"I know without even asking that Graham will have the duck," Audra said.

"Oh, do you still like duck so much?" Elspeth said to him. "It always bothered you that I never cooked it."

It seemed to Graham that a crevasse had opened suddenly, that he was perilously close to falling in. "I do still like duck," he said carefully. "I cook it myself."

"What are *you* having?" Audra said to Elspeth.

"The trout with raspberry vinegar," Elspeth said. Graham could have predicted that, too.

"I'm sorry to interrogate you," Audra said, "but my grandfather always wanted everyone at the table to order the same thing, and it sort of affected me."

This confirmed something that up to now Graham had only suspected: that Elspeth's refusal to be charmed by Audra's eccentricity made Audra act even more eccentric in front of her. The grandfather story was true, he happened to know, but she generally only told it when she wanted attention of some sort.

"Why on earth would he want that?" Elspeth asked.

"He thought it would be easier on the waiter," Audra said. "He thought if we didn't all order the same thing, the waiter would have some sort of breakdown."

Elspeth looked a little astonished. "Did you all do it?"

But it was as though having finally gotten Elspeth's attention, Audra had lost interest. "Oh, sometimes," she said, studying her own menu. "More often, we just changed our orders when he was in the bathroom or something."

It made her sound callous, suddenly, and selfish and insensitive and unkind, and all the things she wasn't.

Then one night they went over to Elspeth and Bentrup's for dinner, and Elspeth answered the door. She had a glass of red wine in her hand and looked exceptionally pale. It took Graham a minute to realize she wasn't wearing any makeup.

"Oh," Elspeth said when she saw them. "I meant to call you and cancel but I forgot."

"What's wrong?" Audra asked. "What can we do?"

Elspeth studied them for a moment. "Come on in," she said finally.

She didn't hold the door for them but walked ahead into the apartment, calling over her shoulder, "Get some glasses from the kitchen, Graham. You know where they are."

He did know exactly where they were. Elspeth never changed anything in the kitchen. He went into the kitchen and pulled two more glasses out of the cupboard.

Audra called, "I think you should bring another bottle of wine, too." She said it exactly the way she told him to bring Tylenol and the thermometer when Matthew had a fever, so Graham picked up another bottle from the counter and hurried into the dining room.

The table was not set, the only things on it were a mostly empty wine bottle and Elspeth's glass. She sat at the head of the table with Audra on her left. Graham sat across from Audra.

"Where's Bentrup?" he asked.

This question seemed to make Elspeth take a very long drink of wine. "I don't know," she said finally. "He left. I told him to leave."

"Oh, Elspeth," Audra breathed. "How terrible. What happened?" She motioned impatiently for Graham to open the wine. He obeyed.

"Well," Elspeth said. "Last night he said—"

"Wait, wait," Audra interrupted. "Where were you? What were you doing, exactly?" Audra liked her stories to have context.

"Oh-kay," Elspeth said slowly, in a we'll-do-it-your-way-if-we-must voice. "Last night we went to a farewell dinner for this man who works in my department. Yes, Audra, it was at a *restaurant*." She took another enormous swallow of wine. Graham wondered if she would be able to finish her story at this rate. "And the people at our table were discussing movies and Bentrup said that he saw *Accidental Love* last week, at a matinee."

Audra moaned.

Elspeth nodded.

Graham knew something had passed between them—that some essential piece of information had been exchanged—but he didn't have a clue what it was. "I don't get it," he said.

Both women looked at him impatiently.

"No man would go see a romantic comedy by himself," Audra explained. "Especially not in the afternoon. He obviously went with a woman."

And then Elspeth said something else but Graham didn't hear what it was because it was almost like he had physically left the room. It seemed as though he and Elspeth and Audra were all carts going along a track in a coal mine, and his cart had suddenly been shunted off on a separate track into a dark shaft while theirs continued ahead. Graham was so enveloped by emotion that he was utterly unaware of his surroundings, and the emotion was vindication. He was not the only person who couldn't be faithful to Elspeth! Bentrup couldn't do it either!

When Graham reentered the conversation, only a few seconds had passed and Elspeth was saying, "So this morning, I hid his iPhone and he looked and looked for it but finally he had to go to work without it and I took it into the office with me and hacked the pass code—"

"You hacked the pass code?" he asked, distracted despite himself. "How long did that take you?"

Elspeth waved her wineglass dismissively. "About five tries. It was his birth date but done the European way, with the day first."

"Oh," Graham said.

"Anyway," Elspeth continued, "I entered the pass code and there were all these sexy text messages from some woman."

Audra shook her head. "What a fucking idiot," she said.

Graham and Elspeth both looked at her. Now, Graham thought, Audra would say Bentrup was an idiot to cheat on Elspeth, and he felt a momentary pride in Audra for knowing what to do. But what Audra actually said was "Everyone knows you get caught with text messages."

Elspeth rolled her eyes. "I called him at work and we came home to discuss it and he admitted everything. It's apparently some thirty-year-old woman and it's been—"

"Thirty!" Audra exclaimed. "What *sort* of thirty-year-old?"

"Does it matter?" Elspeth asked, her voice cool.

"It would matter to me," Audra said thoughtfully. "I mean,

was it a thirty-year-old bombshell or some sort of chunky, messy girl who keeps pigeons?"

Elspeth stroked her chin with the side of her forefinger and looked at Audra for a long moment. Audra gazed back, unperturbed. It occurred to Graham that here, finally, was the similarity between the two women he'd chosen to marry: they were both totally unrufflable, one out of iciness, the other out of obliviousness.

"At any rate," he interposed hastily. "You threw him out."

Elspeth finished her wine. "Yup," she said, and he knew she must be very drunk, because she always said *yes*, never even *yeah*.

"Have you had anything to eat?" he asked. "I could fix you a sandwich."

He was a big believer in food as the answer to most of life's questions.

She shook her head. "I think I'd like you to go, if you don't mind."

"Are you sure?" Audra said, as though there had been anything even slightly equivocal about Elspeth's words or tone.

Elspeth nodded, and so Graham and Audra gathered up their coats, which hung over the backs of their chairs since Elspeth had never taken them.

"We can let ourselves out," Graham said.

Elspeth smiled, a wry complicated smile. "I know."

He regretted his words now. Wasn't that a version of how their marriage had ended, Graham letting himself out?

And so they left. Graham made sure the door locked behind them in case Elspeth got too drunk to get up and check. He didn't want to be held responsible for her being murdered in her bed, along with whatever else she held him responsible for.

They rode the elevator in silence, and as they walked through the lobby, Audra sighed deeply. "She hates us."

"What?" Graham said, startled.

"She hates us now."

Graham cleared his throat. "I think that might be—premature."

"Didn't you see the way she looked at us?" Audra asked. "We're not her friends anymore, we're one of *them* again: the cheaters, the trollops, the bastards."

She sighed a second time, and Graham put his arm around her as they went out through the revolving doors and into the cool night air. Audra was not quite as oblivious as he thought.

Graham waited for Audra to say it and when, after five days, she didn't, he couldn't resist saying it himself: "I guess you can't use that Barneys discount anymore."

"I know!" Audra said. "I thought of that right away."

They were in the kitchen, drinking wine on one side of the breakfast bar, while Matthew sat on the other, folding an origami creation called a Snake Dragon. Audra was folding origami, too, some part of the dragon's tail. Just like the Old Masters had had apprentices who filled in the backgrounds of paintings, Matthew had Audra, who sometimes did the easier folds on very complicated projects.

"But we have to be loyal to Elspeth, even if she is ignoring us," Audra said.

Graham had called Elspeth twice and left messages, asking if there was anything she needed, if there was anything at all that they could do. She hadn't returned either call. Now both he and Audra glanced at the phone on the kitchen wall, even though they both had cellphones, and multiple email accounts, and Graham had a phone at his office. There were probably a dozen avenues Elspeth could use to ignore them.

"Why do we have to be loyal to Elspeth?" Graham asked.

"You're doing that fold wrong," Matthew said from across the counter.

"Sorry," Audra said absently. To Graham she said, "Because Elspeth's more, like, family or whatever. We have a connection to her. Besides, what are we going to do, have Bentrup and his new girlfriend over for dinner? That would be so—tangential."

Graham could not help thinking that they'd certainly had more tangential social interactions. Last year the locksmith who came to fix the dead bolt ended up sleeping in the den for two nights because his wife had stopped speaking to him due to the fact that he insisted on cutting the dead skin off his feet with a very small pair of scissors instead of using a pumice stone. ("Have you ever *heard* of anything so ludicrous?" Audra asked. Yes, he had: letting the locksmith sleep over. Although the locksmith had repaired their toaster for free.)

"It's supposed to be a valley fold," Matthew said.

"Hey, I'm doing my best," Audra answered. She took a new square of origami paper from the stack on the counter and started again. "You know," she said, "I used to have this fantasy that Elspeth had a terminal illness and asked me to give you back for six months, and I did."

Graham was speechless for a second. "I can't imagine who would hate that more, me or Elspeth."

"Well, in my fantasy, she was very grateful to me, and you were very dutiful, and you sort of even fell back in love a little," Audra said wistfully. "You had these beautiful months together, and I used the time to paint."

"Good God," Graham said. (When she came out with things like that, it was like being married to a less talented, prettier Van Gogh.)

"Could you *concentrate*?" Matthew asked, in such a perfect imitation of Audra's own exasperated voice that both Graham and Audra laughed.

"Okay," she said. "Show me what I'm doing wrong."

She and Matthew bent their heads together over the counter, and Graham, momentarily excluded, stared at the phone again. Audra had a theory (talk about ludicrous!) that when you called someone and they were home but not answering, the ringing sound had an ever so slightly different timbre to it. Although Graham had made fun of this for years, he could not help wondering now if maybe the reverse was true and the *silence* of this phone had a different quality because Elspeth wasn't calling it. A dry, chalky, guilt-inducing silence, which filled his throat like dust.

They had taken to going to an Asian supermarket Elspeth had told them about on lower Broadway on Saturday mornings while Matthew was with his dyslexia tutor.

The supermarket was owned by a Chinese man and his mother-in-law, and the man had once called them at home to tell them that Audra had left her purse in the frozen foods aisle, actually *in* the freezer full of dumplings. ("I guess I put it in there when I took the dumplings out," she'd mused, undisturbed. "Some unconscious check-and-balance thing.") So now while Graham shopped, Audra went into the back room and drank tea and talked to the man and his mother-in-law. She called them Hwang and Li, which amused Graham since he suspected that those were their last names and Audra was unaware that Chinese people say their surnames first. This didn't seem to keep her from getting to know them, however, and advising them about colleges for the oldest son.

And on this Saturday, while Graham was pushing his cart along the dusty, spicy, fragrant aisles, he saw Elspeth. She was wearing a pale blue linen coat buttoned all the way up, even though the weather was warm, and her hair and makeup were as flawless as ever. Graham had given up leaving messages two weeks before.

"Hey," he said, pushing his cart to the side so it was nose to nose with hers. "I've been meaning to call you."

She looked annoyed. "I hate it when people say that," she said. "Like you remind them of some forgotten chore."

Actually, Graham sort of hated that, too. So why had he said it and why did he hate hearing she hated it so much?

"Well," he said, choosing his words carefully. "Maybe it would be more accurate to say that I have been thinking about you. Wondering how everything is."

"If that's your way of asking about Bentrup," she said, "he's gone."

"It was my way of asking about *you*," Graham said softly.

"I'm alone," she said.

There didn't seem to be much of an answer to that, but he tried. "Would you like to come over sometime, maybe for lunch? Audra and I—"

Elspeth slumped against her cart suddenly, forsaking her usual perfect posture. "Could we not do this anymore?" she said. "Not pretend to be friends? I really don't need you and Audra to show me how great your marriage is and prove to me that you were meant to be together."

"That was *never* my intent," Graham protested. But at the same time, a very soft dissonant chord chimed once in his chest. They hadn't meant to do that. Had they?

Elspeth turned and walked away. It took Graham a moment to realize she had abandoned her cart and was leaving the store, and by the time he did, the bell over the front door was already jingling as she walked out.

He was still standing there when Audra came down the aisle behind him and said, "Guess what? Hwang's son got into NYU! They gave me some spring rolls to celebrate." She was carrying a small Tupperware box. "Are you almost done? Because we should go get Matthew. Oh, look, someone went off and left a shopping cart."

Graham thought he could ask any of the women he knew how motherhood had changed them, and they would all sigh and talk about how their hips had widened or their skin had coarsened or their feet had flattened (Audra claimed her *arms* were hairier), but Graham thought the real changes were mental. The real changes were a tendency to give ten-minute warnings before leaving the house; a restlessness at school pickup time even on weekends and holidays; a previously unsuspected knowledge of the lyrics to folk songs; and the strange compulsion to comment aloud on everyday sights. Oh, look, a drawbridge. Oh, look, a fire truck. Oh, look, a mother duck and her ducklings. Oh, look, someone lost a glove, someone dropped an earring, someone forgot a math book, someone went off and left a shopping cart.

Audra glanced into Elspeth's abandoned cart briefly, and then continued on down the aisle. She didn't comment further, perhaps because Matthew wasn't there, or perhaps because she was still thinking about Hwang's son, or perhaps because she just didn't care.

. . .

One week later, Graham got a check in the mail at his office. The check was from Elspeth. There was no letter with it, only a careful notation in the memo line of the check: *Proceeds from the sale of Sotheby's item.* Ah, his half of the value of the marble kitty cat, which must have finally sold. It came to slightly less than two thousand dollars.

Graham sat at his desk and looked at the check for a long time. Not much doubt now. He was "out" with Elspeth, if he had ever been in. For once, he didn't feel particularly guilty. He didn't think this was his fault, or Elspeth's, or even Bentrup's. Maybe in some relationships there was so much history that fondness and guilt and curiosity and familiarity remained separate elements and could never be melted down into friendship. He had a sudden urge to tell Elspeth this.

Instead, he gathered up his things and left the office.

Olivia was on the phone to her roommate. "I'm *pretty* sure our stove is gas," she said. "You know that little circle of fire? I don't think you get that on an electric stove."

She trilled her fingers at Graham.

It was early evening. He went across the street to the bank and put Elspeth's check in the night deposit box. Then on impulse, he walked the fifteen blocks to Barneys. He went straight to the housewares department and discovered that they had a whole counter dedicated to "Home Fragrance."

"What's the most expensive scented candle you have?" he asked the girl behind the counter.

The girl's carefully made-up face betrayed no surprise. "That would be the Joya Coup de Foudre," she said. "It's two hundred and twenty-five dollars. A limited edition candle with notes of cassis, cedar leaf, suede, and smoke."

Graham resisted the urge to make a joke about how all candles were sort of limited edition by nature, and all must smell of smoke, given that they were on fire. "That's perfect," he said. "Can you wrap one up for me?"

"Certainly," the girl said, and then Graham waited forever while she wrapped the candle and put it carefully in a tiny carrier bag with tissue paper and even sprinkled some rose petals on top. He paid with his credit card and went back out on the street.

Graham decided he would walk home.

He knew that Elspeth's check was still in the deposit box, that it wouldn't be added to his account until tomorrow, and wouldn't clear for at least two days after that. But it felt as though he'd purchased the candle with Elspeth's money. It was extravagant, and it came from Barneys, and Audra would love it. These things were as deeply pleasing to Graham as the nap of velvet against his fingers, though he could not have explained exactly why.

It was late September now. On Wednesday evenings, like this one, Graham picked Matthew up from Clayton's apartment. Wednesdays were half days at Matthew's school, so Audra dropped Matthew off at noon, and Matthew and Clayton did origami together until Graham picked him up at seven. Matthew loved it and it was a break for Audra (and for Clayton's wife, Graham suspected).

Graham pushed the buzzer and heard footsteps, and Clayton answered. "Come in, we're just finishing up."

Graham followed Clayton down the hall, past many framed origami creations, to the dining room, where Matthew was still folding.

"Hey, buddy," Graham said. "Time to go."

Matthew frowned. "We're working on the Tadashi Phoenix."

They had been working on the phoenix now for several weeks. Pieces of paper lay all over the table in various states of complicated folds. Graham couldn't tell which were parts of the phoenix and which were unsuccessful attempts that had been crumpled up and discarded.

"I know," Graham said. "But we have to go. Get your backpack and stuff, okay?"

Matthew moved away reluctantly and Graham was left to talk to Clayton. "This is very impressive, very detailed," Graham said, gesturing to the phoenix parts on the table. It was a kind of all-purpose origami remark, but it usually worked.

"Thank you." Clayton beamed. "This particular phoenix is very difficult, as you may be aware. We're working from crease patterns."

Audra was right. They couldn't let Matthew grow up to be like this guy. If he was going to spend his Wednesdays here, maybe they should insist Matthew take alligator wrestling on Thursdays, or else apprentice him into some seedy, messy occupation, like emergency plumbing.

Matthew showed up with his backpack and they said goodbye to Clayton and went out on the street.

"Are we going to get a hot dog?" Matthew said worriedly. Graham had bought Matthew a hot dog from a street vendor on the way home from the first lesson, and with Matthew, anything done once became a routine that had to be followed forever.

"Sure," Graham said, and Matthew relaxed.

They walked toward Tompkins Square Park in companionable silence. Graham thought, as he did every Wednesday, that if they walked around the south side of the park, they would pass a gourmet shop that Elspeth had taken him and Audra to weeks earlier, when they were still double-dating. They had gone there one Sunday. Audra and Bentrup had stayed at the front of the store, sampling about a dozen kinds of lavender honey and calling to each other, "Try this one!" "No, this one!" "Wait, here, here—it's like paradise on a breadstick!"

But Elspeth had taken Graham over to the mushroom bins and shown him the shiitakes and the oysters and the portobellos and even rarer ones like hen of the woods and blue foot.

"They have the most beautiful chanterelles in the autumn," Elspeth had said, her voice almost dreamy. "I sauté them in butter with cream and veal and a tiny bit of tarragon. I'll have to make it for you."

She had looked at him and her eyes were perfectly blue, so clear that he felt like he could see all the way to the back of them. She could have been fifty, or twenty, or no age at all.

Graham and Matthew had reached the edge of the park.

"There's a hot dog guy," Matthew said happily.

Graham gave him some money and let him run ahead. The hot dog would be Matthew's dinner but Graham didn't know yet what he and Audra would have.

He thought about the chanterelles, which would be in season now. He would like to make the dish that Elspeth had described. He could imagine it, how the ridges of the chanterelles would hold drops of tarragon-flavored cream like dozens of gently cupped hands. He thought about it, about how simple it would be to walk home on the south side of the park with Matthew and stop at the gourmet shop. But he didn't think he would. He never went there now.

Three

It was the night before the origami convention. Audra said that they could still change their minds and get their deposit back. Graham was pretty sure they couldn't get their deposit back, but he knew if he pointed that out, she would say she didn't care. She said whether they went or not all depended on how much they loved Matthew.

"That's easy, then," Graham said. "Because we love Matthew more than anything in the world." They were in the kitchen, speaking softly so Matthew wouldn't hear.

"Exactly!" Audra said. "And I *still* don't know if I can bear to go to a whole weekend of origami lectures in Connecticut."

It was kind of startling, Graham thought, how true that was.

"Well," he said slowly, "there are two of us, so one of us can go to the classes with Matthew and the other one can relax. We'll take turns. Maybe it won't be so bad."

"There's a *dinner dance*," Audra said.

"Dear God," Graham said.

"I know!" she said. "I think maybe it's some sort of divine punishment for how superior I felt last summer when the Bergmans had to take their little girls to that American Girl Doll Museum in Chicago."

"The Bergmans survived," Graham said. "And so will we."

"I guess," Audra said gloomily. Then she brightened a little.

"Maybe we'll meet Matthew's future wife there. Some nice Japanese girl who likes origami and who doesn't mind that Matthew is quiet and wears sweatpants all the time and has an extensive Pokémon collection."

It was awful to hear Matthew summed up that way, and yet Graham knew exactly what she meant.

An hour later, Graham found the phone number.

He was in his study, feeling unsettled. They hardly ever went away for just one night. They went to Long Island for a month during the summer and usually took a week at Christmas to go somewhere warm and tropical—although not *too* warm or *too* tropical given how scared Matthew was of bugs. Graham hated coming home from the Christmas trip, hated how unlived-in the apartment felt, hated the stale smell, the air pockets in the pipes making the faucets spit, the lack of food in the refrigerator, the sense that night was coming on and he didn't have enough provisions, hated how chilly it was until the furnace woke up and drove the cold air out again.

He realized he was out of stamps and went to ask Audra if she had any.

Audra and Matthew were in Matthew's room and she was saying, "Now, I'm going to put out everything you need to take on your bed, but I'm expecting you to pack it all in your suitcase," and Graham experienced the wave of weariness he sometimes felt when he considered all the steps it would take to make Matthew—any child, but especially Matthew—a functioning adult.

Audra's handbag was on the hall table and Graham opened it and took out her wallet. He knew she sometimes kept an extra stamp or two behind her driver's license, where they wouldn't be lost amid the shuffle of bills and receipts and business cards in the main part of her wallet. But Graham didn't find any stamps. Just a small scrap of yellow paper with the name *Jasper* written on it and a phone number.

Graham looked at it for a long moment. The handwriting wasn't Audra's.

Audra knew hundreds of people. She had Lorelei and then her other friends and her mom-friends (as she called them) and her work-friends and her professional contacts and her army of acquaintances and the man at the bodega and the girl at the library and the woman who ran the bake sale and the college student who found Audra's sweater at the library once and ended up coming to Thanksgiving dinner. (Graham could never quite figure out how that happened.) She knew all those people and probably all of their phone numbers, too, and maybe even one or two of them were named Jasper, but Graham didn't think this particular Jasper fell into any of those categories. Otherwise his phone number would be in Audra's phone or her Rolodex and not folded up and hidden here.

He heard Audra's footsteps and knew she was about to enter the hallway where he stood, but he made no move to put the paper back. Oh, he was not the secretive one here. Let her see him with that yellow scrap of paper, let her say, *Oh, Jasper? He's a commercial artist I work with over on Broadway and I have his number tucked in there because—*

But Audra crossed the hall from Matthew's room to their bedroom without noticing him.

Graham slipped the yellow piece of paper into his pocket and returned Audra's wallet to her handbag. He went into the kitchen and poured himself a glass of wine. He looked out the window for a long moment. Then he started chopping onions to make chili for dinner.

He felt no need to reach into his pocket and make sure the number was still there. He could sense it there, bright, like an ember, or a luminescent watch face, or an isotope of radium that would glow for hundreds of years.

They were up early the next morning. Matthew didn't have to be called to the table for once—he showed up before breakfast was even ready, dressed and chattering about the origami classes he wanted to take. As she put Matthew's plate of pancakes in front of him, Audra said, "I can't help but feel that across town, Clayton's wife is doing exactly what I'm doing: making breakfast and listening to an excited male talk about outside reverse folds."

They had agreed to give Clayton a ride to the convention, and when they drove up to his apartment building, Clayton did indeed seem excited; he was waiting outside with his backpack already on. That and the fact that Clayton's wife was with him made him seem very juvenile to Graham, as though they were picking up a contemporary of Matthew's rather than a grown man.

Clayton and his wife resembled each other: tall, lean, white-haired, bespectacled. The only real difference seemed to be that Clayton wore an outfit so mundane it defied description and his wife wore a cherry-red warm-up suit and matching red earrings made of extremely small paper airplanes.

"Hello, Pearl!" Audra said as they got out of the car, and Graham was grateful because he couldn't have remembered Clayton's wife's name if he'd been left in a prison cell for five years with nothing else to do.

"Hello, Audra," Pearl said cheerfully. "Hi, Graham, and hi, Matthew!" She had to lean down to say the last through the car window because Matthew hadn't gotten out.

"Let's get going, shall we?" Clayton said.

"Goodbye, dear," Pearl said.

Clayton was already getting in the backseat with Matthew. "Bye!" he called.

Audra and Graham said their farewells, too, and Pearl smiled and waved. She turned to walk back into the apartment building, off to enjoy a presumably origami-free weekend. Graham felt a pang of envy so sharp it was like being snapped with a rubber band.

The feeling that Clayton was ten instead of in his fifties persisted. He took forever to buckle his seat belt, and he adjusted his air-conditioning vent far more than could have actually been necessary. He opened and shut the cup holder quite a few times, and probably would have rolled the windows up and down, too, except that Graham had locked them as soon as he'd noticed Clayton's preoccupation with the cup holder.

Audra must have felt it, too, because after a few minutes, she said, "Clayton, can I ask you to not bang the armrest like that?" exactly the way she would have said it to Matthew.

Clayton stopped his fidgeting but still didn't sit back in his seat. "This is my favorite weekend of the whole year," he said—which was so depressing that Graham thought he might involuntarily plunge the car into the East River.

As Graham wove through the Lower Manhattan traffic, Clayton and Matthew talked about origami—about double rabbit ears, crimps, double sinks, closed sinks, and their shared disdain for people who could not fold a bird base from memory. (Graham gathered this last was necessary to qualify for the more advanced classes.) Then they moved on to discussing *Star Wars*, which Matthew loved, and apparently Clayton also loved, although he pretended to be interested in it only in an academic, linguistic sort of way, talking about whether Old Galactic Standard was based on a mix of Durese and Bothese, or whether it was influenced by Dromnyr, which they speak on Vulta.

Audra said something, but Graham was so busy wondering how he and Audra could have been such *idiots* as to leave their beloved child in the care of someone so clearly insane that he didn't hear what it was.

"What?" he asked.

"I said that it made me feel old, the way they're talking about Anakin Skywalker, and I can only remember Luke Skywalker," Audra said.

"Oh, well, now, Anakin—" Clayton began from the back.

"It's okay," Audra said hastily. "I don't need to know."

The traffic and the conversation were making Graham's head ache, but then suddenly they were out of the city and on I-95 and the day was beautiful and the trees along the highway were as red and gaudy as candy apples. The hum of tires on the highway seemed to make both Matthew and Clayton sleepy, and their conversation dwindled to sporadic half sentences like, "But if Cloud City is on Bespin . . ."

Audra put in a Leo Kottke CD, nice and soft and gentle. If it weren't for the piece of paper with the phone number on it in his pocket, Graham would have been almost happy.

As soon as they got to the hotel, Matthew and Clayton went off to look at the model menus set up in the conference rooms, and Graham and Audra waited in line in the lobby to check in. Audra was carrying her overnight bag with both hands and leaned back slightly to balance the weight, bouncing it against her knees.

"What I don't understand about origami," she said to Graham in her normal speaking voice, "is why can't anyone like it a *little* bit? Why aren't there nice, well-rounded people who enjoy a bit of origami, the way there are nice, well-rounded people who enjoy a bit of bondage?"

It seemed to Graham that a silence spread out from them, like ripples from a pebble thrown into a pond. But with this crowd, it was hard to imagine whether they were more offended by her first sentence or by her second.

Audra continued, oblivious. "I mean, it's like miniature trains or dog shows. It takes over people's lives and they end up going to conventions. It's not like, you know, gardening or sailing or something you just have as a hobby."

Like bondage, Graham was sure the rest of the lobby mentally added.

A portly Asian man in line in front of them turned around. "I take it you don't fold," he said stiffly to Audra.

She gave him her friendliest smile. "No, I don't."

"Then why are you here?" he asked.

"We're here because we love our son," Audra said in a bold, preachy tone Graham had never heard her use before. Then she looked thoughtful and added in her usual voice. "Plus, we didn't want to be outdone by the Bergmans."

"And your son," the Asian man continued, "is he passionate about origami?"

"It's pretty much a way of life for him," Audra said. "But we're hoping he'll outgrow it." She stuck out her hand. "I'm Audra Daltry."

The man shook her hand. "I am Li."

"The Amazing Li!" Audra exclaimed. "You teach the class where they fold the praying mantis! Matthew can't wait."

It was remarkable, Graham thought, that even origami geeks were susceptible to pretty women flattering them. It was kind of comforting, actually. It gave him hope for Matthew.

There were only five people in line ahead of the Amazing Li, but by the time Li reached the front desk, Audra had found out that he had once broken both wrists in a tree-climbing accident and thought he'd go crazy not doing origami for six weeks, and that he was having trouble finding a girl his parents would approve of because they were so old-fashioned and, well, Chinese, and that he really disliked the taste of canned soups, chicken noodle in particular.

Graham had often wondered how Audra got people to tell her everything about themselves so quickly. Once he had asked her and she'd said vaguely, "Oh, I don't know. I guess I think life is too short for all that crap about 'Where are you from?' and 'Do you play the zither?'"

The zither! On what planet was "Do you play the zither?" considered normal small talk? But no matter. What mattered was who Jasper was, and all the things Audra no doubt knew about *him*.

Graham took Matthew to his first class: the F-16 Fighting Falcon. The man teaching the class called himself Captain Jim, and he fit the part: tall, imposing, silver crew cut, solid jaw, commanding voice. But Graham wondered whether he was actually a retired Air Force captain who had figured out how to fold an incredibly complicated design, or a crazy origami person who figured out the design and then adopted the military persona. Graham sighed. There were so many crazy people in origami.

Matthew had been allowed to attend the more advanced classes only if accompanied by an adult, but Graham knew that Matthew wouldn't need any help. They sat at a table together and Matthew began folding along with Captain Jim's instructions.

Graham read *The Wall Street Journal* and drank a cup of coffee and wondered what Audra was doing—had she noticed Jasper's number was missing from her wallet? Even if she had never called Jasper, did she sometimes take that scrap of paper out and smooth it against the leg of her jeans? And then Captain Jim was standing at their table and admiring Matthew's work.

"Well, look at this," Captain Jim said in his authoritative voice, startling Graham. He picked up Matthew's partially folded airplane and flexed it slightly, checking the folds. Then he looked sharply at Matthew. "How old are you?"

"Ten," Matthew said. "Can I have my paper back?"

Captain Jim gave it to him. "It's interesting," he said. "You are two folds ahead of my instructions. How did you know what I was going to say?"

"I just knew," Matthew said.

Captain Jim nodded. He didn't seem to find Matthew's answer odd, or care that Matthew didn't want to discuss it. He looked at Graham and said, "He has very unusual ability."

Graham smiled but said nothing. He thought, as he sometimes did, that Matthew's origami ability was like a rampart they'd erected to shield them from the rest of the world, and Graham and Audra crouched behind it. People looked and saw only the handsome little boy with the unusual talent. They did not know of the struggles to teach Matthew to tie his shoes, or ride a bike, or try new foods, or wear clothes with scratchy tags, or have his toenails clipped, or understand sarcasm. They did not know that sometimes Graham would be willing to exchange all that origami talent for just a little sarcasm.

After class, they met Audra in the hotel coffee shop for lunch. Matthew was so dazed and dreamy that Graham had to keep reminding him to take bites. He practically had to remind him to chew and swallow.

When Audra asked Matthew how class was, he said, "Great!" and his face glowed with happiness but he didn't elaborate. Audra glanced at Graham, looking amused, but she didn't press. They knew how to handle Matthew by now, and when he was this overwhelmed by something, even overwhelmed in a good way, they let him be.

Instead Audra told Graham that while he'd been in class (she made it sound like he was the one who wanted to go), she had unpacked their suitcases, removed the macadamia nuts from the minibar so Matthew wouldn't eat them, called down to the front desk for extra conditioner, explored the fitness room, done some yoga, and bought a knockoff of a Chloé handbag in the parking lot from a Hispanic man named Smoke.

She had the handbag with her, in an ordinary plastic grocery bag, and she took it out and showed it to Graham. It was a deep mahogany color, with about a hundred zippered compartments, and looked large enough to hold a terrier comfortably.

"How much did you pay for that?" he asked.

She beamed. "Fifty dollars!"

"That's amazing," he said. "I think you've done really well."

He didn't actually think that. He actually thought there was a limit on how many handbags any one person needed and that limit was probably one. But Graham thought that the secret to understanding women (if in fact there was a secret and they could be understood at all) was to admire their purchases. Approve of the stuff they brought home after shopping and they thought you were wonderful.

Audra looked at him happily and put the handbag on the table and began showing him all the little compartments and telling him what she planned to keep in each one.

"Now Smoke told me that the lining is actually the same as

the lining in a real Chloé bag," she said. "Apparently the factories in China always make extra fabric and sell it and the companies know but they just consider it part of the cost of doing business. So the only real difference is the quality of leather, and . . ."

There was more like this, but Graham didn't listen to it, although he kept an attentive look on his face. He knew Audra hated it when he did this, but he still couldn't stop himself. She didn't understand that it wasn't that he wanted her to be quiet; it was that he didn't want to be held accountable for paying attention. He liked the sound of her voice, which was warm and bubbly, and it flowed over Graham, as cozy as bathwater, as comforting as milk.

The name Jasper and the fact that the number was written on a fragment of legal-pad paper caused Graham to picture a lawyer, someone older and respectable and dependable. Someone like Graham himself. And wouldn't that make sense? Didn't most criminals get caught because they made the same mistakes over and over, because they couldn't break familiar patterns?

So when Audra took Matthew to his afternoon class and Graham went into the bathroom and changed the settings on his cellphone to disable his caller ID and dialed the number written below Jasper's name, he was expecting a mellow confident voice to answer. Instead it went straight to voicemail and a man said, "Hey, this is Jasper. Leave a message."

There was a hurried quality to the voice that Graham associated with young people: breathless, staccato, busy.

He rapidly abandoned the mental image of the older man with the short white hair and the blue eyes and the long, interesting face (who, Graham realized suddenly, was the lawyer who'd drawn up his will) and replaced it with the image of a tall thin young man with unruly dark hair and horn-rimmed glasses. Then he realized he was thinking of a children's folksinger he'd taken Matthew to see last month. Apparently he was so lacking in imagination that he couldn't visualize someone he'd never met.

"Hey, this is Jasper. Leave a message." Hardly words to haunt you.

He knew he should throw the piece of paper with the phone number away or, better yet, flush it down the toilet. Graham had a poor memory for phone numbers and he wouldn't be able to recall this one—even this one—a week from now. That would be the sensible thing to do. Get rid of the number, clear it from his phone, forget about it, let Audra think it had fallen out of her wallet.

But instead Graham put the number back in his pocket and splashed cold water on his face, already thinking about when he might call again, and what he might say. Criminals were not the only people who made the same mistakes over and over again.

Graham put on a suit for dinner and then sat on one of the beds in the hotel room and waited for Audra to get ready. They were late but he didn't try to rush her. By now he was used to being late wherever they went. She was wearing a long butterscotch-colored velvet dress. She had owned it for many years—in fact, it had been her backup choice for a wedding dress. But she'd stuck with her first choice and married Graham wearing jeans and an ivory blouse of shattered silk. Graham could still remember the feel of that blouse, its silky-rough texture against his fingers when he put his hand on the small of Audra's back.

He watched as she pinned her hair up. It always surprised him that a woman whose hair was not even long enough to touch her shoulders could have so many hairstyles. She clipped on dangly earrings and then turned to face him.

"You look beautiful," he said sincerely. "I'm sure you'll be the most beautiful woman there tonight."

She laughed. "I'm not sure that's all that much of a compliment, given this group," she said. "But thank you."

They retrieved Matthew from the lobby, where he was examining a display of origami animals, and went in to dinner and found the table with their name cards. Graham was sitting between Audra and Matthew, and next to Matthew was Clayton, and next to Audra was Li. ("Li!" Audra exclaimed, the way someone might cry "Grandma!" at Thanksgiving.) On Clayton's other side was a girl of about thirty, who Graham thought would be really pretty if she weren't so full of hard edges. Her flat blond hair hung past her shoulders and was cut straight across with what appeared to be razor precision. She had a nice but very square jaw, and her eyebrows were straight lines without a hint of arch. She wore wire-rimmed glasses, and the lenses were perfect rectangles. Her dress was stiff and white, with a row of gold buttons marching down the front.

Her name was just as hard-edged. "Trina," she said when Graham introduced himself and Matthew. "And you must be the Matthew everyone's talking about."

Matthew looked puzzled. "Why is everyone talking about me?"

"Because you're so good at origami," Trina said.

"But everyone here is good at origami," Matthew said. "Well, except one lady who couldn't collapse multiple creases."

Graham expected the service to be awful, but to his surprise the waitstaff were efficient and he was pleased that instead of taking individual drink orders, they put entire bottles of wine on the tables. As Graham filled up his glass and Audra's, Li and Trina and Clayton pulled stacks of origami paper from their bags (Clayton had his backpack and Li had a man-purse of some sort) and began folding. Audra laughed and reached into her own handbag and produced a stack for Matthew. "I don't leave home without it."

With four of them folding, conversation was somewhat stilted, although conversation was never that stilted with Audra around. Soon she had them telling her about last year's convention and how someone named Joe got locked in the men's room and missed all of lunch and part of the advanced snowflake workshop.

Graham reached for the bottle of red wine nearest him and found that Audra's hand was already on it. They traded looks. *Let's get drunk,* his look said. *How else can we get through this?* hers answered. Audra took her hand from the bottle and held out her glass, and he recognized a tiny flourish in the gesture, a sign of Audra making the decision to let herself go. He knew her most minute movements, her most subtle turn of mind. There was no way she kept a secret—a meaningful secret—from him.

Graham went to the men's room between the first and second courses and took a circuitous route back to the table, hoping it would take a long time and spare him having to make conversation with Clayton and Trina and Li. And so it was that he was walking aimlessly past a set of French doors leading to a balcony on the other side of the hotel and he looked out and saw Audra.

She was talking on her cellphone and pacing back and forth in the cool October evening, her long velvet dress whirling prettily around her ankles every time she turned. The balcony was in darkness, except for the squares of light that fell from the windows of the hotel along one side, and it was through these patches of brightness that Audra moved. Her auburn hair appeared much darker and her skin much paler than usual, and her butterscotch-colored gown was a hundred shades of gold where the folds of it caught the light.

Oh, Audra was wrong when she complained that Graham was not a visual person, that he had no memory for specific hues, that he could not recognize the simplest pigments, that he grew impatient when she got out her color boards. (Actually, she was right about the color boards.) For here was Graham, drinking in the very sight of her, and wishing he were a painter or photographer so he could capture the way she looked forever. Here he was thinking that her eyes were like pools of still water when she looked up at him and that the lock of wavy hair the wind blew across her face was like a dark tendril of ivy on a marble statue.

She saw him and gave a slight wave. Then she said something into the phone, and took it from her ear, turned it off, and slid it into her handbag.

Graham opened the French doors and she came inside, along with a gust of cold air.

"I was talking to Lorelei," she said, slipping her arm through his. "I wanted to tell her about my new handbag."

It didn't strike Graham as at all unusual or unbelievable that Audra would call Lorelei to talk about her new handbag (Audra had called Lorelei from their *honeymoon* to describe a coconut-curry sauce), but suddenly he wondered if it was unusual for Audra to tell him who she had been talking to. Did she normally do that? Or was she trying to prevent him from asking, from wondering? Graham tried to remember, and since Audra talked on the phone constantly, he should have had millions of incidents to compare with this one, millions of incidents to use to calibrate her behavior. And yet he couldn't remember a single time.

He put his hand over hers on his arm. Her fingers were cold and he wondered suddenly how long she'd been out there.

He could be certain of one thing only: he couldn't go on like this.

The wine was working. Dinner no longer seemed to Graham like an extended running track with a long series of conversational hurdles he had to force himself over. In fact, he didn't have to talk at all. Matthew was quiet beside him, happy with the endless French fries and milk shakes that the waiters brought, and his stack of origami paper.

Clayton and Trina were deep in discussion about something—Graham couldn't hear what, exactly. But Clayton was even more hyper and worked up than usual, and Trina nodded when he spoke in a manner that reminded Graham of the way North Korean delegates nodded when the Dear Leader gave political speeches. Occasionally she put her hand on Clayton's arm and leaned closer.

On his other side, Li was teaching Audra how to fold a square of paper into sixty-fourths. Graham felt impatient despite the wine. Audra didn't care about how to fold a paper into sixty-fourths any more than he did. Why couldn't she talk to *him*, when he was sitting right here?

Audra was saying whenever she tried this with Matthew, she ended up with a rectangle, not a square, and Li said that could happen with machine-made paper if you weren't careful, and Audra said why is that, and Li said it was because in machine-made papers, the fibers are aligned, and Audra said that is so interesting, and Li said modestly that he didn't see any problem with having slightly off-square paper for tessellations, and Audra said he must be the most amazing teacher, and Li said, "I am so fucking turned on, you wouldn't believe it."

(Actually, Li didn't say that last part, but Graham was pretty sure it was true. Who wouldn't be turned on having Audra hang on your every word while you talked about your favorite subject and got to look down the front of the velvet dress, which was very low cut?)

Finally the others left to go to the dessert buffet and Audra moved her chair so she was nestled up to Graham. "What do you think of Trina?" she asked in a low voice.

"I think she'd be pretty if she were a little . . . softer," Graham said.

"Oh, I didn't mean her looks," Audra said, "because, please, those shoulder pads! Is there a Van Halen concert I didn't know about?"

She said things like that occasionally, which Graham found absolutely inscrutable. She might as well have been speaking whatever they speak on Vulta.

"What I *meant*," Audra continued, "is, do you think she's flirting with Clayton?"

Graham looked over at Trina and Clayton, who were going through the dessert line together. Trina kept picking desserts up with the serving tongs and inspecting them, and then putting them back. Clayton appeared to be making helpful suggestions.

"That did occur to me, yes," he said finally.

"Look, I know he's making an origami candy cane out of fifty triangular units," Audra said. "And that must be very exciting to her. But honestly, can't she see that he's just a superskinny guy in weird jeans?"

There was no one in all the world he'd rather sit next to.

. . .

Audra was so sleepy and tipsy from all the wine that she wanted to go straight to bed after dinner. Graham had a far greater tolerance for alcohol. The wine had only relaxed him. So he sent her on ahead to the room and he took Matthew to the All Night Folding Room, which was set up in one of the conference rooms.

Graham thought that the main problem with the All Night Folding Room was that there was no one around to make fun of the All Night Folding Room with. Everyone there seemed to take it very seriously. They were gathered in small clusters around different models, folding intently. A few instructors wandered from group to group, but there was little conversation and no background music, just the rustle and snap of many papers being folded.

Matthew left Graham's side and went to one of the tables, and the people there greeted him and quickly made space for him. Their manner was so much more welcoming and accepting than the kids' on the playground at Matthew's school that Graham's heart clenched briefly.

He waited until Matthew was settled and then he stepped out of the ballroom and found a quiet corner. He took out his cellphone and Jasper's number and dialed.

A girl answered, saying, "Jasper's phone."

Graham swallowed. "Could I speak to Jasper, please?"

"Sure," the girl said. "Hang on."

So there was a girl in Jasper's life and he let her answer his phone. Both of those were good signs.

"Hello?" It was Jasper now, the same voice as on the message.

"Hello," Graham said. "You don't know me but my name is Peter and I'm a friend of Audra's and she has a message for you."

"Friend of whose?" Jasper asked. Graham could detect no hesitation.

He sounded open and friendly, honestly confused.

"Audra's," Graham said.

"Who's that?"

"Audra Daltry? Graphic designer?"

"I'm a photographer," Jasper said. Again, Graham heard that breathless, energetic sound in his voice, as though he were hopping on one foot or putting on his shoes while he talked. "I know dozens of graphic designers."

"Who is it?" the girl asked in the background.

"Someone calling about a designer," Jasper said.

"We have to go," the girl said. Graham wondered where they were going at ten-thirty p.m. But that was young people for you.

"I know," Jasper said. "You go on out. I'll be there in a sec. Wait, take my blue— No, right, that one, thanks."

Graham smiled slightly at their shorthand. Every couple had that. "I'm sorry," he said, feeling foolish. "I must have the wrong number."

"No problem," Jasper said.

"Sorry to have bothered you," Graham said. "Goodbye." He could feel his whole body relaxing, relief flowing from the hand that held the phone all the way through him.

"Wait," Jasper said. "What was the message?"

Graham gripped the phone harder. "What?"

"You said she had a message for me," Jasper said. "What was it?"

Graham was silent. Most people are uncomfortable with silence and will eventually say something to fill it. He waited to hear what Jasper would say. "Was it—"

But suddenly Graham couldn't bear to hear any more. "It doesn't matter," he said quickly. "Goodbye." He ended the call.

His heart was thudding and he could barely swallow. It had been a mistake to call. The worst decision possible. If there was anything to know, he didn't want to know it. He couldn't bear to know it. His heart would burst under the weight of it. He realized that now.

In the morning, Audra was so hungover that Graham sent Matthew down to Clayton's room to tell him that they would leave an hour later than they'd planned. Audra stayed in bed with the pillow pulled over her head, and Graham sat in a chair and leaned his head carefully against the back of it, taking small sips from a glass of water. He was hungover, too.

Matthew was back five minutes later. "Clayton was in the shower but the girl said she'd tell him."

"What girl?" Graham asked. "Are you sure you went to the right room?"

Audra sat up on one elbow.

"Yes, I went to the right room," Matthew said. "Room 471." Matthew never made mistakes when it came to numbers. "And I did like you said, I knocked and the girl answered and I said that Mommy had had too much wine and needed more time."

"I didn't mean for you to say that part—" Graham began and then gave up. He also hadn't specified *not* to say that, and Matthew was so literal.

"What girl, Matthew?" Audra asked. "What did she look like?"

"The girl who sat at our table last night," Matthew said. "With the blond hair and the glasses. Can I go downstairs and look at the models since I'm ready?"

"Sure," Graham said absently. "Just don't leave the hotel."

Matthew left, banging the door behind him, and Graham and Audra stared at each other. Audra was sitting all the way up now, and the strap of her pale yellow nightgown slid down one arm. She always wore pale nightgowns, she said, because men liked it when they could see her nipples through the fabric. (She had told him this on their first date, cheerfully, while she ate a cheeseburger.) Graham could see her nipples now, and he liked it. But the thought of Jasper seeing them and liking them made Graham feel as though an unseen person had suddenly laid a cold hand on his chest, directly over his heart.

"I think it is just unforgivable of Clayton to do that to Pearl," Audra said. "Especially considering how she wears those itty-bitty paper airplane earrings all the time."

Graham frowned. "You think wearing paper-airplane earrings is the worst part of being married to Clayton?"

"Sure," Audra said. "What do you think the worst part is?"

"Well, having to talk to him or have dinner with him or go to bed with him. Just Clayton himself, I guess," Graham said. "The earrings might be the *best* part of being married to him."

"I just hate him now, though," Audra said. "I can never forgive him for this."

And Graham thought that someone else might take Audra's anger at Clayton as proof that she would never have an affair herself, but he knew differently. He knew that adultery was just like any other vice—pride or gluttony or overspending or vanity. It was easy to condemn other people for it, but then you went right out and did it yourself. It was all different when it was you.

As they got in the car, Graham thought that he and Matthew and Clayton looked like three of the Seven Ages of Man. Matthew the healthy little boy and he and Clayton the two stooped gray men near the end. He would even put Clayton as the final man, though Graham was probably older by a few years. Clayton's hangover appeared extreme; he looked dull and shrunken, with none of his usual hyper energy.

"No talking," Audra said to Matthew as they drove out of the parking lot. "Everyone has a headache."

"I don't have a headache," Matthew said.

"Well, the grown-ups do," Audra said. "You just sit quietly and think interesting thoughts. You, too, Clayton," she added quickly, leading Graham to believe Clayton must have opened his mouth in protest.

In less than fifteen minutes, Matthew and Clayton were asleep. Graham saw them in the rearview mirror and turned to smile at Audra, but she was asleep, too, curled sideways in her seat with her feet tucked under her and her face resting against the upholstery. Her eyelashes were dark crescents on her cheeks.

What was the message?

Graham pushed the thought away.

Audra woke up an hour later and stretched. "Can we stop at an Arby's?"

"Sure." Graham knew she believed Arby's to be the perfect hangover cure.

They saw a sign a few exits later and Graham pulled into the parking lot. Audra said she had to go to the bathroom so she would go inside and get their food.

Graham stayed in the car. He looked back at Clayton and Matthew, who were still asleep, and saw that Matthew had moved so his head rested against Clayton's shoulder. Graham was flooded with a surge of love so strong it made his throat ache. He had been wrong earlier when he thought he would change any part of Matthew, that he would trade any of Matthew's sweet guilelessness for some sarcastic little kid. Matthew was beautiful, perfect, just as he was. Graham loved Matthew, he loved Audra, at that moment he almost loved Clayton. There, in the Arby's parking lot, he felt almost overwhelmed by love for his family, and a certainty of his course of action. He would forget all about Jasper and who he might be to Audra. He would stop observing her, stop monitoring her, stop snooping and hoping to find proof of anything. He would love her and trust her—he *did* love and trust her!—and his love would bind them together, like the atoms in hydrogen, the compass needle and the North Pole, like the rings around Saturn—

"You will not believe this, but they were out of Horsey Sauce," Audra said, getting in and slamming her door shut. She had a way of bringing him back down to earth.

Graham unlocked the door to the apartment and held it open. Audra walked in, saying, "Home again, home again," and Matthew said, "Jiggety-jig." It was their routine since Matthew's babyhood, and made Graham think instantly of strollers and sippy cups and Cheerios everywhere.

Matthew ran off to his room to do origami, and Audra went to their room to unpack. She always unpacked right away. Graham took the mail and went into his study and sat at his desk.

He flipped through some letters, checked his email and the stock market. He could hear Audra moving around in the bedroom and kitchen. She seemed restless, opening and shutting the refrigerator, pulling out a chair (he heard the scrape of it on the floor) and then pushing it back in.

She appeared in the doorway, wearing an oversize sweater of dark green yarn. Her face was pale and her hair was pulled back messily, but her smile was as warm and sweet as always. He had married her for that smile. "I'm going down to see Lorelei for a while," she said.

"Okay," he said.

"Are you all right?" she asked.

"Sure, just tired."

"It makes me so sad that the best thing I can say about this weekend is that it's over," Audra said. She kissed the top of his head. "See you later."

After she left, Graham went into the kitchen and made himself a cup of tea. He felt the same restlessness he'd sensed in Audra. It seemed like there should be more to do—groceries to buy, laundry to start, bills to pay, lists to make. But there wasn't.

Graham left his tea sitting on the kitchen counter and walked down the hall to the front door. Audra's handbag rested on a small table there.

He took the piece of paper with Jasper's number from his pocket and put it carefully back in her wallet, exactly as he'd found it. He vowed that he would never look to see if it was there, not ever again. Eventually, he would forget about it, he would go back to being the person he was before.

He walked back down the hall, stopping to check the thermostat because the apartment felt cold. But it was set at seventy-two the way it always was, and they hadn't turned the heat down when they left anyway. It was only the fact that they'd been away that made him imagine this coolness in his chest, this feeling that he ought to rub his hands together and start the blood flowing. That was ridiculous. It had only been a little more than twenty-four hours, not nearly long enough for a chill to set in.

Four

No one had canceled Thanksgiving.

Graham found that remarkable. Although maybe that was the most stressful thing about holidays: they couldn't be canceled. The holidays marched in unwanted and forced themselves upon you like Vikings invading a village, or a wet dog who shakes himself next to you, or the dirty and unshaven man who had once pinched Audra's bottom at a midtown salad bar.

Still, this year, when Graham felt so—so unbalanced, so guarded, so wary despite himself—you'd think Thanksgiving might be canceled. Or postponed. But no.

There are rumored to be people who enjoy getting up early, but Graham was not one of them. He had to force himself out of bed at six on Thanksgiving morning. Audra slept on next to him, a dim humped shape under the comforter. Graham pulled on his robe and left the bedroom quietly, pulling the door shut gently.

The kitchen was almost literally bursting with food. The refrigerator shelves were stacked with all the dishes Graham had made ahead—the cheese spread, the crab dip, the three-bean salad, the glazed brussels sprouts—and heaped with balls of pie dough, cartons of heavy cream, and sticks of butter for the dishes he had not yet started. The vegetable bins were stuffed with celery, asparagus, broccoli, carrots, cauliflower, and green beans. No room for the white wine—it was chilling in the dishwasher, which Graham had filled with ice the night before. He could hear the ice trickling as it melted. The counters were crowded with bread set out to stale for the stuffing, and net bags of onions and yams and potatoes. The turkey was defrosting in a roasting pan on the counter. Its skin was pale and dimpled, with a faint purplish tinge as though it were cold. Graham thought he'd never seen anything less appetizing in his life. He was not in the proper frame of mind for this. He wanted to be left alone to brood.

It wasn't as though Audra behaved like someone having an affair—and who would know affair behavior better than Graham? Cheating spouses were supposed to be distant and preoccupied, to be secretive about their whereabouts, to be obsessed with their cellphones.

Well, cellphones! Sometimes Graham wanted to have an affair, just so he could benefit from the ease of cellphones. (It was like he sometimes wanted to take up skiing again now that there were fleece hats, which didn't make your head itch like the wool ones.) But what if your wife had *always* been obsessed with her cellphone? She'd been obsessed with her *landline*! Accusing Audra of having an affair because she made too many phone calls was like accusing Tiger Woods of having an affair because he played too much golf. (Although, you know, maybe Tiger Woods was not the best possible comparison here.)

Graham started the coffee machine and cut open the bag of potatoes. He should peel them while the coffee perked but found he didn't have the energy. Instead he leaned against the counter and stared at the guest list Audra had taped to the refrigerator.

Lorelei
Doug
Bitsy
Clayton
Pearl
Manny
Alan
Dr. Moley, Matthew's pediatrician
Dinah, Dr. Moley's wife
Mr. Vargas, Matthew's piano teacher
Mrs. Bellamy, the old lady on Six

All the lonely people! Where do they all come from? Graham
didn't know where they came from, but he could have told the
Beatles where all the lonely people *go:* they go to Graham and
Audra's house for Thanksgiving dinner.

And the final name on the list: *Elspeth.*

Elspeth! Elspeth was on the list, was apparently coming over
for Thanksgiving dinner.

"I told you," Audra had said last night when she showed him
the list.

"No, you didn't."

"I'm *sure* I told you," she said. Then she looked suddenly
thoughtful. "Unless maybe I only thought I told you, and I actually told someone else."

Why would she remember telling Graham? He was only her
husband.

"But who else would I have told?" Audra continued. "I mean,
it's not like I would say to some random stranger, 'Hey, my husband's ex-wife is coming to our house for Thanksgiving.'"

It was *exactly* like Audra would say that to a random stranger. She would *delight* in saying it to a random stranger.

"I didn't think Elspeth was even speaking to us," Graham said.

"Well, she wasn't," Audra said, "and then I accidentally included her on this group email about Matthew's school auction and she emailed back and said, 'Please don't bother me with your tacky fund-raiser,' and I replied and we sort of went back and forth and I invited her."

Graham was silent.

"Are you angry?" Audra asked.

"No," he said. "I'm trying to estimate the minimum number of exchanges it would take to get from her reply to your invitation."

"Oh, well." Audra shrugged. "Not that many, actually. Fewer than you'd think."

"And these other people?" he asked. "Why is the pediatrician coming? Why is Mrs. Bellamy from downstairs coming, when I've never spoken to her except once when she got a package for us?"

"Because none of those people had plans for Thanksgiving," Audra said. "It made me sad to think of them all alone."

Graham hadn't had the heart to say it made him sadder to think of them coming over. He sighed and began peeling potatoes.

Around ten, Audra came into the kitchen in her melon-colored robe, yawning and sighing as though she, and not Graham, had been slaving away in the kitchen all morning. She poured her own cup of coffee and leaned against the counter. "I was thinking"— she interrupted herself with a huge yawn that made her jaws creak—"that maybe we should issue a last-minute invitation to the gay couple down on Five. First of all, they're here in the building, which means that they could bring some chairs with them, and second, I thought they might have a nice friend they could fix Mr. Vargas up with."

"Mr. Vargas is gay?" Graham said.

"Oh, yes," Audra said. "Didn't you know that?"

No, Graham hadn't known that, but he did know the couple down on Five whom Audra was talking about and they were tall glamorous-looking men in their thirties who worked in advertising. It seemed unlikely they would have friends interested in a portly fifty-year-old Argentinian piano teacher.

"Anyway," Audra continued. "When I invited Mr. Vargas to Thanksgiving, I said, 'Now, if there's someone you'd like to bring, you're more than welcome,' and Mr. Vargas said, 'I'd love to but I'm unhappily single right now.' And it turns out that up until about six weeks ago, Mr. Vargas lived with this very nice but very volatile violinist and then one day right in the produce section at Whole Foods, they had a big argument about whether 'The Blue Danube' was written in three-four time or six-eight time and the violinist said, 'I can't believe I've wasted two years of my life on someone who doesn't know the time signature of "The Blue Danube"!' And they broke up then and there and the violinist stormed off, leaving Mr. Vargas holding a bunch of kale. And now Mr. Vargas lives alone and he says that sometimes he plays 'The Blue Danube' in six-eight time and thinks that it sounds better that way, haunting almost, and I said, 'Mr. Vargas, that is just beautiful, you should call the violinist up and tell him that,' and Mr. Vargas said, 'No, because it turns out he also never cared for my habit of whistling—'"

Listen to her. She was still Audra. She still watched him with apparent utter absorption when he spoke and then said something like, "Wait, I think I left my blue sweater in the dryer!"

which showed she hadn't been listening at all; she still believed Cub Scouts was a dreadful organization; she still exclaimed, "I didn't realize how hungry I was!" at the start of *every single meal;* she still flirted with bartenders; she still drove around with the gas tank nearly empty; she still came up behind him in the kitchen and rested her cheek between his shoulder blades. What phone number? What affair?

"For God's sake, Audra!" Graham snapped. "No more guests!"

She didn't seem to notice his tone. "Maybe I could just invite their chairs."

It seemed that Audra's main contribution to Thanksgiving dinner was getting herself ready, which she took over an hour to do, while Graham whipped the sweet potatoes and mixed the stuffing. Though he had to admit that she looked very pretty when she finally appeared wearing a periwinkle-blue skirt and sweater she'd owned for many years but that were still as richly colored and soft-looking as the day she'd bought them. Her hair was pulled back in a silver clasp at the nape of her neck and she wore silver earrings that made a pleasant clicking sound whenever she turned her head.

To be fair, she also set the table, even producing a paper turkey as a centerpiece, the kind you popped open to reveal the round honeycombed tissue-paper body. Then she made little name cards, and irritated Graham unendurably by calling out to him about the seating plan as he struggled to roll out pastry crust. "Now, do you think Elspeth would enjoy talking to Clayton?" she called. "Do you think Doug and Pearl would have things in common? Do you think Dr. Moley would be interested in discussing Bitsy's hives?"

Audra was just saying, "I feel like I'm seating a cat next to a dog," when the buzzer sounded. "Now who could be rude enough to come right on time?" she asked.

The answer was Matthew's origami club, that's who. They all arrived together: Clayton, Pearl, Manny, and Alan. Alan was a large man with freckles and fading red hair. Manny resembled Clayton closely enough that they could have passed for brothers. (Was Clayton *replicating* himself? It was a disturbing thought.)

Graham took their coats and Audra herded them all into the living room, where they clustered around the coffee table with Matthew and pulled origami paper from their backpacks.

"I thought we'd attempt the Roosevelt Elk today," Clayton told them all, and then the buzzer sounded again and Graham went to answer it.

It was Mr. Vargas, wearing a starched white shirt and bow tie. He was beaming and offering a bottle of red wine.

"Please come in," Graham said, and they were halfway down the hall when they met Matthew coming in the other direction, probably headed to his room for his own supply of origami paper.

Matthew's eyes got very big when he saw Mr. Vargas. "Do I have to have a piano lesson?"

"No, no," Graham said soothingly. "Mr. Vargas is just here to have dinner."

At that moment, the buzzer sounded yet again, and this time the door swung open before Graham even had a chance to move toward it, and a woman's voice called, "Yoo-hoo!"

A man and woman entered. It was Dr. Moley, Matthew's pediatrician, and his wife, Dinah. When Matthew saw Dr. Moley, his eyes got even bigger and he clutched Graham's sleeve. "Do I have to have a shot?"

God, they were traumatizing him. The whole dinner was probably going to traumatize Graham, too.

"No, Matthew," he said. "You go on back with everyone else."
And he turned to greet the Moleys.

Audra had always said that she could never make up her mind
about whether Dr. Moley was a genius or belonged in a special
home somewhere. But what Dr. Moley seemed like to Graham
was an aging alcoholic. His eyes were bloodshot and he listed
slightly as he walked. The faint smell of bourbon seemed to cling
to his big gray walrus mustache.

Dinah Moley was a small spry blond woman with black shoe-
button eyes. "I hope we're not going to eat too late," she said to
Audra when they were all in the living room, "because we're flying to Florence tomorrow." Then she looked at Graham and said,
"Vincent needs a drink."

She said this in such a way that it caused Graham to think
Vincent was either a very small dog she carried in her purse or
an imaginary friend of some sort. He was about to ask cagily
whether Vincent liked water or milk when he realized from the
expectant way Dr. Moley was looking at him that she was referring to her husband.

"Certainly," said Graham. "Bourbon on the rocks?"

"That'd be great," Dr. Moley said, not seeming to wonder how
Graham knew.

Graham stepped into the kitchen for ice cubes, and Matthew
came up nervously behind him. "Who else is coming?"

"Just friends of Mom's and mine," Graham said.

"Not Dr. Alpen?" That was the dentist.

"No."

"Would you tell me if he was?"

"Yes, of course."

Matthew looked unconvinced but left the kitchen without further argument. Graham followed him with the ice bucket, figur-

ing that otherwise he'd be making a lot of trips to the kitchen for Dr. Moley.

When Elspeth arrived, Graham was so happy to see someone normal, he nearly cut a caper right there at the door. Instead he said, "Welcome!" in a booming voice unlike his own.

How strange to see Elspeth here in their apartment—a single snowflake from a massive blizzard writ large once again. She carried her coat over her arm and wore a slim black skirt and plain white blouse. He leaned forward and kissed her on the cheek. Her skin was as firm and cool as the skin of a chilled apple.

"Graham," she said, smiling a little.

Before Graham could close the door, the elevator chimed again, and this time it was Lorelei and Doug. Graham sent them all down the hall into the living room.

Bong! went the elevator again. He turned back toward the door, and this time it was Bitsy.

"Graham, hello!" she said in her soft voice.

Graham blinked. "Bitsy, how nice to see you," he said, holding the door open for her.

"It's nice to be here," Bitsy replied, but Graham wondered: *was* it nice for her to be back here, the scene of such unhappiness, the very square footage where she'd realized her marriage had come to an end?

He led Bitsy down the hall to the living room, where Doug was saying, "Origami!" in the sort of falsely excited voice people use when they talk about visiting a museum. "What are we making?"

"We're not *making* anything," Alan said. "We're *folding* the Roosevelt Elk."

Doug was not offended. "Well, let me pull up a chair here and see what I can do to help."

Everyone huddled around the coffee table, reaching casually

for Manny's stack of lokta origami paper, which Graham knew Manny had special-ordered from Nepal.

Audra paused beside Graham and whispered, "I'm so embarrassed that everyone thinks we've planned origami as entertainment!"

Matthew looked wildly relieved to see Bitsy—undoubtedly he was thinking, *One for my team!*—and Bitsy ruffled Matthew's hair as she sat down next to him.

Graham took everyone's drink orders and headed to the corner of the room where he'd set up the bar.

"Everyone, this is Elspeth," Audra said. Graham hoped that Audra wouldn't feel it necessary to say that Elspeth was his ex-wife, but she probably would. She believed, he knew, that you had to give people a little bit of information as a conversation starter when you introduced them. Graham didn't disagree with this policy, it was just that Audra always chose information he'd rather she not share.

And sure enough, Audra said, "Elspeth and Graham were married for eight years, and then separated for—"

Graham turned to the table in the corner where he'd set out the wine and opened the first bottle. It was tempting to drink straight from it.

Behind him, Audra continued introducing people and tossing out conversation starters. "Clayton, this is Dr. Moley," she said. "Dr. Moley once removed a piece of Lego from Matthew's ear. Doug, this is Alan. He's allergic to beets. Dinah, this is Bitsy. She has very clean fingernails. Pearl, this is Mr. Vargas. He's just been through a difficult breakup."

"Nice to meet you," Mr. Vargas said. "Have you ever been to Whole Foods?"

Clayton said aggressively, "I think we should have an advanced table and a beginners' table."

Dinah Moley said to Bitsy, "I hope we eat soon because Vincent and I are flying to Florence tomorrow."

Who were these people? What was Graham doing here? Where was his life, the one he was meant to be living? He sighed. Maybe if he turned up the oven they could eat sooner and everyone would go home. He sighed again and began pouring wine.

Elspeth bustled into the kitchen. She opened a drawer and shook out a fresh dish towel, which she tucked into the waistband of her skirt.

"You don't have to be in here," Graham protested. "You should go out to the living room and have a drink with the others."

Elspeth gave him a sardonic smile. "I'd rather stay in here," she said. "And it looks like you could use the help."

Graham couldn't argue with that. "Okay."

Elspeth opened the oven and looked at the turkey with narrowed eyes. Then she turned back to him and said, "Do you mind if I make the cranberry relish? I have a certain way I like to do it."

"Not at all," Graham said.

Elspeth was washing the cranberries in the sink when the kitchen door swung open and Audra entered with Mrs. Bellamy. Mrs. Bellamy was a short lady in her late seventies, so stout that she appeared to have no breasts and no waist, like a giant pincushion covered in blue fabric. She had fluffy white hair, which curved back from her face in two smooth wings. She was carrying a platter of deviled eggs.

"You remember Mrs. Bellamy," Audra said. "This is my husband, Graham."

"Of course," Graham said. "And this is Elspeth."

"Hello, dear," Mrs. Bellamy said, shaking Elspeth's hand. She looked at Graham. "And aren't you smart, hiring a caterer!"

"I'm an attorney," Elspeth said coolly.

"I'm not sure what you'll make of my deviled eggs," Mrs. Bellamy said, oblivious, "but I always take them to parties. It's my signature dish."

"And we appreciate it," Audra said. "Let me just grab some napkins and we can go on into the living room."

After they had gone, Graham put the butter and milk for the mashed potatoes into a small saucepan and placed it on one of the back burners.

"Oh, do you heat the milk for the potatoes?" Elspeth asked.

"Yes," Graham said. "Some people skip it but I think it makes a difference."

"I use a potato ricer," Elspeth said. "Though for years I used a hand mixer."

What a pleasure it was to have this conversation, thought Graham, who also used a potato ricer. He could remember that when he was having an affair with Audra, he could barely sit through dinner with Elspeth—she struck him as so maddeningly calm and deliberate. Always his mind would turn to what Audra might be doing at that moment, what she might be saying, and to whom. In fact, he *couldn't* sit through dinner with Elspeth, and his main memory of those last few months was a constant restlessness at meals, hopping up and down to refill his glass, fetch the butter, look for pepper. Audra showed none of that restlessness; she seemed as deeply content with her life as she always had.

And yet—and yet—it had begun to seem to Graham that Audra had less time during the day than she used to. All through their marriage, Audra had run countless errands during the week:

going to the liquor store for wine, to the dry cleaner's for Graham's shirts, to the post office for stamps, to the pharmacy for cough syrup, to the bakery for bagels, to the gourmet shop for truffle oil. But lately they seemed to run low on everything, and Audra would say, "The day got away from me! I'll pick up your prescription tomorrow." Or mail your package. Or deposit that check.

But could you really believe your wife was cheating on you because you ran out of truffle oil? Audra didn't even *like* truffle oil. She said it smelled like feet.

As though his thoughts had summoned her, Audra pushed open the swinging door of the kitchen at that moment. "I'm sure it won't be any trouble at all," she called gaily to someone over her shoulder. She looked at Graham and Elspeth and said in a lower voice, "Apparently, Manny only eats food that's *white*."

Then she backed out of the kitchen and the door swung shut behind her.

Elspeth and Graham looked at each other for a moment.

"Is your life always like this?" Elspeth asked.

"Yes," said Graham.

But the truth was more complicated than that. Because although Audra did make preposterous statements at least twice a week (more frequently than that if she had PMS), the truth was that Graham liked it. Or at least, he liked it and he disliked it in equal measure. But he didn't tell Elspeth any of that. He let her think that life with Audra was maddening, and nothing more.

Graham had to admit it: he'd nourished a very small hope that this Thanksgiving would be a success. He had thought it was possible—or well, more accurately, he had thought that it was *not impossible*—that this eclectic mix of people would gel into a party.

But when he finally took a break from the kitchen and joined his guests in the living room, the atmosphere was less like a party and more like a group of strangers stranded at a bus station.

There was even the equivalent of a drunken homeless person—Dr. Moley was nearly horizontal on the sofa, his drink balanced on his stomach. Pearl was perched on the other end of the sofa, speaking to him along the length of his body. "Clayton rearranged my recipe box," she said. "He organized the recipes by frequency of use instead of alphabetically, and I have to say, I find it extremely efficient."

(Graham felt an embarrassing thrill of interest in this, although he chalked it up to the extreme stress of the holiday.)

Doug was stuck talking to Mrs. Bellamy about her cats.

"Now, Arlo," Mrs. Bellamy said in a happy, relishing voice. "Arlo I have to have professionally groomed because otherwise we run into a bit of a hair ball problem. But Iris from kittenhood has always kept herself impeccably clean."

Audra, Lorelei, and Elspeth were sitting together, discussing Starbucks stock performance. Audra said, "The whole Starbucks experience has just been ruined for me since they started listing the calories next to all the drinks."

There was no conversation here that Graham wanted to take part in and, even worse, no conversation that seemed to want him in it. It was dark out now and he could see his reflection in the windows, a lone figure looming over all the others.

He helped himself to one of Mrs. Bellamy's deviled eggs, so it would look like he'd come out just for that, and went back into the kitchen.

The table groaned with food, and despite himself, Graham's spirits rose. The turkey rested on the platter in golden brown splen-

dor, garnished with sprigs of rosemary and wedges of lemon
and bright red pomegranate seeds. All of their flowered serving
dishes were out, filled with the mushroom and walnut stuffing,
the white-wine gravy, the roasted carrots with dill, the pears and
red onions, the maple-whipped sweet potatoes, Elspeth's cranberry relish. The pure decadence and plentitude of Thanksgiving dinner had always appealed to Graham, and he took no less
pleasure in it this year just because he had prepared it for people
he didn't especially like.

"Everyone, come to dinner!" Audra called. Then she said to
Graham in a lower voice, "Why did you switch all the name cards
around?"

"Because I couldn't stand the thought of sitting next to Pearl,"
he answered, but that was not the truth. Graham had rearranged
the seating on a sort of Asperger's continuum, with Lorelei at the
head of the high-functioning end, and Manny and the rest of the
Origami Club at the low-functioning end. Doug sat on Lorelei's
left, Graham on her right, Audra, Elspeth, Bitsy, and everyone
else in the middle. Matthew was seated next to Graham because
Graham couldn't bear to see him down at the other end.

"Well, now!" Mrs. Bellamy said brightly as she sat down next
to Elspeth. "I think it is so modern and lovely the way you have
the caterer eat with us."

Graham thought Elspeth might stab Mrs. Bellamy with her
salad fork.

Graham had prepared a separate plate for Manny: a slice of
white bread with the crusts cut off, some cubes of feta cheese,
a container of plain yogurt, and a few marshmallows. He was
really quite pleased with his ability to improvise on short notice.
But it turned out that Manny not only insisted on all-white food,
he wanted an all-white plate, too. So while everyone else flapped

open their napkins and filled up their water glasses, Audra tapped off to the kitchen and came back with a white fondue plate. Graham could have imagined it but he was pretty sure the rest of the Origami Club looked at the fondue plate with its segregated compartments wistfully.

"Here you are," Audra said to Manny just as though he were a normal person. "We don't have any white utensils, but if you need some, perhaps Graham will run down to the deli for plastic ones."

"Oh, please, no," Manny demurred. "I'm not particular."

Graham stood up to carve the turkey.

"I'm glad we're eating early because Vincent and I are flying to Florence tomorrow," Dinah said.

Suddenly, Graham seemed to hear drums beating, very low. It was more a gently pounding sensation than actual sound. Random snatches of conversation reached him: Manny telling someone he hadn't eaten colored food since 2002; Dr. Moley (who had perked up a bit) saying that no other animal besides a human can get a rash from poison ivy; Mr. Vargas describing a sexual position called "suspended congress" to Audra, who said, dubiously, "That's not what I'm used to."

The drumbeats were louder now. And then Graham realized he was sick to his stomach. He hadn't been hearing drumbeats at all—it was just the foretelling of nausea. The body knew what was happening before the brain did and tried to send signals, a warning. Graham was having trouble swallowing. His saliva felt thick and mucusy in his mouth. He could barely stand. The carving fork was already buried in the turkey and now Graham dug the knife in, point first, like a pirate sinking a grappling hook into the plank of a ship. He swayed, and his vision swam with black dots. The turkey kept him upright while, fortunately, his vision cleared.

"I feel—funny," said Pearl.

Doug jumped up suddenly and ran for the bathroom, his heavy body tilted forward and thick legs pumping. He looked like a linebacker rushing a pass down the hallway. It was perfect, really, for Thanksgiving, Graham thought distantly.

Then Mrs. Bellamy leaned over and threw up on the rug.

Of course, it was Mrs. Bellamy's deviled eggs. Later, Graham would have an eerily vivid picture of the scene: Mrs. Bellamy tottering around her kitchen, humming to herself while she whipped up her signature dish, using elderly eggs and ancient mayonnaise, because how quickly did a single person go through either of those ingredients? Or perhaps she made them in the morning and left them out on the counter to remind herself to take them? And who was to say she didn't help herself to a few deviled eggs for lunch, eating them whole in the greedy, unself-conscious way people are free to do unobserved in their own kitchens? Oh, Graham could see it, the fat slippery egg whites disappearing into her mouth, the yolky yellow smears on the corners of her lips. He would never feel the same about deviled eggs again.

But all that came later. At the time, the emergency was hot and there was only thought for the most basic triage.

"My rug!" Audra cried. "Someone get the salt!"

Pearl bolted from the table. Graham collapsed back into his seat. Lorelei jumped up to kneel by Mrs. Bellamy's chair. Dr. Moley took her pulse, and Dinah Moley began taking a survey of who had eaten the deviled eggs.

It turned out that six of them had: Mrs. Bellamy, Pearl, Graham, Doug, Lorelei, and Audra. Audra felt fine (she had a very strong stomach, like a Doberman); Graham and Lorelei felt shaky; Pearl and Doug were in various bathrooms; and Mrs. Bellamy was tipped back in her chair, panting, her eyes ringed with white, her face pale and slick with sweat, her skin as shiny as greased plastic.

Matthew couldn't stop staring at the puddle of vomit on the rug. "Who's going to clean that up?" he asked.

"Mrs. Bellamy needs to go to the ER," Dr. Moley said. "We can walk her over. It's only a block."

Graham said he would take Mrs. Bellamy to the ER—he felt responsible as the host. Dr. Moley offered to accompany them, and for a few minutes, everyone was frantically pulling on coats and searching for bags and finding a blanket to drape over Mrs. Bellamy's shoulders since her coat was downstairs in her apartment.

Doug and Lorelei left, Doug with his arm slung around Lorelei's neck.

Pearl came out of the master bathroom looking like a woman who had fought hard with a purse snatcher—breathless, disheveled, frightened—and Audra said to Clayton, "You go ahead and take Pearl home."

"Oh, Pearl's a warhorse," Clayton said confidently, rocking back and forth on his heels, his hands stuffed in his coat pockets.

It was then that Graham realized that Clayton and Pearl, as well as Alan and Manny and Mr. Vargas—what Graham thought of as the low-functioning end of the table—were all planning to come with them to the hospital, as though this were a progressive party and the next course might be served there.

They left Matthew with Bitsy—how quickly Bitsy fit back into her old role as houseguest and nanny, Graham thought—and they went outside. The night sky was beautiful: thick, frosty, starry.

Graham and Dr. Moley supported Mrs. Bellamy between them. Elspeth walked behind them, carrying Mrs. Bellamy's purse and rooting through it for an insurance card.

"I hope this doesn't take too long," Mrs. Moley said. "We have to fly to Florence tomorrow."

"Oh, are you going to Florence?" Audra asked, deadpan, and Graham's heart, which had been cold with suspicion, flamed with desire for one bright moment, and then was ash.

The ER was mercifully uncrowded. Dr. Moley signed Mrs. Bellamy in at the front desk and she was whisked back to an exam room. The rest of them drifted over to the waiting room and sat in uncomfortable chairs with curved wooden arms. Alan complained that there were no flat surfaces for folding.

It began to seem as though Graham was trapped in some awful social quicksand and the more he tried to free himself, the deeper he sank. It seemed that he would never get out of the hospital and back to the apartment without at least one unwanted guest.

Mrs. Bellamy was admitted to the hospital overnight for observation, so she was no problem, but everyone else seemed determined to return. The old Graham might have let them; the new Graham could not bear it. And yet what could he do when Alan began wondering aloud about turkey sandwiches and Manny said he had low blood sugar and Clayton said Thanksgiving didn't seem like Thanksgiving without at least one slice of pumpkin pie? Graham was afraid to open his mouth for fear the quicksand would flow in and choke him. He would sink without a trace.

Of course it was Audra who saved him. "Goodness," she said to Manny and Alan, "weren't you smart to bring your backpacks! We won't have to go back for them."

"We *always* bring our backpacks with us," Manny told her. "We don't want to get trapped somewhere without origami paper."

"Well, now, that's very forward-thinking," Audra said. "Perhaps after you and Alan help Clayton get Pearl home, you can all fold something together."

"I guess we could order Chinese food," Clayton said thoughtfully.

"White rice, though," Manny said quickly.

"So let's see," Audra said. "We'll need one—two—three taxis. One to Clayton's house, one for the Moleys, and one for Mr. Vargas. It's so late! You all must want to get home. Thank goodness no one has any travel plans tomorrow."

(It was possible that she didn't say that last sentence, that Graham only imagined she did because he wanted to say it so badly himself.)

"Dr. Moley, can I ask you to flag the taxis for us?" Audra said. "Come on, everyone." She put her hand on Graham's arm and whispered, "I'll see you at home."

And they were off, everyone obediently trailing behind Audra like the world's oldest human ducklings, and Graham and Elspeth were alone.

Elspeth wore a pale yellow coat, almost the same color as her hair. She looked, as always, tidy and poised and slightly starched, more like Graham's vision of a nurse than any nurse actually here in the hospital.

"What a night," she said to him.

He smiled. "It won't be good publicity for your catering business."

Elspeth gave him a narrow look. She had never liked his humor very much.

She tightened the belt of her coat. "It was good to see you," she said formally.

"Very good," Graham said, trying to make up for offending her.

She paused. "Perhaps we'll see each other again soon."

"I'd like that," he said.

Her eyes flashed up to his instantly.

"We'll figure this out," he said. "How to be friends."

She nodded, lifting her chin slightly. "If you want."

Without really planning to, Graham stepped forward and took her in his arms. He felt her stiffen, and then she sighed and relaxed. She leaned her head on his shoulder, and he thought of how long and slender her neck was, how vulnerable. He put his hand on the back of her head and held her that way for a long, long moment, not caring if anyone saw them. He didn't do it because he felt guilty, or because he felt he owed it to her, or even because he wanted to. He did it because it was the one thing he felt he could do right.

He waited on the sidewalk with Elspeth until a cab came. She got into it the primly sexy way women wearing narrow skirts always get into cabs: with a slight swing of her hips and a little hop. Graham leaned forward to close the door, but she was already pulling it shut from the inside. That was Elspeth.

He began walking home. He should have been exhausted but he felt energetic. Maybe Audra would be waiting for him with a bottle of wine. He would make turkey sandwiches and they would drink wine and discuss Thanksgiving, and she would say, as she did after every dinner party they had, "On a scale of Delightful to Never Again, where would you rate it?"

Graham looked forward to that suddenly, looked forward to being with Audra.

And then tomorrow he would call Elspeth and that was something to look forward to also. He hadn't realized he intended to call her until the plan was there, already in his mind. He would call Elspeth and they would meet for drinks. It felt like the right decision, as certain as death and taxes, as inevitable as bifocals and paper cuts and bad TV on Saturday nights.

This was where he had gone wrong all those years ago, he saw that now. He had gone too suddenly—too completely—from Elspeth to Audra. He was finally at a place where he and Elspeth could have a relationship that was free of bitterness, free of guilt. They could be close again. Not romantically—he didn't want that—but close, intimate, even loving in some way that only former spouses could be.

This idea seemed so clear to him that for a moment he wondered why he hadn't thought of it before. He felt something in his chest clutch and release, the way it felt when he thought he'd left his wallet in a restaurant and then touched his pocket and realized he still had it with him. Of course. He remembered. Things were different now.

Five

So this is how it works, Graham thought.

Life went on. You learned the unimaginable, but life went on. The earth should have stopped spinning, or at least have tilted another twenty-four degrees on its axis, creating new seasons, new weather—a new, harsher world for everyone. But it didn't. Everything went on as normal. Your child folded origami and your wife obsessed about United Nations Day and the afternoon doorman, Julio, lived in your den because—because—well, Graham wasn't exactly sure why. Bedbugs? Landlord dispute? He couldn't remember.

Graham looked out the window sometimes and expected to see a postapocalyptic world, with a cold gray skyline and abandoned cars clogging the street, not a living soul in sight. But when he looked outside, he saw only the normal Manhattan traffic and people hurrying around, with their shopping bags in their hands, or cellphones to their ears, gesturing at no one. The postapocalyptic world was inside him but no one seemed to notice.

Right now, for instance, Audra was talking to Julio in the kitchen. Julio was a good-looking Dominican guy in his early twenties who was so grateful to be staying with them that he did everything he could to be helpful. He and Audra had just returned from the vegetable stand. Graham was reading the paper in the living room but he could hear them perfectly.

"I've devised this whole new system for dividing the population into two groups," Audra was saying. "It's very simple: if you don't like United Nations Day, you can be my friend. If you do like it, then you can't."

"What's wrong with United Nations Day?" Julio asked.

"I don't mean the *actual* United Nations Day," Audra said. "I mean, United Nations Day at Matthew's school, which is this day where every classroom is decorated like a different country and the children visit each country and learn about different cultures and stuff."

"Well, what's so awful about that?" Julio asked.

"It might be easier to tell you what *isn't* awful about it," Audra said. "Which is nothing. See how easy that was?"

But then she plunged ahead anyway and outlined the awfulness for Julio: the decorating of the rooms, the painting of murals, the hanging of bunting, the making of little passports, the sewing of costumes, the preparation of the food, the endless meetings to plan all this, and then the day itself, with the overexcited children and the visiting dignitaries from the real United Nations and the stressed parents snapping at each other.

"And some of the parents are really into it," she concluded. "Actually, all of the parents, except me. At least they pretend to be."

Last year, Graham remembered, Audra had worked in the England Room and had had to wear a low-cut Renaissance dress while she warbled on about humanism and art, and the Italian ambassador's assistant had stuck a rolled-up dollar bill between her breasts. (Although later he realized that it was not the act that offended Audra so much as the amount. "A dollar!" she'd said. "Not even a twenty!") This year she'd volunteered to be in charge of the Food Committee and had sworn that she would not interact with another soul on the actual day.

"But why do you have to be on any committee?" Julio asked. "Why can't you just blow it off?"

"Because then everyone would say bad things about me later and not invite Matthew to birthday parties and things like that," Audra said. "It's like if you lived in Japan and gave someone a gift using only one hand. You're supposed to use both hands—I learned that the year I worked in the Japan Room."

And on she went, her voice rising and falling in the normal way as she washed the fruit and vegetables, quite as though she hadn't broken Graham's heart.

Graham had found out about Audra from an unexplained charge on their credit card.

He was going back through old statements to check his interest charges and there it was: a restaurant he'd never been to—a place called Le Vin dans les Voiles—and he *knew*. He didn't think it was a mistake or identity theft or an online purchase. There seemed to be no originality in the world anymore. Somehow that made it even worse.

"Audra?" he had called from his study. She was in the kitchen with Matthew, making pancakes, but she came and stood in the doorway.

"What's up?" she asked. She had a smudge of flour on her cheek.

He didn't get up from his desk. "There's a charge on the credit card," he said. "Back in December. A French restaurant in the Village."

She opened her mouth slightly and then paused. He could

almost see her considering various explanations and rejecting them. It seemed to him that each excuse was a slight ripple across her expression, a minor adjustment. Then she came and sat in the chair across from his desk.

"Oh, Graham," she said. "I've wanted so many times to tell you."

"You're having an affair," he said flatly.

"Not an *affair*," she said, as though scandalized. "More of a—a flirtation that got a little bit out of control. His name is Jasper and he's a photographer."

"How old is he?" Graham asked.

"Thirty," Audra said. "That made me feel so awful, how young he was. I felt like a dirty old man."

Graham didn't want to hear about how awful she felt. "And you and he had a relationship?"

"Yes, but not what you think," Audra said. "Well, not as bad as you think, probably. It wasn't because of you, Graham. It wasn't because I'm unhappy with you. It was more that it was exciting. And I thought, well, I could have you and Matthew and I could have this other thing, too. And by the time I realized I couldn't, we were too serious, and he said—"

Graham interrupted. "I don't want to know any of that."

He could have sworn she looked disappointed. "What *do* you want to know?" she asked finally.

"Is it over?"

"Yes," she said. "It was over by Christmas. I felt so conflicted and he had this girlfriend—"

"Stop!" he said.

"Graham," Audra said. "We were never lovers—it didn't go that far. We almost—"

He must have winced because she stopped. "I have to get back to Matthew," she said softly. She got up and walked toward the door.

"Why did you use the credit card?" he asked suddenly. "You must have known it would show up on the bill."

"That was an accident," she said. "They charged the card I made the reservation with and I didn't know how to undo it."

"But why use the card to even reserve the table?"

He could see in her face that this was not something he should have asked. She tilted her head slightly. "It was his birthday," she said simply. "I wanted to take him somewhere special."

And then she let herself out of his study, very quietly, closing the door gently behind her, like a nurse leaving a patient alone to deal with a difficult diagnosis.

Once, years ago, Audra had been stuck in an elevator for over three hours with a man who raised ferrets for a living and she told Graham later that she was sort of sad when the elevator began moving again, because she and the man were still getting acquainted. How ironic was it that Graham should be married to someone who loved to talk that much, and now not want to talk to her?

He had forbidden her to talk about her almost affair, her almost lover. He didn't want to know any details, felt he could not survive if he was forced to hear any details, and Audra was a very detail-oriented person. (She knew the names of the children of the man who owned the Mexican restaurant on the corner, for example, knew the oldest one, Tiffany, was working for Senator Schumer.) So Graham refused to discuss it.

And strangely, there seemed nothing else to talk about. Which was another layer of irony, since once Graham and Audra had gone to Vermont for a week, for Christmas, to a remote farmhouse, and Audra had said worriedly, "What if we run out of things to talk about?" and Graham had had to suppress a smile.

Oh, life was thick with irony now. Sort of like baklava, layer after layer pressed down on each other, with grit in between the layers and honey glossed over everything to make it sweet. He was pleased with this analogy, or as close to pleased as he got in these days where it seemed all his emotions lay under a cool frost. He wanted to tell Audra about it. But he didn't, because not only would she have gasped and said, "Baklava! Jesus, I'd better order some for the Greek Room," but because he didn't want to give her anything right now—no gift, no peace offering—no matter how humble.

When Graham got home from work about a week after the discovery, Audra was talking to Lorelei outside the building. She and Lorelei did this constantly—bumped into each other and said they wished they had time to talk but they didn't, and then stood around talking for an extremely long time anyway. Graham guessed they'd been standing there for at least forty-five minutes.

"It's like I've *turned*," Audra was saying. "Like I've become someone else. This perfectly nice lady called me and offered to work on the Food Committee between two and four, and I said I was really hoping for people to work all day, and she said she could only do that one shift, and I was like, 'United Nations is a big day and I need a big commitment.' And then I stopped and thought, *Did I just say that? What's happened to me?* I think when United Nations Day is finally over, I'm going to need deprogramming."

Normally Graham would have stopped and joined the conversation, or at least said hello. But suddenly he realized that Lorelei must know all about Jasper—that surely Audra had shared it with her on a minute-by-minute basis as it happened, for there was nothing that Audra didn't share with Lorelei immediately.

And so instead of stopping to talk to them, he continued on into the building, feeling that losing Lorelei on top of Audra was entirely too much for him to bear.

I have been in United Nations Day meetings *all* afternoon," Audra said the next evening, banging into the apartment and slamming her purse down on the table where Graham and Julio were sitting, drinking beer. Julio had just gotten off duty and was still wearing the red-and-gold pants of his doorman uniform with a plain green T-shirt.

"It was excruciating," Audra said, going into the kitchen to get her own beer. "As head of the Food Committee, I had to stand up and give a progress report and afterward everyone said, 'Things used to run so *smoothly* when Mrs. Adams was in charge of the Food Committee,' and '*Mrs. Adams* had such a serene, efficient manner,' and then they'd look at me sideways."

"What's up with that shit?" Julio asked. "Where's this Mrs. Adams now?"

"She moved to Ohio," Audra said. "Which is apparently *my* fault. People kept saying, 'It was such a *shame* she had to move.' Honestly, it was even worse than the time Grandpa Sandoval French-kissed me under the cuckoo clock."

Julio looked extremely startled by this piece of information but Graham wasn't. Audra had five events that differed in degrees of awfulness and she was always using them as reference points, as though she were plotting all the events of her life on some chart. One: the time when her grandfather French-kissed her one sunny afternoon when she unsuspectingly wandered into her grandparents' kitchen looking for a Fresca. Two: the time when her car ran out of gas in the driveway of some man she was having an affair with while his wife was at work. (Graham didn't imagine this was one of the *man*'s particular favorite memories either.) Three: the spectacular case of food poisoning which had put her off Taco Bell forever. Four (sometimes this moved up to number three temporarily, displacing Taco Bell): the time when she gave a man she was dating a blow job and immediately afterward, he said, "Well, I don't know if I would call you my *girlfriend*." Five: the Cub Scout camping trip when Matthew was six and they woke up with two inches of rain in the tent.

She didn't include even worse events, like the day they got Matthew's Asperger's diagnosis, or her miscarriage the year before Matthew was born, or when her college roommate took an overdose of sleeping pills, though Graham supposed maybe she kept a more private roster of them.

"Your *grandfather* French-kissed you?" Julio asked.

"Yes," Audra said. "He had Alzheimer's, although we didn't know it then. I think maybe he thought I was my grandmother and it was 1930."

"How old were you?" Julio asked.

"Nineteen."

"That's terrible," he said. "I don't know how you're, like, still a functioning member of society."

Graham said nothing, though he wanted to. He wanted to tell Julio that you could go through much worse than that and still function. You could learn things about your wife and marriage that you never suspected and still function. You could go around completely shredded inside and no one could even tell.

· · ·

It turned out that Julio had a girlfriend. He brought her over one night to introduce her to them. At least Graham *thought* it was just to introduce her, but maybe the girlfriend was going to move in with them, too. Lately the mesh of his brain had widened—too much information slipped through.

Julio and his girlfriend arrived at dinnertime, when Graham was in the kitchen, braising peppers and onions.

"Mr. Cavanaugh, this is my girlfriend, Sarita," he said. "Sarita, this is Mr. Cavanaugh." (He called Audra by her first name, but not Graham.)

Sarita was a slender black-haired girl in her early twenties, with enormous brown eyes fringed by thick dark lashes and full red lips that even Graham could tell were free of lipstick. She looked extremely nervous, and Graham wondered if her promotion to Julio's girlfriend was something that had happened very recently.

Audra came down the hall from Matthew's room to greet Julio, and when she saw Sarita, her face became carefully neutral and her eyes took Sarita in from head to toe with a long look and a slow single blink, like a lizard's. Graham knew she was assessing Sarita's outfit—jeans and a tight-fitting pink satin cowboy type of shirt with pearly snap-buttons—and comparing it to her own. He waited to see whether she would decide that Sarita's outfit was sexier.

She must have, because in the next instant, she gave both Sarita and Julio her most dazzling smile and said, "It's such a pleasure to meet you, Sarita! Give me a kiss, Julio!"

Graham marveled for the hundredth time that out of all the women he knew, Audra alone seemed to understand that the prettiest woman in any room would always be the one with the most confident smile.

For a second there, he almost admired her.

．　．　．

Audra asked Graham and Julio to collect food for United Nations Day from the people who had it frozen and ready a week in advance. She said people needed motivation to plan ahead because everyone is basically so lazy.

"Our car's in the shop, remember?" Graham said happily. (Sometimes the gods smile on you for no reason at all.)

"Oh, honestly," Audra said, as though this were a piffling detail.

She was standing in front of Graham and Julio, who were unfortunately both sitting on the love seat in the living room. The love seat was very deep with a short back, and anyone seated on it tended to look recumbent and idle.

"I've already told everyone to expect you tonight," Audra said in a wheedling tone.

"I could probably find us a car," Julio said to Graham. Julio looked guilty. (He didn't know that Graham never needed to feel guilty again where Audra was concerned.)

"I can go with you," Audra said. "If Graham wants to stay here with Matthew and label two hundred bags of Korean scorched rice candy."

Well, Graham wanted to do *that* even less than he wanted to drive around with Julio. So off they went, in a blue Honda Accord that Julio had somewhat magically supplied. Graham suspected it belonged to another tenant who had no idea the car was out and about. He hoped they didn't spill sweet-and-sour sauce on the upholstery.

Julio seemed unconcerned, driving fast and well, although he whistled when he saw the list of addresses. "How are we supposed to make twenty stops in two hours?" he asked Graham.

"Maybe we can do it if we call people and have them meet us in front of their buildings," Graham said.

So Julio drove while Graham dialed his cellphone and they made a series of stops, putting on the hazard lights amid much honking, while a variety of parents ran out and thrust Tupperware boxes full of frozen food at them through the car window.

One woman handed Graham a bag full of cylindrical objects wrapped in plastic and then leaned in the window and gave them a long blast of information about rolling out the dough and brushing it with butter and afterward sprinkling each individual roll with egg wash and then a little pearl sugar or possibly almonds unless that was a danger due to nut allergies, which schools were way too paranoid about in her opinion.

Graham thanked her and rolled up the window.

Julio pulled the car back into traffic. "Do you remember one word of the shit that woman said?" he asked Graham.

"No," Graham admitted.

"Shit," said Julio. (He used the word *shit* all the time, Graham had noticed: as a noun, as an adjective, as an interjection, and sometimes just as a sort of filler, where another person might take a breath.) "I feel like my brain can't hold one more piece of information about United Nations Day. It's like my head's *full*. I hear shit but I can't absorb it."

Graham had been unable to absorb any information for three weeks now, ever since the credit card finding. Julio was right; his head was full.

Julio continued. "You know, in the beginning, I *cared* about all this shit Audra said. I was *concerned* that nobody would work in the China Room even though one out of every four people in the world is Chinese or whatever. I thought it was *terrible* that the India Room wouldn't acknowledge the Pakistan Room. I got *upset* when the bunting for the cafeteria was fifty feet too short. Bunting? I don't even know what that shit is. But I cared because Audra cared."

"I know—" Graham started to say, but Julio was too worked up.

"Now she talks and I don't hear it," he said. "It's like I *can't* hear it. It's like there's a limit to how much any one person can hear about United Nations Day and I'm there."

"I think I reached it three or four United Nations Days ago," Graham said.

"Audra says she's going to be the happiest person on the planet when United Nations Day is over," Julio said, "but she's not. She's going to be the second-happiest person, because the happiest person is going to be me— Oh, look, there she is."

They were only a few blocks from home now and there was Audra, standing in front of the flower stand with Matthew. Audra was pointing at one bunch of flowers and then another and asking Matthew something. (Probably she wanted his opinion; she could never understand that men don't have opinions on flowers.)

She was wearing her short swingy green coat and a little green beret, and just the ends of her hair curled from beneath it. Julio and Graham were stuck at a light so they watched as Audra finally decided on both bunches of flowers. She tucked them under one arm and took Matthew's hand and began walking. Their clasped hands swung easily between them.

Julio blew out a breath. "A fine, classy lady," he said.

And there was a little pause, a little space, where Graham was supposed to say "Yes, a very fine lady." But he didn't.

On the last Friday of every month, Graham and Olivia ordered Chinese food for lunch and ate it in Graham's office.

Graham was fairly sure that Olivia looked forward to it—she always reminded him on Thursday nights, saying, "Tomorrow's our lunch!" But sometimes he wondered if Olivia viewed their lunches as a form of community service. Perhaps she thought she was having lunch with some sort of shut-in. (It never pays to overestimate yourself.)

Today they had sesame noodles and shredded pork with snow cabbage and sliced beef with black bean sauce. Graham always ordered; he was trying to expand Olivia's palate. She'd told him that before she came to work for him, the only Chinese food she'd ever had were egg rolls and sweet-and-sour chicken, and she'd only had that once at a restaurant in her hometown. (Graham did not want to even *think* about how bad Chinese food in Kentucky must be.)

Now Olivia was curled in the chair across from Graham's desk, her feet tucked under her. She was wearing a black skirt and a white blouse with a Peter Pan collar and looked about eight years old. She ate rice dreamily, grain by grain with her chopsticks. "I love Chinese rice," she said. "Whenever I make rice at home, it burns and we have to throw out the pan."

It was news to Graham that Olivia ever tried to cook *anything* at home and he felt mildly encouraged for her future. "Just set a timer," he said. "Then you won't forget about it."

"I guess," she said, still dreamy. "But I wish there was, like, a machine that cooked the rice for you, like a coffeemaker makes coffee."

"There is."

Olivia looked confused. "There is what?"

"A machine that cooks rice," Graham said. "It's called a rice cooker."

"What—you're saying it really exists?"

"Yes."

Her eyes were very round. "Where can I get one? Do I have to go to Chinatown?"

"Oh, no," Graham said soothingly. "I'm sure you can get one in any department store."

Olivia looked worried. "Will you write down the name of it?"

"I'll tell you what," Graham said. "I have an extra one. I'll bring it in on Monday and give it to you."

It wasn't true that he had an extra one, but he did have one he hardly ever used. In fact, he could picture it, sitting in its box at home in a high cupboard that was hard to reach. He could see in his mind the thick layer of greasy dust that seemed to collect on all seldom-used kitchen utensils. He would give it to Olivia, and she and her roommate would eat rice all the time for a month and then she, too, would probably put it in a cupboard and maybe it would follow Olivia on a few of her moves, or maybe she would forget about it and it would remain in her kitchen for the next occupants. It made Graham feel, all at once, very sorry for the rice cooker, for anything that got left behind.

It was really just amazing the way life kept grinding forward, demanding things of him. He had to get up and go to work and earn a living and cook dinner and be a parent, all on days when he didn't know if he could manage to brush his teeth. And he had to take Matthew to Origami—some special meeting where Matthew's club was joining forces with another origami club. (Graham had gathered that there was bad blood between the two clubs—some sort of turf war over who could and who could not shop at a certain paper-supply store in the West Village—but evidently they had all moved past it.)

"Do you think it's safe just to drop him off?" he asked Audra in the kitchen as he shrugged into his coat. "What if these other men are child predators?"

"Oh, I'm sure they're not child predators," Audra said, in her maddeningly calm way. She was paging through an Italian cookbook.

"Why wouldn't they be?" Graham asked. (Sometimes, they did accidentally drift into conversation.)

"Well, because think how much trouble it would be for a child predator to learn to fold that Tadashi Mori Dragon—"

"Leviathan," Matthew corrected from the hallway.

"Leviathan," Audra said. Then she lowered her voice. "Why does he always listen when we don't want him to and never when we do? Anyway, the Leviathan has about five hundred folds and they can all do it by memory and I don't think a child predator would go to so much trouble. I think he'd just go out and buy an Xbox. Besides, Clayton will be there to look after him and bring Matthew home."

Clayton! If there was someone of more questionable emotional maturity and moral fortitude, Graham couldn't think who it was.

But Matthew called from the door, "We're going to be late if we don't go now," so Graham left and he and Matthew took a cab down to the diner.

The other Origami Club members were already there—plus a few men Graham didn't recognize, who must have been from the other club—clustered around a table.

"Hello, everyone," Graham said.

They'd saved a chair for Matthew, who slid into it, already unzipping his backpack.

"You're five minutes late," one of the other members said—a large man wearing a camouflage jacket. Graham hadn't seen this particular man before. He looked like he ought to be sitting in a duck blind somewhere.

"Well, traffic," Graham said, shrugging.

"You should *allow* for traffic," said the duck-blind man. (Graham had noticed that OCD was somewhat widespread in the origami crowd.) "Anyway, now that Matthew's finally here, we can start. First we need to make fifty triangular units each."

All the salt-and-pepper heads and Matthew's brown-haired one bent over their stacks of origami paper.

"Um, goodbye," Graham said, feeling like an idiot. He always expected to feel suave and sophisticated in front of the Origami Club and yet he never did. "You're bringing him home, right, Clayton?"

Clayton looked up and gave an impatient nod and then looked down again.

Graham took another cab back home, thinking that before, he would have looked forward to a Sunday alone with Audra. Even if they were both working on separate projects, he would have enjoyed her presence in the apartment, would have looked forward to meeting her in the kitchen, would have persuaded her to come out with him somewhere. But now he didn't want to go home and see her. He wouldn't have gone home at all except that he couldn't think of anywhere he did want to go.

Julio was on duty when he got back to the apartment building, nearly unrecognizable in his uniform. "Hi, Mr. Cavanaugh," he said.

"Hey, Julio," he said. "Should I count on you for dinner tonight?"

"Absolutely," Julio answered. "I finish at seven."

One of the other tenants, a man about Graham's age, was

reading the newspaper in the lobby and he peered at Graham over the top of it. He probably thought Julio was Graham's rent boy. Well, let him think that. Graham was too dispirited to care.

He took the elevator up and opened the door to the apartment.

Audra's voice reached him. Not the careful, solicitous voice she used with him now, but her normal voice, warm and full of laughter. "Tell me about it," she said. Then there was a pause. "Well, I don't know."

She was on the phone. Graham paused. He left the door open behind him, and hoped no one would take the elevator up to this floor and cause the bell to ring. He stood and listened.

"Yes, me too," Audra said. Pause. "I know, but what can we do?" Pause. "I hate it, too." Pause. "I know."

Graham tried very hard not to fill in the pauses. But then what was he standing here listening for, if not to do that?

And then Audra said, "What am I supposed to do with a hundred Ethiopian cookies when there's no Ethiopia Room, though? I didn't even know they *had* cookies in Ethiopia. I thought there was a perpetual famine there."

Graham sighed and let the door bang shut. He felt a sudden longing, sharp enough to cause his chest to tighten. He wanted his life back.

They sat in the living room, making a cozy family picture: Graham in the armchair with a newspaper, Audra curled on the couch with a magazine, Matthew next her, Julio on the floor, tapping out texts on his phone.

"Can we all watch a movie together?" Matthew asked.

"Only if I pick the movie," Audra said.

Matthew frowned. "What's up with that shit?"

There was a pause, long enough for several blinks, and then Graham said to Julio, "If we get called in for some sort of school conference about this, you have to go," and Audra laughed.

Graham had noticed that it was easier for him and Audra now to communicate by bouncing conversation off Julio. He wondered if they would become like Graham's mother, who projected her feelings onto her elderly spaniel and said things like, "Bilbo doesn't like it when people forget to hang up their coats." Maybe Graham would say to Audra, *Julio doesn't know if he'll ever feel the same about you.*

"What's up with that *shit*," Audra said to Matthew, "is that after *Spy Kids 4*, I absolutely cannot watch another bad children's movie. I feel like I was never the same afterward, like some vital part of my brain was destroyed."

Ironic that she would say that when it was Graham who knew all about vital parts of yourself being destroyed—Graham who knew all about never being the same afterward. He couldn't stop thinking about ironies, and before, and after.

"So what will we watch?" Matthew asked.

"Oh, I don't know," Audra said. "Something scary and inappropriate, probably. Maybe a disaster movie."

"Will you watch with us?" Matthew said to Graham.

"Of course."

"And Julio?"

"If he wants to."

"I'd love to," Julio said, not looking up from his phone.

Graham envied him suddenly. Julio could drift in and out, partaking of family life, and yet leading his own romantic life (he was frequently out all night). Julio could stay on the surface, where everything was fine, where the happy family watched movies and ate dinner and sat around in cozy clusters. Julio never had to look deeper and examine the foundation. That was Graham's job.

Graham was standing at the kitchen counter, trimming the fat off the pork chops for dinner, when Audra appeared in the doorway. She was wearing jeans and a bright red flannel shirt that he'd always liked.

"You're going to think I'm a horrible person," she said.

No, he wouldn't think that. Or maybe he thought that already.

"But someone just called to say she was bringing two hundred pork sausages for the England Room, but the England Room already has tons of food. Do you think anyone will notice if I put the sausages in the German Room and call them *wurst*? Because the German Room hardly has any food at all."

Graham decided to cut up the pineapple. It was nice and noisy and required lots of attention. "No, I'm sure no one would notice," he said.

"Graham—" Audra began, and then stopped.

He kept cutting the skin off the sides of the pineapple, concentrating on making the knife follow the curve. He could tell she was still standing in the doorway.

But when he finished with the pineapple and looked up at her, she had already turned to go, her shirt leaving an afterimage of red that hurt his eyes.

Graham and Julio were assembling an IKEA bookcase for Matthew's room.

"Shit," said Julio. "I think it'd be easier to *build* one, from scratch, with no instructions, than to follow these."

They both squinted at the instructions spread out on the floor between them, along with the little plastic bags of screws and bolts, and those maddening Allen wrenches.

Graham had grown very fond of Julio, although he knew better than to get too attached to houseguests, which he and Audra seemed to have perpetually. Julio was moving back to his apartment next week.

"Well," Graham said, "we could just wait until Audra and Matthew get back and then have Matthew put it together. He'll take one look at the instructions and just *know*."

"Yeah, I remember he fixed Mrs. Allman's dryer down on Four," Julio said.

"Before we had Matthew to do this," Graham said, "I used to tell Audra that I would divorce her if she brought home another piece of flat-pack furniture."

And then he wished he hadn't said that because it made him think of the time when marital troubles were something they laughed at, nothing to do with them.

He realized Julio was watching him closely. "But you don't want to do that—divorce her," he said. "You and Audra, you're good together."

"You don't understand," Graham said flatly.

"Oh, I understand enough," Julio said. "I know that when you two sit on the couch, you leave enough space for, like, an invisible person to sit between you. I know that when we watch some shit on TV and one of the characters is having an affair, you grab hold of the arms of the chair like you're an astronaut in liftoff. I see Audra walking around looking like a dog just before someone shouts at it. I know what's going on."

"Well, then," Graham said, annoyed, "you know how I feel." But Julio didn't know how he felt. Julio couldn't imagine the effort it took just to carry on this conversation.

"But that shit doesn't mean anything," Julio said. He saw the startled look Graham gave him and went on. "I mean, I know it means *everything* but it doesn't really *mean* anything."

It was yet another irony, Graham thought, that something so inarticulate should make so much sense, and that it should turn out that Julio would be the one to understand exactly how he felt.

The phone rang at six in the morning on United Nations Day, with the news that some woman had burned ninety Swedish meatballs and didn't know what to do.

"That's easy," Audra said. "Just buy frozen meatballs from the supermarket and we'll stick toothpicks with little Swedish flags in them and no one will ever know any different."

She hung up and said to Graham, "Honestly, do you think people bother Ban Ki-moon with nonsense like that?" And she flounced off to take a shower.

A little while later she came into the kitchen, where Graham and Julio were sitting at the counter, drinking coffee. She was wearing jeans and a purple silk shirt and long dangly earrings. Her clothes were casual and yet she looked vaguely corporate. Graham supposed that was just her determined expression.

"Have you made Matthew's lunch?" she asked abruptly. "Have you made sure he's awake and started his breakfast?"

"Am I supposed to take Matthew to school today?" Graham asked.

"For God's sake," Audra said irritably. "*Yes.* I have been telling you for weeks that I was going to leave before seven today. Do you just sit there and think about porn while I talk?"

Now, why was it exciting to hear a pretty woman say the word *porn,* no matter what the context? Graham glanced at Julio and saw that his eyes had unfocused slightly, too. Evidently it was a common phenomenon.

"Okay," Graham said finally. "I'll get Matthew going."

Audra and Julio packed up and called questions to each other while Graham made Matthew's lunch.

He went into Matthew's bedroom to wake him. "Hey, buddy, time to get up," he said, poking Matthew's sleeping form. He opened the curtains to let some light into the room and saw Audra and Julio on the sidewalk below, setting out for United Nations Day. Audra was walking ahead, carrying a single tray of cookies, while Julio followed, loaded down with bags and boxes in a way that reminded Graham of a Sherpa guide.

He felt very sorry for Julio, who had taken a day off work to help Audra, and then he experienced a rush of relief that he was able to feel something—anything—for another person at all.

Graham was already home from his office, pouring himself a glass of wine, when Audra got back. He heard the door open, and Audra sigh and dump her bags on the floor with a muffled clatter. He didn't call to her.

She walked past the kitchen into the bedroom. Graham followed, still holding the bottle of wine and the glass.

"How was it?" he asked.

"It was horrible," she said. She looked tired. The purple silk shirt was rumpled and the auburn highlights in her hair seemed to draw all the color up and out of her face.

Graham poured wine into the glass he was holding and handed it to her. She drank it in one long swallow and handed the glass back to him. He understood that she wasn't giving him the glass because she was finished with it. He refilled it and gave it to her again, and then he sat on the bed to watch her.

"The Irish storyteller ate the cream tea that was on display in the England Room when no one was looking, and the England Room got all upset and demanded an apology. I'm sure if it had been anyone but someone from the *Ireland* Room, they wouldn't have cared."

Audra sipped her wine while she stood on one foot and then the other removing her boots. "Julio took Matthew out for pizza but I didn't want to go. Pizza only reminded me of the Italy Room. I want to eat something tonight that has no cultural associations whatsoever."

Was that possible? Graham felt a slight stirring of interest. Almost all food has cultural associations. What could they have? Not hamburgers or pasta or chili or quiche. Baked potatoes? Too Irish. Maybe scrambled eggs.

She came and sat by him on the bed.

"Still, it's over," she said, stretching her legs and wiggling her toes, "and I haven't been so happy since, well, right about this time last year when United Nations Day was over."

Last year! This time last year, he had been happy. This time last year, none of this had happened, he hadn't even been suspicious, he had been living life just as he wanted to.

"Lorelei says she doesn't want to hear about United Nations Day ever again," Audra said. "She says no matter how long or short the rest of our friendship turns out to be, it's off-limits, which I think is so unfair. It's like when I told Matthew I didn't want to hear any more about double rabbit-ear folds and now he looks so guilty when he brings it up, or when you—when you said you didn't want to know any details. Everywhere conversations are being *aborted*."

She sighed on the last word, making her sound like a pro-life person describing a very sad truth. And yet, he knew Audra did genuinely feel the loss of these conversations, of any conversation that she didn't get to have. (She often claimed to regret not getting the phone number of a very nice woman she sat next to on a bus when Matthew was a newborn.)

"Do you really *want* to tell me the details?" Graham asked. He was not sure what he would do if she said yes.

"Oh, Graham," Audra said suddenly, putting her hand on his arm. "I just want you to love me again."

Well, love. Of course he loved her. He didn't know if he could forgive her, or trust her, or go on living with her. But he still loved her. He couldn't help it.

"I do," Graham said. But it came out impatiently: I *do,* with so much emphasis on the second word that it sounded like it had two or three *o*'s. He swallowed and tried again. "I do." That was better, but he said it again anyway. And again. Until he got it right.

Six

It was just like an affair, Graham thought, except without the sex or love or excitement or other good parts. There weren't even the bad parts—shame or betrayal—because Audra knew and approved. Or at least she offered no objection and sometimes she even looked relieved. (She seemed overwhelmed lately.) No sex, no secrets, no guilt, no debauchery greater than gourmet potato chips.

So why then did Graham's heart beat faster every time he climbed the steps to Elspeth's building?

The reason Audra was so distracted was that she was getting the apartment ready for houseguests. She did all the usual things—set up a cot in Matthew's room and put fresh sheets on the foldout bed in the den and stocked the bathroom with miniature toiletries and cleaned out space in the hall closet and made Graham wrestle the armchair out of the den and down to their storage space—this last part was reason enough never to have houseguests, Graham thought. But even for Audra, having these houseguests bordered on the extreme. *Strangers. Two* of them. For a *month*. (It seemed to Graham to get worse with every phrase.)

Over Christmas, Graham and Audra and Matthew had spent a week in a Miami resort and met another couple who were so unremarkable that if you got on an elevator with them, you not only wouldn't remember them, you might not even notice they were there. They had an eleven-year-old son named Noah, and he, too, was completely unremarkable except for one quality—he and Matthew had become friends. The kind of friendship Graham had always hoped Matthew would have—easy and uncomplicated and heartfelt. Matthew and Noah explored the resort together and called each other on the hotel phones and went swimming and ordered milk shakes and stayed up late. Graham supposed they had fallen in love a little bit—the bright, sweet kind of love you feel when someone asks you to sit with them at lunch.

Naturally, Audra had spent hours talking to Noah's parents and stayed in touch with them after they'd left. In some long complicated email thread (Graham imagined that printed out, it would stretch the length of a basketball court) Audra and Noah's mother had worked out an arrangement where Noah would come and stay with them for the month of February, since he went to an international school with a long half-term break. And since Noah couldn't travel by himself, he would bring his grandfather.

Oh, listen to Graham! Making it sound like this was all some crazy scheme of Audra's. As if Graham hadn't agreed to it, as if Graham hadn't leapt at the chance, as if Graham didn't want to live, however briefly, in that golden world where your child romped happily through the enchanted forest of friendship.

Graham knew that other people didn't do this. Other people had children and those children had friends and they went over to the friends' houses and watched TV and hung out and slept over and sometimes they drank the friends' fathers' whisky and then added water to fill up the bottle and kept doing that until the whisky was the color of dry sand. That was how it was supposed to work. That was how Graham remembered it working. But what happened when it didn't work that way? What happened when your kid never seemed to make that kind of connection?

Before you had a special-needs child, you probably thought, *Okay, special needs means a tutor, maybe a specialized school.* You didn't know then that having a child with special needs would seep into every part of your life, like rain through topsoil. Who would ever think you would be happy to host a strange boy and his *grandfather* for a month just so your kid could have a best friend? Your old self wouldn't believe you would agree to such a thing. Your old self would stick his hands in his pockets and shake his head and give a little disbelieving whistle. But your old self knew nothing at all.

Noah's grandfather was not what they were expecting. Graham had pictured a genteel, urbane older gentleman with a pointy white beard who would make witty conversation about his travels and possibly have a passion for the early works of Edward Bulwer-Lytton. But in reality Noah's grandfather was a balding red-faced man who swayed alarmingly even when using a cane. He wheezed badly just from taking the elevator, and his first words to them were "These long flights are murder on my kidneys."

Even more startling than this was that Noah's grandfather was accompanied by a barrel-chested chocolate Labrador named Brodie, who lumbered past Graham and Audra as they stood at the door. Graham could hear Brodie's claws scrambling madly for purchase on the hardwood floors.

At least Noah was the same as they remembered—pallid and thin, with no-color hair and pale eyelashes, and a gap-toothed smile. It was true: you really cannot help who you fall in love with. He smiled waifishly and Matthew beamed at him and then they disappeared into Matthew's room.

Meanwhile Brodie pushed through the swinging door to the kitchen, letting out a little yelp as the door closed on his tail.

Graham pointed at the kitchen. "Did you know about this?" he said to Audra. Noah's grandfather was in the bathroom.

"What—Brodie?" Audra said, as though Graham could possibly be referring to something else. "No. No. Well. No. Anyway, Graham, forget about the dog! What about *him*? He's so old! What if he falls over and breaks his hip and we have to take care of him for three months? What if he wakes up tomorrow and can't move the left side of his body? What if he has to be in rehab for months!"

"That's not going to happen," Graham said.

"But how do you know?"

"Because I won't let it. Because if he falls and breaks his hip or has any other health problem, I will pay for him to be medevaced back to California."

"Really?" Audra said. Her eyes were shining and she was gazing up at him as though he knew all the world's secrets.

This was an actual conversation. Graham meant every word.

Graham and Audra had never had a dog; they were not dog people. And Graham thought that probably even dog people weren't *Brodie* people. Graham could not get used to the way Brodie's nails scraped constantly on the floors, or the strings of drool that hung from the corners of Brodie's mouth, or Brodie's sudden fits of scratching, which seemed to go on endlessly, his tags jingling noisily. Brodie panted constantly, even though it was February, and he barked almost as much as he panted. He barked when the elevator dinged, or the phone rang, or when they opened and shut the cabinet doors (or when their neighbors opened and shut *their* cabinet doors). He barked for almost half an hour at an African mask in the den until Audra pulled it off the wall and put it in a closet. Brodie carried their shoes around and chewed the laces out of the eyelets. He also got into the coat closet and chewed the pockets out of all their coats (there must have been crumbs in them), which they only discovered when their keys kept falling on the floor. He jumped up on everyone who came into the apartment, and he tipped over the wastebaskets and spread garbage on the floor, and he stole a whole loaf of bread off the kitchen counter.

"Brodie, sweetie," Papa Stan said. "You have to behave! Remember your manners! These nice people are our hosts. This is their home. Now show them what a good boy you can be. Please? Can you do that? Brodie? Brodie! I asked you a question."

That's the way Papa Stan spoke to Brodie: long complicated sentences that didn't contain one single command. Clearly, this was what happened when you were a lonely old man and a dog was your only companion. It was only too easy to imagine them watching the nightly news, Papa Stan trying to elicit Brodie's opinion on same-sex-marriage appeals.

When Papa Stan spoke to Brodie like that, Graham's throat tightened and he had to turn away. Sometimes other people's pain is more than you can take. You have to seal yourself off.

Elspeth's apartment was as simple and stylish as a showplace. Part of it, Graham supposed, was that she was one person living in a two-bedroom apartment, but he didn't like to think about that. And anyway, he knew that the main part of it was just Elspeth. She liked to keep things extremely neat. That had driven him fairly crazy when they were married. She could not relax— she was always moistening her finger to pick crumbs off the table or stretching to pluck fluff off the carpet—and she'd had a way of watching him, too, as though silently daring him to spill his drink or crumble a cracker. And—this was the worst—often when Graham himself neatened up, when he pushed in the dining room chairs, or centered a candlestick on a table, Elspeth would come along right behind him and readjust the chair or candlestick by an inch. It was as though she didn't want objects in the apartment to get the wrong idea and start thinking Graham was the boss.

But the apartment seemed overly tidy, even for Elspeth. Graham found it depressing. It was like when you were young and single and cleaned your apartment and then realized you still didn't have a date—you were just a person with a clean apartment who didn't have a date.

Even her handbag on the hall table looked staged, like something out of a magazine, perhaps because otherwise the tabletop was bare, with no jumble of keys or scattering of mail. In the kitchen, the counters were free of crumbs, the appliances shining; there was no dish drainer because Elspeth dried dishes and put them away as soon as she washed them (and if you think *that*'s relaxing, think again). The carpet was far cleaner than a twice-a-week cleaning service could account for, and the furniture was dustless but without the smell of Pledge—Graham seemed to recall that Elspeth polished it with lemon oil. The dining room table gleamed so deeply it was reflective, and Elspeth always had a different centerpiece—a candle floating in a crystal dish, or a square tray filled with blue stones, or a bowl of perfect green apples. Real apples, too. But what did she do when they started to ripen? One person couldn't eat a dozen apples in a day or two. Perhaps she got all economical and whizzed them up into applesauce. But how often does a single person eat a dish of applesauce? Oh, everywhere Graham turned, he stumbled into the fact of Elspeth's aloneness.

Still, it was a nice apartment—no getting around that.

Graham and Elspeth's evenings were full of intimacy. Graham arrived at Elspeth's building and the doormen no longer bothered to make him wait while they called up, they just waved hello, and there was intimacy in that, and when Graham got to Elspeth's apartment, the door was propped open on the dead bolt and Graham could let himself in, and there was intimacy in that. The wine would be on the counter, chilling, and there was intimacy in that, and often Graham would have done some shopping on the way over and he would put the food in the refrigerator, and there was intimacy in that, and usually Elspeth would be in the bedroom changing clothes with the door slightly ajar and there was intimacy in *that;* oh my, yes.

But Elspeth did not come out of the bedroom in a silky robe or floaty negligee. She had merely changed from her suit into wool pants and a silk blouse, or maybe black leggings and a black sweater. This was, Graham knew, her equivalent to putting on her bathrobe. And she always wore high heels. She was the only woman Graham had ever known who didn't kick off her high heels with a moan of pleasure as soon as she got home. (That had been another unrelaxing component·of their married life, that she never lounged around in her bathrobe. Try lounging around in *your* bathrobe while your spouse clicks around the house in stiletto heels and vacuums the back of the television set. It gets to you.)

Elspeth would join him in the kitchen and they would make dinner together, stepping around each other as neatly as square dancers. They never touched, not even accidentally. It seemed to

Graham that they went out of their way *not* to touch, that they didn't touch even when they should. Elspeth would put her glass on the counter and step back while Graham filled it, and then he would step back and she would reach for it. *Do-si-do,* Graham would think. *Promenade. Swing your partner. Big foot up and little foot down.*

Honestly, sometimes he wondered if he was losing his mind.

They spoke mainly of whatever they were cooking, for they were both ambitious cooks, and often whatever they were making led them to plan future meals: chicken gumbo leading to chilaquiles verdes to chicken vindaloo Vesuvius. There was never any doubt that they would do this again.

And then after dinner, they would sit on the couch and drink more wine. Elspeth did not sit directly beside him, but she always turned toward him, extending her arm along the back of the couch, her face as open and calm as a pansy.

Eventually, it would be nine o'clock and Graham would rise (though Elspeth wouldn't; he saw himself out) and thank Elspeth for dinner and she would smile as though he'd said something ridiculous and he would say, "We should do this again soon," and she would say, "Well, how about the day after tomorrow?" and he would say, "That would be great, if you're not tired of feeding me," and she would say, "Don't be silly. But are you sure they won't need you at home?" and he would picture Audra and Matthew and Noah's grandfather and Noah and Brodie (God, there were so many of them!) and say, "Oh, no," as if his family were a power station or fresh water supply, one of those things you were very grateful for but didn't think about all that much.

There *are* some good houseguests—people who know why your dishwasher is making that clunking noise, and friends with all-day meetings and big expense accounts—but Noah's grandfather wasn't one of them. (They were supposed to call Noah's grandfather Papa Stan. "I'm almost sixty years old," Graham said. "I'm not going to call a man ten years older than me Papa anything." But he did. Of course he did.)

From the very first morning, Papa Stan took to wandering around in a ratty old blue bathrobe. Didn't houseguests understand that the point of growing up and buying a house and all the responsibility that went with it was so that you didn't have to see anyone but your spouse in a bathrobe? Papa Stan set the television in the den to Fox News at a high volume and he seemed to dirty a fresh cup for every sip of coffee and he used up all the half-and-half in a single morning. And that was just for starters. He wanted attention *all* the time—he wanted you to show him how the shower worked and where you kept the butter and give him directions to the nearest supermarket. He wanted you to watch the news with him and fix him sandwiches and listen to his opinions on police brutality. He was as helpless and needy as a newborn baby.

Papa Stan also had the hearing of a lynx. Graham had to set but one toe on the floor outside the bedroom—quietly, quietly—and suddenly Papa Stan would appear and say, "I was just thinking about breakfast myself." But what he meant was, *Ah, someone to make me breakfast!* And if Graham lied (yes, Graham had done this) and said he wasn't going to the kitchen at all, he was actually going to change a lightbulb or put some laundry in, then Papa Stan would trail along behind him, plucking at his sleeve and asking questions and telling boring stories until Graham wished he'd just gone ahead and made Papa Stan breakfast and been done with it.

Except that he *wouldn't* have been done with it. There was no being done with Papa Stan. If you made him breakfast, he wanted you to keep him company while he ate it. If you read the newspaper, he read aloud from the page facing him. If you unloaded the dishwasher, he leaned on his cane right in front of the silverware drawer and talked to you. If you checked your email, he breathed over your shoulder. If you said you were going for a walk, he said the exercise would do him good. If you said you were also going to run a bunch of errands, he would say that he didn't mind that. If you said they were *really long, boring errands,* he said he would bring a book. If you said that now that you thought about it, you had a really important meeting on the other side of town, then he just looked disappointed and let you go, and if you felt like a horrible person for dodging a lonely old man, it served you right. (It was worth it, though.)

Like all affairs, Graham and Elspeth's involved a lot of alcohol. At least, Graham assumed all affairs involved a lot of alcohol, just as he assumed that people who didn't drink had fewer affairs. But he didn't really know. Maybe they had *more* affairs because they had more time, what with no trips to the liquor store or hangovers to deal with.

At any rate, whenever he got to Elspeth's apartment, she would have a bottle of dry white wine chilling in an ice bucket on the counter, along with two balloon wine goblets—the kind of glasses that Audra claimed made her drink too quickly. Graham would pour the wine and they would start drinking.

Drinking, for Graham, had always been like traveling down a gently curving country road, clearly marked with speed limits and traffic arrows. He knew this was not the case for everyone. Some people, like Audra, rocketed down the road from a sober starting point with no control or caution and they were as surprised as anyone else when they missed that last curve and ended up vomiting in someone's potted plant and had to call the hostess and apologize the next morning. But not so for Graham.

For Graham, the road was clearly signposted in two-glass intervals, and the brake was always within easy reach. The first drink was unbeatable: delicious, relaxing, restorative—practically medicinal. He had read that alcohol didn't enter your bloodstream for twenty minutes after the first sip, but everyone knew that was nonsense; it started working as soon as you poured it into the glass.

The second glass was nearly as good as the first, and this was what Graham thought of as the Relaxed Stage. During the third glass, he passed smoothly into the Euphoric Stage. He could almost read the sign, white letters on a reflective green background: WELCOME TO EUPHORIA. It was a mellow, blissful kind of euphoria, but euphoria nonetheless. Words flowed more freely, his outlook was brighter, his muscles more relaxed. Sometimes Graham could extend his stay in Euphoria to three glasses by eating dinner—like pulling into a scenic overlook on the road to drunkenness, he supposed. He and Elspeth cooked elaborate meals—crab jambalaya or lamb shank ragù—and the food could stabilize his sobriety level, at least briefly. Between the fourth and fifth glasses, Graham entered the Mildly Confused State—the country road had sharper turns now, more yellow warning signs, even guardrails. Sometimes Graham was aware that he could not remember a particular word, or realized that he had no idea what time it was. But these were small things. Between the sixth and seventh glasses, Graham would reach a stoplight that flashed red and warned him to go to bed. If he passed that light, he would be sorry the next day, so he almost never did.

And so it was, one night when he was in the Mildly Confused

State, and he and Elspeth were sitting on the couch after dinner. Elspeth was wearing a thin white sweater and long wide-legged pants, which made her look like a stilt walker. And yet, Graham liked them. They swirled around her legs when she moved.

Elspeth took a drink from her wineglass. Her eyes over the rim were as clear as blue bath beads.

"I always knew," she said, "about the affair you had with that teenage typist."

Graham's fingers tightened on his wineglass so abruptly that he was surprised it didn't shatter. She wasn't a teenager and she wasn't a typist, but Graham knew exactly who Elspeth was talking about. Her name was Marla and she had been the temporary receptionist in his office. And, well, yes, she was twenty-two, which, Graham supposed, was still young enough to see your teen years if you glanced back over your shoulder.

Marla had lived in a studio apartment with a pet iguana named Leonard, and whenever Graham came over, Leonard would inflate his dewlaps and rock back and forth on his front legs and get ready to charge. Marla said this was because Leonard thought Graham was a male iguana. Graham would have to wait in the hall while Marla chased Leonard around and forced him back into his cage, which he was outgrowing. And then Graham and Marla would have sex on Marla's daybed while Leonard bobbed his head up and down in the background and whacked the wall of his cage with his tail. After about a month, it had begun to seem to Graham seedy rather than sexy, and Marla's temp job ended and they stopped seeing each other. Graham almost never thought of her except for a brief time when Matthew was five and had played a song called "I Wanna Iguana" endlessly, and then Graham had thought of her—more precisely, of Leonard— all the time.

He supposed his affair with Marla was unforgivable on a lot of levels, but the absolute worst part of it was that it took place while Elspeth's mother had been dying. Not just dying (if there is such a thing as *just* dying) but dying a horrible, undignified death from a series of strokes. The strokes had come quickly—the first at home, the rest in the hospital. The medical staff had been unable to prevent them, unable to do anything to shore Elspeth's mother's brain up as it crumbled like an eroding cliff. The last stroke had left half of her face frozen in an ugly sneer that belied her sweet nature. Elspeth's father was dead by then, and she had no siblings, so Elspeth did everything you do when someone is in the hospital—visited and comforted and consulted and stayed awake and feared the telephone—alone. Alone except for Graham, when he wasn't with Marla. (Which really had been hardly ever, he told himself.)

Graham swallowed. His throat made a clicking sound. "You must have hated me," he said finally.

Elspeth looked thoughtful. "I guess I did. A little bit. For a little while. But in a way it made it easier. Well, not easier, but more straightforward. I had to rely on myself. There was no other choice."

Graham drank the entire contents of his enormous wineglass. His mouth remained as dry as a volcanic plain.

Elspeth was still staring dreamily ahead. "And, of course," she said, "then I fell in love with Mr. Dutka, and I could hardly hate you after that."

"Mr. Dutka?" Graham said.

Elspeth leaned forward and refilled her wineglass.

"I know it must sound strange to you," she said.

Strange? *Strange?* Mr. Dutka was an elderly Hungarian man who had lived in their apartment building when Graham and

Elspeth were married. Elspeth used to do his grocery shopping on Saturday mornings and once she helped him when his umbrella had gotten stuck in the lobby's revolving door, and that was *it*, as far as Graham knew. That was the extent of their involvement with Mr. Dutka. He would have bet his life on it. But evidently that would have been a mistake.

"But you weren't—" Graham said. "It wasn't— This was an *emotional* connection, right?"

"No," said Elspeth. "We were lovers."

"You and Mr. Dutka? Mr. Dutka, who was, like, seventy?"

"Yes," she said. "He had incredible stamina."

He could remember Elspeth arising early on Saturday mornings—she didn't like to sleep in; that was yet another unrelaxing habit she had—and he could remember hearing her move about the bedroom as he slid deeper under the covers. He remembered the final soft *click* of the bedroom door on her way out and how that made sleeping in seem extra-decadent, yet also more pleasant—to lounge in bed while his selfless philanthropic wife went off and did some old man's grocery shopping. Or *did* Graham actually remember those things? It seemed like he did. It felt like he did. But maybe he was only adding them in, now that he knew the truth. If he did know the truth. If the truth was, in fact, knowable.

"You have to understand," Elspeth said. "No one had ever seen me as sexy before. I used to think, *Well, I've always been slender, so I'm not one of those people who have to struggle with their weight,* and then I'd think, *Thank God I'm intelligent and don't have to worry about that,* and I would sort of add up all my good qualities, like being organized and well-read and self-motivated, and I'd feel so much luckier than almost everybody, and *then* we'd see some girl—I mean, some awful waitress with the flashiest earrings, and I'd realize all over again that I wasn't sexy."

Ah, that waitress! She worked at the Cuban diner and Graham remembered her well. She used to give you a slow smile when she served fried plantains that could just about make you sob. And Graham thought again, guiltily, of Marla's nipples poking at her blouse—like puppies' noses or pencil erasers.

"But then Zoltan came along," Elspeth continued, "and he thought I was the sexiest woman in the world! Why, I barely had to touch him—"

"Could we just get something straight?" Graham interrupted. "Did you ever in fact buy the man's groceries?"

"Oh, yes," Elspeth said. "But after a few weeks, we began having them delivered. So we would have more time."

More time. Really, it was amazing how people always feel the need to add some little flourish, some extra element that you didn't want to know. It was like they could not stop themselves.

"If you were in love with him—" Graham said, and his voice was as acidic as the space creature's blood in *Alien*. He couldn't help it. "If you were so in love with him, why didn't you leave me and run off with him?"

"He wouldn't hear of it," Elspeth said simply.

Honestly, it was lucky that Graham could take a taxi home. If he'd been driving, he would have surely crashed the car.

Papa Stan turned out to be allergic to nearly all interesting food. Not that anyone *told* Graham this—no, indeed. He had to find out from Audra through the most irritating sort of process of elimination. Every morning, she would come up to him and ask casually what he was going to make for dinner and no matter what he answered, she would say "That sounds delicious!" in a falsely hearty voice and then add anxiously, "It doesn't have scallions in it, does it?" Or olives. Or basil. Or almonds. Or feta cheese.

Audra had obviously been given a list of Papa Stan's food allergies—probably it was in the same email that had announced Brodie would be visiting—so why didn't she just *tell* Graham everything that was on the list and get it over with? Instead she backed him into a culinary corner until he found himself asking what Papa Stan wanted and that was what they wound up having: canned soups and grilled cheese sandwiches and sloppy joes and hot dogs and macaroni and cheese. Honestly, was it any wonder Graham wanted to go over to Elspeth's for dinner?

Brodie was the only one who seemed to appreciate Graham's cooking. One night Graham made a rib roast (let them eat hot dogs on a night he was out), and the aroma was almost more than Brodie could bear. He stood in front of the oven, drooling and moaning desperately. As the rib roast cooked, both the drooling and the moaning escalated, until Brodie was nearly gargling.

"It's like living on Dagobah with Chewbacca," Graham said to Audra.

She frowned slightly. "Was Chewbacca ever actually *on* Dagobah?"

"No, he wasn't," Matthew called from the living room.

"What?" Papa Stan said, and Matthew and Noah began giggling like crazy.

This was Graham's life. His real life.

During the meals Graham ate at home, Brodie sat at Papa Stan's elbow, moaning with desire every time someone passed a dish. Finally, Audra, who could be surprisingly handy, installed a baby gate across the doorway to the dining room, so now at meals, Brodie no longer groaned and slavered at the dinner table. He groaned and slavered behind the gate.

"Sweetie!" Papa Stan called to him. "I know it's hard, but be patient! Let the nice people enjoy their dinner! I will give you a special treat later! You and I can watch *Masterpiece Theatre* together!"

(He didn't really say that last part.)

Matthew and Noah ate as fast as possible, so they could go back into Matthew's room and do whatever it was they did on the computer. (What *were* they doing in there? Graham wondered. Was anyone monitoring them?) Graham ate as fast as possible, too, so he wouldn't have to listen to Papa Stan.

If it had been up to Graham, they would have ignored Papa Stan—politely, of course—and talked to each other, but Audra seemed to feel the need to include Papa Stan, to draw him out, even.

"Now, Papa Stan," she would say warmly, "tell us about your day."

"Well," Papa Stan would say slowly. "First thing, Brodie and I checked the stock market and found that Pfizer had announced a tax inversion. Was it Pfizer? Or Walgreens? Pfizer, I think. Then we went for a walk and I stopped and got the newspaper, and then I went around the corner for a cup of coffee. Now, what is the name of that place?"

"Starbucks?" Audra said helpfully.

"No, no, the other one."

"Tea Leaf?"

"Well, now, maybe it was, maybe it was. It was on Broadway and was it Seventy-second, or Seventy-third . . ."

Graham wished they could put Papa Stan behind the gate, too.

". . . And then we came back and Brodie and I watched something on the History Channel. What was it, Brodie? Something about America's Doomsday plans, maybe. Or was it about sharecropping? Let me think . . ."

"And tell me, what is the Doomsday Plan?" Audra said. She sounded like a TV talk show host. Graham thought he might strangle her and Papa Stan both if he sat there a moment longer.

He pushed back his chair so abruptly the legs screeched against the floor. "I'll take Brodie out," he said. "He looks restless."

Brodie did look restless, but it was no doubt because he was eager for table scraps. It was Graham who was restless for escape.

Nevertheless, Graham would snap the leash on Brodie and drag him, nails clawing and scraping, out the door, into the elevator, and out on the street.

Walking Brodie was less like walking a dog and more like trying to fly a kite in a hurricane, or possibly windsurfing. Brodie lunged at people, dogs, lampposts, mailboxes. For Graham, it was all a matter of keeping himself firmly anchored and ready for Brodie's next leap. How did Papa Stan manage?

Graham didn't speak at all on these walks—there was no point since Brodie didn't know any commands. Graham was sure the silence rang in both their ears.

And not only did they have to talk *to* Papa Stan, they had to talk *about* him, too.

"So today," Audra said as they were getting ready for bed, "I told Papa Stan that I wished the dishwasher was either bigger or smaller because I keep running it three-quarters full. And I look up and he's staring at this spot over my shoulder and he looks like he might faint and I'm thinking, *Oh, no, this is what I've been afraid of! He's going to die right here in the kitchen!* And then I realize, no, he's bored."

She flexed her elbows in a brief chicken-wing formation while she undid her bra, and then pulled her nightgown over her head.

"*I bored Papa Stan,*" Audra said. "How awful is that? I feel I've hit an all-time conversational low. It's like—I don't know. Like I should go live in a cave or something. I'm apparently not fit for human society."

Graham didn't say anything. He was thinking that Audra wore satiny nightgowns and Elspeth had worn tank tops and pajama bottoms and you'd think it would be the other way around. He was thinking that maybe people weren't meant to get married twice; it only led to comparisons.

Graham had to spend the first half hour of his workday—just think, thirty minutes during which no medical research was accomplished, no capital raised, no venture undertaken—examining a tiny little raised freckle on Olivia's hand and reassuring her that it wasn't skin cancer.

"But what *is* it?" Olivia said worriedly. "It was never there before."

She rested the hand with the new freckle in the bright circle of light cast by the gooseneck lamp on Graham's desk. Her hand was like an actress's hand in a commercial for paper towels, slim and white and red-nailed.

"It's a skin tag," Graham said.

"Skin tag!" Olivia looked like she would be happier to hear it was cancer.

He turned the light off now, the afterimage blooming behind his eyelids like a bruise. Olivia pulled her hand away. "It's a harmless lesion—"

"Our *dog* has skin tags!" Olivia nearly wailed. "And she's like a million years old in dog years!"

"If it really bothers you," Graham said, "you can have a dermatologist remove it."

"Our dog has them *all over* her body," Olivia continued. "Is that going to happen to me? Is this thing"—she gestured at one hand with the other—"going to get brothers and sisters?"

"I don't think it will repopulate the area, no," Graham said drily.

Olivia examined her hand suspiciously. No doubt about it: there were too many women in his life.

Graham called Audra to tell her he wouldn't be home for dinner and caught her just as she was going out the door.

"What?" she said. "Well, okay. Right now I have to take Papa Stan to a playdate and Brodie to the tutor and Noah to get his shots. Matthew's staying with Julio."

"Wait," Graham said. "You mean you're taking *Noah* to a playdate and *Brodie* to get his shots and *Matthew* to the tutor?"

"No, I meant exactly what I said." Audra sounded harassed, but she never hurried a conversation. "Papa Stan met an old man in the park and the man's daughter called me and we set up a time for them to get together for a couple of hours. They want to watch some History Channel special about Vikings. Isn't that a playdate? I don't know what else to call it."

"Well, I guess—" Graham started.

"And it turns out Noah is allergic to Brodie and has to have these superstrength allergy shots every week while he's here," Audra said, "and I found this dog trainer for Brodie who specializes in difficult cases so today I'm taking him over for his assessment."

"Assessment?" Graham asked.

"The trainer calls herself the Alpha Dog," Audra continued as though he hadn't spoken, "and everyone else has to call her that, too. Can you imagine how I felt calling up and asking for her? This woman answered and I said, 'Could I speak to the Alpha Dog, please?' and I thought the woman would say something like 'You lousy kids and your prank calls!' but she just said, 'Speaking.' So we had this normal conversation about setting up the assessment, but the whole time I couldn't shake the feeling that I was talking to a standard poodle. But apparently she's excellent. Mrs. Swanson recommended her after Brodie bit her hand in the elevator."

"Brodie bit someone?" Graham asked. It seemed to him that biting was the one piece of bad behavior Brodie didn't indulge in.

"Papa Stan said it wasn't *biting*," Audra said. "He said it was *mouthing*, which is apparently some instinctual way that dogs communicate with each other, only Brodie does it to people, too. He did it to Mrs. Swanson in the elevator and Mrs. Swanson felt that what Brodie was trying to communicate was that he wanted to bite her hand off. But she said the Alpha Dog would fix him right up and it seemed like the least I could do was agree to take him."

Graham wondered if the Alpha Dog would agree to work with Papa Stan, too. Perhaps they could book a double appointment.

"So Matthew's going to stay with Julio because I didn't know what else to do with him," Audra finished. "Why were you calling?"

"Just to tell you I'd be out for dinner," Graham said.

Surely it was possible to love your family from a distance. People must do it all the time.

It seemed that now that they knew the worst about each other, Graham and Elspeth could relax for the first time in twenty-three years. Sometimes silence rolled out between them like a cottony soft cloud Graham could float on. And when they did talk, not every subject had to be pursued until Graham nearly collapsed under the strain of it. (Conversations with Audra often felt to Graham like asymptote curves on a graph, where the distance between the curve and the line approaches zero but never actually gets there; that's how endless they were.) But Graham and Elspeth were just two people making a delicious meal that no one complained about. Heaven.

Sometimes Elspeth would reach around him in the kitchen and her blouse would whisper sweetly against the silk of her camisole, and it would seem to Graham that he had retained the muscle memory in his fingertips of all those wonderful, maddening layers that Elspeth wore—blouse, skirt, slip, camisole, bra, stockings. It was like unwrapping an Eskimo who wore only silk. And underneath all those cool slippery layers, the warmth of her skin. He remembered, too, that Elspeth's breath had always tasted sweet and faintly spicy, like cinnamon or cardamom. The first time Graham had ever had a chai latte in Starbucks, he'd had a flashback to kissing Elspeth that was so powerful he'd nearly dropped the cup. And still they never touched.

And then after dinner, there would be the long pleasantly drunk hours on the couch, talking or not talking, no forced chatter, no hearing about people he had no interest in, no breathless revelation about how the cashier at the supermarket had broken her eyetooth on a stale bagel. Instead they discussed their days and current events and sometimes Graham told Elspeth stories about Papa Stan and Brodie that made them seem—just for a moment, in the subdued, tasteful light of her apartment—amusing. And Elspeth smiled but she didn't laugh until she spit wine everywhere. It was all wildly civilized.

All this and afterward Elspeth did the dishes! *Now* you're talking, as Audra would say.

The garlic from their meal had given Elspeth's face a pink, girlish glow. Graham had forgotten that, how garlic made very fair women flush like they'd just had the best sex of their lives. (If you only ever got that look from a woman after shrimp aioli, you were doing something wrong, was Graham's view.)

But maybe it was more than just the garlic because Elspeth took a long sip from her wineglass and then said, "There's an ABA Leadership Conference on Thursday and I get a room at the conference center even though I live here. I thought I would stay there—you know I like hotel rooms."

That was true—she did. Something about all those clear surfaces and empty drawers. Elspeth loved them the way other women love hot fudge sundaes.

"I was thinking," she said slowly, "that you could meet me there, maybe stay the night."

She looked at Graham and her eyes were like two cups of Easter egg dye—that blue, that clear.

"You don't have to tell me now," Elspeth said. "Just think about it."

So there it was. Graham had known it was coming, and yet its arrival startled him and made his heart race—like the first shotgun-rattle of rain against your window from a storm you've been following on the Weather Channel.

Graham was waiting for a sign. If he told Audra he was going to be out late and she objected, that would be a sign that he shouldn't go.

But Audra didn't object. He stood in the bathroom doorway

while she put on her makeup and told her that he had a very late business dinner on Thursday in Hoboken.

Audra rooted around in the drawer that held her jumble of cosmetics and said, "That's Papa Stan's last night," which momentarily startled Graham into silence. For so long he had viewed Papa Stan's departure as a wondrous event that was promised but never materialized, something like the seventh astral plane. But he should have remembered because he had made arrangements for Papa Stan and Noah and Brodie to go out and stay at the airport Marriott on Thursday, since their flight left so early on Friday morning. Graham had paid for the hotel and he was happy to do it. He felt like he would pay $150 a night for the rest of his life, just for the pleasure of not having Papa Stan and Brodie in the apartment.

"Anyway," Audra went on, "it's fine if you want to go out, because he asked if we can have tuna casserole for dinner."

Graham could tell by the slight smoothing out of her forehead when she spoke that she was relieved not to have to sell him on the idea of the tuna casserole (which would have been an impossible sale, by the way).

"I might be really late," Graham said. Here was another chance for Audra to object.

"Okay," she said. She was putting on mascara and looking down her own nose at her reflection.

"If it runs past midnight, I might get a hotel room," Graham said. "You know how impossible it is to get back from New Jersey."

Stroke, stroke went the wand of Audra's mascara. "All right," she said. "Whatever's easiest on you."

"I'll be sure to say goodbye to Papa Stan and Noah on Thursday morning before I leave for work."

"Okay," Audra said.

Good God, woman, give a sign! Make an objection! Show some possessiveness! But she just dropped the tube of mascara in the drawer and shut the drawer with a bump of her hip.

So Graham was free to meet Elspeth, it seemed. And it was odd because at this point in his life, Graham could not imagine going to meet a stranger in a hotel room—that had once seemed exciting but now the idea just seemed stressful. He did not have the energy to worry about what some new woman would think of him or what expectations she might have or what judgment she might pass on his body—the body that had served Graham so well and faithfully for all these years. It seemed less like his body and more like a devoted servant. He could not bear the idea of someone insulting it.

But meeting Elspeth—that was different. He knew exactly how she would behave. He had been in countless hotel rooms with her. He knew her body well—it, too, was like an old friend. (Perhaps it would be like doubles tennis or a bridge foursome, Graham and Elspeth and their bodies getting together for an evening.) And Graham knew Elspeth—he knew the scent of her perfume, and the sound of her footsteps, and the curve of her face. He could predict exactly her pleased smile when she opened the hotel room door and saw him standing there. And wasn't that the weird thing—sorry, one of the *million* weird things—about marriage? That the familiarity that drove you so crazy at times— Audra had a particular three-tiered yawn that Graham thought might cause him to throw himself out the window if he heard it again—was the very thing you longed for in the end.

When Graham got to the hotel lobby, he realized that he didn't know Elspeth's room number. He sat down in an armchair so deep it nearly swallowed him and took out his phone to call her.

Just then Elspeth arrived. She walked through the revolving door wearing a tightly belted trench coat and carrying a single leather satchel. Graham had always admired the way she traveled—such economy and simplicity. Not like Audra, who invariably wound up putting a whole bunch of last-minute items in a paper shopping bag, which then broke in the middle of the airport and stuff scattered everywhere. (Seriously, that happened every single trip they took.)

Graham watched as Elspeth went to check in. His chair was to the side of the reception desk, and she could have seen him if she'd glanced even slightly to her right, but she didn't. The chair was too shadowed and the lobby too softly lit for her to notice him, which, Graham supposed, was probably the point.

The reception clerk was a young man with full cheeks and a high, scratchy voice. Graham could hear him clearly when he asked for Elspeth's name.

"Elspeth Osbourne," she said, "I'm here for the conference."

The clerk rattled the keyboard of his computer. "The ABA conference or the NASA conference?"

"The ABA."

The clerk smiled. "Do you know how NASA organizes their conference?"

"What?" A tiny line appeared between Elspeth's eyebrows.

"Do you know how NASA organizes their conference?" the clerk repeated. "They planet!" He laughed.

Elspeth was so close to Graham and her face so perfectly illuminated by the reception desk spotlight that Graham could see her expression clearly. The skin around her mouth tightened and her eyes hooded slightly. Her lips made a perfect little circle, just enough to let out an annoyed breath that was one shade too deliberate to be called a sigh. But even if he hadn't seen her so well, Graham would have known exactly how she looked. He had seen that expression a million times—a *hundred* million times—when a person made a joke that Elspeth thought was unfunny or inappropriate. Most of the time, that person had been Graham.

Silently, she held out her hand for the key.

The clerk shrugged good-naturedly and handed Elspeth a little envelope. "You're in room 917," he said. "The restaurant is open until eleven."

She picked up her leather satchel and started toward the elevator bank. Now was the time for Graham to stand up and intercept her, to take her hand and tuck it in his arm.

But Graham sat in his chair.

Elspeth had never found him funny—she had only found him tiresome. How could he have forgotten that?

The desk clerk was already greeting the next customer, his scratchy voice cheerful and confident. Well, he didn't have to go up and face Elspeth. But then, neither did Graham.

His cellphone was still in his hand. He hesitated for a moment and then typed out a text: *I'm sorry. G.* He didn't add any sort of explanation, not because there wasn't one, but because she wouldn't want to read it, she wouldn't *care* to read it. And if you didn't believe that, you didn't know Elspeth as well as Graham did.

Graham left the hotel and walked all the way home, sixty-two blocks, his heart as heavy as his shoes.

Was he doomed to be never faithful, but never unfaithful? But that was ridiculous. He had been faithful, for years and years, and he had been unfaithful, too, also for years. So why now did it seem like he was caught in some horrible limbo where he was destined to disappoint everyone? Perhaps that was why some men got married five or six times. Everyone hates uncertainty.

He headed down the block toward his apartment building and realized that even though he would be home hours earlier than he had said—he would tell Audra the dinner was awful, a waste of time—it was still after eight, the time that Papa Stan and Noah and Brodie left. There was no loss without some small gain.

He realized suddenly that his feet were sore and his ears were cold and his stomach was empty and he wanted a drink so badly that his throat clicked drily when he swallowed. Food, shelter, alcohol, love—he wanted it all and he wanted it now. And yet he paused in front of the door to the lobby, his breath making white plumes in the air. He was suddenly afraid that no one would be home or, worse, that no one would recognize him, that his key wouldn't open the lock, that strangers lived there now and they wouldn't let him in.

This is what life had taught Graham about houseguests: they drained your batteries. The very best of them left you a little juice, just enough to miss them once they'd gone. He suspected that everyone felt that way about houseguests. Except Audra. Then why had he married her? Sometimes that was an impossible question to answer.

Graham let himself into the apartment and did a quick emotional survey. Did he miss the click and scrabble of Brodie's claws on the floor? Did he miss Papa Stan's wheezy greeting? No, on both counts. If he had hooked himself up to an emotional battery tester, the needle wouldn't have moved at all.

Still, the apartment was too quiet. Graham checked the bedroom and then went to Matthew's room. Matthew was sitting at his computer, a peanut butter sandwich on a plate at his elbow.

"Where's Mom?" Graham asked.

Matthew took a bite of his sandwich. "Up on the roof."

Graham hesitated. "Are you okay?" he asked. "Do you miss Noah?"

Matthew glanced up at him and nodded. "It was so much *fun* to have him here."

Fun. Wasn't that really the beauty of childhood? That you measured experiences by how much fun they were, not by how much work or inconvenience or tedious conversation they caused you? Of course you didn't think of the tiresome things if you were a kid, because you didn't have to do them. And that was just as it should be, in Graham's opinion.

But still he could not bring himself to be sorry Papa Stan and Brodie and Noah were gone. Apparently there were limits to what you would do for your child. Graham had never realized that before. He leaned down and kissed the top of Matthew's head.

Graham went into the kitchen and poured himself a glass of wine, but suddenly he could not stand to be in the apartment. He left his wineglass on the counter, grabbed his coat, and went up to the roof deck.

Audra was there, standing coatless at the railing, slender and pretty in a powder-blue sweater and jeans. She looked over at him and smiled. It had started to snow, just a few thick shaggy flakes that looked more like ash than like snow. Graham was reminded of a nuclear winter, a long volcanic season, sunlight blocked for years.

Audra never altered, Graham thought. Infidelity, illness,

houseguests, natural disaster, the end of the world—it would all wash over her and she'd still be there, looking fresh as a flower and wondering if there were any blueberry muffins left. It was the very best and the very worst thing about her.

Suddenly, Graham yearned for her. She would rescue him from this terrible feeling of not belonging, of being adrift. She always had. She was an absolute certainty in a horribly uncertain world. Other people could try to make sense of the world by doing crossword puzzles and installing dead bolts and eating peas one at a time. Graham only needed Audra.

He had paused in the doorway, and she started toward him, snowflakes catching in her hair and glinting on the shoulders of her sweater. She would reach him, Graham thought, and he would hold on to her. As long as he held on to Audra, let the world try to do its worst. Just let it.

Seven

The problem with so much makeup sex, Graham thought, was that sometimes it led to a makeup baby. At least that's what Audra said. She said she was almost certain. She said she'd walked past a hot dog vendor and the smell made her want to throw up and that meant definitely. But then again she said maybe *not*, because the other two times she'd been pregnant, she'd had a sexy dream about Anthony Hopkins very early on and she hadn't had the dream yet. (Graham trusted this person to manage birth control; sometimes he shocked even himself.)

He was standing at the kitchen counter, pouring himself a glass of wine and struggling to comprehend what she'd said— trying to gather up her sentences like someone trying to gather up the loops of a garden hose—when she called out, "Matthew! Be sure to pack long underwear!"

How could she think of something as mundane as long under- wear when they may actually be expecting another child? Was her mind that compartmentalized? What about the compartment that monitored the birth control? Perhaps she had been thinking about long underwear or frozen burritos when she should have been concentrating on putting her diaphragm in correctly.

It was the last day before spring break and Matthew was leav- ing for sleepaway camp—a unique sleepaway camp where all the kids had special needs, all the kids were like Matthew. And appar-

ently, at this camp, Matthew would learn to love hiking and swimming and canoeing (which were all things he did not care for),
and learn not to mind mosquitoes and wasps and mud between
his toes and freezing cold water and being away from his family
(which were all things he minded a lot). This was what everyone
said. Other kids from Matthew's school were going, and Matthew
had wanted to go, too. So why was Graham so scared, so certain
that Matthew would be the camp's first failure?

And then the phone rang and it was Mr. Sears, the principal of
Matthew's school. Mr. Sears was calling, he said, to tell them that
Matthew and another boy had used a school computer to access
porn.

The evening was off to a very poor start, in Graham's opinion.

The other boy almost certainly was Derek Rottweiler," Audra
said.

It almost certainly was. Matthew's new best friend was a sly,
feral child named Derek Rothmuller but whom everyone, including Matthew, called Derek Rottweiler. He was a sweet-looking
child with a heart-shaped face and curly black hair, but his eyes
were like lasers, constantly scanning for trouble. He was the
worst-behaved student in the school, a constant discipline problem, and his own parents had advised Audra to put her purse in
a dresser drawer when Derek came over. And yet, Graham and
Audra welcomed him into their home and tried to feel fond of
him. Maybe other parents had the luxury of turning away their
children's friends, of telling their children to look for more suit-
able peers, but Graham and Audra did not. They took what they
could get.

"What did Mr. Sears say, exactly?" Audra asked.

"Just that Matthew and another boy had used the computer in

the school computer lab and later the computer-science teacher checked the history and found they'd been looking at porn."

"Matthew, though?" Audra said. "Our Matthew?"

It was easy to believe that Derek Rottweiler would look at porn on a school computer, or on any computer at all. But not Matthew, their good boy, their sweet handsome well-behaved son. Why, last year, when the teacher had implemented a system where each day every student was assigned a color based on behavior—green, blue, yellow, orange, or red (just like the original Homeland Security System)—Matthew had never moved off green, not one single time. (Derek Rottweiler, it almost went without saying, shot straight to red on the first day of school and stayed there, the sixth-grade discipline equivalent of Khalid Sheikh Mohammed.) Matthew was the opposite of disruptive. Matthew had beautiful manners and the gentlest nature—everyone said so.

But when they called Matthew out to the living room for a family meeting, he looked alarmed (which was normal—he hated change of any kind and always feared that family meetings were called to announce a move or a new school), but he also looked guilty.

"What is this meeting about?" he asked.

"Well," Graham said, and then found he didn't know quite how to continue. "It's about watching porn."

"What's porn?" Matthew asked. For a moment Graham thought Matthew was being sarcastic, but he should have known better. Matthew was never sarcastic. He actually didn't know.

"Pictures or movies of people having sex," Audra said.

And then it was clear that Matthew *did* know; he just hadn't known the term. Remorse and shame swamped his small face.

"I don't do that," he said. "And I *especially* didn't do it today in my room between four-thirty and five."

Graham felt his heart twist. Matthew was so guileless, so defenseless against the world.

"Well," he said slowly, "be that as it may, Mr. Sears called and said that you and another boy had been using the school computer to look at porn, which is against the rules."

"There's nothing wrong with porn," Audra said. (Immediately Graham imagined Matthew repeating that to the school guidance counselor.) "It can actually be very, sort of, nice, and enjoyable sometimes. Relaxing, even. It's just that we want you to wait until you're a little older."

"How *much* older?" Matthew asked.

"Twenty," Audra said. "No—thirty."

Graham had the feeling this conversation was so far off track that they couldn't see the rails anymore. "At any rate," he said deliberately, "the point is that you and Derek broke a school rule and there will undoubtedly be consequences. Mr. Sears is trying to decide now what your punishment will be."

Graham wondered why Mr. Sears hadn't just told them what the punishment would be. Didn't the school have a policy in effect? Were they supposed to stress about that all through spring break? What if Matthew got expelled?

Matthew went back to his room and Audra slid down on the couch until her head was resting against the back of it. "I feel like this is some sort of cosmic payback," she said. "Just last week, Derek Rottweiler was over for a playdate and they were in Matthew's room and I sat in the kitchen and felt all superior. I thought they were watching Robert Lang's TED Talk on origami! I sat there and thought, *Well, other mothers may have to worry about sex and drugs and alcohol, but not me. My son is in there improving his mind.* I actually thought that, Graham! Those very words!"

"Well," Graham said, "he has watched that TED Talk—"

"I haven't felt so—so *ridiculous* since that time I worked the PTA bake sale with Penny Fitzgerald and I said, 'Uh-oh, some creepy man with an awful mustache is watching us from that car over there,' and she said, 'That's my husband.'"

Audra slid even lower on the couch. Soon she'd be sitting on the floor. "And now after all this I can't even have a beer because it might be bad for the baby," she said.

Baby! Twenty minutes ago she had said she wasn't even sure she was pregnant and now it was a baby! Did she not understand what that word did to Graham—how it wrenched him?

Matthew left for camp the next morning. He stood in the hallway by the door with Graham's huge old backpack on his shoulders. Was there any sight more heartbreaking than a small boy with a big backpack? Well, yes, of course, there was. Think of the photos of victims of the Nepal earthquake, of the starving children in South Sudan. But those weren't the same. Those photos made you sad for a little while, but they didn't make you want to run out on the balcony and drop to your knees, promising God anything if only He will protect your child from bullying and motion sickness.

Audra was standing next to Matthew, wearing sweatpants and a T-shirt, jingling her car keys and sipping her coffee, just like this was a normal morning. Graham hugged Matthew goodbye, and then Audra and Matthew were both out the door, gone from his protection, out in the big bad world. Graham could not shake the feeling that the next time he saw Matthew, Matthew would be in tears.

Depressed, Graham got a cup of coffee for himself and went into his study to work. An hour later, Audra leaned around the doorjamb. "Matthew went off on the bus so happily!" she said. "He was sitting by Derek Rottweiler. Now I'm going to call Dr. Medowski and see if I can have a pregnancy test this early."

She liked to do that—announce she was going to do something, then do it, then come back and tell him about it. It was as though their lives were being televised, with a lot of buildup and recap, like the Academy Awards or election results.

"Okay," Graham said.

He heard her walking around the living room and the small beeps as she dialed her phone. "Oh, hello," he heard her say. "This is Audra Daltry. Can I speak to Dr. Medowski?"

She must have been pacing because her voice grew fainter and then indecipherable as she moved away from him and then louder as she moved back and crossed the doorway of his study again.

"I know I should have gotten up and taken out my diaphragm and used more contraceptive gel," she was saying. "But Graham was so eager, and I didn't want to break the mood. Also, I sort of thought, my eggs are so old and his sperm is probably pretty slow by now—it just seemed so unlikely!"

Graham's face was suddenly scorching, as though he had thrust his head through the trapdoor of a smokehouse. He could not have been more embarrassed if he'd appeared naked in front of the Origami Club.

Relax, he told himself. Audra was speaking to her gynecologist. It was probably nothing the man hadn't heard before.

"So I knew at the moment that it was fairly unwise," Audra said. "But I thought everything would probably be just fine."

That was pretty much her theory of life, Graham thought—this belief that everything would be just fine. He wondered how often that actually turned out to be true for her. He would guess at most—at *most*—half the time.

Audra paced out of his hearing again, and he tried perfuncto-
rily to compose an email. But he was listening for her footsteps,
and sure enough, she came back along the hall and into his study.

"You won't believe this," she said, collapsing into a leather
armchair, "but they're out of the office! Until Thursday! Because
of Easter! I wanted to say, 'You think people don't have pregnancy
scares on major holidays? You think you can just close up shop
and leave all your patients sweating and anxious?'"

Graham frowned. "So you didn't speak to Dr. Medowski?"

"No, I just told you," she said impatiently. "The office was
closed."

"So who *were* you talking to?"

"Some woman at the answering service," Audra said.

The answering service! Graham's face felt hot again.

"She said Dr. Medowski is playing golf in Florida, which I can't
help feeling is sort of frivolous, but I guess he couldn't know I was
suddenly going to need him," Audra said, and she sighed.

Graham studied her. If she really was pregnant, it agreed with
her. She looked pretty—pink-cheeked and bright-eyed, her wavy
auburn hair like a hint of autumn color. He remembered suddenly how she'd looked in the months after Matthew was born.
Her face had been thin, with too-prominent cheekbones, and
her hair had grown dry and brittle, as though motherhood were
draining her of all vitality.

"Lorelei says that the doctor would probably tell me to wait
anyway," Audra said.

"Lorelei knows, too?" Graham asked.

"Yes, I stopped by her apartment on my way back from taking
Matthew to the bus," Audra said. "We talked about how terrible
it is that you spend so much of your life hoping you're not pregnant. Like this time in college when Lorelei had a one-night stand

with the guy who lived in the apartment below us. He was handsome but he had this very distinct unibrow. Lorelei and I used to call him Bert because of that. So, anyway, after the one-night stand, Lorelei said she had these very vivid dreams about being in a delivery room and the doctor holding up a baby with Bert brows. And even after she knew she wasn't pregnant, she would have, not nightmares, I guess—more like bad daydreams—where she took little Bert home to her family and they were all like 'But his eyebrows! Where did they come from?' "

Graham closed his eyes and leaned his head back against the chair. He thought that, really, Journey was right: it just goes on and on and on and on.

Graham had been developing a theory lately that the parents of kids with Asperger's also had Asperger's, only less pronounced. A milder Asperger's. The *seeds* of Asperger's. And he'd certainly met enough parents of special-needs kids to know.

Of all the dozens of special-needs kids' parents he knew, one parent of every couple always seemed a bit odd, a bit eccentric, a bit *Aspergery*. One parent would be unable to pick up on social signals—say, for instance, not understanding that Graham's putting on his pajamas and brushing his teeth was a signal the evening was drawing to a close and they should go home. The father of a friend of Matthew's named Lucas used to actually follow Graham and Audra out to their car and keep talking while they drove away. Graham had always been worried about running over the man's foot. Another man had seemed unable to process that he and Graham drove the same make and model of car but that Graham's was a different color. "It's not blue?" the man had said more than once. "I want it to be blue, like mine."

One woman, the mother of a small boy named Jack, used to

respond to anything other than a direct question by saying, "Well, that's news to me." You could say "I'm going to pick up Matthew at six" or "Jack ate some cupcakes"—it didn't matter. She would say, "Well, that's news to me." The first time she did it, Graham thought maybe Jack wasn't supposed to eat cupcakes, or maybe Jack didn't like cupcakes as a rule, but it quickly became clear that this was her all-purpose response to any remark. Graham wondered why she'd settled on that particular statement, because it didn't seem like it would apply to all that many situations. Perhaps it had started as some sort of sports-related thing with her husband: "The Giants are on tonight." "Well, that's news to me." "The Mets won!" "Well, that's news to me."

And food! Dear God. Graham had never met such finicky adults. The kids, sure, he expected that—nothing spicy or exotic or oddly textured went over well with children. But the parents were just as bad, and full of exacting standards—steak was *supposed* to be medium-rare, pasta was *supposed* to be spaghetti, chicken was *supposed* to be white meat, ice cream was *supposed* to be vanilla. "Soup is *supposed* to be hot," one man had said accusingly when Graham served gazpacho. (That was back in the early days, before he truly appreciated the magnitude of the problem— back when he still experimented and hoped for the best.)

One woman had said, "This salad has so many vegetables!" in a soft, startled voice, and Graham had thought at the time that she meant it had too many greens and not enough delicious, high-calorie things like bacon and candied walnuts. But looking back on it now, he thought it was more likely she meant it had too many *ingredients*. She probably wanted just two: iceberg lettuce and beefsteak tomatoes.

They didn't like too many ingredients, these parents of Matthew's friends, or even too many dishes to choose from. And often, he'd noticed, they ate their meals in a certain order—all the meat, then all the starch, then all the vegetables. Every single one of them left the vegetables for last, like overgrown children. They didn't like the different foods to mingle on their plates, and they didn't seem to like meat to be carved at the table, or sauce, or gravy, and there was a near-universal distrust of salad dressing.

Once they had the parents of Matthew's friend Carolyn over and Carolyn's mother had come up to Graham in the kitchen afterward as he was stacking plates in the sink and thanked him for making lasagna. "It was such a treat!" she'd said in a low voice. "Colin doesn't like me to make anything but meat and potatoes."

Graham was startled. "What, all the time? No exceptions?"

"Not really," she said. "I mean, on Fridays we have hamburgers and French fries, but the other nights, it has to be meat and potatoes."

How did she manage that? *Were* there six different combinations of meat and potatoes? He began thinking aloud. "Steak and baked potatoes, pork chops and mashed potatoes . . ."

The woman beamed. "Exactly! And one night I make ham with potatoes au gratin."

"Pot roast," Graham said thoughtfully.

"With roasted potatoes," she finished helpfully.

"Does he eat chicken?"

"Oh, yes, of course," she said. "Roast chicken." She put enough emphasis on the word *roast* to make Graham sure that it was roast chicken only, nothing fried or breaded or sautéed. "With hash browns."

"And what about the seventh night?" Graham asked.

"Cottage pie."

Well, wasn't she the sneaky one with that cottage pie! He hadn't thought of that.

"And that's it?" he said. "No pasta or rice or pizza?"

"Oh, no," she said. "Colin is very old-fashioned."

Old-fashioned? Unacceptably rigid was more like it, Graham thought. Difficult. Impossible. Life without pasta or pizza? Who could live like that? Had she known it when she married him? Were there compensations? (He could hear Colin and Audra talking in the dining room and Colin was saying something about how the law of unintended consequences was affecting gas prices, so if there were compensations, they weren't readily apparent.)

Now—especially now, when Audra might be pregnant—Graham began to wonder with more and more frequency where he and Audra fit on this sliding scale of parental Asperger's. He didn't have a problem with food, and Audra would eat anything—literally anything, it seemed. Twinkies, Spam, pork rolls, beef jerky, Lucky Charms, Hot Pockets, tapioca. He wondered sometimes if her genes had been spliced with a goat's. And as far as he could tell, they had good social skills. Why, Audra was the most social person he had ever known.

But still. But still. There were other family members' genes to consider. Graham's uncle, for instance, who was so scandalized by the price of food that his wife used to stop by the side of the road on her way home from the supermarket and scrape the price tags off all the groceries to prevent him from going berserk. That same uncle had very rigorous criteria when it came to how the carpet should be vacuumed. "In an expanding wave pattern!" he used to say. "Like a seashell! Is that too much to ask?" (Well, yes, it is.) And Audra had a cousin who could not understand or recognize even the most common idioms. You could say, "It's raining cats and dogs," and he'd look out the window with a slightly fearful expression. And Graham's own cousin with the miniature-train collection that no one else was allowed to touch. And Audra's uncle with the fear of acorns. The great-grandmother with the alphabetized linen closet. The aunt—

It really did not bear thinking about, all the strange relatives, all those peculiar genes floating around in their gene pool. But Graham could not seem to stop.

I feel so bad for the baby," Audra said to Graham. "It's going to have such old parents."

"Bad for the baby?" Graham said. "What about *me*? I'll be seventy-five by the time the baby graduates high school."

Another baby? Impossible. Really impossible.

"If I am pregnant," Audra continued, "the first thing we're going to do is invest in a Bugaboo stroller. Remember that awful stroller we had when Matthew was a baby? The one that was, like, two inches too wide to fit through any doorway? And I would have to lift him out and hold him and then try to get the stroller to snap shut with one hand? Because it was supposed to just col-lapse if you pressed this one button, but I could never do it. I tell you, that is my worst memory of Matthew's babyhood, standing there in doorways, shaking this stupid stroller while people tried to get past me."

That was her worst memory of Matthew's babyhood? What about the sleep deprivation? Graham could remember realizing that if they had ten minutes, he and Audra ate something; if they had twenty minutes, they slept. He remembered seeing Audra walk down the hall toward the baby's room in the very early morning, trailing her hand along the wall. At first he thought it was to help her find her way in the dark—then he realized that it was already light. She was touching the wall to help her stay upright.

From his earliest days, Matthew awoke with the birds. Or the neighbors. Or the traffic. Or the whine of the elevator. Nothing, it seemed, could induce him to sleep beyond 5:00 a.m. Not blackout curtains, not a white-noise machine, not even the special sound-absorbing cork they used to line the walls of his nursery. The early rising lasted through infancy, through babyhood, through the toddler years. Graham would look at the clock every morning as soon as he heard Matthew's cries and do a sort of internal calibration—4:45 or later meant a good day, a survivable one. By the time Matthew was three years old, Graham and Audra were so desperate for sleep that they would bring Matthew into their bed and try to snuggle him down between them, to lull him with their body heat and slow breathing. Occasionally this would work and Matthew would drift back to sleep and then inevitably assume the dreaded starfish position in the middle of the bed, a little hand flung into each of their faces, a little foot poking into each of their hips.

But more often Matthew was just awake for the day and would squirm and wiggle and toss around until Graham felt like he was trying to sleep next to a bag of something that clattered, like a bag of aluminum cans. On those days, Graham would force himself out of bed and entice Matthew to the kitchen for breakfast while he drank coffee with an extra shot of espresso in it. And then they would leave the apartment together in the early morning and Graham would push Matthew in the stroller to the playground on Ninety-sixth Street, usually stopping at Starbucks for another coffee. (The thought of Matthew's babyhood made Graham's mouth feel sour with the heavy saliva left over from so much coffee drinking, made his head feel light with remembered caffeine.)

Sometimes they skipped the playground and pushed on to the pond by the boathouse, where they could rest and have animal crackers or Cheerios or vanilla wafers—that was another thing about Matthew's early childhood: crumbs everywhere, always, as inescapable as sand in the desert—before Graham would begin the long walk home. They had the park to themselves at that time in the morning—almost too much to themselves; Graham worried about muggers sometimes—but one day as they sat by the pond, another father came along. He was older than Graham and his son was older, too, a boy in his mid-twenties with Down syndrome. They sat on a bench near Graham and Matthew, and Graham felt moved by a spirit of shared suffering to offer small talk.

"Nothing like an early morning, is there?" he said to the man.

The man grunted. "We're here a lot," he said. He looked at his watch. "Come on, Timmy."

Graham was startled. It has been his experience that adults on outings with children liked conversation with other adults— loved it, *craved* it, would rustle up a conversation based on the most artificial and flimsy connection. *Where'd you get that T-shirt? You don't have a Band-Aid in your bag, do you? Do you have four quarters for a dollar?*

The man and Timmy moved off, having stayed only a moment. Graham realized that Timmy was even older than he'd first assumed, maybe in his thirties. How many years, how many decades, had Timmy's father been bringing him here, on made-up outings, in the early morning? No wonder he was cranky and antisocial. He must be exhausted. And for him, there was no end in sight. At least for Graham, the end was in sight. Matthew would mature, perhaps more slowly than other children, and certainly more slowly than he and Audra might desire, but he'd get there. He would not always awaken before first light, and even if he did, he would eventually be able to make his own breakfast and get dressed and entertain himself. In fact, at age eleven, Matthew could already do those things. (Pretty much. If he didn't touch the stove.)

It would be unbelievably—cruelly—frustrating to start all over again. It would be like finding your own footprints while lost in the jungle and realizing you had been walking in circles.

Julio came over for dinner the next night, and while Graham was pouring him a beer, Audra came rustling out of the bedroom and said, "Julio! How are you? Did Graham tell you I might be pregnant?"

One of the very best things about Julio was that he was nearly impossible to embarrass. Graham supposed that came from being a doorman.

"Well, now, no, he didn't," Julio said, leaning forward to accept Audra's hug. "Congratulations!"

"It's not for certain," Audra said. "Especially since I haven't had my Anthony Hopkins dream, but—" She paused suddenly. "Where is Sarita? Why didn't you bring her?"

Julio sighed. "We broke up."

"Oh, I'm so sorry to hear that," Audra said, putting a hand on Julio's arm. "Was it because she refused to go to your sister's wedding?"

"What?" Julio looked very startled. "My sister's wedding? No."

"Then why *did* you break up?" Audra asked.

"She said we wanted different things and that she—" Julio stopped. "Can we just go back to what you said before? About my sister's wedding? Because Sarita said she had conjunctivitis that weekend. She said her eyes were redder than stop signs! And now you're saying she just plain didn't want to go?"

"Well, she mentioned some detail about your mother not liking that Sarita took such long baths," Audra said. "And Sarita said *she* didn't like people standing outside the bathroom door and saying in loud voices, 'I sure hope Julio makes a good salary to pay the hot water bill. Must be nice to lie in the tub while other folks set the table and chop the vegetables!' Sarita said baths are her way of relaxing and she didn't deserve to be criticized. Sarita said not every woman relaxes by drinking an entire pitcher of sangria at four o'clock in the afternoon the way your mother does."

Julio was looking positively alarmed.

"But I could be wrong," Audra added hastily. "Maybe I'm thinking of someone else."

Hear those hoofbeats? Graham thought. *Those are the horses running away after you forgot to lock the barn door.*

Graham was making dinner: pork tenderloin with herbed wild rice. No need to cater to the crazy whims of picky eaters tonight. Julio was a pleasure to cook for. He not only ate whatever you put in front of him but said it was the most delicious meal he'd had in a long time. This might even be true, because the doormen in their building seemed to eat take-out Chinese food all the time. If he'd lived in pioneer times, Graham sometimes thought, Julio would be the bachelor homesteader who came over for dinner in exchange for helping with the spring lambs.

Since there were no lambs needing to be born, Julio repaid them with gossip about the people in the building. Mrs. Mullen in 10E had her brother-in-law visiting and she wanted Julio to find out how long the brother-in-law was staying. "She told me, 'Just ask him all natural-like. You know, inquire as to how long we'll have the pleasure of his company, and then tell me what he says.'" Mr. Coltrane in 3D had sublet his apartment (something strictly prohibited by the building) and the subletter had left the windows open during a rainstorm and now there were mushrooms growing in the carpeting. Mrs. Begay in 9C had received a package labeled "Live Reptile." Mrs. Salerno in 4A had gone on a monthlong bird-watching trip to the Pacific Northwest and her husband was having his girlfriend visit every night, telling the doormen it was his assistant bringing him important papers from the office.

"How do you know it's even his girlfriend?" Audra asked. "Maybe it's a hooker."

"Oh, no—they've been going out for a while now," Julio said. "Mr. Salerno also forgot a lot of important papers at work last fall while his wife was off looking at warblers in New Brunswick."

After dinner, Audra said the baby was making her sleepy and if they didn't mind, she would just go to bed.

Graham and Julio went up to the roof terrace with a bottle of port—it was warm for April. They pulled two chairs together, and Julio lit a cigarette while Graham poured the port into tumblers from the kitchen.

"How do you feel about the baby?" Julio asked once they were settled.

Exhausted, Graham could have said. *Disheartened. Nearly hopeless at times.*

"Nervous," he said. "But it's not for sure."

"Kids are nice," Julio said. He might have been talking about place mats, or tomatoes, or those sprinkles you put on ice cream.

Children were many things—heartbreaking and wonderful and worrisome—but Graham had never thought they were *nice*, exactly.

"Yes," he said. "They are."

He wished suddenly that he had more vices. Perhaps he should begin gambling or start abusing drugs. Even smoking, like Julio. Right now, Graham wanted desperately to be someone like Julio, who smoked cigarettes in the dark, the tips of them red as lipstick, hot as tears.

It was odd, how empty the apartment seemed without Matthew. And even odder that they had only the roughest idea of where he was (camp) and what he was doing (camp things).

Years and years before Apple had launched the iCloud—perhaps before they'd even *thought* of it—Graham had suspected that Audra had some version of it in her head. You could ask her any question about anyone's schedule and her eyes would unfocus for a second (while she accessed the Audra-cloud) and then she would say, "Well, Carrie can't pick Matthew up then because her boys have soccer on the North Meadow and it takes her over forty-five minutes to get home in rush hour," or "Matthew has Science from 9:10 to 9:55 on Mondays, Tuesdays, and Thursdays, but on Wednesday he has Computer Art, and on Fridays, they have assembly," or "The dentist is open on alternate Saturdays but closed on Wednesday afternoons and the orthodontist is open on Wednesdays and also stays late on Thursdays." She just knew it! And she could access it! Sometimes Graham felt selfish, being married to Audra. She was like a national resource, or a piece of farm machinery too valuable to be owned by just one family. At the very least, she should be co-oped.

But even Audra didn't know Matthew's schedule at camp, and

neither of them knew how he was doing. Campers were not allowed to call home. The camp website said, rather euphemistically, that they found calling home "reduced morale." Was Matthew homesick? Was he scared? Was he being bullied? Did he like the food? Could he sleep at night? Had he suffered from bug bites or poison ivy, had he burned his fingers roasting marshmallows? If so, had he cried in front of all the other kids? Could he keep up on the hikes? Did they *go* on hikes? Was he wearing a life jacket when they went canoeing? So many things could go wrong. It wrung Graham's heart just to think about.

"No news is good news," Audra insisted, and Graham supposed she was right. No school or camp ever called to tell you that your child was having a marvelous time and fitting in beautifully with his peers. No, Graham thought (not without a trace of bitterness), they only called with bad news. They only called to tell you that your child had cried in science lab when it was time to dissect worms, or that your child fell on the playground and screamed at the sight of his own blood, or that your child wasn't making any friends. Then they couldn't *wait* to get ahold of you.

But now Matthew might as well be on another planet. The only news they'd had came from Brenda Rottweiler. The camp had called *her* yesterday to say that Derek had flushed sweet potatoes down the staff toilets so that now the staff had to use the same smelly outhouses as the campers.

Graham and Audra had debated this news intensely, like Kremlinologists studying the parade lineup in Red Square. Evidently Matthew wasn't involved because they hadn't gotten a call. Did that mean Derek Rottweiler had abandoned Matthew, or did it mean only that Derek had acted alone? Did this mean the camp was so lacking in fun that the campers had to play pranks to amuse themselves? Was the camp so absent of discipline that the children were running wild like a pack of hyenas? So primitive in its amenities that the campers were striking back at the staff, in the manner of serfs raiding the castle?

Graham and Audra talked about it for nearly an hour, nearly a whole bag of peanut M&M's (Audra said it might be a pregnancy craving), and in the end, they had nothing, except that Audra said she thought she might be in love with Derek Rottweiler.

Graham went to a diner near his office for a quick, solitary lunch, and there—right in front of him!—were Clayton and Manny, sitting in a booth together. When they saw Graham, they looked at each other with unmistakably guilty expressions. What were they guilty of? Dear God—were they lovers? Graham's mind stepped around that thought the same way his body stepped around a puddle of vomit on the sidewalk.

They were both sitting on the same side of the booth nearest to the door.

"Hello," Graham said.

"Hello," they said nearly in chorus. Again, they exchanged that look. They were definitely hiding something.

"Would you like to join us?" Manny said, seeming to indicate that he was several rungs higher on the evolutionary ladder than Graham had suspected.

So Graham sat down across from them and struggled to think of something innocuous to say. "What are you guys up to?" he said, and then immediately regretted it.

Manny shot Clayton a long look and then Clayton blew out a breath and said, "We shouldn't be meeting like this, but we're discussing a new club member."

"It's supposed to be a club decision," Manny added.

"We're supposed to *vote*," Clayton said.

"Those are the rules," Manny said.

They were both looking at Graham challengingly, so he said gently, "But . . . ?"

"But we're very unsure about this new guy," Clayton said. "*So* unsure about him that we decided to meet outside the club and discuss him."

"What's wrong with him?" Graham asked. "Does he belong to a gym or something?"

Clayton and Manny both burst into laughter.

"Good one," said Manny, shaking his head slightly.

It occurred to Graham that this was the first time he had ever made either of them laugh, and he had no idea what he'd said that was funny.

"The main thing wrong with him," Clayton said, apparently having decided to toss caution, or at least discretion, to the wind, "is that he *speed*-folds."

"That makes sense," Graham said, although it actually made no sense. Speed-folding? What was that?

Manny leaned forward. "And at the first meeting, Clayton here happened to mention an eight-petal flower fold and the guy's look was totally blank! No idea! You can bet he's never made anything other than a five-petal."

"I see," Graham said.

"Now, we don't mind taking on someone with limited experience," Clayton said. "Not if he's serious-minded. Not if he wants to *improve*. But this guy. I get the feeling he's—he's—"

"Dabbling," Manny finished.

"Exactly." Clayton nodded. "Especially after what he said about origami sheep for Chinese New Year."

"Well, of course," Graham said.

He was beginning to have more sympathy for the woman

who said *Well, that's news to me* all the time. He was beginning to understand how that could happen. He wished Audra was here. Audra could converse with a statue. (In fact, once in the ER she had had a long talk with a man who turned out to have had a stroke and could only communicate by blinking.)

They struggled along for a while, with Manny and Clayton talking about origami and Graham saying "I understand" or "That sounds wise" or "Of course" whenever a response seemed called for. There was a brief bit of something you might call an actual conversation, if your standards were very low, when Clayton asked why Matthew wasn't at the club meeting on Sunday.

"He's at camp," Graham said.

"Origami camp?" Manny asked, looking hopeful.

"No," Graham said. "Just camp." He wasn't about to say special-needs camp. Not in front of these two. Not in front of anyone.

"What do they do at this camp?" Clayton asked suspiciously.

"Well, you know," Graham said. "Hiking and campfires and stuff."

"Oh, *outdoor* camp," Clayton said.

"Yes, exactly."

"I never cared for that myself," Clayton said.

"Me, either," Graham said, realizing it was true. Why had he sent his child off to do something he himself would have hated? (He kept forgetting that Matthew had wanted to go.)

They made it through lunch, just barely. Graham had the fish and chips, Clayton had a grilled cheese sandwich, and Manny had mashed potatoes with a side of cauliflower and a vanilla milk shake. Graham had forgotten that Manny only ate white foods off white plates. It seemed impossible to forget such a thing, but he had.

"We come here because they don't insist on garnish," Manny

said. "It can ruin a whole meal for me if someone puts a little colored doodad on my plate."

Afterward, Graham went back out on the street, feeling sad because he had liked the diner very much and now he knew he would never go there again, for fear of running into Manny and Clayton. This seemed to him sometimes to be the essence of aging: that the places and people you loved were ruined for you, or you ruined them for yourself, or they stopped serving the complimentary breadbasket, and before you knew it, you were left with nothing but memories.

But he wouldn't go back and risk putting himself through another lunch where he felt like such an outsider. And then Graham felt even sadder than before, because he wondered suddenly if this was what life was like for Matthew all the time. Guessing at people's meanings and relying on stock phrases to get you through? Knowing that you weren't connecting but not knowing why, or how to fix it? He had read somewhere that people with Asperger's had to work very hard to exist in this world, the normal social world, with all its complicated nuances. They preferred their own worlds, but Graham wanted Matthew to live in *this* world, with him.

I'm finding the no-alcohol thing really hard," Audra said that night. "And it's only been three days."

Graham admired her for avoiding alcohol before they even knew for certain that she was pregnant, but he couldn't help noticing that even without alcohol, she got a little loopier around seven o'clock every evening. Perhaps she didn't *need* alcohol anymore. Maybe she was so conditioned from years of happy hours that her brain was now spontaneously releasing some organic form of a cocktail at the same time every day.

Right now, for instance, she was sitting on the living room couch with him—her bare toes gripping the edge of the glass coffee table—and eating a bag of Cheetos while he drank a Scotch. She said the baby loved Cheetos. Apparently the baby had likes and dislikes now, perhaps even an opinion on Hillary Clinton.

Audra tossed her nearly empty Cheetos bag on the coffee table. "Cheetos are just delicious while you're eating them," she said. "But then you feel yucky afterward. Sort of like porn." She frowned. "I feel like porn is becoming the underlying theme of our lives."

Graham ignored that. "Do you ever worry," he said slowly, "that another child would be like Matthew?"

Audra was licking orange dust off her fingers, but they weren't getting any less orange. "Like Matthew in what way?"

Well, that was a good question. Because Matthew had a million sterling qualities—sweet, affectionate, brown-haired, dimpled, good at math, kind to animals, smelled faintly like maple syrup even though he sometimes went days without a bath. So why when Graham said "like Matthew," had he only meant "with Asperger's"?

"Well," Graham said. "With the same learning differences and challenges." Now it seemed he was speaking some sort of school missionese.

"Oh, I see what you mean," Audra said. "No, I guess I don't worry about that, because Matthew has always seemed to me like a little bit of an outlier. Like, if we had one hundred children, would Matthew represent the minority or the majority? I mean, if we had one hundred children, maybe sixty or seventy would be just like him in all sorts of ways. But I always thought Matthew would be Matthew, unique, and the other ninety-nine would be, I don't know, sort of *standard* children. Like child actors from central casting. Not so special. I always feel like Matthew is the child we were meant to have. If anything, I worry that another baby won't be *enough* like Matthew."

They were so different, and Audra didn't even know it. She didn't know how often Graham had wished for a more standard son. She didn't know that sometimes he thought a child actor from central casting would have suited him just fine.

It seemed that sleep deprivation was not the only thing Audra had forgotten. When she talked about the baby (that word again!), she only said things like, "I definitely wouldn't get a bottle sanitizer this time," or "Remember baby food? Remember that sort of liquefied ham?"

Liquefied ham! No, Graham didn't remember that. He remembered Matthew as an easy but peculiar baby, slow to walk and even slower to talk, but smiley and sweet, obsessed even at an early age with the stroller's wheels and lift-out puzzles and lining toy cars up in precise rows. But at about eighteen months the constant toddler meltdowns started—over nothing, very close to literally nothing. Taking a different route home or drying Matthew off with the wrong bath towel or missing the first thirty seconds of *The Wiggles* would cause Matthew to scream and kick and turn nearly geranium-colored with rage. Constant battles over getting him dressed. For one solid year Matthew had refused to wear anything other than a flimsy Spider-Man costume. Audra had even bought a second one, but Matthew could be satisfied only with the original, which grew thinner and limper and more faded as the months and months and months passed. Audra quickly washed it and dried it every night while Graham spun out bath time as long as possible. Surely Audra couldn't have forgotten that! They had a photo album to prove it, an entire one in which Matthew wore nothing else. My son, Spidey.

The tantrums didn't go away. The terrible twos seemed to have a magical stretching ability when it came to Matthew. They went on for *years*. Eruptions over milk served in anything other than the Buzz Lightyear sippy cup, over music that was too "tinkly," over carpet that was too scratchy, over people who stood too close, over the smell of sunblock, the prospect of butter on biscuits, the sight of cheetahs in an animal documentary. The littlest thing could set Matthew off, and there seemed to be no way of calling him back from the land of the tantrum—in an instant, he would be flat on the floor, back arched, legs rigid, mouth a wide-open circle of angry scream. They would do anything to prevent it. Graham could remember once frantically Scotch-taping the last banana in the fruit bowl back into a banana peel so Matthew could eat it monkey-style. Graham's hands had been shaking with desperation.

Matthew had woken from all naps in the foulest mood imaginable, yelling with outrage—over what? Graham always wondered. Being pulled back into the waking realm that seemed to so aggravate him? The only solution was to rush into the nursery at the first hint of Matthew beginning to stir and hand him a grape Popsicle. Grape was the only flavor he would eat—they threw away dozens, probably hundreds, of orange and yellow ones. They needed the freezer space for the purple ones. Once Matthew had a Popsicle, he would consent to be wrapped in a blanket and sit in Graham's or Audra's lap and be rocked and soothed, gently coaxed into the world again. It was an arduous process. Graham could remember being on vacation once with Matthew sleeping on the hotel room bed, he and Audra out on the balcony, shivering and drinking wine from paper cups because they dreaded the prospect of waking him. Surely, Graham had thought, not all parents lived like this.

Public places were the worst. Once Matthew had screamed so loudly and forcefully during a haircut that they'd been blacklisted from the salon—and it was a place that specialized in children's haircuts! And at a supermarket one time Matthew had taken a big bite out of a doughnut with jam in the middle and you would have thought he had bitten into a caterpillar from the way he carried on. Other shoppers rushed over to help, but there was nothing to do except scoop Matthew up and carry him out to the car while he wailed like a siren. Oh, how they tried to tell themselves this was normal.

Preschool to Matthew had been like a blowtorch held to a bare foot. He had screamed all the way there, every day, and continued to scream while Graham gently pried Matthew's fingers from the car seat and the doorframe and carried him into the school, where he handed him over to the sweet, saintlike teacher who ran the place. (It was months before Graham actually heard the woman's voice—all he saw were her lips moving.) Matthew screamed in the teacher's arms while Graham left, and the sound of his cries followed Graham out the door and back to the car and all the way to his office, it seemed.

Sometimes Matthew screamed all morning at preschool, although sometimes he calmed down for a while, until something else set him off—a glass breaking, another child using his pair of scissors, a smoke alarm beeping. When that happened, the teacher or one of the assistants would come out and wait to speak to Audra at pickup time—the other children waited inside and were released one at a time when their parents arrived. Audra had told Graham that once she had driven up and seen the teacher standing outside with Matthew and had wanted to keep going. "I thought, *Has she seen me? If she hasn't seen me, I could quick turn around and she'd never know. I could go to Starbucks and have a coffee and wait until I felt stronger.*" Could Audra have forgotten that?

And then finally, when Matthew was four, they had taken him to an educational psychologist, someone who had told them gently but firmly that Matthew's behavior was very similar to that of children with Asperger's, and had outlined the ways in which Matthew's symptoms fit the criteria for diagnosis. The doctor had talked about the psychological assessment, and the communications assessment, the long questionnaires filled out by Matthew's teachers, and by Audra and Graham, too. Hundreds of questions on those behavior forms were boiled down to a few numbers, expressing Matthew's profile in terms of what is typical for a four-year-old.

The doctor's voice was soft and soothing and a little bit singsong. "As you can see," he said, "Matthew's score on the questionnaires for oversensitivity to stimulation ranked more than a full standard deviation above the average for children his age." He pointed to the peak on the graph of Matthew's scores. "His score for social development problems is also elevated, again by more than a standard deviation."

Standard deviation! Graham was appalled. Was that what they were discussing here—statistics? And who's to say that there isn't a standard deviation *from* the standard deviation? Who was this doctor to say that because of standard deviation, Matthew stood firmly on the stark cracked-earth desert of Asperger's, that he would never feel the long cool green shade of *normal*?

Graham had wanted to argue with the doctor. He had wanted

to say, *Go back and spend a little more time with him! I don't think you know him well enough to be saying these things.*

They had left the doctor's office and Graham could still remember another couple sitting in the waiting room. He had looked at them, wondered if they were about to receive a similar diagnosis, if this was what the doctor did all day—broke devastating news to parents in his Mary-had-a-little-lamb voice?

In the elevator, Graham had put his arms around Audra and she had pressed her face against his chest and slipped her hands into his coat pockets. It had been years since she'd done that. "How are you feeling?" he'd asked softly.

She'd sighed and leaned against him. "Blacker than midnight," she'd said.

Had Audra forgotten that day, too? Was that even possible?

They were going to have dinner with the Rottweilers. Audra had arranged it.

"This way if we end up in some sort of school conference, they'll side with us," Audra said. She had the shrewd, hard instincts of a good hunter.

And so on an evening when Graham could have been sitting in the comfort of his own house, drinking whisky and watching the news, he and Audra went to an Italian restaurant in midtown and met the Rottweilers.

Brenda Rottweiler was a petite woman with the same bright brown eyes as her son, and a halo of curly hair that looked like someone had drawn swirls with a brown crayon. She had a small, soft-looking mouth and an anxious expression. Jerry Rottweiler was a bearded man with very round rimless glasses. He looked something like a furry owl.

After they were seated and had ordered wine—"Just mineral water for me," Audra said—Brenda leaned toward them and said, "Thank you so much for suggesting we get together. This has been the worst experience."

"I know," Audra said, giving Brenda her warmest smile.

"We checked Derek's computer as soon as he left for camp," Jerry said.

Audra sighed. "We did, too. We found a lot of porn sites."

"I don't even like to think about it." Brenda lowered her voice. "It was so upsetting! They were looking at the most terrible, graphic things! Threesomes and bondage and double entry."

Audra looked at her thoughtfully. "I think it's called double *penetration*."

The waiter was just approaching their table with a wine bottle, and he paused uncertainly.

"You're quite right," Jerry Rottweiler said. "*Double entry* is an accounting term."

Graham sighed and waved the waiter forward with the wine. Apparently they were going to need it.

But actually it was okay. It turned out that Jerry was a civil-litigation lawyer, and, surprisingly, Brenda was a real-estate agent. (Surprising because Graham thought she must be a substitute teacher or perhaps someone who worked in customer service, but evidently her scared, beaten-down expression came from being mother to Derek.) They weren't without quirks. Brenda spoke to Jerry as though he were a child—"Napkin on lap," she said firmly, just before the appetizer arrived. And Jerry tended to say unremarkable things as though they were scandalous announcements: "Brenda likes dry white wine." "I started at the firm almost ten years ago." "You say Matthew is eleven now?" Almost everything he said had an unspoken *Can you believe it?* attached to the end.

But on the whole, they were well traveled and well-read and they had a seemingly endless supply of parenting horror stories about Derek Rottweiler, including (but in no way limited to) the fact that the only person who would agree to babysit Derek was a parole officer who lived in Queens.

"That wasn't so bad," Graham said to Audra in the cab on the way home. "I kind of liked them."

"Oh, I don't know," she said. "All those I've-been-to-France stories get so old."

"They lived in Marrakesh for three years," Graham protested.

"I guess," Audra said glumly, looking out the cab's window. The streetlights threw fleeting lines of shadow across her face, like prison bars. "It's just that there's only so much mineral water you can drink."

Graham and Audra were in the kitchen, putting away groceries.

Audra had been playing tennis with the Akela (who apparently had a killer backhand), and she still wore her tennis dress, with a baggy sweater over it, and white shoes and socks with those hilarious little pom-poms at the back. It never failed to amaze Graham that Audra played tennis. First of all, how did she make it through a game without talking? Maybe she didn't. Maybe she frequently called the Akela to the net and said, "Oh, now, before I forget, did I tell you about this book my book club is reading?" Second, he had always admired women in tennis skirts—the smooth tanned legs, the springy steps—and here he was married to one. Life was strange.

"Do you ever think," he said now, "that you and I might have Asperger's of some sort?"

"Oh, no," Audra said immediately. "Not at all."

She was so definite that Graham felt better.

"Although," she continued, frowning. "You do have that habit of saying *north* and *south* instead of *left* and *right*."

"That's called 'having a sense of direction,'" Graham said. He didn't add that Audra seemed to have been born without one. Actually, it was even worse than just having no sense of direction—it was like some sort of direction *deficit,* something that steered her in the wrong direction. They could go to the restaurant across the street from the apartment building— literally *across the street*—and when they came out, Audra would turn and wander down the block. Graham had told her once that when she was lost, she should close her eyes and try to sense which direction felt like the correct one, and then go the opposite way. (She had reported back that this was extremely helpful.)

"And there's also the way you behave in the elevator," Audra said. "I mean, we get in there with anyone from the building, and you just stand there, stiff as a soldier! Ignoring people like we don't all know each other, like we haven't all lived in the building for years and years. Flipping through your mail like the other person is not dying for you to say, 'Now, Mrs. Pomranky, I have been meaning to tell you how nice your hair looks,' or 'Mr. Fielder, please tell me all about how your daughter's getting along in med school.'"

Were the other people dying for him to say those things? Graham wondered. He'd always assumed that everyone would rather ride in peace, desperate as they all were to get up to their apartments and have the first whisky of the evening, thereby restoring the will to live.

"And then when *I* ask one of the neighbors to water our plants or turn down our thermostat," Audra said, "I have to work extra-hard because you've been so antisocial. I have to say, 'Now, we're going to be away for the weekend and I'm wondering if you could take care of such-and-such, and by the way, I'm terribly sorry that my husband acts like you're a spider plant.'"

Spider plant? What was she talking about?

"First of all, I would never say that I've been meaning to compliment someone's hair," Graham said. "What if she hadn't had anything done to it in, like, years and years—"

"Also," Audra interrupted, "you have this, I wouldn't call it an obsession, but certainly a *rigidity* about reading the newspaper in the morning."

"Hey," Graham protested. "I'm sure ninety-nine percent of all men read the paper in the morning. Ninety-nine percent of all *people*, probably."

Audra herself never read the paper, never even watched the news. North Korea could bomb the entire Eastern Seaboard and she wouldn't know about it until someone mentioned it on Facebook.

"But do they read it every single *day*?" she asked. "Even on their wedding day? Even on the day their child is born? Even while their wife is in labor and needing to go to the hospital?"

"I was checking the stock market!" Graham said. "You said the contractions were still fifteen minutes apart."

"Don't get so defensive," Audra said mildly. "I don't think you have Asperger's. I just think you have it more than me."

And then she picked up the water bottles and went off to put them in the hall storage cupboard, the pom-poms on the backs of her socks bobbing up and down like twin sailboats on a choppy sea.

Graham didn't admit this to anyone, even Audra, but part of him was secretly pleased that Matthew had been caught looking at porn on a school computer. Wasn't that—wasn't that something normal kids did?

Graham remembered how he felt the first day Matthew went to school without crying (which hadn't happened until he reached the second grade), and the first time Matthew had made it through a movie without throwing a tantrum, and the first time he'd eaten a grilled cheese sandwich made with whole-wheat bread instead of white, and the first time he'd consented to go over to some other kid's house. Graham had felt relief and happiness and pride, but most of all, acceptance. He'd finally been granted entry into the world that other parents lived in, the one where children behaved sort of like you had expected back when you were young and foolish and thought child-raising was effortless.

And wasn't this porn thing another version of that? Another developmental milestone that Matthew had achieved? And getting around the school's content controls—didn't that show initiative? Problem solving? Maybe this whole episode was something to be proud of.

He felt that way right up until Mr. Sears called and said they had to come into school for the conference.

The first thing Graham thought at the conference was that Audra had been right to take the Rottweilers out to dinner. Jerry and Brenda were already in the little waiting room outside the school conference room when Graham and Audra got there, and Brenda jumped right up and linked her arm through Audra's. So not only did they present a united front, but they handily outnumbered the two school officials with whom they were meeting.

Mr. Sears, the principal, and Mrs. Costello, the guidance counselor, were already seated at a long conference table. Graham did not care for the conference table. He wanted this meeting to take place in some nice cozy office with pictures and a rug—the kind of place where they only told you good news.

As always, when Graham met Mr. Sears, his mind flashed back to a long car journey during which he and Audra had played Kill, Shag, or Marry and she'd chosen to shag Mr. Sears. "I feel obligated because he's helped Matthew so much," she'd said. "Remember when Matthew first started school and was so afraid? Plus I'm so grateful to Mr. Sears for overturning the school cafeteria's ban on caffeinated drinks. He's very petite and gentle—I don't think it would be such a bad experience. I think he'd just be kind of grateful."

(Audra had chosen to marry the art teacher, Mr. Menendez, because she felt they could do some interesting art collaboration, some sort of stained-glass mosaic. She'd ended up killing Eugene, the school custodian, a very nice man who'd never done anything to anyone.)

Mr. Sears *was* petite and gentle—a little man with a soft white pointy beard and silver-rimmed spectacles. He looked like the elderly cobbler in "The Elves and the Shoemaker." He smiled at them now from his place at the table.

Mrs. Costello was a slender woman in her fifties, with pronounced circles under her eyes, the skin there looking bruised and crepey. She always looked like that, Graham knew from previous meetings, which he thought wasn't a great advertisement for the school: was being the counselor there so incredibly stressful? Today she was wearing a terry-cloth dress, which along with the circled eyes, made her look like someone who'd been dragged out of bed with a terrible hangover.

"Thank you so much for taking time to meet with us!" Audra said, as though she and Graham had requested this meeting instead of the other way around. She shook hands with both of them in an eager, confident way. She reminded Graham of a politician.

When she got to Mrs. Costello, she said, "Now, Lois, you won't believe this but I think we have the same hairdresser!"

Mrs. Costello looked startled. "Who, Bruno?"

"Yes." Audra nodded. "I've been getting my hair cut by him for years. I always get the last appointment of the day and then he and I have a glass of wine together first." Suddenly, she looked thoughtful. "I mean, I assume he only does that before the last appointment, but maybe he does it before *every* appointment. Maybe he's hammered every time he cuts my hair. When do you get *your* hair cut?"

"Oh, well, Saturday mornings, usually," Mrs. Costello answered. She had the look of someone unsuccessfully searching for the off button.

"Of course, of course," Audra said soothingly. "You're so busy at school, it would have to be on the weekends. Does Bruno offer you a glass of wine ever?"

"No—" Mrs. Costello said.

"Although for a while Bruno was coming over to our place on Mondays," Audra said in a reflective tone, "and I never saw him drink during the day. The reason he came to our apartment on Mondays was that his mother-in-law had begun spending that day at his house. Bruno said that when he and his wife got married, the wife said, 'If you're going to go out with your friends on Thursday nights, then my mother is going to come for dinner every Sunday.' So Bruno said fine and they got married—this was all ten years ago, I gather—and then abruptly the mother-in-law began coming over on Mondays, too, which, you know, for a hairdresser is part of the weekend. So Bruno said to his wife, 'I agreed to Sunday but I never agreed to Monday—you never so much as *mentioned* Monday,' and his wife said, 'What am I supposed to tell my mother? That she's not welcome here?' and Bruno said,

'Tell her whatever you like. Tell her I'm taking a class in ombre processing on Staten Island!' and his wife said, 'What? For six months?' and Bruno said . . .'"

Yes, this was the woman who had told Graham he was the more Aspergery of the two of them.

Normally, Graham got very restless when Audra went off on a conversational tangent like this, but now he was grateful. Furthermore, he thought it might actually have a purpose. Perhaps Audra was hoping they would run out of time, or that if she went on for long enough, no one would remember what they were here to discuss.

"Anyway," Audra was saying, "Bruno came over on Mondays for quite a while and he was very easy to have around. He did my hair on Monday mornings and I saw how people get used to that, you know, like movie stars. I read once that Princess Diana had her hair done professionally every day of her life. I guess that's why it looked so good all the time. My hair didn't look that good on Mondays, though better than the other six days, certainly. But then Bruno and his wife worked it out. I think that maybe now the mother-in-law still comes on Mondays but she babysits for them on Friday nights."

She suddenly turned to include Mr. Sears in her smile. "Now, what can we do for you nice people?"

Mr. Sears had curled up a little smaller in his chair while Audra was talking and now he stroked his tiny beard and said, "I'm going to cut out leather for a pair of shoes and see if elves come in the night."

(He didn't really say that but Graham was so tense that he was sure for a moment that he would.)

What he did say was "Well, ah, thank you all for coming in. The school takes internet safety and propriety very seriously, and Derek and Matthew have violated our policy. I'm sure you remember that all students and parents have to sign an internet-usage agreement at the beginning of the year."

They did? They had? It was hard for Graham to remember. They had signed so many forms.

"However," Mr. Sears continued. "We, ah, have reached a decision about the internet incident and we feel that while this has been a serious matter and both boys have shown very poor judgment, we don't think a suspension is called for."

"Hurray!" Audra cheered in an excited whisper. Graham wished he had a sock he could stuff in her mouth.

"So what is the punishment, exactly?" Brenda Rottweiler asked timidly.

"We'd like the boys to write a letter of apology to the computer-science teacher," Mrs. Costello said. "And to stay after school two days next week and clean the computer lab."

"Clean the computer lab?" Jerry said in his can-you-believe-it? voice.

"Oh, it's probably dirtier than you can imagine," Audra said. "Once this salesman came to my office trying to sell this special little vacuum for cleaning keyboards and I said my keyboard was perfectly clean and he said, 'Turn it over and shake it,' and I did and all these cracker crumbs and a fair bit of lettuce fell out and the salesman said, 'Well, see now! You could make a chef's salad from what you got there.' It was very disturbing."

Nobody said anything for at least fifteen seconds. Graham was sure they were all afraid of inadvertently starting Audra up again. Finally, he said, "I think that's very fair. We will see that the boys write the letter."

"Oh, yes," Brenda Rottweiler said. "Immediately."

They all shook hands again, which was very awkward with everyone stretching across the conference table and supporting themselves with their free hands.

Graham waited for Audra to say something else, to talk about baby names or ask what everyone thought of the color chartreuse. But she only smiled and slipped her hand into the crook of Graham's arm. Perhaps, for once, she was as eager for something to be over as he was.

When Graham opened the apartment door on Thursday evening, he heard the gasp and pop of a cork being eased out of the wine bottle. It was so perfectly timed that he wanted to close the door and reopen it to see if would happen again.

"Graham?" Audra called from the kitchen. "I have the best news! I went in to Dr. Medowski for a blood test and I'm not pregnant!"

Graham set down his coat and briefcase and walked down the hall to the kitchen doorway. Audra had poured two glasses of wine and she handed him one.

"I'm so happy and relieved," she said, drinking deeply from her glass. "Oh, I have been without the gentle touch of alcohol for far too long. Anyway, cheers!"

Graham lifted his glass automatically to clink against hers, but he didn't take a sip. He sat down slowly on the kitchen chair.

"I just got back about two minutes ago," Audra said. Graham saw that she was more dressed up than usual in a suede skirt and silk blouse. "Dr. Medowski called me this morning and I went in this afternoon and the nurse drew some blood and while we were waiting for the lab, Dr. Medowski showed me about a million photos of his golfing vacation, and then they got the results back and I was so happy I could have hugged him." She frowned slightly. "Well, I *did* hug him goodbye, I always do. But I could have hugged him there in the middle, too."

Audra wasn't pregnant. Now that Graham knew that, he could allow himself to feel longing for a baby—a regular old baby, nobody special, a baby who would reach all the developmental milestones right on time. Sorrow swept through him like cold water through a faucet. Why was he always conflicted? Always two steps behind Audra?

"Anyway," Audra said, pacing rapidly around the kitchen, taking plates from cabinets and silverware from drawers. "The Rottweilers are picking Derek and Matthew up from the bus and they're all coming here. I invited them for dinner, I hope that's okay." She took another drink of wine. "Although at this rate, I'll be sloshed before they get here."

She stepped past him and went into the dining room to set the table. "I asked Brenda if they had any food preferences and she said Jerry doesn't eat fruit or vegetables," she called. "And I said, 'Well, what about onions?' because I know you put them in almost everything and Brenda said, 'Onions are okay if you grate them superfine so he can't detect them,' and I didn't ask what happens if he *can* detect them. Like, does he just stop eating or does he have some sort of meltdown? And I wonder about his health, too. Does he have scurvy or rickets or whatever it is you get without vitamin C?"

Chicken and potatoes, Graham was thinking. No, chicken and *rice,* because Jerry Rottweiler might consider the potato a vegetable. Chicken and rice, then, with French bread and butter as a side dish. Gravy served in a separate bowl. Vanilla ice cream for dessert. A fattening and joyless meal, but undoubtedly it would do. Graham sighed. The innkeeper and his wife at the House of Picky Eaters.

Just then the door burst open and Matthew came running in, followed by all three of the Rottweilers. Graham caught a glimpse of Derek Rottweiler's face and wished he'd thought to close the door to his study and put their new camera out of reach. But then Matthew was standing in front of Graham and he could think of nothing else.

Matthew was suntanned and grass-stained and mosquito-bitten. His lovely thick brown hair was matted and greasy, and a long red scratch traced along one cheekbone. A cluster of red dots that might well be poison ivy showed on his neck.

"Camp—was—fantastic!" Matthew said, and Graham gathered him close.

Camp was fantastic, which meant life was fantastic. Audra was fantastic. The Rottweilers were fantastic. Chicken and rice was fantastic. Who needed fruit and vegetables? Not Graham, not now.

Graham's only regret was that he hadn't known ahead of time that Matthew would love camp, that Matthew could go off in the world and sleep in strange places and have new experiences and love doing it, just like any other kid. If Graham had known that, he could have enjoyed this week, relished it, even. He could have lived life like other parents, the way he'd always wanted to.

Graham leaned down and pressed his cheek against the top of Matthew's head. Matthew smelled like woodsmoke and pine needles and sweat, but Graham could still smell maple syrup. Camp had worked its miracle, but underneath Matthew was still Matthew.

And then Graham understood that it was almost too late. He had spent so much time wishing Matthew were different, wondering how to *make* Matthew different, when it was actually the process of living that did it. Life forced you to cope. Life wore down all your sharp corners with its tedious grinding on, the grinding that seemed to take forever but was actually as quick as a brushfire. What Graham had to do was to love Matthew right now, right this instant—heart, get busy—before Matthew grew up and turned into someone else.

Eight

It was a Friday night not so different from any other. Graham and Audra were having dinner in their apartment with Doug and Lorelei and Doug's mother, Mrs. Munn.

Whenever Mrs. Munn came to stay with Doug and Lorelei, Audra invited them all over for a meal. Graham was unsure whether this was a higher level of friendship or more a type of community service, but he knew Audra did it in hopes of relieving Lorelei of the stress of having houseguests. Only it didn't really *relieve* the stress, it just sort of diluted it. Now, for example, instead of just Doug and Lorelei spending the evening making small talk with Mrs. Munn, Audra and Graham had to spend the evening making small talk with her, too. You know, it would be far simpler and more effective if you could march your houseguest over to a bench in Central Park and say, *You just sit right there while I go home and read the newspaper in peace. I'll be back to pick you up in two hours.* And if your houseguest was of the older, feebler variety, and you feared they might be mugged or beaten in the park, you could take them to a movie, possibly a matinee. Actually, there should be a houseguests' club, like the kids' club in a resort, where your houseguest could watch movies and play games and have a snack while you recharged your batteries. Although, Graham recalled, Matthew had refused to attend kids' clubs since babyhood, screaming so loudly that the staff always called them back within the hour. Now, casting a seasoned eye on Mrs. Munn, Graham suspected she would object just as forcefully.

Mrs. Munn was an overweight woman in her seventies, with extra bolsters of flesh under her chin and stacked on her midsection. She had a deceptively obliging and soft-spoken manner. She had softly complimented Audra on the "lived in" feel of the apartment, and gently praised Doug for not checking his phone all the time in company the way he did at home. She had quietly admired the long hours Lorelei worked and said it was no wonder Lorelei looked so tired. She had commented sympathetically on how boring grown-up conversation must be for Matthew and how she understood completely that he would rather have a sandwich in his room. She had sweetly congratulated Graham for feeling comfortable enough to leave guests while he spent long stretches in the kitchen (he was having some trouble with the gravy) and remarked how unpretentious it was of him to use supermarket salad dressing. She had serenely dominated the dinner conversation talking about how she understood why people lived in New York City but that it wasn't for her while she ate large forkfuls of roast chicken and sweet potatoes. (Graham was beginning to truly comprehend how long this visit must be for Doug and Lorelei.)

Mrs. Munn pushed her plate away slightly and reached for her water glass. "I'm sorry," she said. "This was delicious, but I'm afraid my eyes were bigger than my stomach."

"How big *is* your stomach?" Audra asked in the sort of sincere but idle way she might wonder aloud how long a hummingbird's life span was.

Mrs. Munn's glass knocked against her teeth with a startled *clunk*.

The phone rang and Graham leapt out of his chair so quickly, he nearly knocked it over.

"I'll get it," he said unnecessarily. He ducked into the kitchen. "Hello?"

"May I speak to Graham Cavanaugh, please?" A man's voice, unfamiliar.

"This is he."

"My name is Ronald Perkins," the man said. "I am a senior partner at Stover, Sheppard, Perkins, and Lemke."

Elspeth's firm. Graham gripped the phone more tightly. "Yes?"

"I'm terribly sorry to be the one to tell you this," Mr. Perkins said, "but Elspeth has passed away."

"She what?" Graham said.

"She passed away," Mr. Perkins repeated politely. "She died."

He paused and waited for Graham to say something, but Graham couldn't. Died? Elspeth *died*? The word had no more meaning than any other. It was like playing Balderdash with the dictionary and choosing a word you were pretty sure no one knew the definition of. *Bibble, cabotage, ratoon.* It was a nonsense word. He could make nothing of it.

Mr. Perkins cleared his throat. "I'm sure it's a tremendous shock to you," he said. "It was to all of us."

"What happened?" Graham asked finally. "Was she—in a car accident?"

"Elspeth failed to show up for work on Wednesday," Mr. Perkins said. He had a precise way of talking, as though his sentences were perfect strings of pearls with knots between the words. "She missed several meetings and that was completely out of character. Naturally, we grew concerned, but we waited until noon, thinking perhaps Elspeth had a personal appointment that we knew nothing about. In the early afternoon, her secretary, Miss

Zapata, went to Elspeth's apartment in person. She thought perhaps Elspeth was ill. She had a spare key and let herself in after ringing the doorbell repeatedly. She found Elspeth on the bathroom floor. It appears she slipped while getting out of the bathtub and hit her head."

"This happened Wednesday?" Graham said. It was Friday. Forty-eight hours had gone by and he hadn't even *known*?

"Tuesday evening, we believe," Mr. Perkins said. "Miss Zapata said that the bed was not slept in and some"—he coughed delicately—"nightclothes were laid out."

So Elspeth had lain there all night and all the next day. When—*when*—would Graham learn not to ask questions?

"Of course," Mr. Perkins said, "it goes without saying that we are all extremely regretful that we didn't check on her sooner."

Well, yes, regrets. Everyone had them. But Mr. Perkins hadn't left Elspeth waiting in a hotel room and then never contacted her again. Mr. Perkins wasn't the one who had divorced Elspeth and left her to live alone. And die alone.

Mr. Perkins cleared his throat again. It was clear that Graham was leaving too many pauses in the conversation. "I thought you would want to attend the funeral on Monday."

"Yes, of course," Graham said.

Mr. Perkins gave him the details and Graham wrote them on the scratch pad by the phone. They said goodbye and hung up and Graham rested his forehead against the kitchen wall.

Shocking. And perhaps most shocking of all was that even at this moment, a part of Graham was happy that now he wouldn't have to sit through dessert with Mrs. Munn.

It was a strange weekend. It had no—no *rhythm*.

Graham woke up at five in the morning on Saturday and then

fell back to sleep at his normal waking time. He woke up again in the late morning and the light was all wrong—dark golden, like rancid honey.

He made cooking mistakes he hadn't made in years. He burned the toast for breakfast, and his scrambled eggs were tough and dry. He crowded the meatballs in the frying pan and forgot to add salt to the pasta. His hamburger patties crumbled like damp sand castles and he undercooked the potatoes, making the potato salad inedible. His timing was off, too. He served lunch early and dinner late on Saturday, and then lunch late and dinner early on Sunday, as though he were a traveler trying to trick his metabolism into some new time zone.

Audra's rhythm was affected, too. She wanted to talk about Elspeth's death and she would begin speaking in a sad, serious tone and say things like, "Of course, we must go to the funeral" and "You must reach out to mutual friends and let them know."

Her voice was subdued but not *very* subdued. It wasn't quite as effervescent as the first glass of champagne out of the bottle—it was more like the third glass—but there were still bubbles aplenty. Then she would get a little more upbeat and say, "Who takes baths anymore? Except for, I don't know, eccentric millionaires and maybe very elderly British people?" and "Did she take a lot of baths when you were married?" and "Who was the last person she spoke to, do you know?"

"No," Graham said. "Maybe someone at her office."

"I hope it was someone she liked a lot," Audra said. "I hope that they had a nice long satisfying conversation and the very last thing Elspeth said was 'It made me so happy to talk to you!'"

Graham wasn't sure Elspeth had ever said that to anyone, let alone as her last words.

"I wonder about last words, sometimes," Audra continued.

"What if your very last words were, you know, 'I think maybe I left my curling iron on'? When Matthew first started going to elementary school, I would make sure that the very last thing I said to him every morning was 'I will always love you,' so that if something happened to me, that would be the last thing he remembered me saying. But that sort of fell by the wayside and now when I drop him off, I say, 'Don't tell me you forgot your backpack again!' or 'Jump out quickly before someone honks!' You know, in general, I feel my standards of mothering have declined over the years. Doesn't it seem like I would have gotten *better* after so much practice? Like by this point, I should just be able to snap my fingers and—poof!—Matthew's dressed and fed and loved and secure? But instead it's more like *Downton Abbey* and I had a couple of very strong seasons there in the beginning and now I'm cutting corners like crazy."

Downton Abbey? What was she talking about?

Audra looked suddenly abashed and reverted to her semi-sentimental voice. "Do you remember when Elspeth said she liked my topaz earrings?"

(This was apparently the fondest memory she had of Elspeth, which was upsetting on a number of levels.)

Elspeth's death was like—like—well, like a few years ago when they pulled up the carpet in the bedroom and had the hardwood floor restored. Graham had not realized his muscle memory was so strong, but for weeks, every time he entered the bedroom, he stepped down too hard, expecting the floor to be an inch higher than it was. The fact of Elspeth's death was like that little jolt, surprising him from time to time.

How awful that Elspeth should die and his only symptoms of grief were a faint muscle memory and bad potato salad. Was that truly all he was capable of? But that was why the weekend had no rhythm, Graham realized. He was treating sorrow as a formality, or a temporary condition—like a room he was passing through and shortly he'd enter another room where some other, happier emotion was going on.

Before the funeral service started, Audra leaned across Graham and said to the elderly woman seated next to him on the pew, "Excuse me, but would a nice pretty lady such as yourself have a breath mint?"

The old lady gave a pleased, full-cheeked chortle. "Well, now certainly," she said and began rooting through her purse. She was the old-ladiest type of old lady, with feathery white hair, bright red lipstick, and a little hat with white flowers on the brim.

"Here you go," she said at last and held out a roll of pepper-mint Life Savers.

"Oh, thank you!" Audra said, taking one. "I had a roast beef sandwich for lunch and I can still taste the horseradish."

"For me, it's garlic bagels," the old lady said.

"Garlic is the worst," Audra said. "Did you know it comes out your pores and not just your breath? Once Graham here had lunch in Little Italy and he smelled so garlicky afterward that his office sent him home! Apparently everyone else was having trouble concentrating because there was Graham, smelling like an Italian sausage and not even aware of it."

"Mercy!" the old lady said. She pulled back and gave Graham a long look, the flowers on her hat bobbing in a startled way.

"And don't even get me started on tuna fish," Audra said.

"Goodness, no," the old lady said.

"Although," Audra continued thoughtfully, "as I get older, this whole freshening process seems to me like a lot of upkeep. I mean, brushing your teeth, okay—that has health ramifications.

But deodorant? And scented shower gel? Followed by scented lotion? And different scented lotion? And different scented shampoo, and then scented hair spray? Sometimes I think, *Where does it all end? Why not just go around with bad breath and smelly armpits?*"

She gestured at Graham slightly, and the old lady flicked him a little glance. Evidently he was now the world representative of body odor.

"I know," the old lady said. "When I think how many minutes of my life I've spent putting on lipstick!"

"I read once that the average woman spends seventy-two days shaving her legs over the course of a lifetime," Audra said. "And—"

Graham cleared his throat and made a little motion with his head toward the front of the chapel. Both women fell silent, although nothing had happened yet. No minister had appeared. The coffin was there, closed. The octagonal maple coffin with brass trimmings—it reminded Graham intensely of Audra's earring box.

Audra leaned back across Graham and said, "Speaking of lipstick—"

And so it was that even on this day, the day they buried Elspeth, Graham had to listen while Audra talked to strangers about tuna breath. He supposed there was a life lesson in there somewhere. He just didn't know what it was.

It wouldn't be accurate to say that no one came to Elspeth's funeral—at least two dozen corporate types, presumably colleagues, were there—but almost literally no one came to the wake. All the corporate types had pulled out their phones and checked their email as soon as the service was over, and then all of them slipped away. Even the old lady who'd given Audra the breath mint, and Graham had pegged her as the type who would almost certainly stay, especially if refreshments were involved.

But the only people who followed Graham and Audra to the tiny room in the back of the funeral parlor were the minister and an elderly man in a heathery purple sweater.

The minister had wild curly gray hair and eyeglasses with pink-tinted lenses. He looked like someone you'd meet at a Grateful Dead concert. He had delivered a strange, second-person eulogy so generic that it sounded like a horoscope. ("You were reliable, hardworking, kind, and considerate. You were a quiet person who liked to be alone.")

Now he stood next to the buffet eating a sandwich.

"*Virginia* ham," he said to Audra, who stood next to him.

"*American* cheese," Audra responded carefully, evidently thinking the minister was some sort of eccentric. (Or, alternatively, she may have thought he was attempting to play a word game—she loved word games.)

"No," the minister said. "I meant, this sandwich is made with Virginia ham. I can tell from just one bite. That's how many wakes I've been to."

"Is that so?" Audra said in a pleased voice. "I'm that way about doughnuts. I could eat the teeniest crumb and tell you exactly what kind of doughnut it came from because one summer in high school I worked at Dunkin' Donuts. And at the end of the summer, the manager took me aside and said, 'It's my policy to let employees eat as many doughnuts as they like because I've found they get tired of eating doughnuts all the time pretty quick. But you never got tired!' I felt so self-conscious! I thought, *Well, you awful, awful man. See if I ever clean behind the spiral mixer again!*" Suddenly she looked contrite and laid her hand on the minister's arm. "I'm sorry—I guess that wasn't a very Christian thing to say."

"Well, it wasn't very Christian of the manager to point out how many doughnuts you'd eaten," the minister said.

"No, indeed," Audra said, immediately cheerful again. "Now, tell me, were you and Elspeth close?"

The minister reached for another sandwich. "Who?"

Graham sighed and turned away. The old man in the purple sweater was right behind him. "Mr. Cavanaugh?" he said. "I'm Ronald Perkins."

"Yes, of course." Graham shook hands with him, and Audra left the minister's side and joined them. She was wearing a Mexican sundress, and even though it was plain black with no sparkles or embroidery of any kind, there was something about the drawstring neckline and flowing sleeves that struck Graham as inappropriately festive.

"How nice to meet you," she said to Mr. Perkins. "Were you and Elspeth close?"

"I was the one who hired Elspeth originally," Mr. Perkins said. Graham saw that Mr. Perkins must be approaching eighty—his hair was a baby-fine white and he had the pointy coat-hanger shoulders old men get. "I had the greatest respect for her, but I didn't know her very well personally."

"Oh," Audra said in a disappointed tone.

"However," Mr. Perkins continued. "I am the executor of Elspeth's estate. I was going to call you, Mr. Cavanaugh, but then I thought I might see you here today. Elspeth left you a bequest." He pulled a slip of paper out of his pocket and then held it at arm's length so he could read it. " 'In light of our previous relationship, I would like my former husband, Graham Cavanaugh, to choose one item from among my personal effects to keep.' "

"That's it?" Audra said.

Mr. Perkins nodded. "Yes, just one item."

"No," Audra said. "I mean, that's all she said about him?"

"I believe so," Mr. Perkins said. "There is no further mention of Graham in the will."

"That is so typical of Elspeth," Audra said. "Now we have no way of knowing whether she meant, you know, 'In light of how great our love was,' or 'In light of what a low-down dirty dog he was.'"

"Audra," Graham said gently, although he was thinking the same thing.

"Oh, well, now," Mr. Perkins said. "I don't imagine she would have left him anything at all if she disliked him."

(Which just proved that he really hadn't known Elspeth at all, Graham thought.)

"But didn't you *write* the will?" Audra persisted. "Weren't you *there* when she said that? How did she sound? Did she say it like she was still in love with him, or like she couldn't stand him?"

"She worded the document herself," Mr. Perkins said. He sounded very relieved to be able to say that. He turned to Graham. "Perhaps we could meet at Elspeth's apartment one evening this week? I would like to handle this soon, so that we can dispose of the estate."

"Of course," Graham said. "Whenever is most convenient for you."

Mr. Perkins handed him a business card, and Graham put it in the breast pocket of his suit.

"So you're saying Graham can go to her apartment and choose absolutely anything he takes a fancy to?" Audra said. "Or is it, like, all the good stuff goes to someone else and then whatever Graham doesn't take gets hauled away by the Salvation Army?"

"No, no," Mr. Perkins said. "He can come and choose his bequest before anything else is disposed of."

"Choose from the whole apartment?"

"Yes, absolutely."

"Well, cool," Audra said so abruptly Mr. Perkins blinked.

After that, there really seemed to be nothing to do. Graham wandered over to the buffet, but the minister had eaten most of the ham sandwiches, leaving only the cheese ones, which looked thick and dry, like they would stick to your teeth. There was a tray of carrot sticks growing warped, and two platters of cookies. It reminded Graham of a church day camp he'd gone to as a child where they watered down the apple juice.

In the cab on the way home, Audra ate a handful of Oreos and got crumbs all over the taxi's upholstery. "I was hoping Bentrup would be there," she said thoughtfully.

"Bentrup?" Graham said. "Why would he be there? They broke up on such bad terms."

"Well, maybe not Bentrup but *someone*," Audra said. "Some nice older man who was Elspeth's lover."

Now, it wasn't an affair if you didn't go through with it, right? If you never so much as kissed the person in question? Then why was Graham's mouth so dry suddenly that his tongue felt small and shriveled?

"I don't believe she had anyone," he said at last. "Not for a while."

Audra pried open an Oreo and licked the filling off. "But there must have been someone," she said. "Even if it was just sex and not a serious relationship. But everyone at the funeral just up and disappeared right away! I kept thinking some man would come up and say, you know, 'Elspeth and I were very close,' or 'Elspeth meant the world to me,' or some other thing that would be code for them having slept together. The only person who even spoke to us was that Mr. Perkins, and I couldn't picture him and Elspeth having sex, though I *tried* to picture it, a little, while he was talking about codicils and stuff."

"As far as I know, there hasn't been anyone since Bentrup," Graham said carefully. "I think she was going through a dry spell."

Audra looked at him in astonishment. "What? No sex at all?"

"I don't think so."

"Not even a one-night stand with a drunk migrant worker she picked up in a bar or something?"

Graham couldn't imagine anyone less likely to do that than Elspeth. He shook his head. "I don't think anyone, ah, touched her," he said.

"Well, I had dry spells when I was single, too," Audra said. "But those were times when I didn't have a steady boyfriend. I mean, there were still men who touched me. And then some."

Mercifully, the taxi pulled up to their building. Graham paid the driver and Audra hopped out to hug Julio, who was on duty, and then there was the mail to collect, and homework to supervise, and dinner, and dishes, and all that stuff you do every day that sometimes seems pleasurable and sometimes seems pointless but never seems to end.

Later that night, in bed, when they'd turned off the lights and the darkness of their bedroom was as soft and deep as mink fur, Audra sighed.

"I hope Elspeth was at least *fingered* by a drunk migrant worker," she said.

Graham pretended he was already asleep.

The worst thing, the most unjust thing, about Elspeth dying— well, okay, obviously, the worst, most unjust thing about Elspeth dying was that she died at age fifty-four and didn't get to lead a long and happy life, and nobody seemed to even miss her all that much. But the *second* worst thing, the *second* most unjust thing, was that Graham never got to tell her he was sorry they argued about the All-Clad frying pan.

He could remember—vividly—splitting up their belongings on the day when Elspeth had moved out of their apartment all those years ago. It was a Thursday, he recalled, because Mrs. Batista, their cleaning lady, was there. He and Elspeth had moved from room to room with Elspeth pointing out which possessions she wanted and Graham obediently marking them for the movers. So great was his guilt over their separation that he had disputed no request, had relinquished every article she asked for, but every item he agreed to give up just seemed to make Elspeth angrier. By the time they got to the kitchen, her face was so flushed that her blond eyebrows stood out like white lines. Her skin was sweaty, and strands of her hair kept escaping her ponytail and sticking to her cheeks. She pointed angrily to the KitchenAid mixer, the Sabatier knives, the Le Creuset casserole dish, the copper-bottomed pots, the baking tins, and the antique cobalt glassware. Graham agreed to all of it.

Then she snapped, "And don't for one minute think I'm leaving you the All-Clad frying pan!" and she took the pan out of the cupboard and banged it on the counter so hard it startled Mrs. Batista (who was trapped in the far end of the narrow kitchen, discreetly polishing the stove top).

And Graham had hesitated. It was true that the frying pan had been his originally. He had brought it in to the marriage and he had expected to take it out of the marriage, too. It was true that the frying pan felt as good and right in his hand as a baseball bat does when you're on your way to the park on a sunny summer morning. He could have just said, "Fine." Instead he'd said, "If you must." He wanted to make Elspeth feel *guilty* about it. He wanted her to feel ever so slightly *bad* when she used the frying pan. Despite Audra, despite Marla, despite all the other Marlas, Graham had wanted to diminish Elspeth's pleasure in a *frying pan*. He wanted to taint her association with it, to make her feel a little bit dishonest. God, he was a small, small person. He knew that.

The movers had come the next day and taken all Elspeth's belongings, and even though he still had plenty of furniture and dishes and lamps and candlesticks, the apartment had the sad, deserted look of a dorm room on the last day of the year, when all that's left on the wall are four tacks and the corner of a poster.

The next Thursday, Mrs. Batista had left him a note: *I miss some of the things around here.* It was difficult to tell whether this was a note of condemnation ("All your pretty things are gone, serves you right") or commiseration ("I can't believe she walked off with that Waterford pitcher!"). Graham guessed the latter, though, since Mrs. Batista had continued working for him, not Elspeth. In fact, Mrs. Batista *still* worked for him, only now she was older and brought her daughter along to do the vacuuming.

(And if you think Graham's longest, most consistent, most satisfying relationship with a woman was with his cleaning lady, you'd be wrong. It was with his dental hygienist, Louisa. He had been her very first patient, back when he was twenty-nine and she was twenty-four. She had been a young, pretty, intense, black-haired girl who cleaned his teeth silently and thoroughly, and now she was not so young, but still just as pretty and just as intense. Every time Graham came in for an appointment, Louisa would greet him and then say to the receptionist, "He was my first patient! Can you believe that?" Then she would clean Graham's teeth and afterward she'd say, "Still not a single cavity! You're amazing!" and Graham would say, "I owe it all to you," and then they would both say bad things about people who don't floss, and that would be the end of it for six months. They never argued, never got jealous, and Graham didn't have to remember her birthday. It was, he often thought, everything a relationship should be.)

Audra had moved in shortly after Elspeth had moved out, and they had lived in that apartment until they got married a year later. Audra had brought her own mountain of possessions and formed her own relationship with Mrs. Batista (and many of Mrs. Batista's relatives). In no time at all, Audra's cosmetics had littered the bathroom counter where Elspeth's cosmetics used to be, and Audra's jewelry rested on top of the dresser, and Audra's clothes hung in the closet, and Audra's books lined the bookshelves, and her prints went up on the walls, and her beaded lamp stood on the nightstand, and her former roommate's ex-boyfriend's grandmother's sister's quilt covered the bed for some reason Graham could never quite figure out. Soon the apartment lost that sad abandoned dorm room look, and took on the happy cluttered look of home.

But Audra had owned no kitchen equipment because Audra never cooked, and it was weeks before Graham got around to replacing the frying pan. He kept forgetting. He would forget all about it until he needed it. Then he would reach down to the low cupboard where Elspeth had kept it and his fingers would touch nothing but the bare dusty shelf and he would realize all over again that it was gone.

Graham opened the door of the apartment, and Audra and Julio were standing right there, two steps away. Julio wore his door-man uniform and looked oddly out of place, like a suit of armor propped up in your living room.

"That is just terrible news," Audra was saying.

Graham felt suddenly hollow. "What is?"

"Well, Julio's uncle— I'm sorry, Julio, what's your uncle's name again?"

"Enzo," Julio said.

"Thank you," Audra said. "Julio's uncle Enzo and his family live in Queens and the people in the apartment above them hadn't had their water boiler serviced in, I don't know, like a million years and it burst and leaked through the ceiling and they have just untold water damage to their apartment now."

"I see," Graham said carefully.

"And apparently insurance will cover it," Audra continued, "or some of it, which is the good news, but they can't live there for at least several weeks, which is the bad news. So Uncle Enzo and his wife, Dominga, are going to move in with Julio's mother," Audra said. "But Julio's mother and his aunt Dominga have not spoken since 1986—"

"Actually, the very last day of 1985," Julio said.

"Because Julio's father—whom I now believe is deceased?" Audra paused and looked at Julio, who nodded.

"Sorry to hear that," Graham said, and Julio made an accepting sort of face.

"Well, apparently Julio's father got very drunk at a New Year's Eve party in 1985," Audra continued, "and patted Aunt Dominga's bottom in the kitchen and Julio's mother happened to be coming into the kitchen right at that split second and saw it. And I'm sorry to interrupt myself here, but, Julio, shouldn't your mother have been mad at your father instead of Aunt Dominga?"

"Oh, she was mad at both of them for quite a while," Julio said. "But my father convinced her it wasn't his fault—he said, 'Now, honey, you know that men are just powerless over their lower urges.' So after a while Mama decided that Aunt Dominga had encouraged it by wearing dresses that were too tight and flirting with every man in sight. And my aunt Dominga said, 'What are you talking about? I was minding my own business, just checking the rosca de reyes in the oven!' and Mama said, 'It's the *way* you were checking the oven, bending over like that,' and Aunt Dominga said, 'Do you know another way to check the oven?' And Mama said, 'You were all but horizontal!' and Aunt Dominga said, 'Well, it's not my fault he prefers my behind to yours.' "

Julio was an even better storyteller than Audra. Audra told stories in her usual voice, no matter who was talking, as though the whole world spoke with breathy excitement. Julio's voice went with the dialogue, rolling into the deep baritone of his father, rising to the indignant tones of his mother, sliding into the smug tartness of his aunt.

"And they truly haven't spoken since then?" Audra asked.

"Pretty much," Julio said. "Though at my sister's wedding last year, Mama went up to Aunt Dominga by the punch bowl and said, 'I might have guessed you'd wear red—it suits you.' "

Audra was shaking her head slightly and clucking. "So now," she said to Graham, "Julio's mother feels that she must open her home to her brother but she refuses to sleep under the same roof as Aunt Dominga, so she's moving into Julio's apartment, which is just a studio and nowhere near big enough, so I told Julio he should just stay with us."

"Of course," said Graham, who, for several minutes now, had been secretly fearing that Aunt Dominga was coming to live with them. "Of course. We would be happy to have you."

That was the truth. Julio was an easy houseguest and Graham was fond of him. And anyway, Graham was so relieved that the terrible news wasn't that Julio had been fired and was moving away. Graham couldn't stand to lose anyone else right now.

. . .

Olivia arrived at the office the next day pulling a suitcase that looked about the size of the love seat in Graham's living room. Actually, maybe the love seat was a little smaller.

"Phew!" Olivia said, blowing out a breath. Her bangs were stuck to her forehead.

"Going somewhere?" Graham asked.

"To Kentucky to see my parents," Olivia said, fanning herself with the collar of her blouse. "I have to leave for the airport straight from here. You will not believe how much this thing weighs!"

Graham looked at the suitcase. "How much *does* it weigh?"

"I have no idea," Olivia said. "That was just an expression."

"But, I mean—" Graham paused doubtfully. "Won't you have to pay a fee for oversize baggage?"

"What are you talking about?"

"Well, if your suitcase is over a certain size, the airlines charge you a fee."

"They do?" Olivia looked shocked. "How much?"

"About a hundred dollars, typically."

"A hundred dollars!" Olivia cried, dismayed. "That's like twenty Frappuccinos!"

"Well, yes."

"How heavy can it be before they charge you?" Olivia asked.

"Fifty pounds, I think."

They both regarded her suitcase suspiciously, as though it were an alien spacecraft.

Olivia looked over at Graham. "How much do you *think* it weighs?"

Graham picked up the suitcase, the tendons in his arm creaking. "More than fifty, I think. You might have to repack."

He didn't mean right then and there, but Olivia immediately knelt down, her blue skirt pooling around her like a puddle of water, and undid the clasps on the suitcase, resulting in an explosion of cosmetics and shoes and bras and phone chargers. A bottle of shampoo rolled over to rest against Graham's shoe and he nudged it until it rolled back.

"You see," he said, "you're better off buying stuff like shampoo and lotion in Kentucky, or taking really small bottles. And why are you taking a jar of pennies and that little Statue of Liberty figurine—"

"What am I going to *do*?" Olivia interrupted, nearly wailing.

"Let me get my gym bag," Graham said. "And I think I have some shopping bags, too. We'll figure it out."

She looked up at him and nodded, her cheeks as pink as a Dresden doll's.

He went into his office and dumped his gym stuff onto the floor of the closet there. When he returned, Olivia was still kneeling by her open suitcase, looking like someone who'd just been evicted from a very crowded apartment.

She had her cellphone to her ear and Graham guessed she was speaking to her roommate. "Yes, a hundred dollars!" she said. Then her eyes fastened on Graham. "I don't know *how* he knows this stuff, he just does."

He felt—just for the tiniest instant—very wise, very old.

You could bet Graham wasn't going to choose the frying pan. That was certain. But what *would* he chose from Elspeth's apartment? He was due to meet Mr. Perkins at Elspeth's apartment in an hour. He went into the kitchen to say goodbye to Audra, but she jumped up immediately from her seat at the table.

"Of course, I'll come with you, darling," she said cheerfully. "It's bound to be upsetting. I wouldn't want you to be alone."

Clearly Audra just wanted to have a good poke around Elspeth's apartment, but it didn't seem worth arguing about. She wore jeans and a white blouse embroidered with flowers around the neckline. Why was it that everything she wore lately struck Graham as inappropriately lighthearted?

They left Matthew at home alone. This was a new development and Matthew tended to call them on their cellphones and say things like, "I'm thirsty. Do you think I should get a drink of water?" But, hey, progress is progress. It gave Graham hope that Matthew could live independently by age thirty-five or so.

He and Audra took a cab down to Elspeth's apartment and met Mr. Perkins in the lobby. Mr. Perkins wore a checkered blazer that made him look like an elderly bookie. Graham said hello and avoided the doorman's eyes. Did they remember him?

"Well, I'm sure Graham will start in the kitchen," Audra said to Mr. Perkins in the elevator. "So let's you and I just have a little mosey around."

Mr. Perkins looked a bit startled but he just said, "Certainly."

"I can't wait to look in her closets," Audra said in a soft, happy voice.

Graham didn't have any intention of starting in the kitchen. As soon as they got to the apartment, he went straight to Elspeth's bedroom. He was looking for *the drawer*. Everyone had one, at least he assumed that. A drawer, or maybe a box on your closet shelf, where you ended up storing things of sentimental value. Graham's own such drawer was the bottom drawer of his desk. Audra's, oddly, was in the kitchen, and in addition to some letters and photos she treasured, it held bits of string and stretched-out rubber bands and spare batteries of uncommon sizes. (How like Audra to have everything mixed up together, the priceless and the useless.)

Graham opened the door to Elspeth's bedroom. It was immaculate as always. It looked so much like a showroom that Graham had the sudden conviction that if he pulled back the bedspread, he would find only a bed-shaped piece of Styrofoam beneath it.

He steeled himself and stepped into the bathroom. Nothing there. But what had he expected? A pool of blood on the floor? A chalk outline of Elspeth's body? He didn't even know if there had been blood. Who came and cleaned up after someone died at home? It was something he'd never thought of before. Who knew death left so much garbage behind for others to take care of?

A silky lavender robe hung on a hook behind the bathroom door. Graham lifted its folds to his face and breathed deeply. It smelled of soap and maybe hair spray, but it didn't bring Elspeth to mind the way he had hoped. He went back into the bedroom.

"Just look at this linen closet!" Audra said admiringly from the hall. "Everything folded and stacked so neatly. God, these towels look brand-new. Some of them *are* brand-new—I can see the tags! All this stuff is just in perfect condition. Where do you suppose she kept the old ones?"

"Old ones?" Mr. Perkins said.

"You know," Audra said. "The faded or torn ones. What did she do when the dishwasher overflowed? Just run out and throw a brand-spanking-new towel with a scalloped edge on the floor?"

Mr. Perkins said something inaudible.

Graham opened the drawers of the nightstand on the side of the bed closest to him. Hand lotion, nail clippers, notepad, pen, phone charger, lip balm. This was not what he wanted. The drawers of the nightstand on the other side of the bed were completely empty, which was somehow even worse.

Audra was still marveling over the linen closet. "This makes me want to go home and replace all our towels. We have towels older than Matthew. We might even have towels older than *Graham*. My mother was the same way. In fact, when I got married, the very morning of the wedding, we had all these relatives staying with us and my mother put out the nice new towels for them, and I—the *bride*—had to use a thin little towel that still smelled like the cat and the cat had been dead ten years by then."

Graham began opening the dresser drawers. Sweaters, panty hose, a whole drawer of slips, another whole drawer of camisoles. And finally—here we go. The bottom drawer was empty except for a Valentine's Day card and a small jeweler's box. The card had no envelope, and when Graham picked it up, it felt dusty to the touch. On the front was a silhouette of a couple under a heart-shaped umbrella. It was signed *All my love, M.* Well. Indeed. Graham didn't need Audra to tell him that men only signed with their initial when they were married. He put the card back. The jeweler's box held two wedding rings. One was Elspeth's mother's—he recognized it instantly. A silver octagonal ring that had always struck him as uncomfortable-looking. Or was that because he had only ever seen it on an arthritic finger? The other ring was slim and gold and, he realized with surprise, was Elspeth's own, the one Graham had given her long ago. He put the ring in his palm and closed his fingers over it, trying to remember what Elspeth's face had looked like when they said their vows. But all he could recall was the minister's face—a very pink face, the color of smoked salmon, and beaded with perspiration. The minister had either been rushing from an earlier wedding or had some sort of cardiovascular disease because he had puffed and wheezed so heavily throughout the ceremony that Graham had feared the man would have a heart attack. Now all Graham could summon up of Elspeth at their wedding was a faint memory of a cool white presence in a gauzy veil standing next to him in the church, as though she had been a ghost already.

He put the rings back in the box and shut the drawer gently.

Audra and Mr. Perkins had apparently finished their tour of the apartment. (Graham later learned from Audra that the closet in the guest room was completely empty, which not only disappointed her but made her feel inadequate as a housekeeper.) They were seated at the dining room table with cups of tea. Graham walked past them into the kitchen.

"Graham and Elspeth had the most teenage type of relationship imaginable," Audra was saying. She frequently talked about him even when he was standing right there. It was sort of like being a supporting character in a book someone else was writing. "Always either best friends or worst enemies. Actually, more like hostile roommates, even after they stopped living together. This sort of mind-set like 'Well, *you* kept me up all night playing your stupid music so *I'm* going to hide the carrot peeler.' That's not an actual example, but that sort of mentality. You know what I mean?"

"Well, yes, I think so," Mr. Perkins said tentatively.

Graham sighed and looked around the kitchen. He checked the lower cabinets and found the All-Clad frying pan, right there with the others where it should be. He took the frying pan out and held it for a moment. It was just as he remembered—the perfect weight, the perfect size. (All-Clad had discontinued this particular model, which is why he didn't have his own. Plus Audra put everything in the dishwasher and their frying pans didn't look as glossy and perfect as this one.) Graham put it back.

"Their whole marriage was like that," Audra said in the other room. "Graham told me once that he moved the living room furniture around and the very next day while he was at work, Elspeth moved it all right back. And neither of them said anything about it! Both just as stubborn as could be! They just had this sort of falsely civil supper and pretended that furniture arranges itself."

Graham had forgotten that furniture episode, but it was true. Elspeth had gone out and bought special casters to put under the legs of the sofa just so she could push it back into place without having to ask him to help. *Had* he and Elspeth been like teenagers? It seemed to him that their relationship had been so complicated, so layered, so *intricate,* that it was beyond anyone's understanding, but maybe not.

"And even after their divorce, it was like that," Audra said. "We never knew where we stood with her. You could call her up one day and she'd be so happy to hear from you, and the next day, she'd be all 'What? What? I can't hear you! Speak up!' even when the connection was totally clear. *That* kind of conversation—you know?"

"Oh, yes," Mr. Perkins said unexpectedly. You could never be sure, with Audra, exactly how much of the conversation the other person would be able to follow.

"Personally, I think that's why Graham married Elspeth in the first place," Audra said. "He was attracted by her unpredictability. Men are so gullible! He liked the way she was cold one minute and then loving two seconds later. It was really a sign of how incompatible they were, but Graham thought it showed, I don't know, her passionate nature or something."

"My wife was like that," Mr. Perkins said in a soft, contemplative tone. "Fire and ice."

"I believe 'fire and ice' is a certain type of oral sex," Audra said. "But, yes, that sort of idea."

There was a very startled silence. The apartment itself seemed shocked—Graham imagined he could hear teaspoons rattling in the silver chest.

"Well," Mr. Perkins said. He had to make another start. "Well."

"So what's going to happen to this apartment?" Audra said. "Who did Elspeth leave it to?"

Undoubtedly that was confidential information, but Mr. Perkins was either too flustered to recall that or too grateful for the change of subject to protest. "Elspeth had no close relatives," he said. "The apartment and all the contents are to go to the Global Fund for Women."

"Even those pretty towels with the pink rosebuds?" Audra asked wistfully.

"Yes, everything," Mr. Perkins said.

Graham turned back to the kitchen. What to take? Not something decorative—he didn't want to stare at a reminder of Elspeth in his living room (and he didn't want the decorative object to stare at *him*, either). And not something distinctive, because he didn't want Elspeth sneaking up on him in the form of a vintage nutmeg grater when he opened the cupboard and least expected it. Of course, he could take nothing at all and just go home, but he didn't feel right about that. And he planned to *use* whatever he took, because taking some little knickknack and sticking it in the closet and then throwing it out one Saturday when the clutter of your closet got too overwhelming—well, that was too apt a metaphor of Elspeth's existence.

At last Graham chose a plain rectangular wooden cutting board. Because although Graham loved many things about cooking—the predictability and the orderliness and the almost immediate gratification—he loved the mindlessness of chopping vegetables most of all. When he was chopping vegetables, he could achieve a mildly stoned state of reflection. Sometimes, on weekends, he made a very complicated minestrone from scratch just because it involved so much chopping. It went without saying that he owned several cutting boards, and one or two were nearly indistinguishable from the cutting board he held in his hands now. That was why Graham chose it. Maybe, if he was lucky, it would get mixed in with all the others, and after a while, Graham would never know which one it was.

Julio moved in on Friday night. He brought with him only a Tupperware container, a small leather toiletry case, and his doorman uniform in a dry-cleaning bag.

"Oh, that is so sad!" Audra whispered to Graham. "Imagine moving through life with so few possessions."

Graham could imagine it. He thought it was probably wonderfully freeing.

Julio handed the Tupperware container to Graham. "Mama sent you this," he said. "It's her one-pot chorizo-and-potato stew for us to have for supper tonight."

Julio's mother sent them supper and they didn't have to even meet her, let alone endure an evening of small talk? Now *there* was a relationship Graham could get behind. It was even better than pizza delivery because not only did you have to pay for the pizza, but the delivery guy had a tendency to hang around and talk to Audra about his romantic life. (He was seeing this girl who posted cat GIFs all the time and— Oh, never mind.)

"Thank your mother for us," Graham said. "I'm sure it will be delicious."

"She said to serve it with sourdough bread," Julio said, "and sends her apologies for not having a fresh loaf ready for me to take."

Homemade bread? It was very possible that Graham might be in love with Mama Julio.

"Oh, I'm sure just regular bread will be fine," Audra said. She would think that. She was so—so offhand about food.

"I'll go out and get some," Graham said. "I don't mind."

He just had time to walk to the bakery on the corner. They closed at six. He took the Tupperware container into the kitchen and opened it. Even cold, it smelled delicious.

He walked back along the hall toward the door. He could hear Julio and Matthew in Matthew's room. Julio was speaking in a mock-tough voice, "What's this shit about you watching porn on the internet? You better not do that while *I'm* here." Matthew's laughter was soft and pleased.

Graham had never wanted a big family—all that noise and disruption—but maybe he'd been wrong about that. Maybe he just wanted a family that consisted of people who'd already grown to adulthood, of kind and funny young people who had been expertly raised by women thoughtful enough to send whole meals. That kind of family would suit Graham just fine.

Outside, Graham walked through the warm evening air to the bakery. He pushed open the door, and even this late in the day, there was a line of people waiting and the smell of fresh bread was everything you wanted love to be, but it so often isn't: hot, sweet, comforting, full of promise, and so heartwarming it made you want to do nice things for other people.

He had read once that *everyone* responded to the smell of freshly baked bread that way—that it was merely a common physical reaction to the aroma of fermenting yeast and not anything to do with a sentimental flashback to one's grandmother's kitchen. But knowing this didn't make Graham appreciate it any less. He inhaled deeply.

How strange. How strange. Here was Graham smelling fresh bread and Elspeth was doing nothing at all. She wasn't chopping celery or doing her taxes or drinking wine or yelling at a cab-driver. Graham felt a second of sorrow, but it was like a spark from a campfire—shrinking to a pinpoint and then blinking out. You couldn't even see where it had been.

Graham sighed, which caused the woman in front of him in line to shoot him an annoyed it's-not-my-fault look. But Graham didn't see her. He was thinking about the time Matthew had gone through a period of intense infatuation with geocaching, and Graham and Audra had had to spend all their weekends hiking through the woods, searching for worthless trinkets and leaving their own trinkets there for others to find. (It was either geocaching or origami—when would Matthew become a sullen teenager who spent his free time getting stoned on the fire escape? It couldn't happen soon enough.) Graham thought his relationship with Elspeth was a little like geocaching. They went long periods without speaking and then one of them would leave some sort of emotional coordinates (a phone call or an email), and sometimes the other one followed the coordinates and located the treasure, and sometimes they didn't. But Graham had assumed that the treasure would always be there, that it was just a matter of finding a free weekend to track it down. He didn't know until now that sometimes it just stays hidden, forgotten—that it will always remain something you meant to do.

Nine

Everywhere Graham turned, relationships were crumbling, hearts were shattering, romances were dying—the fragile golden fabric of their lives was being ripped apart by giant, uncaring hands. (Audra said that last part.)

But it was sort of true.

First of all, Lorelei and her husband were moving to Boston.

Audra couldn't get over it. "But we only bought this apartment because Lorelei lived here," she said.

This was, amazingly, true. They had moved out of the apartment Graham had originally shared with Elspeth and had actually bought a piece of Manhattan real estate and undertaken all the responsibilities that went with it—maintenance fees and school districts and property taxes—because Lorelei lived on the third floor and Audra had wanted to live in the same building. It was like being married to someone in junior high.

"I can't believe she's going to move because of her husband's stupid *job*," Audra kept saying. (Graham felt that it was likely that if he were transferred to Boston, or anywhere else, Audra would stay in New York to be near Lorelei—it was *extremely* likely.)

Second, Matthew wanted to quit Origami Club. He had told Graham and Audra he didn't want to go to the meetings anymore, he didn't want to get the newsletter, he wasn't even sure he wanted to do origami at *all* anymore. Graham's first thought was entirely selfish: *No more Origami Club! No more conventions! No more origami people!*

But Audra had looked dismayed. "Who's going to tell Clayton?" she'd whispered.

Oh. That was a good question. Clayton and the other members of the Origami Club would be so disappointed. They would have to be let down easily, with many flattering and completely untrue excuses. (Dealing with the Origami Club was also a lot like being in junior high, come to think of it.)

Third—and by far the worst—Derek Rottweiler appeared to have broken up with Matthew. No argument, no insult, no explanation—just all of a sudden Derek wouldn't sit with Matthew at lunch or talk to him on FaceTime or accept his invitations to sleep over. Matthew said Derek's best friend now was some kid named Mick Blackburn, who was the meanest, worst-behaved kid at school.

"It scares me to think that there *is* a child meaner and more badly behaved than Derek Rottweiler," Audra said.

Matthew came straight home from school now and went to his room. He said he didn't want to go to that school anymore. He said he didn't want to have other friends over. He said he missed Julio, who had moved back to his own apartment. He didn't want to go to the movies, or watch TV, or go buy candy at the store. He didn't want anything but to be Derek Rottweiler's best friend again. This was also a lot like junior high, but since Matthew was actually *in* junior high, that was probably to be expected. Still, Graham doubted if Matthew realized life would always be this way, pretty much.

Audra told Graham that she thought she could heal the rift between Matthew and Derek Rottweiler by calling Brenda Rottweiler and persuading her to speak to Derek about it privately. And so with a kind of serpentine wiliness, Audra called Brenda under the guise of asking her about the School Fundraising Plant Sale. Graham was sitting on the sofa next to Audra, reading the newspaper. Matthew was still at school.

Brenda answered in her usual shy, scared voice—perhaps she feared every call would be the school telling her that Derek had scalped someone. "Hello?"

"Brenda, hello!" Audra said.

She set the phone on the coffee table and put Brenda on speakerphone, which was something she'd taken to doing lately. (Graham found it about as appealing as listening to your neighbors have loud sex, only less so.) Graham had to hear the whole thing—did Brenda think it was fair to let the parent volunteers have first crack at the plants? Well, the perennials and the annuals, sure, but remember last year when Mrs. Sandberg up and bought all the bonsai trees before the sale even *opened*? What did people think when they came to the plant sale and there was a big sign saying BONSAI TREES and then no bonsai trees? It made them look downright amateur, was Audra's opinion. Maybe they should put a limit on what the parent volunteers should buy. Or maybe just a limit on what Mrs. Sandberg could buy. Or maybe let all the other parent volunteers buy as much as they liked, but ban Mrs. Sandberg altogether—

After about fifteen minutes of wearing Brenda down, Audra must have judged her sufficiently vulnerable, because she said, "You know, Brenda, there's one other thing I'd like to talk to you about. It seems that Derek and Matthew have had a falling-out."

"Oh?" said Brenda. If she was trying to sound innocent, she failed miserably. Audra gave Graham a slit-eyed look.

"Yes, well, they have," Audra said, "and it's really upsetting Matthew because he likes Derek so much."

She paused, clearly hoping that Brenda would say that *Derek* liked *Matthew* a lot, too, but all Brenda said was "I'm sorry to hear that."

"So I was wondering if maybe you could have a little word with Derek and ask him to perhaps sit with Matthew at lunch—"

"Oh, I don't know about that," Brenda said tentatively.

"Or perhaps you could encourage Derek to come over here," Audra said. "I know Matthew would love that."

"Derek's grounded for taking all the bolts out of his bunk bed," Brenda said. "It collapsed and his five-year-old cousin got a concussion."

"Well, then, maybe Matthew could come over to *your* place," Audra said. Push, push, push.

"I'm sorry," Brenda said softly. "But we don't believe in interfering with Derek's social life."

"What?" said Audra. She swung her feet to the floor.

"I said, we don't believe in interfering—"

"I heard you," Audra said, standing now. She was barefoot, in jeans and a gray sweatshirt. She looked very strong to Graham. "But what does that mean, exactly? That you don't interfere in his social life?"

Brenda sounded confused herself. "Just—just that we tend to let him choose his own friends," she said. "And when there's a disagreement, we try to stay out of it."

"But that doesn't make sense," Audra said. "Isn't that basically what parents *do*? Interfere in their kids' social lives and teach them about the value of friendship and the meaning of loyalty and stuff?"

"Well—" Brenda began.

"I mean, children need help making choices!" Audra said. Graham had never heard her talk this way. She must have read some parenting book. "They need to be taught compassion and empathy! They need to learn acceptance and respect!" Audra paused and then said in her regular voice, "Honestly, Brenda, being a good mother is not just about making peanut butter sandwiches."

"Derek can't have sandwiches anymore," Brenda says. "The doctor has put him on a gluten-free diet."

This happened much more frequently than you might think: Audra said something crazy and the other person responded with something even crazier. It made Graham doubt the sanity of almost everyone.

"So what are you saying?" Audra said. "That Derek could— could go off and become friends with Robert Mugabe and you wouldn't interfere unless pasta and cookies were involved?"

"Robert Mugabe?" Brenda sounded confused. "What grade is he in?"

"Never mind about that," Audra said, leading Graham to believe that she didn't know precisely who Robert Mugabe was, either. "The point is that Derek needs to make better choices."

"We believe in letting Derek learn from his own mistakes," Brenda said, a statement so flawed—if you knew Derek Rottweiler even slightly—that apparently Audra didn't know where to start.

The conversation didn't end then, so much as dribble off, like when you knock over a soda can you thought was empty but it spills sticky droplets all over your newspaper. Brenda thanked Audra for calling and Audra said she had a good recipe for gluten-free cake and Brenda said she would see Audra at the plant sale and Audra asked what shift was she working, and on like that.

Then Audra hung up and said to Graham, "She is the most amazingly misguided woman!"

But the really amazing thing about this phone call, to Graham, was that apparently Audra believed there were two kinds of breakups: the kind that's obvious and inevitable and permanent, and then some other kind that's more like a clerical error. The second kind of breakup is reversible. It's like when you get home from the supermarket and realize you left a gallon of milk at the checkout lane instead of putting it in the cart, and so you go back to the store and show the receipt to the manager and he looks at you kindly and says, "Why, certainly, take another gallon from the shelf." In other words, you haven't really been dumped because it's just a matter of going back and presenting a little paperwork and having the person who dumped you quickly and sincerely realize their mistake. Actually, *all* people believe there are two kinds of breakups—the kind that happens to other people, and the kind that happens to them. But in reality there's just the one.

Olivia wanted to do role play with him. Not the sexual, exciting kind of role play where Olivia played a nurse and Graham played a patient, but a vaguely insulting one where Olivia played herself and Graham played her father.

"You're about his age," Olivia said. "Well, maybe he's, like, ten years younger than you, but whatever. So, okay, I'm going to be me and you be my dad. All right, now, here, I'm starting." She paused and cleared her throat a little. "Dad, I'm moving in with Brian."

"Who's Brian?" Graham asked.

"My boyfriend!" Olivia said impatiently. "But my dad would know that. You have to stay in character. Okay, let's start again— Dad, I'm moving in with Brian."

"Fine."

Olivia frowned. "Do you mean, 'Fine, we can start the role play now,' or are you being my dad saying 'Fine'?"

"I'm being your dad."

Olivia turned her palms up in frustration. "My dad would never say that! That's the point!"

"Well, what would your dad say?"

"He'd say something like this," Olivia said. She sat up straighter and drew her eyebrows together. When she spoke, her voice was deep and incredulous. "'Moving in? I'm not paying a thousand dollars a month for you to cohabitate with Brian! This could affect your credit score! Your joint assets will have no protection! What are Brian's long-term financial goals?'" She paused and nodded. "Like that. He's like you—talks about money and finance all the time. Throw in some percentages, too."

Graham decided to ignore the unflattering portrait of himself that was emerging: old and boring. Instead he said, "Your father pays your rent?"

"Yes."

"Even though you work full-time?"

"Yes. He pays my sister's rent, too," Olivia said. "Now, can we get back to this?"

"I think maybe *you* should be your dad," Graham said. "And I'll be you."

"Okay!" Olivia said happily. "Ready, set, go."

Graham made his voice higher than usual. "Dad, I know this is a big step but Brian and I have decided to move in together strictly for financial reasons. Brian's rent is nineteen percent more than what I'm currently paying, but we'll be splitting the cost evenly, resulting in nearly a forty percent overall savings for you."

"Oh my God," Olivia moaned. "This is fantastic. Keep going."

Graham wondered if she said the same thing to Brian during

sex. "Furthermore, as two single wage earners, we will remain in the twenty-eight percent tax bracket, whereas if we got married, our combined net income would put us in the thirty-one percent bracket—"

"Wait!" Olivia cried. "I have to write this down!"

She dashed out of his office to her desk.

Graham followed her, pulling on his suit jacket. "Later," he said. "Right now I'm going out for a walk."

He did this every afternoon to clear his head. It drove him insane to sit at his desk all day.

"Okay," Olivia said agreeably, scribbling on her steno pad. "All that tax stuff you were saying—is that true?"

"Yes," Graham said. "I can explain it to you when I get back."

Olivia looked overwhelmed by that prospect. "Maybe you should just call my dad directly," she said uncertainly.

Graham left her still making notes and took the elevator down and walked through the lobby out into the sunshine. Yes, the outside world still existed. The sky was blue and an early-summer sun was shining, making the city seem filthy and stinking, but somehow even more alive.

He was on Fifty-third Street when a woman in a pale blue shirtdress with white cuffs came out of the Hilton Hotel. Graham watched her appreciatively from behind. Her hair was pulled up in a ladylike little knot and her dress reminded him of an old girl-friend of his who used to wear one of Graham's shirts around the apartment with only bikini underpants on beneath it.

Men, he realized, only like clothing that reminds them of other, *sexier* clothing, and they only like the other, sexier clothing because they hope the woman wearing it will soon stop wearing it and get into bed with them. Graham believed this was the reason men were so hopeless at fashion, unless they were for whatever reason not hoping some woman would soon be taking off her clothes—i.e., they were very old, very young, gay, or women themselves.

He was just taking his interest in the shirtdress woman as a sign that he wasn't all that old yet when the woman stepped to the street and hailed a cab. She looked uptown, her arm already held up and her face a delicate oval.

It was Audra.

Graham caught Audra's attention just as a taxi pulled over to pick her up. She waved it on with one hand and came hurrying to greet him.

"Hey!" she said. "Fancy meeting you here." She sounded genuinely happy to see him.

"What are you doing in midtown?" Graham asked her.

"I was having coffee with the Akela," Audra said easily. "But now I can have coffee with you, too. Do you have time?"

Coffee with the Akela didn't really explain why she was coming out of a *hotel*.

"Well, sure," Graham said, and they went into an Italian restaurant that had the depressing air of having been some other kind of restaurant very recently: red and gold wallpaper, ornate carpeting, tasseled light fixtures.

"Two, please, just for coffee," Audra told the hostess. The hostess led them to a booth in the corner, and took their orders.

Audra pushed a stray lock of hair off her face and smiled at him happily.

Genuinely. Easily. Happily. Graham was only inserting these adjectives. He had no idea whether he was interpreting Audra correctly. Right at this moment, she seemed as opaque to him as obsidian.

"So, listen to this," Audra said, leaning back against the banquette. Her face was lightly sheened with perspiration. "The Akela wants me to go to some training weekend with her so we can become certified BALOOs. And I'm, like, 'Baloo? From *The Jungle Book*?' and I swear for a second I thought she was talking about the two of us trying out for a musical! But, no, she says, 'It stands for Basic Adult Leader Outdoor Orientation,' like I should know that. And then she's all 'Now, I think we should go the second weekend in July,' and I was like, 'Maxine! That's just crazy talk!'"

What was crazy here was that Graham could have sworn that Audra had met with the Akela last week and told him this exact story. But it was hard to remember. Sometimes he thought Cub Scouts had given him low-level brain damage.

The waitress set their drinks down. Audra's cappuccino cup looked large enough to be a small punch bowl. She picked it up with both hands and took a sip, still talking. "So then she's going on about how there has to be at least one BALOO-certified person on every camping trip, and I'm like 'As far as I'm concerned, that's a good reason to *not* get certified, ever.' You would not *believe* how pro-BALOO she was."

Well, actually, Graham *would* believe that. Graham would believe just about anything. Audra should know.

Normally, Audra drove Matthew to school, and Graham took the subway to work. But today Audra had a meeting with a client near Matthew's school, and Graham had to take the car in for an emissions inspection, so they all drove together.

This meant that Graham exchanged the normal thirty minutes in which he peacefully commuted to work—the time in which his thoughts untangled from the messy knot of home life and smoothed into the sharp clean lines necessary for the office—for a raucous, disorganized departure with his family. Matthew had to go back up to the apartment once for his lunch box and Audra had to go back up for her keys, all while Graham sat double-parked with his blood pressure skyrocketing. And then Graham realized that he'd forgotten the emissions inspection notice and he had to go back up, too. (Once Audra had told him, "Nobody but *nobody* gets out the door smoothly. At least not people with children." It helped to remember this.)

Now they were finally driving toward Matthew's school—Graham at the wheel and Matthew in the passenger seat and Audra in the back, where she was shuffling papers and rummaging in her bag. She reminded Graham of a hen trying to settle, all that ruffling of feathers and shifting around.

"Don't ask me why I agreed to work with this man—" she began.

"Why did you agree to work with this man?" Graham asked. It was an old joke, and a favorite of Matthew's, but Graham noticed Matthew didn't smile.

"So this man asks me to design a brochure for his landscaping business and he wants me to draw a monkey, you know, on every page, sort of swinging around on vines, and stuff," Audra said. "So I do that and show him the mock-up and the man says, 'The monkey doesn't look like Curious George,' and I say, 'Curious George is a trademarked illustration,' and the man says, 'I thought he was a monkey,' and round and round we go, with me doing more and more mock-ups and every single time, the man says, 'Make him look more like Curious George,' so finally I say, 'Why don't I just make him look *exactly* like Curious George, and then you and I can go to prison for copyright infringement,' and the man says, 'How soon can you do that?'"

Graham pulled the car up in front of the school. Some kids

were milling around in front, and one of those kids was Derek Rottweiler, his arm hooked around a pole, spinning lazily. It was horrible to look at him—this small dark-haired boy in a faded T-shirt—and realize that he held the key to your happiness in his grubby little hands.

Graham turned to say goodbye to Matthew, and caught Matthew looking at Derek, too. In that instant, Matthew's face was as starkly revealed as a Mount Rushmore sculpture. Matthew's eyes were wet and his jaws were clenched, his mouth a straight line. Graham reached out to touch his shoulder, but Matthew shoved the car door open and stood on the sidewalk for the briefest of moments, pulling his backpack on.

"Goodbye, Matthew!" Audra said from the backseat, but Matthew shut the car door without speaking.

Derek Rottweiler stopped spinning around the pole and his face lit up—lifting Graham's heart with it for the tiniest of seconds—and then he ran to the other side of the school yard, where a heavyset man in yellow work boots and army pants had just arrived. No, not a man, Graham saw—a big heavy kid, with a moon face and a diamond-shaped body. This must be Mick Blackburn, the new object of Derek's affection. Derek had dropped his backpack to the ground and was rooting through it excitedly, looking up at Mick. Matthew stood on the school steps, looking very hard at nothing.

Graham put the car in gear and drove away. Audra now moved from the backseat to the front seat—legs first, back arching, struggling and kicking. It was like a giraffe was being born next to him.

"Don't knock the steering wheel," Graham said.

Audra plopped into the passenger seat and buckled her seat belt.

"Was he crying?" she whispered, although they were at least half a mile from the school now.

"A little bit, yes," Graham said.

"And did you see Derek Rottweiler run up to that other kid?" Audra said. "Like he couldn't wait to see him?"

Graham sighed. "Yes."

"That's it," Audra said. "We're converting to Hinduism."

"Hinduism?"

"Don't Hindus have arranged marriages? Or tell me some other religion that does arranged marriages and we'll convert to that. What about the Amish?"

"I think Hindus do have arranged marriages, yes," Graham said. "But why do we need that?"

"So we can pick some nice pretty girl for Matthew to marry and set it all up when he's fifteen," Audra said. "Because I absolutely cannot go through this again. What's it going to be like when some girl dumps him? And the girl after that? And the girl after that?"

She was right. Life was just a long stretch of people breaking up with you, really. Of course, it wasn't *all* people breaking up with you. There were good things, too—ruby-red sunsets and afternoon naps and onion rings and whatnot. But when you looked back, you really only remembered the breakups, and it seemed unfair to have to live through all those breakups and then have to *relive* it—a hundred times more painfully—through your child.

Of course, life *is* unfair. People say that all the time, but they're usually talking about some sort of capital-gains tax, or the fact that every once in a while Christmas falls on a Sunday, which is a day you'd have off anyway. They weren't talking about the really awful, searing, painful kind of unfair. Most people didn't know a thing about it.

. . .

The week before Lorelei and Doug were set to move, Graham and Audra took them out to dinner. They met up in the lobby and Audra said, "Greek or French?"

She sounded like a prostitute frisking with a john, but when Doug said "Greek," they all knew without discussing it that he meant the Greek place two blocks down and one block over, because that was the Greek restaurant they all liked, and that unspoken agreement was one of the extreme pleasures of the friendship. It's actually one of the extreme pleasures of *any* friendship. Don't kid yourself—emotional attachment and common hobbies are great, but not having to defend your choice of restaurant is hard to beat.

At dinner, they ordered a bottle of red wine and discussed, as they always did, current events. They started on a very micro level: their apartments. Obviously Doug and Lorelei had a lot going on since they were packing to move.

"I have two questions," Doug said. "Where did all this stuff come from and why do we keep it?"

Audra and Lorelei pondered whether it was better to pack your lingerie and nightgowns yourself, or let the movers do it and live the rest of your life knowing that some coarse man had handled your underwear. (They decided it depended on how stressed you were feeling on the actual day.)

From there, they adjusted their conversational focus outward slightly and discussed current events in the building. Julio had told Audra that the building was currently debating whether to replace some of the storage units with a fitness center.

"Fitness center," Graham and Lorelei said at the same instant. They were like that sometimes.

"Storage," Doug said. "We have to have somewhere to keep all this stuff we never use."

The waiter brought their entrées and another bottle of wine. Then they moved the conversation up a level, and discussed current events in the neighborhood. What did Doug and Lorelei think of the bakery that had opened up across from Nam's Bakery and seemed determined to run Nam's out of business?

"What do you suppose the profit margin on cheesecake is, anyway?" Doug said.

(Friendship doesn't get any sweeter than this.)

The price of baked goods led them straight to national current events, i.e., the stock market, which was Graham's favorite part of the conversation. He and Doug discussed the Beige Book and the FOMC and Chipotle stock performance until Audra began making impatient sounds through her nose.

And then, as always, just as they finished the meal, they talked about world current events. Conversationally, it was just like the zoom-out feature on Google Maps and no less satisfying. The waiter brought the check (none of them liked to stay for coffee; it was one of their compatibilities), and afterward they walked back home and said goodbye in the lobby.

"I might not see you again before you leave," Graham said. "So let me say goodbye now."

He shook hands with Doug, and then he turned to hug Lorelei.

Lorelei had intensely green eyes, and Audra had a raincoat of exactly the same shade of green, and sometimes when Audra wore that coat and stood next to Lorelei, Graham felt a strange sense of doubling, as though Lorelei were wearing the wrong coat or Audra had the wrong eyes.

And now, as Lorelei hugged him, he felt the same sort of doubling—it seemed he was hugging Audra goodbye. He held Lorelei against him briefly, inhaling the scent of the patchouli oil she wore in place of perfume, and feeling the soft roughness of her hair against his chin. His thoughts were jumbled and he could only think, *You and I share the heart of my one true love.*

But maybe that was just the wine, because by morning, Graham felt like himself again.

This was Graham's favorite slice of the day: that hour when Matthew had done his homework, and dinner was cooking, and the dishwasher was chugging, and the sunbeams came through the kitchen window like dusty gold searchlights. If you made a pie chart of the day, Graham would color this wedge that same shade of gold.

He didn't always get to enjoy this hour. Sometimes Matthew got frustrated with his homework, and there were tears, or Graham and Audra had to attend some awful school function. Or he was late, or Audra was. It was all so precarious! But tonight it had worked. Matthew had done his homework relatively cheerfully and with minimal assistance from Audra. (Elsewhere in the world, parents said, *Hey you, go do your homework,* and the kid said, *Yeah, okay,* and went and did it in his room. Graham hoped to reach this stage by the time Matthew was maybe thirty.) Beef Stroganoff was simmering on the stove, Audra was working on her laptop at the kitchen table, and Graham was drinking a glass of merlot as soft and red as a rose petal. Why, then, did he feel so sad?

"I'm beginning to believe," he said to Audra. "That there is just too much love loose in the world. Too much love with nowhere to go."

"Oh, sweetie," Audra said, looking at him over the lid of her laptop. "Is it because of that man in the Japanese restaurant?"

"What man in the Japanese restaurant?" Graham asked.

(And no—it was because their son was brokenhearted, because their friends were moving, because his mother was alone in her old age, because the world was falling apart. Man in a restaurant?)

"You remember," Audra said. "We were having sushi last week and this old man at the table next to us tried to tell the waitress about how he visited Tokyo once and she was like 'I don't have time to listen to this!'" She frowned. "Was I with you or was I with Lorelei?"

"It wasn't me," Graham said.

"No, I think it *was* you," Audra said, nodding slowly to herself. "In fact, I'm sure of it, because I wanted to invite the old man to sit with us and tell us about his trip to Tokyo, and you wouldn't let me. You said you didn't want to hear about it any more than the waitress did, and at least she was getting a tip. And I said, 'It's not about us wanting to *hear*, it's about him wanting to *tell*,' and you said that was exactly your point."

That did sound like something he would say. Graham had no memory of this, but he was secretly proud of himself for not having let the old man sit with them.

Audra continued, "And I felt so bad for the rest of lunch that I couldn't even look at him! I made you change places with me, remember? And you were all like 'No problem! I can look at him without feeling a morsel of pity!' And now you tell me that he's up and changed your whole view of the world!"

"Well," Graham said. "I don't know—"

"And it's really not all that *helpful* a worldview," Audra said. "It's like suddenly telling me, I don't know what. That you think there's too much boiled wool in the world. What can we do about it? I mean, I could throw away all my vintage peacoats and a couple of sweaters, and as a family, we could stop wearing boiled wool, but that wouldn't have much effect. And it's the same with this unrequited love business. We could start having weekly dinners where we invite the most unloved people we know, like Manny and, well, there's this very nice woman at the deli—"

"I don't want to have weekly dinners with unloved people," Graham said firmly.

"What about a happy hour?" Audra asked. "Maybe not weekly, but monthly—"

"No."

"Well, okay, but even if we *did* do something for the unloved people we know," Audra said, "it wouldn't solve the problem. Love would still be out there, roaming all over the place."

"Yes," Graham said. "That's my point."

"But I don't think it's *much* of a point," Audra said. "It's like when Matthew found out that the actors who played C-3PO and R2-D2 in *Star Wars* can't stand each other in real life. It's just sort of extraneous upsetting information."

She gave him a dark look and went back to her laptop.

The Origami Club wanted to come over and talk about what went wrong. It looked like it was going to be one of those bad, complicated breakups.

But was there any such thing as a *good* breakup? Graham wondered. A good, uncomplicated, friendly breakup? Had there ever been a time in the history of relationships where a couple sat down to eat breakfast and one of them said, *You know, I think we should split up,* and the other person said, *I agree! It's like you read my mind!* and the first person said, *What about our season theater tickets, though?* And the second person said, *I'll go and take your mother with me—I've always been so fond of her,* and the first person said, *I'm hoping your mother will give me her watermelon pickle recipe. I'm sure she'd be delighted. What worries me is our trip to France.*

Oh, that's no problem. I bought trip insurance.

I think one of us should keep the apartment since we just had those expensive curtains made for the den.

Well, you stay and I'll find my own place.

Really? Then, I insist on paying you three percent above fair market value for your half—

"Graham!" Audra said. "Stop daydreaming! They'll be here any minute."

He sighed. He doubted Audra knew what *fair market value* meant, anyway.

Just then the buzzer sounded and Graham went to answer. Clayton and Manny stood there, with a third man, who was presumably Alan.

Graham had met Alan before, but he remembered a large, soft man with freckles. This man, though, was a lot bigger—a *lot*. Graham could not even begin to estimate how much weight Alan had gained, but he seemed to fill the hallway. Manny and Clayton looked like twin Pinocchios next to him. Alan's face was now too wide for his features—his eyes and mouth and nose seemed all clustered together in the middle—and his shoulders had taken on a sloped, shambling look.

"Come on in," Graham said.

Audra was just coming out of the kitchen, and when she saw Alan, she gave a startled squeak.

Then she said, "Hello, everyone!" in a hearty voice. "Just go on in the living room! We'll be there in a sec."

As soon as they went by, she grabbed Graham's arm. "What happened to Alan?"

"He gained some weight, I guess," Graham said.

"Some!" Audra whispered. "He looks like a—a bear. He's crossed species!"

Graham went into the living room. Clayton and Manny and Alan were all sitting on the sofa expectantly. Graham walked over to the corner of the living room where they kept the liquor and began taking drink orders. He suspected that this would be an alcohol-required sort of meeting.

Of course, nothing was ever uncomplicated with the Origami Club—Alan wanted light beer, which they didn't have, and Manny wanted to know what was in a Rob Roy, and Clayton had to do some sort of calculation on his iPhone because he was counting carbohydrates.

In the middle of this, Audra came out of the kitchen with a little silver serving bowl filled with Canada mints—those thick pink candies that taste like Pepto-Bismol. Those mints had been in their kitchen cupboard for months, if not years. It was possible the mints had been in the apartment when they first moved in. So right away Graham knew that she considered this a B-list sort of get-together.

This is one of life's secrets: the status of the guest is directly proportional to the freshness of the snack food offered by the host. This secret had been revealed to Graham only after he had wandered the earth and sought enlightenment for nearly sixty years. (Others of life's secrets are: baby carrots are in fact just regular carrots cut into smaller pieces, and there is no scientific or medical reason you need to wait an hour after eating before you go swimming. About everything else, Graham was still pretty much in the dark.)

"So," Clayton said, after deciding he couldn't have any alcohol and asking for seltzer. "What's this nonsense about Matthew wanting to quit Origami Club?"

Graham didn't feel that this indicated much open-mindedness on Clayton's part, but he started in dutifully anyway. "Matthew's getting a little older now, and he's finding it hard to prioritize things."

"What things?" Manny asked.

Audra spoke up. "Well, you know, he has so many interests now that it's hard to find time for everything."

Clayton looked suspicious. "What sort of interests?"

"Ohhhhh," Audra said, and Graham could tell by her drawling tone and the way she tipped her head back slightly that she had been caught unprepared. So had he. They really should have thought this out more. Audra began speaking very slowly. "Minecraft, of course, and he wants to take banjo lessons, and he's tremendously interested in astronomy, and he's learning to speak Spanish."

What fascinating information! Matthew did love to play Minecraft—that was true. And once when Matthew was, oh, maybe six years old, Graham had taken him to hear an entertainer named Mr. Knick Knack, who played the banjo, and Matthew had liked that quite a bit. And sometimes on a rainy Sunday afternoon, if there was absolutely no other movie playing nearby that they wanted to see, they took Matthew to the Hayden Planetarium. And Julio had taught Matthew how to say *El burro sabe más que tú*—"The donkey knows more than you"—in Spanish. But basically, everything Audra said seemed to be pure fabrication. It was like leaning over someone's shoulder while they falsified their résumé or wrote their Christmas letter.

Audra was picking up speed. "He's also developed an interest in photography and botany. And of course, he spends lots of time with his friends."

"But *we're* his friends," Manny said, and Graham had to close his eyes for a second. (There *was* too much love loose in the world—way too much.)

"Well, of course you are," Audra said. "And you and he will still see lots of each other. After school, and weekends, and holidays." She paused, but evidently she couldn't think of any other times they might see Matthew. "It's just he prefers not to go to the club on Sundays anymore."

"But origami will teach him many skills that are valuable in later life," Alan said.

Was that true? Graham wondered. Certainly you could live a full, rich life without ever having folded an origami *T. rex.* Oh, he supposed origami taught you something about patience and attention to detail, but did that really prepare you for life? Graham was of the opinion that nothing prepared you for life, unless maybe you were forced to run an Indian gauntlet as a toddler.

"That's right," Manny said. "You shouldn't *let* him quit. I quit piano lessons in the third grade, and my mother let me even though the teacher said I had great promise and could become a professional musician."

"Oh, I think all piano teachers say that to anyone who wants to quit," Audra said. "It's a way of keeping up business."

Manny frowned. "Are you saying I *wasn't* talented?"

"Sort of, I guess." Audra looked thoughtful instead of contrite. "I mean, did the teacher ever say that you were very talented *before* you wanted to quit?"

"Well, no," Manny admitted. "Up till that point, she mostly just said that my shoes scuffed up her hardwood floors too much."

"She sounds like a dreadful person," Audra said sympathetically.

"She was," Manny said, in the tone of someone just realizing they've been scammed. "She also said that the Beatles were overrated and she wouldn't let me learn any of their music."

"Now, Matthew's piano teacher, Mr. Vargas, would never say that," Audra said. "He is the nicest, most patient man, and he lets

Matthew learn whatever songs he wants. Plus, he told me about this great Cuban diner in the Village where they make the best fried plantains."

"What's the difference between a plantain and a banana?" Manny asked. "Because I've never known."

"I don't think there is a difference," Audra said. "It's like turtle and tortoise."

Alan had been struggling valiantly for the past five minutes to separate a single mint from the others in the dish—they had apparently adhered together at some point (possibly during the heat wave of 1977)—but now he looked up and said sharply, "There most definitely is a difference between turtles and tortoises. Turtles live primarily in water, and tortoises live primarily on land."

"I'm not sure that counts as a difference if no one knows it," Audra said.

"*I* knew it," Alan said. "Most people know it."

"Well, then, perhaps you know the difference between plantains and bananas," Manny said challengingly. "Or don't they have shows about that on Animal Planet?"

"I didn't learn the difference between turtles and tortoises on TV," Alan said. "I learned it in school."

"What grade?"

"Fourth, I believe."

"Well, I guess Audra here and I both happened to be sick on the selfsame day of our respective fourth grades," Manny said. "Because neither of us knew that."

"I guess so," Alan said, missing the sarcasm completely. "It was in the Life Science unit. And to answer your earlier question, there's a difference between plantains and bananas."

The conversation seemed completely out of control, topic-wise, but suddenly Clayton said, "Now, look here. Has Matthew joined some *other* club?"

Ah, so this was the crux of it, as with any breakup. They thought Matthew was seeing someone else. It actually surprised Graham that it had taken them this long to ask. Wasn't that pretty much the *first* thing anyone wondered in a breakup? And wasn't it usually true? And what was worse, finding out that the person you loved was seeing someone else—possibly meeting someone else in midtown hotels—or finding out that they'd just sort of outgrown you?

"No, no," he said. "It's really a matter of more demanding schoolwork."

After that, there didn't seem to be much point in further discussion, so they finished their drinks and Alan managed to separate another mint from the pack. Then they all made their way down the hall to the door, with the usual rumble of disjointed conversation—Clayton saying, "Tell Matthew he's welcome on a drop-in basis," and Alan saying, "I suppose you think a cold *spell* and a cold *snap* are the same thing, too," to Audra.

Graham found himself suddenly reluctant to close the door behind them while they waited for the elevator. They looked like such a ragtag, dispirited group. He had to remind himself that they always looked that way. And yet, he felt infinitely, unbearably lucky as he stood there with his arm around Audra.

Manny looked at Graham and shrugged. "One door closes and another opens," he said.

Graham didn't think that was really the right metaphor for this situation. It was more like an emotional food chain: Derek Rottweiler had broken up with Matthew, and Matthew had broken up with the Origami Club, and now the Origami Club would—would—would tell some new club member his creases weren't sharp enough and force him to leave. And meanwhile, that awful kid, Mick Whatsit, reigned triumphant as the apex predator (Graham was certain this term was applicable in a thousand ways). But sooner or later someone would break up with Mick, too.

The thought made Graham so happy he gave Audra a little squeeze.

Audra had come up with a new idea to win Derek Rottweiler back.

"He loves to go fishing," she said. "So we'll invite him to spend a day fishing with us—I already researched it and there are lots of places on City Island where they do these all-day fishing trips—and he won't refuse because he likes fishing so much. Matthew told me that. And then Derek will spend all these happy hours with Matthew and remember how much he likes him and all the good times they've had together and they'll be friends again."

Was it just Graham or did that sound a lot like the sort of bad idea you had sometimes where you called your former girlfriend up and asked if you could stop by because you were pretty sure you'd left your green T-shirt at her apartment but really you just wanted her to fall back in love with you, and when you got there, your former girlfriend (a) had forgotten you were coming, (b) was there with her new boyfriend, or (c) both.

He must have looked skeptical because Audra sighed softly and said, "Well, at the very least, maybe Derek will be nicer to Matthew, hoping we'll invite him again."

Graham did have doubts, of course, but he was as eager as

Audra was to reinstate the Matthew-Derek merger, so he agreed. And then Audra gave him this big rap about how fishing was a *manly* activity and so Graham, being the man, should be the one to call Jerry Rottweiler, another man, and invite Derek, a very small man, to go fishing with him and Matthew. Graham suspected that Audra just didn't want to talk to Brenda Rottweiler after the last phone call, but he agreed anyway and called.

Brenda answered in her scared-rabbit voice. "Hello?"

Graham decided not to bother asking for Jerry and instead just said that this weekend they were going on a family fishing trip— "Striped bass fishing trip!" Audra whispered urgently—and they thought perhaps Derek would like to join them.

"Just a minute," Brenda said, "I'll see if he's available," as though Derek Rottweiler were the prime minister and Brenda his humble secretary.

She was gone somewhat longer than it would have taken for her to say *Do you want to go fishing with Matthew?* and Derek Rottweiler to say *I'd love to,* but she eventually did come back and said, "Derek would like that very much." (Thank God.)

She and Graham worked out the logistics, and as soon as they hung up, Audra went online and booked them tickets on a fishing boat called the *Sapphire* for Saturday morning. The tickets cost one hundred dollars each, which seemed like kind of a lot of money for a trip that three of them didn't really want to go on, but Graham didn't hesitate.

Though it did occur to him: were they not, in effect, *bribing* Derek Rottweiler? Were they not attempting to *buy* his friendship? Were they not offering *payment* for something that ought to be freely and naturally given, something that was in fact priceless? Yes, indeed. Just show me where to sign.

.   .   .

They picked Derek Rottweiler up at five-thirty in the morning on Saturday. The things we do for love! (Walking in the rain and the snow? The person who wrote that song knew nothing about love. And clearly did not have children.)

Derek and Brenda Rottweiler were waiting in front of their building. Brenda was dressed in a blue sweat suit but her face was still sleep-creased and her hair was unbrushed. Derek was wearing jeans and a T-shirt and his hair was a curly mass of black ringlets. He clambered into the car and then they all waved to Brenda and pulled away from the curb.

"Hi, Derek!" Matthew said in a soft excited voice.

Derek stared out his window. "Hey," he said tonelessly.

Graham's fingers tightened on the steering wheel. Children were monsters. He didn't like a single one of them.

"How's school going, Derek?" Audra asked.

"Okay."

"And your parents?"

"Okay, I guess."

A small gap opened up in the conversation then and seemed to spread. It got larger and larger and Graham thought someone might actually fall into it, but then Audra suggested brightly that they play Twenty Questions. "Now, Derek, you're the guest, so you go first. Do you know how to play?"

"Yeah," Derek said, and his voice sounded agreeable. "Okay, I'm ready."

Graham felt his hands loosen slightly on the wheel.

"Now you can ask the first question, Matthew," Audra said.

They all took turns guessing but nobody got it and after the twentieth question, Derek revealed that he was Ivan the Terrible.

(It wasn't like he chose Hitler or Jeffrey Dahmer, but that was really the nicest thing you could possibly say about his choice.) Fortunately, the game lasted until they got to the marina.

The blue-trimmed *Sapphire* was moored at the dock and looked promising, with an enclosed cabin and the upper deck shielded by a bright blue canopy. In an ideal world—the one Graham pictured—the captain of the *Sapphire* would be a young, handsome guy, perhaps resembling the Brawny Paper Towel Man, who was kind and enthusiastic and good with children. Instead they walked down the dock to find an old man with whisky blooms on his face and a harsh expression standing next to the boat with a clipboard. He wore stained shorts and a faded T-shirt and uneven grizzled whiskers.

"Hello," Audra said cheerfully. "Are you the captain?"

"Uh-huh," said the man, his breath damp with the smell of Budweiser. (It was just past six-thirty in the morning.)

"It's so nice to meet you!" Audra said. "I'm Audra, and this is my husband, Graham, and our son, Matthew, and his friend, Derek."

Graham and the boys looked at the captain expectantly, but he just grunted.

Audra was undeterred. "And what is *your* name?"

"Captain."

"But Captain what? What's your first name?"

The man had a cough drop in his mouth and he caught it between his teeth for a moment. "Some people call me Salty."

Audra smiled encouragingly. "Like Salty Dog, the drink?"

For the first time, the captain looked even mildly interested. "What's in that?"

"Oh, let me think," Audra sounded thoughtful. "Vodka and grapefruit juice, and maybe gin, too."

"How much vodka?"

"I guess half vodka, half grapefruit juice."

"Then where's the gin come into it?"

"I'm not sure," Audra said. "But any bartender should know how to make them."

A few other people came up behind them then, so Captain or Salty (or whatever the hell the man's name was) checked them off on his clipboard and they went aboard the boat. Audra carried a cooler, and her sneakers squeaked on the deck's varnished boards. Two crew members—Graham noted with satisfaction that they were younger and friendlier than Salty—took the boys over to a rack in the center of the boat where the fishing rods were stored.

Both Derek and Matthew seemed excited, and the water was as blue as a marching-band uniform. Even the ropes tethering the *Sapphire* to the dock seemed to creak with anticipation. Salty rang a bell and the boat pulled out of the marina.

It seemed that in the excitement—excitement? that was the wrong word—in the *distraction* of arranging this trip to woo Derek Rottweiler, Graham had forgotten how prone to seasickness he was. Within twenty minutes of the *Sapphire* leaving the harbor, he felt dizzy and nauseated and sweaty. Saliva was thick in his mouth, like a raw oyster, like a blood clot.

He glanced down and saw that Matthew looked as bad as he felt.

"Hey," he said. "You okay, buddy?"

Matthew shook his head. "I don't think so." He was standing near the railing next to Derek, but now he slid down until he was sitting on the deck.

Graham and Audra crouched beside him.

"What's up, sweetie?" Audra asked, rumpling Matthew's hair.

Matthew's eyes were huge. "I want to lie down," he whispered. Graham could barely hear him over the sound of the boat's engine.

He helped Matthew to his feet. They left Audra with Derek, and Graham led Matthew toward the cabin. "It'll be better when we're at sea," he said, having no idea if this was true. The deck seemed to sway beneath their feet until Graham felt like they were trying to walk across a floor made of cargo netting.

The cabin, which had looked so inviting when the boat was docked, smelled like fish and oil and vomit—the olfactory history of a thousand fishing trips, a thousand miserable souls. Matthew groaned and slumped down on one of the hardwood benches.

A lady about Graham's age was sitting on one of the other benches, knitting, and she looked up and smiled at them. "Oh, is your little boy seasick? That's a shame."

Even to Graham's inexperienced eye, something was wrong with the way this woman was dressed. She wore a high-necked flowered blouse with a ribbon around the collar, a vest that seemed to be made of a furniture doily, and a patchwork skirt. Her clothing wasn't just unseasonal and inappropriate for a fishing trip—there was some other thing wrong with it, too. It took Graham a moment to figure it out: her outfit was homemade. Way too many patterns and frills and embellishments. He seemed to remember from high school that girls dressed that way for a while when they first mastered the sewing machine.

Graham sat on the end of the bench where Matthew lay. Matthew had closed his eyes, but his face was pale and slick with sweat. Graham squeezed Matthew's ankle.

"Seasickness can be just terrible," the lady said. *Click* went her knitting needles. "Luckily, I have never suffered from it. Otherwise I couldn't accompany my husband on all his fishing trips."

"Is your husband the Captain?" Graham asked politely.

"Oh, no," the lady said. "I'm Mrs. Wilcox. My husband is one of the men fishing. I'm just with him for company."

"I see."

Matthew's breathing had already deepened. His skin had a pinched, lavender look, and his eyebrows were drawn together. Graham had never seen someone look so pale and wretched in his sleep. The rocking of the boat made Graham feel like a bubble of air was blocking his throat.

Click, click, pause. Mrs. Wilcox picked a small pink square off her knitting needles and showed it to Graham. "I'm making an afghan for my niece's baby. Pink and blue squares because she doesn't know if it's a boy or a girl. Don't you think that'll be pretty?"

"Oh, yes," Graham managed to say.

Mrs. Wilcox's fingers began working her knitting needles again. "I don't believe married couples should spend too much time apart," she said. "When Gordon tells me he's going fishing, I'm right there with a packed lunch and my embroidery bag."

Graham leaned his head back against the wall and closed his eyes. Almost immediately it seemed to him that his mother spoke from directly behind him. Graham's mother said, "Oh, sweetheart, I wouldn't have had that happen for a million dollars," and Graham looked down at his forearm and saw the deep gash he'd gotten climbing over Mr. Danbury's picket fence. He clamped his left hand over the cut and watched the blood well up between his fingers, just like rainwater rising through the gravel in the sidewalk. And then he was sitting on the long bench seat in his mother's Buick Century and they were driving to the hospital and his mother was saying, "Keep the towel on it! Hold on!" The Buick took the corners in long swooping turns, swaying like a ship, making Graham's head rock on his shoulders and his elbow slam against the car door . . .

He woke up with a start.

Mrs. Wilcox was still talking. "I made Gordon the nicest fishing vest, and I embroidered it with every kind of fish I could think of and—can you imagine!—he won't wear it. Says it's too tight in the armpits and runs around wearing his smelly old canvas one."

Graham didn't know whether he'd been asleep for hours or minutes or seconds. He had a feeling it didn't matter—Mrs. Wilcox would still be talking no matter what.

Matthew looked a little better. At least he was no longer frowning in his sleep.

"I did most of that embroidery using fishbone stitches, too!" Mrs. Wilcox said indignantly. "And that's a very difficult stitch— you might say it's only for people who are very advanced. I thought it would be a cute sort of pun, fishbone stiches on the fishing vest, but—"

"Excuse me," Graham said. "I'm going to go up to the deck for a minute. If my son wakes up, will you tell him I'll be right back?"

"Why, certainly," Mrs. Wilcox said, and as a sort of punctuation, her knitting needles spat forth another soft pink square.

Graham went up to the deck and stretched. He got out his phone and saw that he had slept for almost ninety minutes. The boat had stopped moving, and all along the rails, he could see people with fishing rods. He went in search of Audra and found her on the top deck, talking to Captain Salty. Evidently she'd broken through his taciturn nature and they were discussing how Salty's wife was mad at him for staying out all night.

"Now my suggestion," Audra was saying, "would be to buy your wife a very nice classic leather handbag."

"I think that might make her *more* suspicious," Salty said.

"But that would be overridden by her love of the handbag," Audra said. "If it's the right handbag."

Salty scratched his chin. "Sounds mighty expensive. Flowers'd be cheaper."

"Yes," Audra said. "But a handbag would last for years! For a lifetime, even. And every time she'd look at it, she'd think, *What a thoughtful, loving gift! Salty is such a romantic, devoted husband! I love him so!*"

"That's not really the way she talks," Salty said.

"But *inside*, she'd be feeling that way," Audra insisted. "In her heart, she'd be thinking, *I don't care if he did stay out all night—I don't want to be married to anyone else.*" She pushed a strand of hair behind her ear. "I tell you what—you come into the city some-time, and I'll take you shopping for the handbag. My last name is Daltry, remember? We live on West Eighty-fourth Street. I can put my number right into your cellphone if you like."

It was fairly remarkable that they had all not been murdered in their beds, the way Audra handed out their names and address. (Once she'd told a man in line at the hardware store that he should come right over and she'd give him some old drawer pulls they had and the man had said, politely, that he couldn't come over because he was on work release from a correctional facility and had to be back by four o'clock. Graham had feared for a while that they would have to move.)

Salty's eyes were flickering over Audra, whose hair had gone curly in the sea spray. Her lips were prettily chapped. She gazed up at him trustfully.

"Maybe you and me could have a drink after we go shopping," he said. "Maybe one of them Salty Dogs you were talking about."

"I don't drink those anymore," Audra said. "Not since that time

I told you about earlier, when I woke up in Astoria not knowing where my purse was. But a glass of wine, sure—"

"Hey," Graham interrupted. "Matthew still feels pretty sick. Where's Derek?"

Audra looked around her in a startled fashion. Goodness, where *was* that child they were looking after? Dearie me, did he fall overboard back a ways? Graham sighed.

Eventually, they found Derek on the other side of the boat, wearing a filthy yellow slicker that one of the crew must have lent him. A bucket next to him contained two fish, swirling around like three a.m. thoughts.

Audra handed Derek a ham sandwich from the cooler she'd been dragging around and offered one to Graham. He shook his head and reached for the thermos of coffee.

And so the morning passed—as slowly as the morning passes when you're waiting for a baby to nap so you yourself can sleep. Graham stayed with Derek, leaning against the side of the cabin and drinking coffee. The wind off the sea made conversation impossible—just the way Graham liked it. Audra went down to check on Matthew and presumably got sucked into the Mrs. Wilcox conversation vortex, because Graham didn't see her or Matthew again until the bell rang. The crew announced they were returning to dock and made everyone reel in their lines.

Audra showed up then, Matthew stumbling after her, both of them blinking in the daylight. Graham put an arm around Matthew's neck and kissed the top of his head, but Matthew was looking at Derek's bucket of fish.

"How many did you catch, Derek?"

Derek shrugged, his eyes on his fishing rod. "Six or seven."

"That's fantastic!" Matthew's eyes shone with admiration. He wasn't even jealous.

"Whatever," Derek said.

"No, seriously," Matthew said. "It's great."

"I *know*," Derek snapped impatiently, and went back to reeling in his fishing line.

Matthew shrank back as though bitten, and Graham looked at Audra. Her eyes were dark with pain, bleak-looking. She leaned forward to stroke Matthew's hair.

Eventually, they got back to shore and into the car. They drove home in a silence that not even Audra broke, except once to ask Graham, "Have you ever heard of fishbone embroidery?"

Graham drove straight to Derek Rottweiler's building without even stopping at McDonald's because he felt that he could not physically endure being in the car with that ghastly, heartless child one minute more than absolutely necessary. And then they drove to their own building, where Matthew had some delayed seasick reaction and threw up in the hall outside their apartment door, and Audra discovered she'd left her phone charger aboard the *Sapphire*.

It was not the *least* fun Graham had ever had for four hundred dollars—that honor was reserved for a mule ride up a mountain trail in Puerto Vallarta, where Graham's mule had *died* and Graham had had to hike back down with the sobbing guide—but, oh man, it was pretty close.

Graham expected Audra to be weepy on the day that Lorelei moved, but when he got home after work, she and Matthew were both pink-cheeked with pleasure.

"Lorelei gave me her Coke machine!" Audra said excitedly. "The movers couldn't promise not to break it so she had them move it down here."

"Come look, Dad!" Matthew said.

Graham set down his briefcase and followed them down the hall. Lorelei's vintage Coke machine stood proudly in their living room, as immovable as a tree whose roots have cracked and lifted the sidewalk.

Audra showed him how to use it, as though he'd never seen a vending machine before, let alone this *exact* vending machine, which had stood in Lorelei's den for years. Audra had always been enamored of it.

"Now you just put a dime here in the coin slot," Audra said. "And then you press the button and your drink comes out! It can hold up to nine different flavors or whatever—including beer bottles!—so Matthew and I stocked it from the fridge and Matthew had his very first Coke!"

Perhaps caffeine was responsible for the bright-eyed looks on both of them? For a second, Graham had thought Audra was going to say that Matthew had had his first beer, so he was actually relieved that it was just a Coke. Although up until now they had refrained from giving Matthew caffeine, fearing that it would be as disastrous as introducing television to a primitive culture. Oh, well, who cared? It had to happen sooner or later.

Then suddenly Graham was reminded of the time when Matthew was four and they had made him give up his pacifier. (Yes, at age four, he still used a pacifier; they were tired of hearing about it.) They had promised Matthew that once he'd gone without a pacifier for ten days, they would take him to Chuck E. Cheese's. Matthew had been surprisingly—joyously to Graham—cooperative, letting Audra collect all the pacifiers from around the apartment (she threw them away the next day while he was at preschool) and watching Graham carefully each night as he wrote a big black X on the calendar. The ten days went by like syrup sliding down a stack of pancakes, and they went to Chuck E. Cheese's, and in the car on the way home, Matthew said, "That was great. And now I get my pacifier back!" He had not understood the deal at all, and when they explained to him that the pacifiers were gone for good, his wail of outrage had made Graham's eardrums pulse. Graham suspected that they might be in for something similar now—the novelty of the vending machine would wear off and Audra would want her friend back.

"Press the button, Matthew!" Audra said now, inserting a dime into the coin slot.

Matthew pressed and the machine rumbled and clunked but no beverage dropped into the little glass-fronted dispenser.

"Huh," Audra said, fumbling for her phone. "Lorelei said this might happen. Let me just call her—"

"Mom, you said we could go out and get more drinks," Matthew said. "Special, interesting ones."

"We will, sweetie," Audra said, pressing buttons on her phone. "Just let me ask Lorelei about this." She put the phone to her ear. "Oh, hey, it's me! Are you guys at the airport yet? Remember that time you dropped me off at the airport and we were so busy talking that you dropped me at Arrivals instead of Departures and I had to—"

"Mom!" Matthew protested.

Audra pressed the phone against her chest. "I know, honey. Just give me two minutes." She put the phone back to her ear.

Matthew looked at Graham. "Does she mean the long two minutes or the short two minutes?"

Graham sighed. "The long two minutes, I think. But I'll take you."

So Graham and Matthew went to the supermarket and bought ginger ale and root beer and cherry Coke and cream soda—all those strange drinks that you forget were once actually popular—

and some cold beer in case Audra hadn't been able to get the Coke machine working again. While they were shopping, they called the pizza place and ordered a large pizza with pepperoni and basil leaves.

They picked up the pizza on the way home. Audra was off the phone, amazingly, and the vending machine was working again. Matthew stacked the new drinks on the machine's shelves while Audra updated them on Lorelei's move, which was now less than three hours old—"So they leave for the airport, and Lorelei was all emotional, you know, watching the building get smaller and smaller in the window, and Doug starts talking to the cabdriver about mortgage refinancing and the Federal Reserve! She wanted to kill herself!"—and Graham set the table.

The Coke machine made sort of conversational noises, like an elderly relative—rumbling and shuddering and switching a fan on and off—but the drinks were ice-cold and Graham agreed that it was very satisfying to get them from your own personal vending machine. It was like being the proprietor of a general store, but without the pesky customers.

Say what you will about fat and sugar and salt and alcohol— it's all true. But the meal really did—in a way, for a moment, under the circumstances—make them all a little bit happier, even Graham.

Graham and Audra were going out to dinner—just the two of them—while Matthew had a playdate with a new friend from school named Theo. Evidently Theo was going to be Matthew's rebound relationship. Graham didn't hold out much hope. Rebound relationships never worked. Not even when the rebound person was superior in every way to the previous person, not even when the rebound person owned a PlayStation 4.

They were all going to walk over to Theo's apartment and then Graham and Audra would go on to the restaurant. Graham and Matthew waited for Audra by the door and at last she came clacking down the hall. She wore a rose-colored sheath dress and thin gold hoop earrings and a pair of platform cork sandals so high that it seemed as though she were standing on a stack of telephone books. Graham looked at the sandals doubtfully. "Are you sure you can walk to the restaurant and back in those?"

"Oh, yes," Audra said. "They're new."

Graham wasn't sure how the fact that they were new sandals made them any easier to walk in, but he supposed it was her decision. They left the apartment at five, which meant they would probably get to the restaurant at about five-thirty. Of course, five-thirty was earlier than Graham and Audra cared to eat, but it was like when Matthew was a baby and they watched TV with closed captions for an entire year because otherwise the sound woke him up: theirs was not a perfect world.

Out on the street, the new sandals forced Audra to walk as though her legs were short lengths of limp rope. She took Graham's arm and they all walked very slowly.

"We're going to be late," Matthew said worriedly.

"Just fashionably late," Audra said. "I tell you, these shoes looked so cute online! Who knew they'd be impossible to walk in?"

Graham and Matthew exchanged a look—the shared knowledge that it would be wiser not to answer that.

"Anyway," Audra continued, "Matthew, would you like to invite Theo to go to the Natural History Museum with us tomorrow?"

"Derek Rottweiler can't go to the Natural History Museum at all anymore," Matthew said, "because he took a slingshot into the butterfly conservatory." He spoke in the sorrowful voice of someone who has known great love and loss, and for whom there can be no one else.

"Well, all the more reason to invite Theo," Audra said.

"Maybe," Matthew said. "I don't know."

It took them fifteen minutes to walk the five blocks to Theo's apartment building. The doorman called ahead, and when Graham pressed the buzzer on Theo's apartment door, it was immediately opened by a smiling man with hair sticking up like bulrushes, and wide-open eyes. He looked like he'd just escaped from a psychiatric ward (a medium-security ward, where everyone was pretty high-functioning, but still).

"Hello!" Audra said. She put her hand on Matthew's shoulder. "This is Matthew. Is Theo here?"

The man smiled even more broadly but said nothing. Graham wondered if perhaps he was a deaf-mute.

Fortunately, a plump woman with dark hair came bustling up from behind the man and said, "Hello, Audra! Hi, Matthew!"

"Hi, Marcia," Audra said. "This is my husband, Graham."

Graham shook hands with Marcia, who said, "And this is my husband, Steven."

"Hello!" Steven said with eager happiness. (Apparently he wasn't a deaf-mute.) He didn't offer to shake hands.

"Theo's in his room, Matthew," Marcia said. "He's building something with Legos. Do you like Legos? We didn't know if you liked them. I told Theo you might want to play something else. I said, 'We don't know Matthew very well yet, maybe he wants to play a different game.' Graham and Audra, do you want to come in for a drink? Or maybe you're on your way out. I told Theo I didn't know if Matthew's parents would stay or not. I said, 'Maybe they're on their way someplace.'"

She was clearly one of those people who chased themselves

through conversations—asking questions, answering them, explaining their reasoning—and never realized that their words were like a revolving door spinning faster and faster while the person they were talking to waited in vain for a chance to step in. Graham had met others like her; he knew the type. But Steven—beaming benevolently at them—seemed to be a whole new level of peculiarity.

Marcia finally paused for breath, and Audra quickly spoke up and gave Marcia a pre-playdate rap about Matthew: he had already eaten dinner at home, he really doesn't like loud noises, and he could call them on his phone if he wanted to be picked up before seven. Marcia had a little Q and A with herself about children and cellphones—"Are you glad Matthew has an iPhone? Has he lost it? I'm afraid Theo would lose it. I told Theo, 'I'm afraid you'll lose it'"—while Steven fixed Graham with the most intense look of benign craziness imaginable, like a smiling Phil Spector.

A boy's voice called, "Hey, Matthew, come here!" from inside the apartment, and Matthew squeezed between Marcia and Steven and ran down the hall. Graham and Audra said goodbye and left. They left. They *left*.

Just think about it: If Steven interviewed for a job at Graham's office, Graham wouldn't give it to him, even if it was a very menial job, because Steven was so odd-seeming. Graham would not lend Steven money, or trust Steven to house-sit his apartment, or valet-park his car. But leave their only child with him for two hours? Oh, well, sure, no problem! Here you go, his name is Matthew and we're pretty attached to him, so try not to traumatize him, okay? This sort of trust is one of the great paradoxes of parenting, similar in importance to Galileo's paradox of infinity, and no one tells you about it ahead of time. (No one tells you *shit* about parenting ahead of time, really. Well, they do but not anything useful.)

As they walked down the stairs in front of Theo's building, Graham said to Audra, "Didn't Theo's father strike you as a little—off?"

"Hmmm?" Audra reached the bottom of the stairs and gave a slight lurch, like someone starting to hula-hoop, while she gained balance on her shoes. She slid her hand into the crook of Graham's arm. "I think he was just shy."

"People over forty can't be shy," Graham said.

"What are you talking about?" Audra asked. She looked at him, amazed, and a stray lock of hair blew across her face, as curly and delicate as a sweetpea tendril. "All *sorts* of people over the age of forty are shy! What about Mr. Calkins?"

"Who's Mr. Calkins?"

"He lives in our building, on the second floor," Audra said as they began walking. "And he's too shy to answer the phone in case it's a stranger. You have to call him and hang up and then call back, so he knows it's you. Also, Julio told me Mr. Calkins doesn't trust the postal service and won't open any letters unless they're addressed to him with his middle initial."

"That's what I mean," Graham said. "I think at a certain point, it stops being shyness and becomes something else, some sort of actual disorder."

Audra looked unconvinced. "Anyway," she said. "We should probably have Theo's parents over for dinner. You could make spaghetti marinara with garlic bread."

There are not really words to describe how depressing Graham found this idea. Spaghetti marinara with garlic bread was his all-purpose crowd-pleasing picky-eater dinner. Spaghetti marinara was like taking a girl on a first date, actually: nothing fancy, no surprises, best foot forward. The second date would be like golden chicken with coconut rice—a little fancier, but if you encountered some pushback about the flavored rice, that would be a bad sign. The third date should be something like chile-blackened catfish fajitas—hot and spicy, definitely a flashier and more impressive effort. But be open-minded—check with the date first—because not everyone likes spicy food and, you know, you're invested at this point, and are probably liking the sex. The fourth date is the true test of compatibility, and the future of the relationship hangs in the balance: moules farcies and vichyssoise. Can she eat cold soup? If not, you have to stop seeing her and pretend to be your twin brother when she calls.

Graham hadn't especially wanted to date the Rottweilers; he really didn't want to date the Theos. What it came down to was that he was too old for picking up girls in bars, too old to serve spaghetti marinara. He just didn't have the energy.

Even more depressing than the *idea* of having Theo's parents over for dinner was the *knowledge* that they would do so. Just as they would have the parents of the friend after Theo, and the friend after that, too. Then eventually, Matthew would have girl-friends and wives and in-laws and it would all involve a lot of spaghetti marinara, but Graham would do it. He would do it because that was what you did when you loved someone. You kept pushing until you broke on through to the other side, as Jim Morrison may have said. Only Morrison didn't add that on the other side, you found another obstacle and had to keep pushing. Forever.

Graham was so busy thinking about this that he would have kept walking if Audra had not tugged his arm to stop him.

A workman outside a flower shop had dumped an enormous white pail of soapy water on the sidewalk and people on both sides of the stream had paused so as not to get their feet wet. Graham looked down at the rainbow pattern in the oily water—a dark sunburst edged with color, like a reverse paparazzi flash—and, just for a moment, it seemed to him to contain all the future joy and sorrow in the world, in equal amounts.

"My new shoes!" Audra said with a little moan, and then took his arm again. "Come on."

They began walking again, slowly, clutching each other and concentrating on the ground in front of them. Graham took very short steps, and Audra tottered next to him, holding out her free hand, fingers splayed, for extra balance. He wondered what other people thought of them. He and Audra must look like the newest of lovers, or the frailest of seniors, or the drunkest of partygoers—or anything, really, other than the survivors they were.

Acknowledgments

First, thank you to my wonderful agent, Kimberly Witherspoon, who, among other things, changed my life.

Thank you to my editor, Jenny Jackson, who steered me through the murky waters with such brilliant insight and saintly patience. Nobody, but nobody, is better.

Thank you to Felicity Rubenstein, who watches over my work with such wisdom and care, and to Lettice Franklin, whose perception and support are a constant joy to me. Thank you falls short of all I mean to say, but thank you nonetheless.

Thank you, thank you, thank you to all the readers who read early drafts so willingly and so well: Cecile Koster, Samir Rawas Sarayji, Sofia Borgstein, Vanessa Deij, Joel Kuntonen, Vivian Vos, Cathy Cruise, David Kidd, Dana Flor, Elizabeth Cohen, Bill Roorbach, Justine Kenin, and especially Patrick Walczy.

Thank you to the editors who took a chance on chapters of this book and published them: Cara Blue Adams, Robert S. Fogarty, Linda Swanson-Davies, Susan Burmeister-Brown, and Peter Stitt. You have my deepest gratitude.

Thank you to the experts who so generously advised me on everything from statistics to origami: Jim Ohlson, Kevin Kendrick, Scott Tegethoff, Katherine Fortier, Sahjo Brown, Ekemini Riley, Sonya Dumanis, and Robert Lang. Any errors are mine alone.

Acknowledgments

Thank you to the friends who made me laugh and then let me steal their jokes: Jennifer Richardson Merlis, Jessica Hörnell, Kitty Lei Harter, Jojo Harter, and Leila Barbaro. I am forever in your debt.

Thank you to my parents, Richard and Suzanne Heiny, who never told me that my stories needed gunfights and secret caves. To my brother, Christopher Heiny, who is always there when I need him. And most of all to my sons, Angus McCredie and Hector McCredie, who taught me everything I know.